Border Passions

Vivien Harben

Order this book online at www.trafford.com
or email orders@trafford.com

Most Trafford titles are also available at major online book retailers.

This book is a work of fiction. Names, characters, places and incidents
are products of the author's imagination or are used fictitiously. Any to
actual events or locales or person, living or dead, is entirely coincidental

Printed in Victoria, BC, Canada.

ISBN: 978-1-4269-2271-8

Library of Congress Control Number: 2009912299

*Our mission is to efficiently provide the world's finest, most
comprehensive book publishing service, enabling every author to
experience success. To find out how to publish your book, your way, and
have it available worldwide, visit us online at www.trafford.com*

Trafford rev. 1/19/2010

 www.trafford.com

North America & international
toll-free: 1 888 232 4444 (USA & Canada)
phone: 250 383 6864 ♦ fax: 812 355 4082

The author would like to thank everyone involved in the realization of this book. This book is dedicated to the research of Breast Cancer, as such $1.00 from each book sale shall be donated directly to the Canadian Breast Cancer Foundation. Thank you for supporting my dream and furthering the research into Breast Cancer.

Prologue

Oh my God this could not be happening! The slender figure thought looking at the melee around her. She had taken every precaution so as not to draw attention to herself. She had limited the number of men she brought with her. Her clothing had been carefully chosen to be unnoticeable. She didn't think she would draw that much attention to herself. Yet she was somehow noticed and now in the midst of such chaos she feared she would go mad. How did this happen? She replayed the morning's events in her memory in a desperate attempt to escape the horror she now faced.

"My Lady, my Lady." Stephanie Rockforte's old nurse Matilda, rushed into the room.

"Matilda, what is it? What is wrong?" Stephanie couldn't help but feel a flash of panic. If the keep was under attack, without her father here, they were basically defenseless.

"Lady Stephanie, Anne's daughter Mary has arrived at the keep begging for your help."

Relief washed over Stephanie, the keep wasn't under attack "Why? What has happened?"

"It seems Anne is birthing, but there is trouble and no one is there to help."

"Matilda, go to the kitchen. Make sure that Mary is fed and taken care of. She must be exhausted after such a journey. I will dress and join you shortly."

"Yes My Lady."

Matilda left the chamber. Stephanie dressed quickly; barely pausing she made her way downstairs to the large kitchen. When she entered she was glad to see Mary was at the large table enjoying apple tart and fresh milk, all the while Cook made a show of fussing over her.

"Ooh you poor wee thing" Cook was cooing "You must be half starved running all this way. Don't you worry, Lady Stephanie will help you. Come eat up you poor dear."

Stephanie smiled. "Cook I am here now. Thank you for taking care of Mary. Hello Mary. I hear you need to speak to me. What has happened to bring you here in such a hurry with no one to guide you?"

Mary looked momentarily awed being before Lady Stephanie. But when Mary looked into Stephanie's soft green eyes, so full of compassion, she didn't hesitate as she jumped off the stool and threw her young skinny arms around Stephanie's legs. Mary turned her small face up to look at Stephanie pleadingly.

"Oh my Lady, my mother is in such pain. The baby is coming early and there is no one to help her. Everyone else is working in the fields. Please she asked me to find you because you would know what to do. She is in awful pain and there is so much blood. Please, you must come." The little girl's blue eyes filled with tears that spilled over her dirt streaked face. The fear that echoed in her pleas tore at Stephanie's heart.

Stephanie knelt down before Mary and held her close. "Come Mary. Hush. We will go at once. When did you leave your mother?"

Mary sniffed. "Nearly an hour has passed. I am sorry I ran as fast as I could."

"It is all right Mary." though Stephanie wasn't so sure. It was possible that Anne was suffering a breached birth, which would explain the severe pain and blood as the baby tore her flesh. If she did not get to Anne soon, Stephanie feared both Anne and the baby would be dead. She turned to Matilda and spoke her orders quickly.

"While I change, get Edmund, Matthew and Duncan to saddle some horses. Tell them I will meet them at the stables. Mary you will wait for me here. Finish what Cook has given you and when I return we will be on our way."

With childlike resilience Mary happily turned back to her feast, to wait for the Lady Stephanie to make everything all right.

By the time Stephanie had reached her chamber Matilda was visibly and vocally distressed.

"But Lady Stephanie you cannot go out alone! With all of the trouble your father has had with your Scottish neighbors recently, you cannot possibly leave here without a fully armed escort. You know how upset your father will be if I let you go. Please my Lady you must not go."

Stephanie didn't stop her preparations as she spoke. "I know the trouble we have had of late with the raids. I am not unaware of the potential danger, but time is too short. I suspect Anne is in serious trouble. I cannot wait. You know father was going to petition King Edward for aid to end the growing raids against us. Who knows how long that will take. Anne does not have the time to wait."

"But you are unprotected."

"I shall have Edmund, Matthew and Duncan with me. They are capable young men at arms who can wield weapons in our defense if the situation arises. I cannot afford to take any more men with me or else there will be no one left to protect the keep. I am dressed to be inconspicuous and unrecognizable as the Lady of the keep. No, please there is no time to waste" Stephanie rushed out before Matilda could delay her any longer.

Chapter One

This morning's events now felt like days ago. The band of men had set upon their small group quickly and without any warning. Stephanie was pinned against a very broad chest. Hands like bands of iron gripped her arms tightly and held her firmly in place.

The sound of metal on metal was almost deafening. Stephanie watched as the strange men seemed to taunt and tire Edmund, Matthew and Duncan as they attacked from all sides, clearly outnumbering them.

Stephanie struggled. "Let me go. Release me at once." She demanded of her captor.

"Hush" was all the reply she received.

But Stephanie would not be silenced. "No. Let us be. We have done you no harm. We have nothing of value. I travel only to help a local woman in dire need of my assistance. Please."

Even as she struggled, the man's grip became firmer bruising her flesh. Yet he did not acknowledge her plea. Desperate to get away from the torment of these strangers, Stephanie redoubled her efforts to break loose.

"Nay lass. Ye must nae fight me. Ye willna get away an ye are nae help tae those men trying tae protect ye. Ye would only be in the way and most likely end up dead for yer efforts." The man spoke firmly in her ear but without malice or anger.

Scots! These must have been the men leading the raids on her father's lands. Stephanie felt her own anger begin to boil to the surface. "How dare you say such a thing when my men are obviously outnumbered?"

"Nay lass, silence."

Stephanie focused all her rage and frustration into her struggles and yelled to be heard above the sounds of battle. "If you will not release me, then in the name of God make your men stop. It is not a fair fight. My men will be killed. Please you have our horses and our belongings. Let us go, we have nothing else of value. I must get to the village to tend this young girl's mother, who is giving birth as we speak." Stephanie pleaded with her captor.

The man who held her heard her frustration but could do nothing for her. "Alas my Lady I canna stop these men as they are not commanded by me. We are in the service of the Laird of our clan and only he can stop them."

"Then where is your great Lord?" snapped Stephanie. "Why is he not here to witness this cowardly attack by his men? Why is he not here to end this farce?"

Suddenly a voice thundered above the din "ENOUGH!" Instantly everyone stilled. The disembodied voice came from behind Stephanie. From the looks on Edmund, Matthew and Duncan's faces he had to be some creature summoned from the depths of hell. Their faces were frozen at the sight behind her.

Stephanie knew that with no weapon in hand her own terror would be greater; but, she still had to confront the 'voice.'

She turned and saw Mary. Mary, the little girl who braved a long trip on her own, to help her mother. There the little girl stood with her pale face streaked with and dirt, knowing nothing other than her mother might be dying. Her small frame shook with more sorrow and fear than such a child should ever have to face.

All her own fear forgotten, Stephanie whirled and broke free of her captor's grip to face this bodiless voice that had commanded friend and foe alike. She found herself staring face to well…face to chest, an extremely large chest. Actually more like a great wall draped in wool.

Without hesitating, she took a step back and looked up into a pair of dark gray seething eyes. Stephanie didn't think about the cold fire emanating from those eyes, or even the giant frame to which those unholy eyes belonged, she was so lost in her own anger. She took a deep breath and turned all her anger onto the giant of a man.

"You horrible cruel beast! How dare you set upon such a small group with such a large number? We have done you no harm, nor any wrong to provoke such an attack. We are on a mission of life and death and your men are engaged in nothing more than swordplay. So while your men have some sport, this little girl's mother suffers a breach birth with no one to help." Stephanie paused for breath before continuing.

"If I were a man you would be kissing the steel of my sword for this. I do not care who you are or where you have come from, but I demand that you return immediately and let us proceed to save Anne's life."

Stephanie stopped and in the silence she realized what she had just said and to whom she had said it. This man was truly a giant! He towered over her and was built with such muscle, she was sure if she reached out to touch him she would touch nothing but cold hard stone. Then when she looked into the man's face, that was exactly what she saw, cold hard stone. She also saw his jet black hair, black as obsidian rock and just as shiny. His hair brushed the top of his shoulders that were so wide Stephanie was sure they did not belong to just any ordinary man.

Stephanie had no idea how right she was. Iain MacDonald was no ordinary man. He was the Laird of the large MacDonald clan and he was having a bad day. Newly made leader after the sudden death of his father, Duncan MacDonald and his second wife Kaitlyn six months ago, Iain MacDonald at twenty three found himself trying to govern a lot of good people at a very bad time. His people looked to him to discover why their lands were suddenly being raided by their English neighbor, Lord William Rockforte.

Iain had traveled with a small contingent of men in the hopes of finding some clues as to why Lord Rockforte had begun these raids. Iain had no intention of meeting anyone on this mission, let alone engage in any skirmishes. Yet here he was faced with his men playing with the small group of untried men, and with this woman. She was garbed as a peasant but her tone and demeanor was that of a high born lady. She was beautiful, standing before him with green eyes flashing angry fire at him. Her hands braced on her waist accenting the roundness of her figure. Tendrils of honey gold hair had sprung free from the knot at the nape of her neck, more than that she was graceful and extremely tall for a woman. All together she was stunning in his eyes as she railed at him without fear. Suddenly her voice cut into his reverie.

"Let us pass! Do you hear me? We must reach Mary's mother right away!" After her initial tirade Stephanie had managed to gain control of her anger but time was critical, they had to go now.

"Nay" Iain said quietly.

"Nay?" Stephanie echoed. Had this giant heard nothing that she said?

"Nay. I canna let ye pass. If I do then ye shall be free tae go and sound the alarm to have me and my men taken."

"Did you not listen? I told you I do not care who you are, let us by. We have no time to sound any alarm. Anne's life is in peril." Had Stephanie stopped speaking she might have persuaded Iain to let the small group go but she added. "Besides by the time I do sound the alarm, you will all be gone from these lands where you do not belong."

"Aha, so ye would sound the alarm. Well then here is what we shall do. I, along with my men, will accompany you to this woman Anne's home then we shall see what is tae be done."

"Fine. We need to be off." Stephanie tried to move to her own mount but the Scot's hand held her fast. She looked at Iain. "Tell your man to release me so that I may mount my horse."

Iain smiled a mirthless smile. "This man is my brother."

"We do not have time for this. I don't care who he is, just have him release me so we can go."

"Ye will ride with me lass." Her captor said.

"Nay, she'll ride with me." Iain stepped forward and lifted Stephanie onto the back of his horse as if she were nothing more than a feather. She couldn't ignore the flutter in her belly at his touch and his incredible strength. The man made her feel ridiculously fragile.

Stephanie finally got a look at her captor, also a large man like his brother but with bright red hair and whiskers. He had twinkling blue eyes as he spoke.

"Of course, brother, she rides with you." Stephanie watched in confusion as the red haired man walked to Mary. Before Stephanie could speak the large man lifted Mary into the saddle and swung himself up behind her. As the dark stranger mounted behind her his muscles rippled. Stephanie could feel the power of the movement through her rough wool dress. She felt a chill run up her spine and an overwhelming desire to lean back into the solid warmth of the man's body. Her physical reaction to his presence made her uncomfortable so she tried to shift away from him and snapped indignantly.

"I am perfectly capable of riding my own horse. Put me down at once."

"Nay lass. We are going to go together tae look after this woman's birthing, if yer story is indeed true. Until then ye shall be with me so I can keep an eye on ye. Let's be off." Iain spared no glance at anyone as he began to ride.

Mary, who had lapsed into shock, came back with a start at he jolt of the horse's movement.

"Lady Stephanie" she cried out in fearful anguish. "Lady Stephanie where are you? Mama? Mama?" Mary burst into soul racking sobs as she retreated inside herself again.

Iain's eyebrows drew together in a formidable line across the hard planes of his face. He looked quickly over at Fergus, whose face mirrored Iain's own shock at hearing who they had in their grasp. Lady Stephanie Rockforte, Lord William Rockforte's own daughter!

Chapter Two

Stephanie cringed inwardly as Mary called her by her given name. Now the danger was much greater. She had no idea what the band of Scots was doing on her father's lands but because of the recent troubles she knew their presence did not bode well. Unfortunately she couldn't spare much thought to all that. What was done was done. Stephanie had to stay focused on calming Mary down until they reached her home. She spoke to Iain.

"Ride up next to her so that she may see me and speak to me." Iain moved up next to his brother's mount as Stephanie addressed the little girl "Mary, Mary, it is me. It is Lady Stephanie. I am here. Don't cry now, you must still be brave. You have to show these men how to get to your home so we can help your mother. Look, Mary, their horses are much larger than our own. Show…"Stephanie looked questioningly at the red whiskered man with Mary.

"Fergus" he said "My name is Fergus."

"Come Mary show Fergus how to get to your house and we will ride like the wind on these fast brave steeds."

Iain listened as Stephanie spoke. He marveled that she was not only beautiful but also very intelligent. She soothed Mary by making Iain and his men appear to be heroes rather than villains that attacked them. This kept Mary from panicking as they rode to her house.

"We are here." Mary spoke with tears in her voice, afraid that they were already too late to help her mother.

They dismounted and Iain followed Stephanie to the small cottage. Surprisingly, it was neat and well kept, with a small garden in front and chickens happily scratching for grubs. It was difficult to believe that amidst such hominess, life was in peril. Iain watched as Stephanie moved to the entrance with complete ease. She was in no way bothered about entering such humble surroundings, a lady without pretense. All her remarkable qualities aside, now that he knew who she was, his original fact finding mission had changed. Ideas formed in his mind and he needed to talk to Fergus.

Stephanie was fully aware that Iain was behind her. The man shook her to her very core. She tried to convince herself it was because they had attacked her and her group. But her thoughts drifted to his eyes, such intense eyes. Gray and cold like the worst winter storms. His face was hard and strong with sharp cheekbones and square jaw with full lips. His lips were a contrast to the rest of him, so soft and full. She couldn't help but wonder what it would be like to be kissed by him. Her heart skipped a beat.

What was the matter with her? The day's events must truly have shaken her more than she thought, daydreaming about this stranger. Shocked by her thoughts, Stephanie turned without warning to face Iain.

He was so close behind her, he almost knocked her over. Quickly he reached and pulled her forward to prevent her from toppling over backward. She looked up into his searing eyes and blurted out.

"Sir, you cannot enter here. Anne is in great pain and has enough worry already. If she should see your towering frame filling her house, she would likely die of fright."

"Die?"

Stephanie cursed herself for being absurdly over dramatic "In any case she will be frightened enough to make this difficult birth even more difficult."

"Lady I shall be coming in, I canna risk that ye would find another way out and go call for help." Iain suddenly noticed he was holding Stephanie close enough to see her pulse fluttering at the base of her throat. He thought how lovely she looked trying to be so brave. She looked imploringly at him.

"Please. Have a thought for the woman who suffers inside. You are a stranger. I cannot let you enter here."

Iain raised his brows "Ye canna allow me?"

Stephanie shook her head. "No I will not. I must think of Anne. Her well being surpasses anything you think I am going to do."

"Lady, are ye arguing with me? Do I need tae remind ye who is in charge here?"

"I don't care who you think you are, but Anne is more important here. If she dies you will be responsible. Can you live with that?" Stephanie was getting frustrated and desperate.

"Go Lady. We will wait out here for ye." It was the man named Fergus who spoke. He and Mary had just come up behind them to hear the exchange. Iain looked angry and as if he was going to argue. Rather he said.

"Aye brother ye are right. We have much we need tae discuss. Remember lass, when all is done, mother and babe are settled ye are tae come right back here tae me. Is that understood?"

"Yes" Stephanie turned to go into Anne's house hoping to find they were not too late.

Once Iain watched Stephanie go into the small home he turned to find his brother studying him intently.

"Iain, what are ye thinking? We should be long gone by now. What purpose is served by staying here? Every moment we linger we risk discovery or capture."

Though the brothers shared the same father only, they were as close as full brothers. Fergus's mother, their father's second wife, was Iain's wet nurse since his own mother died in childbirth. So the boys were brought up together. As such they were as tough on each other as true brothers. Iain didn't respond so Fergus continued. "Ye canna do this. We must go. Ye ken who we are with right?"

"I ken full well who we are with brother and that is why we are still here. When she joins us we shall be taking her with us."

"Nay Iain" Fergus was shocked. "You ask for war. That is far too dangerous."

"Fergus, we canna get the proof we need in secret like this. We always risk discovery and next time we may not be as lucky as we were today. I dinna want war I want tae prevent one."

"How do ye mean tae prevent war by taking Stephanie Rockforte?"

"I shall question her and see how much she knows of her father's raids against us."

"But if she knows nothing, once she is released she will run back and tell her father everything. He will attack us for sure."

"If he wants to see Stephanie alive again he won't."

"What?"

"We both know no matter what we do Lady Stephanie will run home to her father and tell him she was attacked by Scots. We also know that her father will gather arms and march against us. Up until now he has relied on darkness to cover his attacks. But if he finds we have come to his lands and exchanged blows with his men, he will openly pursue war with us under the guise of seeking retribution for the 'attack.' But, if I have Stephanie with me, I may be able tae delay the battle until we are prepared."

"Are ye sure of this?" Fergus did not look quite convinced and Iain could not blame him.

"Aye, Lady Stephanie Rockforte stays with us until her father confesses the raids or hands over the people he hired to carry out the raiding."

"It seems we have tae to what we must tae try tae protect ourselves."

"Ye have the right of it Fergus. If Lord Rockforte attempts anything, then his daughter's life is forfeit."

Chapter Three

Unaware that Iain and Fergus were deciding her fate, Stephanie entered the cottage with Mary. Mary rushed over to her mother.

"Mama, Mama. I have brought Lady Stephanie. She came to make everything all right."

Stephanie was pleased that Mary made no mention of the attack or their current escort. She stood next to Mary and looked down at Anne's spent figure on the bed. Anne lay in the center of the bed soaked in sweat. Her hair was matted to her head and face. She struggled to stay awake.

"Hush Anne" Stephanie said as she watched Anne try to speak. "Time enough for talk later. We need to get to work and get your baby born into this world. Mary do you have any clean cloths and fresh water?"

Suddenly Anne was hit with another contraction, too weak to cry out she struggled to breathe. Stephanie watched as Mary began to go into shock at the sight of her mother's efforts, she had to stop it. "Mary I need your help now." Stephanie spoke quietly but firmly. Mary reluctantly looked away from her mother's flushed sweat drenched face into Stephanie's calm green eyes.

"Mary I want you to get me all the clean material you can find in your house. Get me a pitcher of water from the table with the ladle. Build up the fire a little, just enough to heat some water."

Mary began to busy herself to complete the jobs Stephanie had given her, obviously trying not to worry about her mother. Stephanie wished there was more she could do to ease Mary's upset but she had to focus on Anne.

She bent over Anne's enlarged belly and pressed to see if she could determine anything wrong. Anne's belly seemed much too taut and there seemed to be more movement than usual. Granted Stephanie had not birthed many babies, but she had been in attendance for enough to know that Anne's multiple contractions might harm the baby or possibly worse. She began to gently massage Anne's writhing belly.

"Oh Lady," Anne weakly groaned, "Thank you. What is happening? Can you tell? Can you see anything?"

"No Anne, nothing yet." Stephanie replied. What could the problem be? She couldn't know for certain but she had to get Anne to relax and not fight the contractions. Perhaps that would speed up the baby's birth.

Anne suddenly cried out and clenched her muscles.

"Don't fight Anne." Stephanie increased the frequency and pressure of her movements, hoping to provide Anne some relief. Suddenly she felt Anne's belly shift. Anne let out a yell and Stephanie finally saw the baby's head. Anne pushed again and the shoulders followed.

"It's a boy Anne! It's a boy!" Stephanie was so happy to see the healthy baby, tears streamed down her face. She cradled the wailing infant as she cleaned him. Mary looked at her mother and said with some fear and amazement.

"Look Lady Stephanie, Mama's not done. Look! Look!"

"It is all right Mary. It is just the afterbirth."

"No my Lady, it is another head."

Stephanie turned around. Suddenly it all made sense! The size of Anne's belly. The extraordinary amount of movement Stephanie had felt when she massaged Anne's girth. All that with the length of Anne's delivery, Anne was having twins. Stephanie handed Mary her baby brother and waited for the second baby to be born. Anne struggled to push, instinct taking over and preventing her from fainting from exhaustion.

"God! I can't do this anymore. I must rest." Anne began to drift into unconsciousness.

Stephanie grabbed her hand "No Anne!" she said firmly "Look at me. You must not give up. Think of your babes. They need their mother. You still have one more baby to bring into the world. God has blessed you with one strong lad already. You cannot give up before the second baby is born. Your babies need you. Come on Anne, push."

Anne looked into Stephanie's eyes and Stephanie could see how exhausted and desperate she was. But Stephanie couldn't let her quit.

"Come Anne" Stephanie coaxed. "You need to get through this so you can meet your beautiful babies. Mary needs you too. Tom is going to come in from the fields and you need to introduce him to his children. You cannot give up. One more push."

Anne met Stephanie's eyes. A flash of strength passed between the two women bound together by the miracle of childbirth. Stephanie watched Anne take a deep breath and give one last push. Mary's second baby brother emerged with as lusty a wail as his older brother. Anne collapsed against the bed immediately asleep.

With great wonder Stephanie and Mary cleaned up the newborn babes as the boys protested their entry. Stephanie wrapped the boys and noticed that Mary had torn up one of her own shifts to swaddle her brothers in. Stephanie smiled to see that already Mary had taken to her role as older sister and protector of her new baby brothers. Mary brought her brothers to her mother.

Stephanie gently shook Anne awake. "Anne one more job to do then you can rest. You have to feed these young warriors. They already have their priorities in order. Eat first, then rest."

A beaming yet obviously spent Anne reached for her two young sons. "Thank you my Lady. I could not have done this without you."

Stephanie smiled "I rather think you would have managed to succeed without me."

Anne shook her head. "No my Lady, I mean just having you here with me gave me the strength to keep going, when I wanted so much to give up. You saved me, my Mary and my new babies. Thank you." Anne turned to nurse her boys a loving peaceful smile on her lips.

Stephanie was so touched by Anne's genuine belief that Stephanie saved her, she was moved to silence. The love and peace that radiated in the small humble cottage was overwhelming.

Unfortunately, the peace did not last for Stephanie and she was suddenly flooded with the memory of what was waiting for her outside.

Chapter Four

"I see all is well at last." As if conjured from her thoughts, there filling the doorway with his enormous frame, stood the Scot. Stephanie was surprised to hear such a large man speak in such a gentle soothing tone. She knew he did that for the benefit of the mother and the new babies but that didn't quell her nerves as she hissed at him.

"What are you doing here? I told you not to enter. You are a stranger and much too imposing to go unnoticed in here. You must leave at once before you upset Anne and her new sons."

Iain raised his brows. "Twins eh? She is a verra fortunate woman. But my Lady I dinna think ye have tae worry about my 'imposing' presence. Tis unlikely she knows I am here. Look."

Stephanie turned and saw that Anne and her new sons were fast asleep on the bed. Their ordeal was over.

"Now, so as not tae wake them I would like tae speak tae ye outside Lady."

Before Stephanie could utter a word, he had her elbow and was firmly guiding her out the door. Sheer exhaustion from the day's events had her speaking before thinking, something she rarely did. She dug her heels in and faced Iain.

"What do you think you are doing? You can't just drag me away from there. I have to check Anne and the babies and make sure they are well and comfortable. What if something goes wrong?"

"Calm yourself my Lady. I dinna think there is any danger. Mother and bairns all looked well in their sleep. Your duty is done and obviously done well. Now we must leave."

"Leave? Well good. Then go. I told you I would not tell anyone what took place today and I meant it. I have no further quarrel with you. Besides I do not even know who you are, so how could I tell anyone about you?" Stephanie hoped her assurance would be enough to convince this burly Scot to leave and take his men with him. She did mean to tell her father's men to watch for the group of Scots but that was all anyone needed to know.

Besides no one had been hurt and Stephanie just wanted to get back inside and make sure Anne, Mary and the twins were well and settled before she went home and cleaned herself up. Maybe she could even have a rest before supper had to be prepared. The sooner this giant was on his way, the sooner she could begin to forget this ordeal.

"Och! Where are my manners? Lady Stephanie allow me tae introduce myself. I am Iain MacDonald, Laird of the clan MacDonald. We are yer neighbors. We have come tae find out why yer father has been raiding our lands, stealing our livestock and burning our people's cottages and crops."

Stephanie's mouth dropped open in shock and dismay. She could not believe what she was hearing. This man, Iain, was telling her everything about himself. Why would he incriminate himself like this? He was admitting to trespassing and spying on her father's land. Why? No, her mind must be playing tricks on her. Iain MacDonald had everything to lose and nothing to gain by revealing himself like this. Iain's words cut into her thoughts.

"Now that we have been properly introduced, and ye ken my purpose for being here, I canna risk ye exposing us so ye must come with us."

"No! You must be mad. Please just take your men and go. I swear I will say nothing to anyone."

Iain shook his head "Nay, I willna risk my men's safety on the word of a woman, especially a stranger."

Stephanie's cheeks flushed at the insult. "I assure you Laird Iain that my word is better than most men in my experience. What you are suggesting though is madness. I am going home and hopefully will wake to find this all a distant memory. Because you are admitting to trespassing on my father's lands leads me to believe one of two things, either you are crazy or I am."

"Well Lady I can speak well for myself, I amna crazy. Ye I canna say for sure. Now we are losing valuable time. We must leave here and ye are coming with us."

"No I will not." Stephanie said emphatically shaking her head.

"Listen Lady Stephanie, ye ken who I am and I willna risk ye telling yer da that I was here with my men. So you will accompany me back to my home. Ye will also remain with me at my home until the raiding stops on my lands and my people. If I have ye safe with me on my lands then yer father will have tae end these attacks against us. Desperate times require desperate measures."

Stephanie was stunned by Iain's accusations. "You cannot be serious" She said angry enough to move closer to Iain and stand toe to toe with him. Her green eyes flashed challengingly at him. "My father would never cause anyone else any harm nor any damage. In fact we, too, are plagued by raids and property damage. I know that evidence shows it is Scots that are perpetrating these attacks on us. Therefore, I could argue your presence indicates your guilt in these raids against us. No one would doubt my claim since you are here without anyone's knowledge. I rather think you need to accompany back to my home to answer my father's questions."

This was how Fergus found them, staring one another down each refusing to back down. Lady Stephanie Rockforte surprised him, she did not seem intimidated by his brother at all. She stood inches from him glaring at him. Fergus thought he should step in because obviously whatever she was doing was angering Iain more.

Even though he didn't agree with Iain's plan he had to help make it succeed. The MacDonald clan needed Iain now. So if Iain wanted Lady Stephanie to return to Scotland then he would do what ever necessary to help his brother. Fergus watched as Stephanie jabbed her finger forcefully into Iain's chest.

"For the last time, no! Who do you think you are? You think you can come onto my father's lands and accuse him of raiding your property without any real proof. And now you mean to take me prisoner to make the raids stop? Even I, a mere woman, can see how dangerous that plan is."

Fergus moved to intervene but Iain spoke in a tone that left no room for doubt or argument.

"Silence Lady. Ye are coming with me and this can be done one of two ways. First, ye can come with me quietly and no one is hurt. Second, ye raise the alarm and everyone who comes tae yer assistance, man woman or child, will be killed tae prevent yer father hearing of us until I am ready. How much do ye care about yer people Lady Stephanie? Will ye come with me quietly or will ye make yer people suffer fear and death for yer willfulness?"

Stephanie's demeanor deflated somewhat, she knew she had no choice in the matter. "You bastard." She said quietly but with the full force of the anger she had inside. "You leave me no choice. I go with you but not willingly. No one must know of your treachery this day until I am long gone for I cannot bear it if anyone died trying to rescue me. Do what you must but I will have your word that no one will die."

"I canna make that promise Lady. But I can promise that no one will come to harm if we remain unchallenged."

Stephanie said nothing so Iain turned and strode purposefully into the small hut. He surveyed the scene before him. Anne lay sleeping peacefully with her two new sons resting quietly in the crook of each arm. Mary moved quietly, cleaning up the space while looking as happy and content as a new older sister should. She turned and smiled shyly at Iain as he filled the doorway.

"Look at my new brothers, sir." She whispered. "Here because you saved us and brought us home quickly, like our own guardian angels."

Iain was momentarily taken aback by Mary's revision of the day's events. She seemed to have forgotten all about the skirmish that had taken place. She had a memory of being saved by Iain and his men, not attacked. Iain was quite relieved by this memory adjustment and decided he would take advantage of her revised view of the events

"Mary, I am glad that you an your family are well. But ye must promise tae keep me and my men secret. We are secret guardian angels and no one must know we are here."

Mary tilted her neck back to look up at Iain. "Can't I tell my ma about you? She'd want to thank you for helping us."

"Nay, Mary." Iain spoke quietly and gently. "Ye mustn't tell anyone we were here. Some people dinna like us and might try tae come and stop us from helping other people like you." Ian felt only a small twinge of guilt embellishing Mary's fantasy but he had to make sure no one followed them.

"You mean the bad men that tried to stop us from getting to my mama in time, will try to stop you from helping others?" Mary looked incredulous.

"Aye wee one. They will do anything they can tae try and stop us. So we need ye tae keep our secret so we can keep on safely doing our work." Iain waited for what felt like an eternity for Mary to answer.

"Not even my mama can know?" Mary asked.

"Nay."

"Well she probably wouldn't believe me anyway. She is always telling me my imagination is running away with me. When are you leaving?"

"Now, wee one. That is why I am here tae see ye. Lady Stephanie will be coming with us as well."

"Forever?" Mary looked fearful.

"Nay, lass, not forever. But ye ken how well she helped yer ma. We need her tae help us do our good work for a while."

"Lady Stephanie is going to help guardian angels? I promise I will keep the secret. But can you bring her back safely soon so she can come and play with me and my brothers?"

"Aye little Mary. I will bring her back as soon as I can." As soon as her father agreed to end his raiding against the MacDonald clan, Iain added silently in his thoughts. Out loud he continued. "Now ye will keep our secret right?"

"Yes sir. Thank you so much for protecting us."

Iain turned and left Mary knowing that he had covered his tracks as best he could, given the circumstances.

Chapter Five

As Iain walked back towards Stephanie he felt some measure of guilt at the pathetic figure before him. Her blond hair hung lankly around her pale face. When she looked up at his approach he was sorry to see the vitality she had displayed at their first meeting, was buried deep under exhaustion and defeat. He felt sorry for her but for the sake of his clan he had to steel himself against the pity and stay his course.

"What about Duncan, Edmund and Matthew? Are you going to kill them?" Stephanie's voice rang small and hollow in her own ears, but no matter how hard she tried she could not find the energy to fuel the anger buried deep inside her. She waited for Iain MacDonald to answer her.

"Nay, they shall be coming with us. Believe it or not, Lady Stephanie, I am as anxious to avoid bloodshed as ye are."

Stephanie bit out a retort. "Excuse me, sir, but I find that very difficult to believe under the circumstances."

Iain scowled at Stephanie and she glared back. Iain wanted to set Stephanie Rockforte in her proper place as prisoner, but he couldn't spare one more moment. They had to leave.

"Fergus it is time to mount up. Get the Englishmen on horseback but gag and bind them until we are off Lord Rockforte's lands. We do not want anyone alerted to our presence. We have been lucky thus far but it does not seem wise to think our luck will hold out. Move out."

Fergus moved to follow Iain's orders. He felt sorry for the three young English boys, who obviously had no experience in any type of battle. Once they had been trussed up and hoisted onto horseback, Fergus noticed the baleful resentful glances the burly Scots were casting in the young boys' direction. Fergus was afraid that the hostility might mount during the ride home. He had to do something. He walked among the Scots with a warning.

"Dinna let Laird Iain see ye judge, nor condemn these men because of their nationality. We dinna ken if these be the culprits who have been raiding us. Sae dinna treat them as guilty with no proof. Set yer anger aside men and let our new Laird guide us through this difficult time. Dinna presume tae know better than he."

All the men looked sheepishly at each other then quickly looked away from the English lads. The young men looked more than relieved that Fergus had stepped in.

Satisfied the men could control their anger for now, Fergus mounted his horse and turned to look for Iain and Lady Rockforte. When he found them he wasn't much surprised by the scene. Iain stood looking down at the top of Stephanie's head and he did not look at all pleased. Stephanie stood with arms crossed and a decidedly mulish glare on her face. Fergus took pity on his brother and called the men to start out.

Iain shot his brother a grateful look. He knew he should have been leading his men out but he was currently engaged in what appeared to be a one sided silent battle of wills with the stubborn woman in front of him. Stephanie was refusing to move from the spot she stood in. She spoke first.

"If you mean to make me go with you, then you must make me move. For although I have said I will go with you I still do not go with you willingly."

"Lady if ye wish tae surrender yer dignity make nae mistake I will move ye myself. But ye willna be pleased by the means by which I use tae move ye from this place."

Stephanie risked a peek at her captor hoping to see that he was only bluffing. But all she saw was his icy glare. She became instantly aware that she may have pushed this stranger too far. She must have taken leave of her senses, she knew nothing about him and here she was deliberately provoking him. She realized that it was fool-hardy to raise his ire when she had no idea what his reaction might be.

"Fine then. Let us be moving. It appears your brother and your men have left you behind." Stephanie swept past Iain with that stinging remark. She uttered a very unladylike squeak of surprise when she found her waist enclosed in the circle of his massive arm. Despite her own height, next to Iain MacDonald she was feeling very much smaller than her actual size.

Iain swept Stephanie up against his side and walked over to his own horse.

"What do you think you are doing?" Stephanie asked indignantly.

"As ye so eloquently put it my lady, my men have gone on ahead of us. I find myself not in my proper place as Laird, because I made the grave error of trying tae reason with ye. My mistake seems tae be allowing ye the opportunity tae leave this place without jeopardizing any of your people's safety."

Iain fairly flung Stephanie on the back of his horse.

"There is no need to toss me like a sack of grain." Stephanie huffed as she tried to arrange herself decorously in the saddle. Her dress was hiked up around her ankles and she was feeling very exposed. "Besides" she added. "There is no need for me to be on your horse I am quite capable of riding on my own."

"That may be so Lady." Iain said as he vaulted up onto the horse and settled behind her. "But yer familiarity with yer own lands puts me at a disadvantage should ye attempt tae escape. And I dinna like tae be at a disadvantage."

They both lapsed into cold silence. In that silence Stephanie suddenly became aware of his proximity. His size crowded both of them in the saddle. Stephanie kept trying to move away from him but each time she moved his sheer size quickly filled the gap between them. No matter how she moved her shoulder or her legs, he was instantly touching her again. The heat in his skin burned through the coarse wool of her dress causing her belly to flutter strangely. Here was this strange man kidnapping her from her home, and rather than fear she felt anger and a very surprising, growing thrill to be near him.

Iain thought he was going mad. He did not know where this desire had come from for his captive. But as she squirmed about in the saddle he wanted to drag her into his lap and kiss her until she was senseless. He could feel the softness of her skin and her scent was driving him to distraction. He had to get hold of himself. She was his prisoner, his collateral for his clan. With her, he could negotiate peace with her father. But he had to maintain his distance. She was his instrument for peace, not a woman he could dally with. All that into account, it was hard to keep his distance when he was pressed against her softness and warmth.

"Ye will cease ye incessant movement immediately!" Iain spoke sharply into her ear and pulled her tightly against his chest so she was firmly planted before him. In response she held herself ramrod straight and still and replied quietly.

"I will sit still, you barbarian, but you might loosen your hold on me. I am quite sure my father will not thank you if I am crushed in your grip and you have to deliver my lifeless body back to his keep."

"Hrumph" was Iain's only reply but he loosened his hold slightly. She was still pinned to his chest but she could at least breathe.

This was their last exchange for quite some time. They caught up with Fergus and the others. Fergus took one look at Iain's thunderous scowl and Stephanie's determinedly set jaw and he knew he had best keep silent and pretend not to notice anything.

Iain said nothing to anyone and he barely acknowledged the others as he took his place at the head of the procession. For the next several hours no one spoke, they had to maintain quiet until they were off English soil.

Chapter Six

After a while Iain realized it was beginning to grow dark and he thought it would be best if they stopped for the night. He found a clearing near a river and gave the order to stop by raising his hand. Iain had not spoken since they left the cottage. All his men did not find that unusual, they all knew he had much on his mind as well as trying to escort them through hostile territory. So they all moved about making up the overnight campsite, not saying much to one another.

Stephanie couldn't help but wonder what kind of men they were. Granted she couldn't expect them to be very friendly to her, she was a prisoner after all, but they didn't seem to be very friendly with each other either. She watched them move about making camp methodically. They must have done this many times before as each man performed specific tasks. In no time at all they were finished. Temporary beds were set up covered with each man's plaid that they had wrapped their provisions in.

Stephanie realized with some surprise that she and Iain remained on his horse while camp was set up. Then she realized with some measure of admiration that despite the sparse accommodation Iain waited until his men were finished before he saw to his own comfort. She couldn't help but be impressed by his selflessness. He broke her reverie when he jumped of the back of his horse, turned and lifted her off. Embarrassed by her thoughts of admiration about her kidnapper, she was going to decline his offer for assistance with all the disdain she could muster. But before she knew it he had hoisted her off and dumped her on a rock at the edge of the clearing.

"Sit." Iain ordered her and turned away before Stephanie had the chance to speak.

Stephanie glared at his retreating form. Her indignation growing until she thought she would scream.

"Stubborn, rude man! Carrying me like a sack of potatoes, dumping me here and walking away as if I were nothing more than a piece of baggage to be tossed around." Stephanie continued to rant to herself feeling somewhat better as she did so.

"Not even enough manners to consider that I might have needs to attend to. It would not take a very clever man to realize that I have not had a chance to relieve myself since before we arrived at Anne's house and that he gave me no opportunity to do so before he forced me to leave. Of course here I am comparing this Scottish behemoth to a clever man. Silly me. But he is a stupid, selfish arrogant lout!"

"Well I guess I shall have to look after myself then." She rose to move around behind the rock she had been dumped on, and promptly crumpled into an undignified heap on the ground. All the standing next to Anne and then sitting on the back of Iain's horse for so long, had made her muscles sore and weak. Suddenly her fatigue hit her and she began to weep.

"Did I not tell ye tae sit?...Why are ye crying?" Iain looked rather surprised and discomfited as he stared down at the rumpled figure on the ground. Stephanie turned her tear streaked face up to Iain and found herself overwhelmed with the urge to kick him as hard as she could. In her current state she told him as much. Iain raised his brows at her.

"Och really now? And why would ye be kicking me lass?"

"Because you are a boorish oaf. That is why." Iain crossed his arms waiting for Stephanie to continue. He didn't have to wait long. "I have been on my feet all day helping Anne give birth. I am tired, hungry, sore and dirty. And I haven't, haven't...Oh never mind it is obvious you don't understand or care. Just go away and leave me in peace."

Stephanie felt her eyes filling with tears again. She quickly swallowed knowing if she had to speak again at that moment, she would lose her composure and begin crying all over again. She didn't want her thin veil of dignity to be shredded in front of this insensitive brute. He was a brute. How could he not know that at the very least she needed a moment of privacy to relieve herself.

Iain had to admit as he stood studying her, that he was enjoying watching her struggle with her pride. He knew she wanted to look after her personal needs, but he wanted the small satisfaction of hearing her ask for his assistance. He was surprised by his petty behavior. It was not in his nature to subject a woman to such embarrassing discomfort. But he did not want the Lady Stephanie to be comfortable with him. At this moment she was his prisoner and he had to remind himself not to get too comfortable with her either.

Stephanie cleared her throat and spoke. Nothing could have prepared him for the words she uttered.

"I need you to lift me up and take me to a sheltered spot near the river so that I can relieve myself and at least wash my hands and face of the dirt I have been wearing for the last several hours. Since you are such an ignorant clod I must reduce myself to sound like a tavern wench just to have such simplicities acknowledged and addressed. So if you would please stop standing there like a mute and help me, we can go back to pretending that I am not here and I can be out of your way."

Iain did not say a word at her castigation because she was right. But that somehow angered him. He took her up and walked her over to a small copse of trees next to the river as she so imperiously requested. He set her on the ground and steadied her until Stephanie's legs were finally able to keep her upright.

"Thank you." She sniffed "You can leave now. You don't have to worry, I am not going anywhere. I have no idea where I am so I am not going to run away. I wouldn't know where to go even if I did leave. Besides, I am not going to run away and leave my father's men behind. I have no idea what you or your men might do to them and I couldn't live with the uncertainty of their fate just to save myself. Now, give me a moment's peace and privacy. I will call you when I have finished."

Impertinent chit! Iain thought. "You have ten minutes Lady and then I will return to take ye back tae camp. Be sure tae have completed yer ablutions because ye will be leaving with me when I return, ready or not." With that declaration Iain turned and left Stephanie without another word.

Stephanie stuck her tongue out at his retreating back. Her childish display of temper helped distract her a bit from the ever increasing pain in her legs and buttocks as the feeling began to return to her extremities. She didn't trust herself to move just yet so she stood in place and rubbed her painful muscles.

Knowing she did not have much time, she forced herself to move quickly, yet stiffly to relieve herself. Then she limped to the river to wash her hands and face. She knelt down and splashed the cold water on her face. The icy chill in the water refreshed her and made her skin tingle. After she took a long drink, she had to admit she was feeling a bit better. However she had no time to linger. Laird MacDonald would be back shortly and she wanted to be ready and waiting for him.

But when she tried to straighten up from the bank, she was stuck! Her back was so stiff and tired she was unable to get up.

She was frozen in place!

Damn! This could not be happening. Stephanie struggled desperately to try to force herself to stand, but she was well and truly stuck. Stephanie was mortified. Iain would be back at any moment, she was sure she would die from the embarrassment of him finding her like this.

Iain strode into the clearing ready to engage in another battle of words with the prickly Lady Stephanie. He certainly did not expect to find her as he did. He wanted to laugh. He watched her nicely rounded derriere pointed skyward moving in the most endearing way as she struggled to get up.

What was happening to him? She was robbing him of his common sense as his thoughts drifted towards enticing fantasies of her in this position. He was no better than a randy schoolboy. Iain had to gain his self control.

"It seems Lady that you are fully occupied at the moment. Perhaps I should return later?"

"No! No, you mustn't. I need your help I am stuck. My back won't straighten. Please don't leave me. Please don't let anyone else see me like this."

Iain felt like such a lout, imagining her naked when she was in quite a predicament. Iain helped Stephanie up, then walked slowly but purposefully back to camp to allow her to move easier on her own. Back at camp everyone was settling in for the night. The light was fading quickly but Stephanie scanned the group until she found Duncan, Edmund and Matthew. She saw they were still bound but they had been covered and were lying out on the ground with one of Iain's men between them so they could not untie each other. They appeared to be all right for the moment. Feeling somewhat relieved, Stephanie allowed Iain to lead her back to the rock. She sat down and Iain gave her some food. It was meager trail food, dry bread, an apple and some cheese; but it was enough to keep her hunger at bay. Iain turned and left her as she ate her simple meal.

Iain walked over to the fire to join Fergus, who studied his brother as he approached.

"Well brother, why do ye sit there staring at me as if I had suddenly sprouted two heads?" Iain asked as he sat next to Fergus.

Fergus chuckled softly "Iain I just hope ye ken what ye have taken on. This Lady is a bit of a handful. I hope she doesna prove tae be more of a problem then she is worth. Ye ken tis not too late for ye tae change yer mind."

"Nay, she comes with us." Iain said a little more forcefully then he needed to. At Fergus's raised brow he continued. "She will be our guarantee that our people will be able tae rest easy and return tae their way of life without being afraid tae wake up the next morning and find that it is all gone. She will ensure this."

"Aye dinna fash yerself, brother. I support ye but I dinna think ye ken what ye have taken on with this lass." Fergus began chuckling. He knew his brother was affected by this tall English beauty. Fergus knew that these two were attracted to one another and he was keen to see what happened as their attraction grew.

Iain wondered briefly if his brother was slightly daft. But Iain was tired, they all were, perhaps that is why they were all acting out of character. No matter, Iain thought to himself. He needed to get some sleep so that he could push home tomorrow.

Iain reached his spot in the camp and found Stephanie already asleep. Her beauty shone through when she was in deep slumber. Her lovely honey hair tousled around her face flushed with sleep. Her sandy eyelashes delicately cast half moons on her cheeks. She looked so fragile, yet desirable. Every breath she took made her breasts strain against the fabric of her dress. The poor garment hid her shapely figure, her curves only hinted at through the rough fabric. But he had held her in his arms, he knew by touch, the softness that was hidden to all others. He wanted to touch her again so he lay down, covered her with his plaid and enfolded her into his arms. Feeling how well she fit against him, he fell into the deepest sleep he had known for a long time.

Chapter Seven

Stephanie woke the next morning to find she was paralyzed from the shoulders down. Momentarily confused, she tried to remember what had paralyzed her. Suddenly the previous day's events flashed through her mind. She opened her eyes and found that she was pinned under a very large muscular arm dusted with dark hair and she was well aware who was attached to this immovable band of flesh.

Stephanie turned her head ever so slightly and sure enough she found herself looking into a pair of intense quicksilver eyes. His careful study of her made her feel exposed as if he could see her body and her emotions as clear as the blue sky above them. His black hair was ruffled from sleep and strands fell across his eyes. She wanted to reach over and brush them aside. Stephanie began to feel the increasingly familiar flutter in her stomach she had each time she looked, really looked, at Iain MacDonald. His steely gaze never wavered as he watched her perusal intently.

Iain saw the emotions flicker across Stephanie's face and he was extremely pleased to find she was as discomfited by him as much as he was by her. He wanted to kiss those full rosy lips to see if she was as soft as she looked. He took pleasure in her struggle for composure because he felt the same way.

"Well mistress it seems ye have finally decided tae grace us with yer presence. We have been sorely delayed by yer slug a bed ways."

Stephanie began to bristle and opened her mouth to give Iain a piece of her mind. Then she noticed his eyes sparkling with silent laughter.

"You might find that I would move faster if I was not trapped beneath this great weight." Stephanie plucked uselessly at Iain's muscular arm still holding her in place. She felt his rumbling chuckle before she heard it. Her cheeks felt warm. How dare he laugh at her? He was responsible for the predicament she was presently in. Bad enough on its own, but Stephanie found that Iain's closeness was causing her growing discomfort and that discomfort was not all together unpleasant. In fact, she wished they could be closer still. If Stephanie let herself forget for just a moment, she wanted to snuggle right up to his warmth.

No! Her mind and heart warred with her traitorous body. What was she doing thinking these thoughts and feeling these feelings about the man who had forcibly taken her from her home? Here she was melting into his warmth and strength while her father's young men were bound and gagged a few feet away. Stephanie stole a peek at them on the other edge of the clearing. She noticed first that their hands had been bound in front of them to provide them some measure of comfort through the night. Obviously they were by no means comfortable, but they were not being abused.

Then she saw their eyes. She saw the concern, pity and fear for her. She felt sure she could hear their thoughts of frustration of not being able to protect her from these strangers. Here she was fantasizing about Iain while her father's men struggled with all their guilt and shame. She felt like she was betraying everyone around her. Tears began to sting behind her eyes; but she could not break down in front of these strangers. She had to be strong.

She spoke haughtily to Iain with some measure of disdain. "You know you may remove your arm now. Having spent the night here and not taking the opportunity to run away while you slept I am hardly going to make a dash now that you and your men are awake. Besides you are too hot, sweaty and you smell rather like a wet dog. Kindly remove yourself and go wash."

Iain looked at the top of Stephanie's head and swallowed the urge to laugh again. He took no offense to her sharp words or tone having spent the night with her curled up against him. Memories of the soft sighing sounds she made through the night, flooded back to him and undid the sting of her words.

"Well then my lady…woof. Let us be off. We have some ground to cover before I shall be provided the luxury of bathing facilities in order to be worthy of your attention and not be such an offense to your person. Until then my Lady…." Iain leaned in very close to Stephanie until their noses were almost touching. For a moment Stephanie thought he would kiss her. A tiny part of her hoped he would kiss her but…

"Until then my Lady ye should know that yer scent is not any better than the rest of us her. 'Wet dog still smells like wet dog' even wrapped up in a pretty little package." With that he took his finger and gently rapped the tip of Stephanie's nose. He turned and ordered everyone mounted up and ready to go. He didn't even spare her a glance.

Stephanie stared daggers at his back. She wished she could throw herself at him and knock some sense and manners into his thick skull. He was so arrogant it infuriated her.

"Come Lady Stephanie we are ready to go. Have ye looked after yer needs then?"

Stephanie flushed pink and rushed away. Fergus came and stood beside his brother.

"Iain why do ye insist on teasing the lass so? Do ye'no think she has been through enough? She is hardly in a position tae give ye what ye deserve and ye continue tae tease her? Anyone might think ye had soft feelings for her."

"Fergus if ye were no my brother I would lay ye out flat and knock some of yer teeth out in the bargain. She is our prisoner an I dinna intend tae coddle her back tae the keep. She is tae know her place and she willna be receiving special treatment. Both ye and the Lady Stephanie had better realize she is a tool tae peace, nothing more. Nay, dinna look at me like that Fergus, she means nothing more."

Fergus looked doubtful "Aye, if ye say so, brother."

Iain felt more than a little twinge of annoyance with his brother. Of course he was riling Lady Stephanie. No one, least of all himself, could forget why she was with them. She could not be treated like a pampered guest if she was their hostage.

"Let's ride on. Mount up the prisoners Lady Stephanie ye'll ride with me. Move out men we have ground tae cover."

The ride was long and tedious for Stephanie and very shortly she felt the effects of the day before. She was still exhausted form the ordeal with Anne and her babies. Not to mention the ordeal of being abducted. Sleeping outside on the cold ground was not an experience she wanted to repeat anytime soon. Come to think of it hopefully she would not have to repeat the experience of sleeping next to Iain MacDonald either. But now riding in front of him made it very hard to forget how good he felt, yes good, pressed up against her back in the chill of the ground and the air. She had slept well but she still felt tired in her bones. Stephanie wanted at hot bath and a change of clothes. She was unused to going unwashed for so long. The rough material of her dress chafed her through her shift. She was feeling decidedly uncomfortable and irritable. Suddenly in a pique of temper she shifted and with deliberate force jabbed her shoulder into the great wall of chest behind her.

"Something amiss my Lady?" Iain asked with deliberate sweetness. He knew what she was thinking as if she had spoken the words out loud. People, not just highborn ladies, who were not accustomed to long hours on top of a horse, became extremely sore and stiff in a very short time. To her credit Lady Stephanie had not voiced her obvious discomfort in any way, nor had she made any complaint as many other women of her station in life were wont to do. She bore everything with great fortitude.

At Iain's question Stephanie uttered a very unladylike snort. "Amiss? Why no my Lord everything is to perfection. Here am I in the finest garb a top the most glorious specimen of horseflesh, paired with the most courteous of gentlemen. What could be better?"

"Ach, Lady, ye have a true gift for accurate descriptions." Iain quipped sarcastically. He enjoyed hearing her fiery spirit issue forth again. But her pallor was still obvious. "The truth of it is we shall reach our destination soon. Although I dinna imagine it is an estate, the likes of which ye are used tae, it is my home and I shall be glad tae reach it."

Without thinking, Stephanie replied. "Truly so will I. I have a headache the likes of which I have never suffered before. I would dearly love to get off the back of this horse so I could make a compress for myself." Stephanie sighed and slumped forward a bit. She did have a headache but she really wanted to go home. Iain MacDonald was not a cruel man she realized. She and her father's men had not been injured in anyway. But his presence aroused unfamiliar sensations and desires within her. These unknown feelings made her long for the seclusion and safety of her own home.

Home! What must her father be thinking? He must surely have reached home by now. What would he do to find her gone? Stephanie thought for a moment and realized that it was probably too soon for her father to be home yet.

It was a long journey from King Edward's estate where he had gone to try to enlist the King's aid against the raiding Scots. More than likely if the trip had been successful, her father would rest before going home. If the quest was unsuccessful then Lord Rockforte would have stopped to speak to their neighbor Eduard Stockton to ask for his assistance.

Reluctantly Stephanie had to admit that some time would pass before her father knew she was gone. Then, even more would pass before he could find out where to look for her. His worry saddened her. Her eyes burned with unshed tears at his concern for her fate, and she brushed her arm across her face.

"Are ye unwell madam?" Iain asked fearing that Stephanie had finally reached her limit of endurance and he would be forced to press her forward with some unpleasantness.

Stephanie, too tired and too heart sore to temper her declaration, "I am physically well enough my Lord, but I fear that I am burdened by what your actions will do to my father."

"Fear not Stephanie. Yer father will learn of yer whereabouts and your fate soon enough. But only at a time and place of my choosing."

At his rather ominous words Stephanie turned in the saddle to look at him, but his expression gave nothing away. "As you wish. But what is to be my fate?"

"All will be divulged soon enough. Look we are nearing my home."

Stephanie looked around her and indeed the landscape had changed. Gone was the seemingly endless wall of trees. The small group was now in a section of cultivated land. The land, which should have been full of crops ripening in the sun, was scarred by patches of scorched earth. Stephanie saw that by the size of the land that was burnt, many people must have been determined to put it out to rescue some of the crops so they would not starve in the winter.

"One of your father's gifts to us, Lady." Iain's bitter angry voice sliced into her thoughts. "It took all of the people of my town, men, women and children to cut off the blaze before the whole crop was lost."

Stephanie was so saddened and sickened to hear that the fire had been deliberately set that it took a moment to hear what Iain had said. When his words penetrated her thoughts she responded with heartfelt anger.

"How dare you accuse my father of causing the damage! You have no real proof. Did you see him set the blaze? How do you know it was him?"

Iain felt Stephanie stiffen in indignation in front of him. He could imagine how she must have felt being faced with the scene and the fact her father was connected, probably directly responsible for the senseless destruction.

"Lady, we had word from some local traders who recognized yer father's men in the area shortly before the fire started. But then saw no sign of them afterwards."

Stephanie's eyes glowed green fire at him as she retorted. "How can you be so sure?" Angry desperation rang through her voice. "All you have is the words of people who do not even live here or on my father's lands. They wander from place to place. That is not enough! It can't be enough! You must search for more. It is your duty as clan leader."

"Lady dinna presume tae tell me what my obligation is." Iain's voice was ice cold. "My obligation is tae my people. Their safety and well being is more important than anything else. Whether ye like it or no, yer father's men were seen on these lands the night of this fire and now it is up tae me tae put an end tae these attacks."

Stephanie knew to stop speaking. Iain was too blind to the obvious lack of evidence against her father. She could not reason with him at present. But she knew her father would never be involved in such heinous, cowardly attacks. She just had to find the right time to convince Laid Iain MacDonald.

Chapter Eight

The group of men, with their prisoners, worked their way through the village up the hill to the entrance of the keep. People came out of their homes to welcome their Laird and men home. Their cheers died away when they saw her and then saw the three men tied up riding through the town. Stephanie could hear their speculative whispers and wondered how Iain would react.

Iain remained stoic riding past their inquisitive stares. He remained impassive until they reached the gates of the keep. He did not speak until they came to a stop in the middle of the courtyard. He called for the horses to be stabled then he spoke to the men.

"Take these three captives to the cells. Make sure they have food and water. Be sure to put them in separate cells and unbind their hands." Iain turned and lifted Stephanie off his horse. She felt a jolt of heat run through her as her body slid the length of Iain's muscular form. The heat from their bodies burned through her rough dress. Stephanie briefly allowed her mind to wonder what it would be like to be kissed by this hard giant. When her feet touched the ground Stephanie looked up.

As her green eyes met Iain's stormy gray ones, the jolt of desire nearly overwhelmed her. For and instant she felt sure he felt some attraction towards her. But when she blinked Iain's eyes were cold and distant again, though he still held her in his arms.

Iain's face suddenly darkened as he half pushed half pulled Stephanie along with him up the stairs to the keep. Iain knew he was getting closer to trouble. The longer he spent with the Lady Stephanie the harder it was to forget that she was not just his captive, she was a woman. A uniquely intriguing woman.

How he wanted to lean in and taste her lush lips. He wanted to get lost in the green depths of her eyes. When she looked at him moments ago, he knew she felt the pull between them. This attraction was a dangerous distraction to him and he had to steel himself against it.

As they moved into the great hall Stephanie stole glances up at Iain and wondered what he was thinking. He looked so severe and angry. Although Stephanie knew she should be afraid all she wanted to do was smooth the fierce frown off his face. Suddenly a flash of movement across the great hall caught her eye and pulled her attention from Iain's face.

A beautiful woman rushed across the hall to greet them. Stephanie knew this stranger was what men would consider a 'perfect' woman. She was small but her figure was perfect, tiny waist with round breasts and hips. Her glossy black hair fell to her waist in soft curls framing a small heart shaped face with alabaster skin. Deep blue eyes shone as she came forward to greet them. Stephanie felt truly large and ungainly as the woman she took to be

Iain's wife came to meet them. Astonishingly, Stephanie realized that she was jealous of this woman.

At that moment the vision reached them and flung her perfect arms around Iain.

"Oh thank heavens you are home."

Stephanie's heart felt a leap of hope, this woman was English! Maybe if Stephanie could enlist her fellow country woman's aid to get away. She just had to be alone with her long enough to tell her tale.

"Judith. Judging by your over enthusiastic welcome things are not smooth here?" Iain held the lady Judith with one arm while still holding firmly to Stephanie with the other. Stephanie shifted slightly and wondered if Iain had any idea how tightly he was gripping her. She might be a giant next to his fey wife, but she could still bruise easily. She tried to glare at Iain but he only had eyes for Judith who was looking up at him with her own loving blue eyes. Judith laughed when she spoke, even the woman's laugh was perfect.

"Iain, you are a terrible man. Everything is well and you know it. I am just hoping that if I welcome you home properly you will give me my husband back. I have sorely missed him and you have had him long enough."

Stephanie felt a thrill of hope that perhaps this wasn't Iain's wife. Just then Fergus came up and roared good naturedly.

"Och, here now, mon. Get yer hands off my wife! Ye had yer chance. Now ye shall have tae go and find another woman tae warm yer bed."

"Ah, brother, I have nay need tae wed myself tae some shrieking shrew tae have a warm bed. There be plenty of willing women tae keep me warm. Truth tell, I would rather not tie myself tae one woman day after day when there are sae many willing lassies around."

As Stephanie watched, Fergus and Judith greeted one another. How could she have mistaken the look Judith had given Iain as love? Judith's love for Fergus transformed her. As their lips met anyone could see that in that moment the world ceased to exist. Stephanie wished that she had been fortunate to find a love such as Fergus and Judith. She stole a look at Iain. In his face there was just a hint of sadness. Perhaps he wished he was kissing Judith, what man wouldn't want that?

Iain watched his brother and his wife. He felt jealous of their love: he was ashamed of his thoughts. He did not wish to be wed to Judith although it had been their fathers' plan to wed them. No he was jealous of the purity of their love.

He wanted a wife and family to build his home and future with. But he could do nothing about his own life until the situation with Stephanie's father had been resolved. One day he would have his own lady wife at his side to give his people the stability they needed.

Iain turned and looked at Stephanie and found her watching him. He wondered if she wished she had got herself married sooner so she could be safely ensconced on her husband's estate. A biddable, docile wife. Not likely! She would be anything but that.

Iain found himself upset of at the thought of Stephanie with another man. He reasoned that it was because he felt pity for the man who would have to deal with her tongue and stubbornness. It had nothing to do with the fact that he found her attractive and intriguing. He mentally shook himself and growled at her.

"Come!" Iain tugged Stephanie along beside him as he strode out. "Fergus, if ye can manage tae tear yerself away from yer piece of baggage, I need ye tae check on the men in their cells. I will meet ye there. Judith I need ye tae unlock the south tower."

"But Iain the south tower hasn't been opened in months. It is very draughty even in summer and we have no spare tapestries or weavings to cover the windows and walls." She implored Iain, "Come, now, that is no way to treat a guest."

Stephanie wondered how Iain was going to handle this. She relished the idea that he might be forced to explain that Stephanie was present as a prisoner not as an important guest. Although, judging by Judith's attitude, Stephanie had the suspicion that Judith thought she was here as a potential bride for the new Laird. The very idea was laughable particularly since the Laird in question hardly showed tender feelings towards her since they had arrived. But now with his choice of her accommodations Iain must have seemed to have taken leave of his senses and Judith with her gentle reminder of how lacking his choice was, appeared to be trying to get him to rethink where she was to be staying.

Iain barely glanced over his shoulder but his words and tone were unmistakable;

"Judith, you are my brother's wife and the temporary keeper of my home; but my wishes are still final. So while you may not agree with my decision I still expect you to follow my orders without question. My guest will be placed in the South Tower."

"But Iain, I thought..." Judith stopped speaking when Iain turned and fastened his piercing eyes onto her. "All right if that is what you want." She turned to Stephanie "Come with me Lady I will show you to your…quarters."

As she passed Iain stopped Stephanie and whispered. "Remember Lady your men are still being held under my watch. Breathe one word about your situation and those men will suffer for your loose tongue. Guard your words well."

Stephanie took a sharp breath in as he seemed to have pulled her very thoughts from her head. "Bastard!" she hissed at him.

Iain gave her a wintry smile and spoke in a kind voice

"Make yerself at home I will check on you later." He turned and walked away.

"Are you coming Lady?" Judith called to her. Stephanie hurried across the hall to catch up with Judith. Judith was chatting away about nothing in particular, just the local gossip, as she led Stephanie up the stairs to the room she would be staying in. Judith's inconsequential chatter allowed Stephanie to collect herself after Iain's warning. How did he know that she had intended to tell Judith everything about what she was doing here at the keep? Stephanie was sure she could have enlisted her aid in getting back to her father. But with Iain's threat hanging over her head, Stephanie knew she could say nothing to risk the lives of the young men.

When they reached the hall at the top of the stairs, Judith led her to one of the two doors. She turned and gave Stephanie an extremely apologetic look as she opened the door.

"Here you are Lady."

Stephanie straightened herself and moved forward through the open doorway. The blast of cold air nearly took her breath away. The room was nicely furnished but definitely in a state of disuse. The layer of dust was clearly visible on everything. Judith looked utterly dismayed as she spoke.

"Oh Lady" she burst out "I am so sorry about these ghastly accommodations."

"Please" Stephanie interrupted "Please call me Stephanie. It seems I shall be here a while."

"Oh Stephanie, I really am so sorry. This used to be Iain's father and stepmother's chambers. After the accident Iain had the tapestries removed that his stepmother had made and moved to his quarters. He closed the doors and told everyone to leave the rooms as they were. Nothing was to be disturbed. He refused to take the rooms for himself. Fergus thinks that his brother is afraid he may betray his parents' memory by moving into the Laird's quarters. Iain has been quite forceful about leaving everything as it is...so protective."

Judith stopped speaking and looked at Stephanie and sighed. "To be truthful I am extremely confused by his actions. He hasn't let anyone come in here, yet he has put you here as a guest. I am sorry but it just doesn't make any sense. He is acting very strangely He hasn't even properly introduced you or presented you as a guest of his keep." Judith looked expectantly at Stephanie. Stephanie knew that Judith was bursting with curiosity to know why Stephanie was there but as much as she wanted Iain to be revealed for the manipulative mean spirited bounder he was, Stephanie's priority was the safety of her father's men. Their very lives depended on her silence and discretion in not revealing anything to anyone. She turned to Judith with true regret and gave a small sigh.

"I am sorry Lady Judith, my purpose in being here is something only Laird Iain may reveal." There that was not exactly a lie but Stephanie still felt like she was abusing Judith's kindness. Heaven knew she wanted to pour her heart out and confide this horrific situation to this lovely kind woman in front of her. But she could not.

Judith looked surprised by Stephanie's short dismissive answer. But she quickly recovered her composure making light of the situation.

"Well I guess I shall have to either curb my curiosity or get Iain so far into his cups that he reveals all to me in his drunken stupor!" She laughed her glorious, infectious laugh and Stephanie joined in, although still feeling ill for deceiving such a sweet natured woman.

Judith spoke again. "I guess I shall give you some time to get settled. I didn't see any of your things. Is your baggage coming along?"

"Well actually I am sending for my things shortly. I wasn't sure exactly what I needed so I thought it best not to arrive on Laird Iain's step with all my worldly possessions."

"But you have nothing?"

"Ah no…not yet."

"I must admit that seems rather strange but for the moment Lady MacDonald's brush and comb must still be about here somewhere so you can start with that and I will have to think about what to do for some spare clothes. Hopefully your things can be sent for quickly.

Let us look about for some clothes then we can see about getting you some water to freshen up."

"Thank you Judith for your kindness. Laird Iain is very fortunate to have you to help with his keep. I am grateful for your hospitality." Stephanie hoped that Judith could recognize her sincerity despite the fact that Stephanie couldn't offer her any of the truth. Once again Stephanie felt an annoying surge of helplessness rage against the high handed Laird MacDonald. Briefly Stephanie entertained thoughts of cracking the chamber pot over Iain's head when he came to 'check on her.' Only briefly though as she looked over at Judith and found her smiling broadly but still with a questioning look in her crystal blue eyes.

"Stephanie, all subtleties aside, I won't ask because you won't tell, but I like you. Your thanks are obvious from the honesty in your eyes. So let us drop the topic of why you are here and move on and settle you in, whatever your purpose. Now, that being said you need clothes. I am too short for you so let us see if anything left behind is fit to wear. Come"

Judith linked her arm with Stephanie and they moved to the corner of the chamber where a large ornately carved chest stood at the foot of the bed. They lifted the heavy lid and looked inside.

"Steffie, a little dusty but I may find something you can wear. Why don't you look in the wardrobe and see what is there."

"All right" Stephanie smiled her first real smile since her ordeal began. Without any conscious thought Judith had fallen into calling her by the pet name her father had always used for her. It meant nothing to anyone else but her. In a strange way she suddenly felt stronger, it felt like she had a piece of home with her.

Smiling Stephanie opened the door of the large standing wardrobe. The dust that assaulted her nose wiped the smile from her face as she choked out

"Whew! Everything really is in a state of disuse."

Judith held up a shift that looked rather dubious. "Iain was devastated by his parent's premature deaths. Even though she was his stepmother, Iain loved Kaitlyn MacDonald as if she were his own flesh and blood. He wasn't ready for any of this so he froze the grief and the memories out. When he issued his order, no one was surprised but no one, not even Fergus, was prepared to try to reason with him during his grief. Until you came today there was no reason to. Now, that we have a guest I, at least, can see our folly." Judith sighed and glanced over at Stephanie. "Have you found anything?"

Stephanie moved the clothes around. "There doesn't seem to be a lot of damage to these clothes. How about this?" She held out a blue mantle with small intricately embroidered yellow and white flowers around the collar and the hem. "I could wear it over this lighter blue chemise? I think that could work well."

Judith studied the clothes "That will do for now I suppose. But we must get to work immediately on sewing you something that will compliment your coloring. Here keep this shift it seems to be in decent shape. Now come with me we are going to the kitchen to arrange a bath."

Stephanie followed Judith down the narrow winding staircase with some hesitation. She actually was afraid they would meet Iain along the way. She didn't like this growing sense of unease and discomfort at the thought of seeing Iain. She knew she would be seeing him again, and often, but she was beginning to dislike the prospect more and more.

Stephanie pushed all thoughts of Iain out of her mind and took the opportunity to look around her. As they came into the great hall Stephanie saw that the space was incredibly clean. All the tables and trestles were pushed back against the wall and the reeds had been thoroughly cleaned from the midday meal. Even between the stones had been swept carefully. She noticed that the hangings on the wall were all vibrant scenes of daily life. The colors were bright because the walls had no residue from the fires in the great hall. Much time would have been spent to keep them so spotless. One fact made very evident by the cleanliness of the main area, Iain MacDonald cared about his home and the people who lived there.

Judith noticed Stephanie's perusal of her surroundings and remarked;

"Quite amazing isn't it? I think the hall is better run now with Iain in charge than it ever has been. Iain kept everyone's mind off the tragic events by keeping us all busy. The usual work along with some extra thrown in, deflected people from being too fixed on his father and stepmother's passing. Finding extra work was easy with the raids suddenly escalating against us. We have all participated in trying to salvage crops and property as well as cleaning up. It has been a strenuous time. I just wish we knew who was behind this. Public stoning would be too good for the likes of such bandits."

"Did Iain or Fergus ever mention who they thought was responsible?" Stephanie held her breath waiting for Judith's reply.

"No. But I am sure that those responsible have to be nearby to always be alluding capture. As hard as it is for me to imagine, I believe it is the English lord bordering the lands. King Edward is so unreasonable in his demands trying to take over the country that he is prepared to do so by any means necessary. Probably his methods are meant to show the Scots, who have nothing, how foolish it is to resist his governance. Of course, he cannot manage to keep up the skirmishes himself. He has to enlist all his lords to do the work for him."

"But why would you think it is your English neighbor? He too has to maintain peace on his own lands."

"Any number of reasons. Most probably with the discontent between the English and Scottish, he sees the opportunity to forward his own position in the court and gain wealth and power from the King. It makes me so angry I wish I could take up a sword myself and go and show them what it feels like to have crops and homes destroyed. What's wrong, Steffie?"

Stephanie's color had all but drained from her face as she listened to Judith's diatribe against her family. The vehemence of Judith's resentment resonated off her own emotions.

"How do you know it is that Lord specifically? Has anyone been caught? Has anyone been specifically identified or confessed to be from this family of which you speak? What if they are the victims of similar events…" Stephanie stopped speaking realizing that she almost inadvertently revealed her identity. She would have gladly shouted for all to hear who she was, such was her anger against these unfair accusations. But she had to think of Duncan, Edmond and Matthew. To make matters worse she didn't know how Judith would react to her if she knew Stephanie was part of "that family." If she were to learn Stephanie's true identity Stephanie didn't think she would be able to bear the censure from such a woman as Judith. She quickly tried to cover her near slip.

"I mean, Judith, you are English born and yet you are quite adamant that it is your English neighbors, your fellow country men, that are guilty of these heinous crimes, without any proof or confessions. They could just as easily or just as likely be victimized by this. Has anyone spoken to the family to find out what they know or what they have experienced?"

Judith studied Stephanie carefully for a moment.

"True I have no proof of the guilty party, but I have spoken to my husband and he and Iain can find no other evidence of anyone else perpetrating the crimes. Nothing else makes more sense."

"What about someone within the clan? Perhaps someone who doesn't agree with Iain as new Laird." At Stephanie's words Judith showed true surprise.

"Who wouldn't agree with Iain being Laird? He is the eldest son of the previous Laird."

With that final declaration the two women reached the kitchen entrance and found that it was a hive of activity. People were scrubbing from the early meal and others had already begun to prepare the main day meal. Even to the untrained eye it was obvious everyone was extremely organized. Stephanie felt out of place and very conspicuous, she was afraid that her sudden appearance would disrupt everyone and their work. She turned to

Judith and spoke as quietly as she could but still be heard above the din.

"Please Judith, everyone is busy. I will wait until later for a bath. I can survive without washing right away."

"Nonsense" Judith looked shocked "You are our guest and must be treated as such." She caught sight of a young boy who was gathering vegetable peels off the floor and putting them into buckets to feed to the pigs.

"Duggan where are your brothers?" When Judith spoke everyone paused in their work as they caught sight of the grubby stranger next to Judith.

"Get the water on for the bath and get it sent up to the south tower and have it done in time for the noon day meal. Iain doesn't want anyone late" With those pointed words and not a glance spared to anyone the activity began again in earnest. No one wanted to disappoint their new Laird. But they still tried to sneak curious glances at Stephanie as they resumed their tasks.

"Remarkable." Stephanie said

"What do you mean?"

"You appeared to be speaking only to Duggan but yet you knew everyone was watching us. Without any confrontation or reprimands you managed to get everyone back to work. I know of one other family that is so careful to be kind to all in the keep." Stephanie smiled "mine"

Judith and Stephanie were laughing as they crossed back to the tower entrance. Iain walked through the doors just then. The sound of their laughter stopped him in his tracks. The scene before him captivated him. Judith was incredibly beautiful and delicate with her small figure. But next to Judith, Stephanie shone as the epitome of elegance. Tall and graceful with tendrils of golden hair spilling down her back. Her smile filled the room with sunshine. She moved so gracefully beneath her simple garb. It amazed him how, even as filthy and ill dressed as she was, her beauty shone through. God no! He couldn't let her under his skin. She was his hostage nothing more and he had to keep reminding himself of that.

"Ladies" His voice echoed steel across the vast hall. Stephanie jumped slightly at the sound of his voice and he found himself getting angrier over that. He didn't want her to be afraid of him yet he couldn't afford for her to be too comfortable around him either. His emotional frustration was wearing on his nerves. The both turned to face him.

"What are you two up tae?" Iain knew his tone was imperious but he was just angry enough at himself that he didn't care.

Judith smiled with some derision "We have been trying to make Stephanie more comfortable as your guest. That is what you want isn't it? To make her comfortable and welcome in your home."

Stephanie held her breath. Now was the time for Iain to tell her exactly what she was doing here. Gone would be the warm friendliness, Stephanie would be treated as the prisoner she was.

Iain knew he should tell Judith why Stephanie was here. But he realized that he could gain more if Stephanie was considered a guest than if he treated her as a prisoner. She would garner more sympathy if Judith suspected she was here against her will and Stephanie might even convince Judith to get her back home. No, better everyone believe she was an honored guest. He would be able to control her much better. Her breeding would not have her behaving in any way to embarrass him if all his people believed her welcome. He smiled a predatory smile. Stephanie felt her stomach lurch nervously. What was he up to? Then he spoke.

"But of course that is wha' I want. My guest, the Lady Stephanie, should be made as comfortable as possible while she visits here."

"Good" Judith said "We have just come from preparing a bath for her. You know Iain that was very remiss of you. You should have looked after her needs before you went rushing off outside. She doesn't even have any of her things with her and we don't seem to have any clear idea as to when they might arrive. This lack of consideration just isn't like you Iain."

"Judith, you are quite right, I have been most remiss in my duties towards Stephanie. I do have to discuss some things with her so I will escort her to her chamber and supervise the set up of her bath."

Iain appeared to offer Stephanie his arm but his eyes demanded she take it. When she placed her hand on his arm he quickly pressed his hand firmly over hers as he moved her briskly across the hall and led her outside.

"You don't have to drag me along like a horse" Stephanie spoke sharply to Iain and tried to pull away. "I am as anxious as you to escape. Judith is a wonderful woman and I cannot let her know who I am or what I am doing here. With men relying on me for their lives to keep quiet, the one person who has been kindest to me I have to keep everything from. I am your prisoner and now I have to pretend to be a willing guest. I believe I am going to go mad."

Iain felt some guilt to hear how Stephanie viewed her current situation in such stark reality. He steeled himself from feeling sorry for her.

"As it happens, my Lady I am taking you to remind you what is expected of you. How long you have to keep up this role depends on you, the men I have captured, and your father. If ye keep up your role as guest in my keep then everything should be concluded quickly."

"You are expecting me to keep quiet while you force my father and our people to accept responsibility for what is happening to you and your people just to ensure my safety. It is ridiculous!"

"Lady I am no' discussing what I am or am not doing. But as I watch ye getting close tae my brother's wife, I dinna think it is such a bad idea tae remind ye what yer priority is, an' should be. Ye are no here tae make friends, ye are collateral tae make sure yer father makes no further attacks against my people, an ye best not forget tha' or what's at stake."

Iain stopped in front of a mound of earth with a large wooden door set into it. On either side of the door stood a very large man, Iain addressed them.

"Open the door please." They pulled the door open and Iain set Stephanie in front of him. She peered into the dark hole and what she saw shook her to the core. She was unable to utter a word.

There was as small opening at the top of the mound which filtered a small beam of light. Not much because as her eyes adjusted to the lack, of light the three men inside covered their eyes from the bright light that flooded in through the open door. Stephanie saw that Edmond, Duncan and Matthew were cramped into a small area that when they sat down their legs nearly touched the other side. Their hands and ankles were bound and they were filthy. Their clothes were torn so badly that they could barely be considered rags. Stephanie was outraged at the horrifying conditions.

"My God, are you insane? How can you treat people this way?"

"Well they are my prisoners. Are ye going tae be motivated tae keep quiet and keep up the performance if yer men are relaxing in luxury? This is my insurance that ye will keep quiet."

"You Bastard! You animal!" Stephanie turned and punched Iain right in the stomach. The impact sent numbing pain right up her arm. She felt like she had just punched a stone wall. Iain didn't move, he didn't even flinch. She took a deep breath and looked him straight in the eyes.

"If you insist on keeping them locked away in such deplorable conditions, at least let me look at their cuts and clean them up some. Please I need to make sure no wound gets infected. In such a place infection could be fatal."

Iain still felt the sting of her blow to his stomach. Damn but that woman had a strong arm. He wasn't sure he had his breath back when he spoke.

"No" his answer came out in a rush, thankfully he didn't sound as winded as he was. "No, you may not"

"Oh please don't make me beg, let me look after them. Please." Stephanie felt anger well up as the tears welled up just as fast.

"You cannot be this cruel. It is not possible that you are the man spoken of so highly and so respected. I will not believe you are capable of such cruelty."

"Madam, ye had better begin believing it because this is who I am. This is who I have tae be tae be the Laird of such hard lands. Now, come, it is time for your bath."

"No wait. Let these men have the water meant for my bath. Let them get clean."

"Are ye telling me that ye, a woman, are willing tae give up yer bath for these men?"

"Yes! Yes without hesitation."

"While I admire yer selflessness I canna have a 'guest' in my home and at my table smelling worse than the pigs. So I am afraid my dear, that yer nobility falls on deaf ears today. Close the door."

"I'm sorry" Stephanie called out as the door closed firmly before her. Tears streamed down her cheeks and she felt again the sting of defeat and futility at her predicament. Her shoulders slumped. Stephanie said nothing further. When they reached the staircase Iain spoke.

"I look forward to seeing ye a' the noon day meal."

For one brief moment Stephanie's eyes flashed green fire at him but she quickly turned away. Stephanie walked up the staircase without looking back. The once anticipated bath now made her feel even more dirty than before. Seeing her father's men being kept in such deplorable conditions, she could take no pleasure in something as simple as a bath.

Iain watched her walk slowly and heavily up the stairs. He felt guilty for the pain he had caused her, but he had to continue with his plan. He turned and walked back outside.

Stephanie reached the top of the stairs and felt like she had just walked miles, her body was heavy with despair and futility. She paused to catch her breath before she opened the door. In order to protect her father's men she had to compose herself and begin to perform again. She straightened her shoulders, and prayed for the strength and resolve to get through the day.

Judith greeted her as she opened the door.

"There you are! My goodness Steffie what happened to you. You look positively ill."

"Oh it is nothing. I am just tired and grubby I suspect." Stephanie replied as heartily as she could. "I think all this traveling has finally caught up with me. Has my bath water arrived?"

Judith didn't look entirely convinced "Yes the bath is set up behind the screen there. I have left a cake of my favorite soap there. I make it with lavender and rose petals. A treat I allow myself. When you are finished, I have laid out your clothes on the bed. I also found the brush and comb that belonged to Lady MacDonald so you can comb out your hair. There should still be enough time to get it mostly dry to put up for the meal. I will come back and check on you later."

Stephanie watched Judith retreat quickly from the room. She imagined it was probably to get as far away from Stephanie and her secrets. How she hated this deception. "Thank you Judith" Stephanie said but the door had already closed.

Alone in the chamber Stephanie undressed slowly. Finally she could abandon the uncomfortable dress she wore. She laid the garment out on the chest at the end of the bed. The tub was large and the water steamed invitingly up from within. There were also more buckets of steaming water waiting for her to rinse her hair with. She stepped into the soothing water and inhaled the luxurious scent of Judith's special soap. For a moment Stephanie felt as if she were in heaven, but her joy was short lived as she thought of the three young men wallowing in their filth. She needed to come up with a plan to rescue them all from this place.

Chapter Nine

After Iain left Stephanie, he walked back over to the mound and waved the guards away. When he opened the door the three men inside winced again at the bright light assailing their eyes.

"All right lads time tae stand up!" Iain called.

Edmund asked "Have our cells and clothes been cleaned of the mold and fleas?"

"Aye" Iain replied "I apologize to have put ye in here but we dinna want ye tae become ill. While ye are here we dinna want ye tae suffer over much."

"Lady Stephanie seemed much distressed to see us here. Surely she does not think that you are keeping us here does she? She left so quickly we didn't get a chance to speak to her. Will she return?"

"Nay Edmund. Ye lads are nay going tae be here much longer. Fergus will be taking you home with a message for Lady Stephanie's father."

As Iain walked away from his men and prisoners, he looked up towards the keep and saw Judith striding to him with grim determination on her face. Iain really didn't want to have to deal with her right at this moment so he quickly veered off to the stables hoping he could evade her questions. Fergus was better able to handle his lady wife than Iain.

Iain needn't have bothered avoiding Judith, she didn't even see him as she made her way over to the practice yard. No, her quarry was her husband. She had questions and he would provide answers. Judith liked Stephanie but she was upset about something and Judith was going to find out what it was and end it. As she marched over to the men practicing, some caught a look at her demeanor and called out to Fergus.

"Fergus, yer wife is coming and she looks in a mood. Ye'd best be finding yerself a fine hidin' spot an quick afore she spots ye!"

Fergus looked over at his wife storming towards him. He knew he was in for a tongue lashing and he knew what it was about too. With some resignation Fergus put down his sword and turned towards her, legs braced and arms crossed. When Judith reached where he stood she put her hands on her hips and looked up at her husband, fierce determination radiated from her.

Fergus spoke first. "Wife. It seems tae me ye have something on yer mind."

Judith opened her mouth to let Fergus hear all about the 'something' on her mind when he cut her off abruptly.

"Wife afore ye speak I will tell ye once, tae breathe deep and think before ye continue."

She stopped and looked around her. With some shame she realized where they were, the field was crowded with men who had stopped their practice when she arrived to confront her husband. Determined as she was to get answers she was not so insensitive as to create a scene to embarrass her husband in front of the others. She took a deep breath and said quietly,

"Husband I would like to have a word with you in private if you don't mind."

"Fine" Fergus said with a small smile "Let us go to our chamber."

He bent over and picked up his small feisty wife in his arms and started back across the field, while the men's good natured jeers and cheers echoed behind them. "Aye, well done Fergus! Well done, mon!"

Judith glared at her husband as he replied

"I ken ye have a bee buzzing around in yer head. I will do my best tae answer ye what I can. But ye must know tha these events are Iain's doings and he will tell all we need tae know when we need tae know it."

"I have to ask Fergus."

"I ken tha' too. But I need ye to understand tha I canna answer all yer questions ye want answers tae."

When they reached their chambers Judith's feet barely touched the floor before she began her questions.

"Who is Stephanie?"

"I canna say."

"Fergus we cannot begin this without an answer to a simple question."

"Tis no simple Judith."

"Something is very wrong here. Steffie is a sweet lady but she is heavy hearted about something. She longs to speak of it I can tell. Yet she always stops herself. Why?"

"Judith dinna ask anymore questions because everything ye want tae ask I canna answer. But I can say I am verra glad ye like the Lady Stephanie. I too like the lass. She has a strong heart and a true spirit. This is a difficult time for her right now and she needs yer unconditional support and friendship. That is all I can give ye for answers for now. Put them out of yer head and spend time with Stephanie. Help her stay strong and make her stay as enjoyable as ye can. Please Judith ask no more but trust me because I trust Iain, and this is his decision. As our clan leader if we want to maintain peace and his true position in the clan then we must trust him. Can ye do that?"

Judith looked up at her husband. "Fergus I cannot lie. I am very concerned about Stephanie but I do trust you and I do trust Iain. I will set my questions aside for the moment. Promise me as soon as you can tell me something, anything, you will."

"All right Judith I promise. Now since I am here and you have effectively ended my practice for today, why not help me get some more exercise in a much more enjoyable way." Fergus bent down and pressed his lips on his wife's soft mouth. He felt her lean into him as he deepened the kiss.

"Oh Fergus" Judith sighed her voice filled with breathy passion. "You will have to wait." She leaned her forehead on Fergus's midsection and sighed. "I must go see to Stephanie before she misses the meal."

She turned at the doorway and smiled seductively at her husband. "But I would be happy to continue the better part of the conversation after supper." She blew Fergus a kiss as she left the room.

Chapter Ten

Stephanie had dressed herself in Iain's stepmother's clothes. Although the fit was not perfect she at least felt better about the way she looked. That gave her a little boost to face the incredible scrutiny she knew would be coming when she went down for the meal. Stephanie was not naive enough to think that the hall would not be packed with all manner of curious people. Stephanie was sitting in the embrasure of the window, sunlight was streaming in as she brushed her hair. With the warmth of the sun and the comfort of her recent bath, she could almost forget where she was. Her window looked out onto the loch behind the keep. The air was cold but fresh and the sun was warm on her skin. Sounds of the keep drifted up from below, children squealing and laughing while they chased scolding chickens. She remembered chasing the noisy chickens at her own home. The memory assailed her with the reality of where she was.

What was she going to do? There had to be some way to help Edmund, Duncan and Matthew. The young men had been through so much to help her and while she was in the keep against her will the relative luxury of her surroundings compared to theirs made her feel like a pampered lady not the prisoner she was. If she was to be a prisoner here then she should be subjected to the same conditions as the men. Here she was, sitting freshly scrubbed in clean clothes, breathing fresh air, while her father's men were holed up in a pile of dirt with barely any air to breathe at all. She had to do something. But what?

There was really no point in trying to escape, she didn't have any clear idea of where she was nor did she have any horses or supplies. Somehow she had to make a stand against Iain to force him to recognize her as his prisoner so he would treat her like one. Then she would not have to live with this guilt of sitting comfortably while they were housed in misery.

"Stephanie?"

Stephanie turned from the window and saw Judith in the doorway.

"Are you having trouble with your preparations?" Judith asked as she stepped into the room.

"No" Stephanie said. "Why would you ask that?"

"Well Steffie there is the obvious fact that currently you have a hairbrush stuck midway down your hair." Judith said with a smile and a twinkle in her deep blue eyes.

Stephanie laughed a little guiltily. She had forgotten that she was brushing her hair when she lost herself in her thoughts of the men.

"I was lost in thought" true "I got completely lost and absorbed in the beauty of the view," an untruth, but she continued anyway "This must be the most beautiful part of the whole keep."

"Oh yes" Judith said "Laird MacDonald had the tower built when he married Kaitlyn. He wanted to give her a new place of her own so she would not feel she was competing with the memory of Iain's mother, Donald's first wife. He was a very rare man. He loved both of his wives deeply. He always loved Iain's mother and always missed her after her death, but that was the wonderful thing about Fergus's mother, she was so young, full of life and laughter. She never discouraged memories of Iain's mother especially in Iain. I think that is why he was so upset when they were both killed in the tragic accident. She had become a second mother to him."

"What exactly happened? How did they die?" Stephanie asked.

"Well it was all so sudden that I don't know if anyone has all the facts. But I do know that the day they died apparently Laird MacDonald received an urgent message to depart right away. The message was of concern enough that Lady MacDonald insisted she go with him as well. Their coach lost control rounding a curve at a high rate of speed, the wheels came off and the coach broke apart when it turned over."

"Oh my how truly awful!" Stephanie felt sick at the horrible deaths these two people suffered. How Iain and Fergus must have suffered as a result. Then with the onset of attacks so recent on the heels of their parent's deaths, so much to take on all at once. She felt some measure of sympathy for Iain in the position he must now find himself in.

"Enough talk of the past now" Judith broke through Stephanie's thoughts. "I came up here to help you get ready. We must make you look your best for the meal.

You are going to be the object of everyone's attention and speculation. First impressions will count for everything."

"Oh" Stephanie moaned "I hate the thought of everyone staring at me."

Judith took the brush and began to gently disentangle it from Stephanie's hair. "You could reveal honestly who you are and what you are doing here. That would end the speculation wouldn't it?" Stephanie took a sharp intake of breath and stiffened. Judith sensed her discomfort and continued talking. "No matter, I see that my homemade soap has brought out the shine in your hair. I did not realize under all that dirt that you had such lovely soft gold hair Steffie. When we arrange it all people will be talking about will be how beautiful you are."

Stephanie was so relieved at Judith's quick change of topic. Her pulse and heart rate had almost returned to normal. This never ending deception was going to drive her insane. "Oh Judith I don't think I could ever be considered beautiful. You are beautiful. I am just passable."

"Is that what you think? We will just have to see about that."

When they had finished they walked down the tower steps with their arms linked. Stephanie felt more conspicuous now than she had before. She had to agree with Judith, Stephanie found herself transformed. The whole time Judith had been 'working on her' she had murmured secretively and giggled like a young girl. She kept saying "That's perfect. That's it." With every little touch she added. She wouldn't even let Stephanie see what she was doing until she was completely finished.

When she had finally finished she had held up a mirror in front of Stephanie and said. "So? Did I not tell you that you were beautiful?"

Stephanie's jaw had dropped. She could not believe that the vision that confronted her in the mirror was herself. She touched her hair which shone and sparkled in a braided coronet around her head. Judith had woven a blue and silver ribbon throughout the entire braid. The effect was probably more elaborate than the meal required but she looked beautiful. Judith had said she needed to make a good first impression, she was about to make an impression, good or bad, that remained to be seen.

Stephanie found herself getting more and more nervous with every step closer to the main hall. They paused before they entered the hall to prepare. Stephanie could hear the voices of all the people gathered and waiting for the meal. Even though Judith had been so incredibly nice to the 'prisoner' Stephanie had never felt more alone or exposed in all her life.

When Judith and Stephanie entered it didnt take long for the din in the hall to quiet. Fortunately the doors to the towers and chambers were close to the dais so the ladies didn't have to walk far to get to the seats at the head table.

"Come let's sit down and wait for Iain and Fergus."

After they sat down Stephanie finally noticed the silence and felt the numerous eyes fixed on her. She sat in the chair indicated by Judith and Judith took the chair next to her. Stephanie kept her eyes low and put her hands in her lap. Outwardly she was the epitome of a demure lady but inwardly her emotions were in turmoil. She kept her hands clenched tightly to stop anyone from noticing their shaking. Judith patted her hand gently and whispered.

"It will be all right for you once Iain and Fergus arrive."

Damn! All of Stephanie thinly managed control started to dissolve. She had forgotten about Iain. It was bad enough that all these people would be watching her, but Iain would be sitting here at the table watching her to make sure she didn't give away who she was. His very size and presence were going to be disconcerting enough but that steel gaze fixed on her the whole meal was going to make her sick with nerves. Stephanie wanted to scream out loud with her desperate frustration.

Instantly she felt Iain's entrance. She didn't hear him enter, even though the hall was still shrouded in silence. She felt the pull of his presence like a physical tug on her whole being. She couldn't have resisted looking at him even if she had tried. The thought suddenly entered, unbidden and unwelcome, that she didn't want to resist looking at him. She furrowed her brow as she met Iain's eyes. His hair was tousled from the work he had been engaged in, he still had a sheen of sweat on him. His shirt clung to his muscular chest like a second skin. One could never say that Laird MacDonald was a poor specimen of man physically but at this point Stephanie had doubts of what kind of specimen he was as a man. According to her sister in law all the people thought Iain's character and justness were as imposing as his physical self. Thinking of her father's men she seriously doubted that.

As Stephanie watched him enter, she saw him look at her first with a flicker of surprise then watched as his face darkened and he began to scowl. Stephanie felt her face grow hot. She quickly looked down in embarrassment. Everyone had to see how much their Laird didn't like the "guest". How could anyone think she was there at his invitation with such a thunderous gaze cast upon her? How dare he stand there at the hall entrance looking, for all the world, like she was there against his wishes. She wanted to yell across the hall at him to remind him that she was there against her will and he had no right to treat her like she was invading his home. She kept her head down because she knew if she saw his sullen face again she would probably not be able to resist walking across the hall and giving him a swift kick in his shins.

Across the hall Iain was struggling within himself. When he had entered the hall he was so taken aback at first glance at Lady Stephanie he nearly stopped in his tracks. What struck him most at first was the fact that she looked like she belonged there. She looked like she was meant to be seated at his table. Then he saw her, just her. She was achingly beautiful! He felt desire rip through his loins as he took in her beauty. Her hair shone around her head like a gold halo. She had been scrubbed clean so her skin was glistening rosy pink. He wanted to walk straight over to her, pick her up and kiss her until she was senseless. Stephanie was every inch a lady as she sat there looking at him. He registered no one else but Stephanie.

Suddenly Iain remembered where he was. This woman was his captive. She was not the Lady MacDonald. How dare she sit there with such an air of presumption? Without his realizing it his face took on the most fearsome of scowls. Iain was also unaware that the people in the hall witnessed his abrupt shift in attitude as he gazed upon the woman they all had believed to be an honored guest. Any of the other tenants who had not arrived would surely know of this exchange before the day was out. Now, without Iain's knowledge, all the people had begun to look at Stephanie with more suspicion than curiosity. Iain was oblivious to how he had affected those around him he was only aware of the effect within him. Ever since he had decided to bring Stephanie back to Scotland with him she had been affecting him more than she should have. As beautiful, shining and radiant as she was there at his table, he could not let himself desire her as a woman, at the risk of his people's need for peace.

After only a moment Iain strode purposefully to the table. Servants jumped out of his way as they served the meal, since he paid them no attention. Iain reached the table and noticed that Stephanie was seated next to Judith at the center of the table. He was momentarily astounded to see that Judith had put her hand over Stephanie's tightly clenched fists. He could see Judith was developing a friendship with Stephanie already. Damn! He could not have these two women getting too close. If Stephanie didn't tell Judith anything, Judith would become more suspicious as days progressed. He needed to keep them apart as much as possible. So he spoke;

"Lady Stephanie how nice to see you here and looking the part of a lady again. Now if you don't mind would you and Judith please move to each end of the table so that Fergus and I might be able to speak during the meal. I am sure Fergus would also like to have his lady wife seated next to him."

His voice was polite but somewhat chilly as he issued his edict. Stephanie looked up at him, not with any sign of despair at being separated from her new friend, no she looked for all the world that she was going to rail at him or at the very least plant a fist between his eyes. He wanted to laugh at her spirit and kiss the frown from between her eyes. Matching his frosty tone she replied.

"Of course, Laird. It would not do for your discussions with your brother to have to try to talk over the idle gossip of women. Let me move to the end of the table where I may sit in silence and be enthralled by your manly conversation as you totally ignore my presence here." She stood up to move. Iain's eyebrows shot up but there was no other sign on his face in reaction to her temerity. She was so refreshing in her speech to him. She stood tall for a woman, he was still taller and broader; yet, she still challenged his every word. Her bravado was ridiculously endearing and he wanted to pull her close and kiss her soundly where they stood. With a genuine smile he said.

"Well Lady let us not disappoint ye." Even though his smile was genuine, to Stephanie he looked like a predator about to take a very large chunk out of its prey. She flushed in anger. Stephanie was finding it very hard to maintain her ladylike manners in Iain's presence. He got under her skin like a persistent splinter that could not be dislodged no matter how much she dug.

She moved to the end of the table and suddenly felt alone again. He effectively reminded her how isolated she was here. She had no one to talk to and everyone was still staring at her. They all watched Iain take his seat and half turn in his chair so that she was faced with his back every time she looked in his direction. Her isolation was complete.

Fergus watched in shock at his brother's ill-mannered behavior. He wondered what was going on with his brother and the Lady Stephanie.

Iain spoke as if Fergus wasn't even there. "She does not have any right tae think that she belongs here. Cleaning herself up and dressing up as the lady of the keep doesn't mean she is the lady of the keep" He turned to Fergus "We have to start putting our plan into action. The sooner we can get her father to agree to stop the raids against us the sooner she can be gone back to her home and out of our lives."

Fergus grunted "If that is the objective can we get on with the plan soon? Ye should never have abducted an English Lord's daughter. If Longshanks had wanted or needed a reason tae launch full scale war on Scotland ye have handed him the very weapon to destroy us all."

"Nay brother, that is not my intention ye ken. The opportunity presented itself at a time when we needed help the most. We both know that trying to have a civilized discussion with the English, as we originally planned, would never have worked. We needed something to get their attention. Now what could be better than to ha' Lady Stephanie here to ensure Lord Rockforte agrees tae our terms? Ye will take a message to him tae arrange a meeting to discuss our terms. When our negotiations are complete and we are all safe back in our homes then she will be released."

"Iain we are speaking of a long period of time here. How can ye be sae certain tha' nothing unforeseen will occur? One error and we shall have war on our hands."

"Ay Fergus there is some risk but I am quite certain Lord Rockforte will not set two countries to war over a woman. It is sheer madness to believe so. Now I would have ye take the three young men back tae Rockforte and then bring him back with ye tae the field on the edge of our lands."

Fergus said nothing because they didn't know what type of relationship Lord Rockforte had with his daughter. It may very well be that Lord Rockforte would not tear up the earth to find his daughter but they could not be sure. While his brother's plan had some merit and certainly the proper motivation, Fergus was afraid that it would prove to be too impulsive. The possible repercussions would be devastating to all. Still, Fergus had to respect his older brother and show him loyalty as clan leader. Then there was the complication of Iain's growing interest in the Lady Stephanie. Iain denied it but Fergus knew she held a fascination for his brother like no other woman ever had.

At that moment, Iain was contemplating how cruel he had been shutting Stephanie off from everyone and everything at the table. He couldn't really even remember why he had gotten so angry with her. He decided he should at least try to engage her in conversation.

"Lady how does the meal fare for ye?" He asked

"The meal is very satisfactory and your cook is very skilled at making a tasty venison stew. But the entertainment, or lack thereof, is what concerns me. I was looking forward to lingering on your every word but find that you have just been muttering to your brother. Therefore I was forced to look around the hall for other entertainment. I found that while there was no entertainment for me it appears there is plenty for everyone else. It would appear that I am the entertainment for everyone else in the hall today." Stephanie was angry and embarrassed and she wanted Iain to know it.

Iain looked around the hall and sure enough Stephanie was right. While people were eating and talking amongst themselves, to a man woman and child, they were all either staring out right at her or taking frequent glances at her when they thought no one was looking. Mostly, the stares were filled with suspicion but underneath the suspicion there was definite hostility. Under the circumstances it was hardly surprising that his people were suspicious, but he had expected some sort of welcome. She had arrived with their Laird and she was seated next to him at the table. His confusion must have showed as Stephanie spoke.

"It is hardly surprising that I am drawing such unwanted attention. You certainly did not hold any welcome in your expression when you walked through the entrance. Your people look to you for guidance and Laird Iain you did not give any indication that you wanted me to be here. I don't think you have any idea the open hostility that showed on your face. The reaction of your people to me is entirely your own doing. I want you to know that I take great pleasure in knowing that it is going to be quite a challenge for you now to convince people that you want me here. I can stand the continuous stares and whispers because everyone knows you don't want me here. I wish you the best of luck trying to change the impression you have created." Stephanie spoke with much more force than she felt. Sitting there like some distasteful object on the table she felt sure she was going to be ill or break down in tears. When Iain spoke to her that was the focus she needed for her nervous energy.

The two of them knew she was his prisoner but she was supposed to pretend otherwise. How was she to succeed in this charade if he made it full known she was not welcome?

After Stephanie's lengthy speech and following silence, Iain looked around and wondered what he could have done to make all the people present so cold and suspicious towards her. She said it was his look when he entered but he honestly didn't remember giving her such a look of displeasure, especially when he first saw her. He felt real pleasure when he first spotted her there. Damn! Then he remembered he was very pleased by her appearance in his hall, but he was not at all pleased with himself for feeling that way. That must have been what showed on his face that everyone perceived to be directed towards Stephanie. He had to do something before everyone left the hall. He had to try to alter their impressions of her based on his own foolish actions. His plan's success relied on no one suspecting anything awry with Stephanie's presence here.

"Lady Stephanie" Iain spoke loudly enough for the first table to hear him. "Knowing that ye are still unfamiliar to our land perhaps ye would like tae take a ride with me this afternoon? Allow me tae show ye the beauty of our lands." He smiled what he hoped was his most engaging smile and waited for her to reply. It was up to her to continue their charade.

Stephanie nearly fell over backwards. She wanted to spit on his feet and smack his perfectly chiseled cheek as hard as she could. No. She wanted to scream and curse him. She would have done just that had she been alone in this predicament. But there were the three young men to consider so she gritted her teeth and looked up at him smiling tightly.

"Why how kind of you. That would be a pleasure indeed." Stephanie looked at Iain and felt a tightening in her stomach. He really was very handsome when he smiled. His stormy grey eyes looked softer and he had a wonderful dimple in his cheek. She felt a ridiculous temptation to run her hand over his face. Without giving in to her desire, she knew that his skin would be warm and solid beneath her hand. Then she wanted to run her fingers through his black hair, knowing that it had to be soft to the touch as well. When he was smiling, everything about Laird Iain became a contradiction. His physical appearance was so large and his muscles so large and strong, yet he smiled and looked like a completely different man. She could see the softness of the child within him. It was such a shame that he was so coldly arrogant. But she would soon fix that. She most certainly would go riding with him and as he showed her the 'beauty' of the land she would try to find her way to escape this place.

She put aside her plan to be housed as a prisoner with the men and she began to plan their escape. With some careful questions she could figure out how to find her way back home. With the comfort of this thought she smiled her most charming smile back at Iain.

She glowed like sunshine. That was the first thought that ran through his mind as she beamed at him. But her smile was too big and that made him wonder what she was planning. He knew how angry she had been a moment ago. Now she was all smiles just like a woman! She had to be plotting something.

"Wonderful." he exclaimed "Why don't ye go change and meet me back here. Once you are ready we shall go to the stables."

It was on the tip of Stephanie's tongue to remind Iain that she had no clothes with her but she thought it best not to rankle him. He might not take her outside the keep then.

"Of course" she said "Lady Judith can come up with me and help. Thank you for your kindness." Stephanie was up and had grabbed Judith's hand before Iain could speak.

The minx. Iain thought. He was actually looking forward to the ride. He had a feeling he would learn much more about Stephanie if he paid attention today. He knew the more he learned about her the better the success of his plan.

Stephanie all but dragged Judith up to her room.

"What is the rush?" Judith asked breathlessly at the door to Stephanie's chamber. Since Stephanie was so much taller than Judith, Judith had had to run to keep up with her leaving the hall.

"I have to prepare for my ride and I have literally nothing to wear!"

"I am sure we can find something." Judith searched through the clothes in the closet and found a serviceable mantle to wear. Stephanie couldn't risk ruining the good one she had on as there was so little in appropriate attire available to her to wear. She left her hair up to make riding easier.

"There. You look lovely and it took hardly any time at all. I hope you enjoy the ride. MacDonald land is incredibly beautiful and I still remembered how impressed I was when I first saw it."

Stephanie knew she would not be paying any more attention to her surroundings then she needed to, in order to plot her escape.

Chapter Eleven

Stephanie walked back into the great hall, mostly empty except for Iain. Stephanie noticed that he had changed as well and had taken the time to wash up. His hair curled damply around his neck and his skin had a freshly scrubbed look to it. She was pleased and flattered that he had done so for her.

"Well sir, where do we begin?"

Iain turned and looked appreciatively at Stephanie. "Let us go down tae the stables. I told them tae saddle two of the quieter mounts so that we might be able to spend more time enjoying the scenery." Iain took her by the elbow and guided her to the door.

As they stepped out the sun was shining brightly on a scene of busy harmony. Stephanie looked around and saw people busily, and mostly happily, getting on with their daily activities. She looked in the direction of the horrible earthen prison where Duncan, Edmond and Matthew were being kept and swore silently that she would help them. She hoped to find a way to get them a message that she was going to try to orchestrate an escape and perhaps give them some hope. Stephanie braced herself and walked a little more briskly in anticipation. They reached the stables and found two grey mares identical to each other, both saddled and looking very calm and relaxed in the sun. Iain spoke,

"These two are twins, Snow and Storm, our most docile to ride. I thought that they would be best for our ride so that you would not be trying to keep up with my destrier."

"They are beautiful. I love riding. These are two of the best horses I've ever encountered." Stephanie stepped forward and ran her hands over the nearest horse. "So soft and well groomed. You are lovely aren't you?" Stephanie spoke softly to the horse as she nuzzled her hands.

"That is Snow. See how her dapples are farther apart than Storm's? It looks like it is snowing on her rump." Stephanie continued to pat the horse not paying much attention to what Iain was saying. She was so captivated by Snow.

"Oh you are looking for treats aren't you beauty? Well if you can manage to enjoy your ride today without unseating me, I am sure I can manage to find you something that you will like." Snow's ears twitched in response to Stephanie's voice.

"Shall we go? I thought it would be nice tae take ye around the loch."

Damn! Stephanie thought to herself. The loch was in the opposite direction from the prisoners but she had to follow Iain. She had to hide her disappointment to avoid casting suspicion on herself. So she smiled "That sounds wonderful. Let us go."

They mounted Snow and Storm and set off behind the keep. As they rode Stephanie said,

"I saw the loch from my chamber window earlier. It is really a stunning sight. I gather it must be rather cold water."

Iain laughed. "Aye, actually the loch is fed by an underground spring. I find it refreshingly cool after long days of work, but I am sure those not used to it would most definitely find it cold. I do swim here often. Shall I show you my favorite spot?"

"I would like that" Stephanie said suddenly shy in the face of their first civil conversation. Iain dismounted and opened the gate to lead them down to the shores of the loch. The scene spread out before Stephanie like a magical picture and took her breath away.

She looked around her and marveled at the colors and the textures of the landscape around her. She had always thought her home was lovely but here the land had such a harsh beauty it touched her soul. All around the heather and thistles were blooming and the smell was intoxicating.

"The air seems to have a purple haze and light to it." Stephanie spoke out loud without thinking. She was completely distracted by the raw wildness.

Iain turned at the sound of the awe in her voice. He was surprised to see that Stephanie was speaking to herself. He could see how she appreciated the beauty around them. He felt no small measure of pride that at the moment all was well around the keep and there had not been any raids for a few days. But he was also surprised at his pleasure in watching Stephanie appreciate his home. He began to feel optimistic that his plan was a good one. Not only would his people see him spending time with Stephanie they wouldn't be able to miss her pleasure in what she saw, and they would certainly see how happy he was to spend this time with her.

"Aye" Iain responded to her comment "I have often seen that trick of the light myself. When the heather and thistles are blooming in such abundance and the day is particularly warm, it does look like the air is shimmering purple."

Stephanie brought herself back to attention and focus and asked with honesty. "You are a warrior, a soldier, a leader. I would have thought that you would not have the time or inclination to notice such frivolous things."

Iain reined in his mount so they were riding side by side. He looked at her thoughtfully.

"Tis true I am all those things and" he said with a smile "thanks to my father I am verra good at all those things as well. But I also had my stepmother. I knew her better than my own mother so she was more my mother. She treated me like I was her own flesh and blood. It was she that taught me how to see the world outside of the warrior's experience. She helped me amass a huge collection of books that I treasure, which taught me much about different places and perspectives. She also used to remind me that I would be head of the clan someday. So if I was going to relate to and communicate with everyone living in the clan I had to learn to view the world in different ways because everyone sees the world and everything in it differently. All our conversations are imprinted on my heart forever."

It was on the tip of her tongue to comment on Iain's education. That perhaps he should try to view her father differently as well. She thought better of it. If she was going to try to get information to help her escape, she had better not bait Iain. He might end their ride early. Best to keep to simple conversation.

"Your step mother sounds like she was an amazing woman. My mother died when I was very young. All I remember of her was that she was very beautiful and always smiling. But now I often wonder if my memories are only based on her portraits my father has hanging all around the keep. I used to spend hours sitting on the floor looking at her. I actually used to talk to her and imagine that she spoke to me in return. You were very lucky to have your stepmother in your life for as long as you did. What I find truly amazing is that you seem to have really loved and appreciated her."

Iain smiled slightly at Stephanie's remarks. Yes, he did love his stepmother and he appreciated her unconditional love. She was a remarkable woman spreading happiness everywhere she went, most especially to his father. His father was the epitome of the rugged Scottish warrior, rough and hard. Then Kaitlyn arrived and with her patient and kind ways she brought light and love back into the keep.

Thinking of them made Iain's heart ache with sadness at the thought of their recent, senseless deaths.

"Iain? Are you all right?" Iain mentally shook himself Stephanie was regarding him with genuine concern.

"Iain you were miles away. What were you thinking of that made you seem so sad?"

"My parents. But, never mind, we came out tae ride so I could show ye the lands. Let us just enjoy ourselves." Iain spoke with some brusqueness.

His abrupt tone forced Stephanie to realize that they were not on a ride like two normal people. No, he was out to show his people that the stranger amongst them was friend and to remind her she had to behave and play his game. She was sorry she had tried to engage him in any kind of conversation. So much for believing he was a man worth speaking to. She needed to get some information now pertinent to her plan of escape. Stephanie needed to find her bearings.

"So" Stephanie began cautiously "Tell me about your lands and what is around them."

"Our lands stretch from the edge of the forest on the far side of the loch. To your left they reach as far as the mountains and to the right they end at the base of the hills. For many generations those mountains and hills have been the source and place of many conflicts and battles. Each family wants to have the lands at the base of them for strategic advantage. It is much easier to defend a territory on flat ground, while the enemy is forced to pick its way carefully down an incline. Many things are changing in the country. There was a time when life would be clan fighting clan to control hills. Now some say for good or bad we have stopped the constant battling to plant our crops and build new homes. It is hard to build a life and home for family when the men are always away fighting and getting killed. I guess one could say there is an unspoken truce."

"So who are the clans surrounding you then?" Stephanie asked turning to survey the lands around her.

"We have the Campbells, the Duncans and the McAndrews. Those are the most powerful clans. Then of course we have your father and some other English lords that we do not know. We didn't need tae know their names until now. When your king decided to march into

Scotland and tried to dictate how to run our country we needed to know our new enemy. Had Edward Longshanks remained out of Scotland ye ken full well that the Scots and the English would get along fine."

"That is an awfully broad statement. You are judging the many by the actions of only a few. I find it very strange that you, as leader of many people, would be so quick to judge the whole clan guilty based on the actions of the one clan leader."

"Good point, Lady. However, that one leader is the King of a country so he determines his country's course of action. The cross border raids and sometimes all out attacks on the country of Scotland by your countrymen, has made your King's position abundantly clear. When the King leads his countrymen to attack, all those participating in the attacks are culpable."

"But Iain men cannot refuse the King's orders. They would have to forfeit their lands, titles and most probably even their lives."

"If yer countrymen disagree sae much with their King, did they sign with King John all those years ago? Wasn't it to gain some independence from the power the King wielded over his lords and their people?"

"Simplified, that was part of it. But the titled men cannot just decide when and where they will support the King. They swear an oath of fealty. The agreement with King John was to stop the incessant random taxation and rally to arms. Men were called to the King's wars overseas so often that their own lands suffered and then they had difficulties paying King John's crippling taxes, which he was using to finance his war with France."

Iain could not help but be impressed with Lady Stephanie's knowledge of her country's situation and history. She was well versed in politics where other ladies would not be interested in or even be permitted to participate in.

"Sae Lady Stephanie, how is it that a lady of yer position, knows about this sort of thing?"

"My father." Stephanie smiled. "He doesn't have a son and he loves to talk politics. Some say it is a drawback for women to be knowledgeable about anything political. Knowledge apparently diminishes our value on the marriage market. Men don't seem to appreciate women who know their minds. I sometimes think my father educated me thus so that he could entertain himself watching the men's jaws drop when I speak. Whatever his reason for doing so I am thankful to him regardless."

"Why?"

"Because it has saved me from any poor matches in marriage. Any man who can see past my unusual height, cannot see past my level of education. The shock on their faces is so comical. So none of the men I have met so far want to have much to do with a giant woman usually smarter than they are, let alone marry one."

"What do ye mean giant? Ye are no so tall. As for yer knowledge there is nothing wrong with a woman with some intelligence provided she does not use that knowledge tae make her husband look foolish in any way. Her knowledge should remain secondary to her husbands."

"What?" Stephanie squeaked "You almost sounded human. A woman is secondary to her man? So what you are saying is that even if a woman has some brains she should keep quiet so her husband doesn't sound like an idiot."

"Stephanie calm yerself. When I say a woman's intelligence should be secondary, it is to save the woman's reputation and her family. After all a woman who displays publicly a vast knowledge, reflects that her family was unable to teach her some measures of proper behavior and decorum. Shall we continue our ride?"

Iain rode ahead while Stephanie sat fuming. How dare he imply that she was a poor reflection on her family? At the moment the only poor reflection on her family was the fact that she still had not managed to glean any kind of information about her present location. That was what she should be ashamed of, not her mind or her thoughts.

"Fine" Stephanie said "You were telling me about your neighbors. Where is everyone located relative to your property?"

Iain gave her a ghost of a smile. "Never mind those insignificant details. I am going tae take ye tae my favorite spot. In fact yer eyes remind me of my favorite spot."

"That is a very odd thing to say."

"No really, wait and see. Ye will agree with me when ye see it."

Stephanie was surprised by Iain's eagerness to show her this "spot" They rode along in silence. Stephanie enjoyed the scenery but all the while hoping to see something familiar from their ride in earlier. She barely remembered anything other than the desolation of the recently burned field. She looked around but saw no sign of that field. That meant the field was on the other side of the keep. The question would be which way. Having at least a direction to turn Stephanie didn't think it would be too difficult to figure out which way to go to get home. Now her next step was to figure out how to free the men. Until that time, now that she roughly knew which way to go, there didn't seem to be any reason not to enjoy the rest of the ride.

The shore around the loch was quite rocky in places but the horse trail meandered in and out of the edge of the trees along the shoreline. The whole journey was very peaceful. Suddenly Iain turned away from the loch and the path and disappeared around a huge boulder. When Stephanie followed she heard the rush of water. The sound had been silenced behind the wall of rock. They left the trees and Stephanie saw the walls of sheer rock surrounding a pool of water dappled with sunlight. There was a waterfall cascading over the edge of the cliffs surrounding the pool. The beauty of the place touched Stephanie.

"See" Iain said as he dismounted and walked over to her. He lifted her down off Snow. As he lifted her Stephanie saw his eyes swirl and darken. He slid her slowly down the length of him. She saw his eyes flash silver and the look he gave her made her feel completely weak. She felt a slow heat begin in her belly. She was lightheaded and felt she should wrap her arms around Iain to keep from falling over.

Iain's whisper shivered down her spine. "Do you see?" He lifted his hand and gently caressed her cheek. He lightly traced her chin with his fingers. "Do ye see how this place reminds me of you?"

Stephanie barely heard the words Iain spoke. The blood was rushing in her ears. She was sure the pounding of her blood could be heard over the sound of the waterfall. If Iain kept touching her like this Stephanie didn't think she could return to her senses. His hand felt so rough yet so gentle as he stroked her cheek. Ever so slightly Stephanie turned her head into Iain's hand.

"Mm… What?" Stephanie lifted her clouded eyes to meet Iain's stormy ones.

Iain felt like he was spiraling out of control, trying to resist crushing Stephanie's lush curves to his body. He wanted to touch her to taste her, to caress every inch of her. Iain pulled himself away from staring at her golden hair, the loose tendrils teasing his hands as he continued to touch her soft cheek. He let his eyes caress her beautiful cheek stained with the faintest flush of the beginnings of desire. His eyes drifted downwards to her full lips parted slightly as her breath started to quicken. She was as affected by him as he was by her. He felt his groin tighten in response

Trying to regain his composure he pulled his gaze from her ripe lips, begging to be kissed and looked down. A very big mistake, as his eyes fell first on the long slender column of her neck then down to her tantalizing breasts. Her chest rose and fell with her quickening breath which made her dress tighten over them, he wanted to hold them and squeeze them in his hands. Quickly he looked up and saw that under the paleness of her skin he could see the flutter of her pulse just above her neckline. Without thinking he moved his hand slowly down the curve of her neck and placed it over her fluttering heart. His hand rested on her heart for a moment before he began to rub his thumb back and forth over her pulse.

Stephanie thought she must be dying for she could barely draw breath. She could feel the heat from his hand burning her through the cloth of her mantle. His soft caresses were making her feel hot and restless.

"Stephanie, look around ye. See the soft green surrounding ye, tis the same green as your eyes. Here in the shadow of your eyes I have spent the happiest days of my life." Iain put his hands on Stephanie's narrow waist. He felt the warmth of her. He felt the small shudder that shook her frame. He drew her closer.

Stephanie didn't even notice Iain's hands move, or the fact that while he pulled her closer she leaned in closer to him. She felt a dizzy longing but didn't know what she was longing for until his lips touched hers.

Their lips touched so gently but the searing heat of their new passion sent shock waves through both of them. With lips barely touching the connection between Iain and Stephanie was almost physically visible. Iain lifted his head.

"Ach lass, What are ye doing tae me? Ye've nigh stole my verra senses from me."

Stephanie didn't think she just spoke the words torn from her "Iain don't stop please"

Her breathless whisper shredded Iain's last resolve. He crushed her to him and took her mouth with flaming passion. He wanted to devour her as she had consumed him. He wanted every part of her.

Stephanie felt the raw barely restrained power coursing through Iain. She knew his hands could kill with or without the aid of a weapon, but his strength was keeping her upright. His hands were bringing life to her whole body, her senses, her soul. His lips pressed hers and she could feel her desire for him right down to her toes. An electric shock flared through Stephanie as she suddenly felt Iain's tongue gently seeking to enter her mouth.

"Tis all right." he whispered on her lips "Trust me. Let me taste ye lass" So Stephanie did just that. As she sighed her lips softened and parted. She felt his tongue slide into her.

Her world spun dizzily around her. His tongue swirled through her mouth tasting every corner. His breath breathed life into her. Iain could hardly believe how sweet Stephanie tasted. He wanted more, he wanted everything. His large hand cupped her breast and he caressed her nipple with his thumb. As he rubbed, her nipple rose to a taut peak through the material she wore. Her breast fit perfectly in his hand as he squeezed the soft firm mound. He wanted to tear her mantle off and run his tongue over every inch of her to see if the rest of her was as sweet as her honeyed mouth. Iain was on fire.

Stephanie wrapped her arms around Iain's neck and held on for dear life. She felt every nerve vibrating. Her skin was feverish and only seemed to be relieved when Iain caressed her. What was happening to her? The restless heat was building in her, building into an inferno that threatened to consume her altogether. The sensations were building to something but she had no idea what. She only knew that she wanted more of Iain's kisses, she wanted to melt into him. As she wavered in his arms Stephanie thought how odd it was that she had never felt more powerfully alive, yet so weak at the same time. Her legs threatened to give out on her so she clung tighter to Iain, her body demanding more.

Iain felt himself falling further into Stephanie's embrace. Her taste was irresistible. He dug his hands into her hair and nearly came undone at the softness. Could this woman be real? Was there no end to her intoxicating scent and flavor? He had to stop! He must stop! He ground his teeth closed and drew his head away from Stephanie. It took all his warrior discipline not to lean in and lick the moisture their kiss had left on her mouth. He hung his head and was unable to speak for what seemed like an eternity. Setting Stephanie away from him made him feel like he was denying himself air. He was sure he was gasping for breath.

Stephanie was absolutely shocked and bereft when Iain forced her away. He might as well have slapped her in the face. What had she done wrong to make him stop? How could he have aroused such feelings in her and then so casually push her away? Her body still throbbed, every nerve raw and jittery. She almost couldn't stand the feel of her own clothes against her. Her breasts were aching and her nipples tingling. The over sensitiveness was almost painful. Almost as painful as Iain's casual disregard of her. Stephanie let her arms drop limply to her sides. Emptiness echoed through her and for some strange reason she felt abandoned. How was it possible for a person to feel so alive in one moment and in the next be as good as dead? She felt herself go numb and cold. She watched Iain but he wasn't even looking at her. What was happening? She wanted to scream at him but she kept a brittle silence around her.

Iain wrestled with his desire. He had to gain control of the situation. He had nearly ruined everything. His feelings for Stephanie were becoming dangerous. He had to stop them. He knew she felt desire for him as well when she responded to his kisses and caresses with such honest passion he nearly exploded. But he had to tamp down the fires that were blazing between them so he could carry out his plan. He had to make her forget the passion they both desired and felt. He had to make her hate this moment, hate him. When he spoke he nearly hated himself too.

"Well my lady, if I can call ye that. That was quite a pleasant diversion for the afternoon. But really ye should no attack me like tha in public. Someone might see and get ideas." Iain brushed invisible dust off his shirt trying not to look Stephanie in the eye.

"What? What?" Stephanie could barely speak from the insult. "You bastard, if there was any attacking you know full well you did it." She couldn't believe what she was hearing. Iain was acting so insufferable and cruel. She felt sick to her stomach.

"Now now dinna get sae upset. Ye mentioned yerself how many suitors had been paraded through yer father's home. Surely given your blatant sexual expertise as just recently demonstrated tae me, ye dinna expect me tae believe that ye are some untried virgin? Some other men might fall for yer maidenly ways, but I am no fool, so dinna treat me like one." Iain knew he was being a bounder. Stephanie's look spoke volumes to that. He felt guilty at the hurt and betrayal that showed in her eyes. While her words were angry, her real feelings were in her lovely green eyes. It took all his will power not to gather her close and kiss the hurt away.

"Is that all you have to say to me?" Stephanie's voice was subdued and tight. "Because if it is I think that we should get back now. People will be wondering what happened to us."

"Not tae worry. I am showing ye around this great land of ours they will not expect us back anytime soon. Let us continue. Unless ye would like tae finish what ye started? I would be happy tae oblige ye lady, but I warn ye dinna expect me tae become one of yer simpering admirers. Ye and I can have a tumble but tha will be it."

"How can you speak to me like that? You are the most insensitive, rude lout I have ever met! I tell you right now, not only will I never 'tumble' with you but I will never allow you to kiss me again. If you insist we continue then let us be on with it. The sooner your 'tour' is over the sooner I can go back to your keep and be the prisoner that I am. I will be staying with my father's men now. After what you have done here today, there will be no more show. I will stay as a prisoner. Let us go." Stephanie mounted Snow and began to turn him around.

"All right my lady. But if ye change yer mind remember it would be my pleasure tae pleasure you."

Before Stephanie could say anything Iain rode ahead. Stephanie thought it was a good idea that she could not reach him from the back of Snow or she would probably strangle him. He would not touch her again. She would never let him have the opportunity to arouse those feelings in her again. Never.

Chapter Twelve

The two of them rode in silence back the way they had come. Having passed this way already Stephanie was not focused on her surroundings she was thinking of how strange the last couple of days had been. If anyone had told her that she was going to deliver babies then get whisked away by a bunch of Scottish barbarians to be held as a pawn to bargain with her father, she would have laughed outright. She was not laughing now. She was certain no one would ever have predicted that she would grow increasingly attracted to the man who had kidnapped her. But Iain's attractiveness could not be ignored for long. She looked at his back thoughtfully as they rode on. He was certainly physically powerful. Even on horseback his muscles were rippling under his clothing and his incredibly large frame dwarfed the mare he was riding. But for his wonderful physical looks Iain fell far short with his temperament. He was the Laird, yes, but he seemed too accustomed to giving orders and directions and having them followed to the letter. No one seemed too concerned about questioning anything that Iain directed, not even Fergus seemed inclined to do so.

Yet for herself Stephanie knew that she and Iain would cross swords often. His high handedness was a source of considerable frustration for her.

My God what was she thinking? Daydreaming about Iain. The sooner she got away from him the better. He was affecting her better judgment and good sense far too much.

"Where are we going?" Stephanie thought a conversation might stop her mind from wandering to inappropriate thoughts of Iain.

They were just rounding the walls of the keep and moving away from the edge of the loch.

"I thought we could ride to the edge of the village and we could walk through town. I should like to show you our village. The people have been working very hard since before my parents died, to make the place a profitable place to settle. Here we are." Iain stopped Storm in the clearing between the gates of the keep and the village. He dismounted easily and quickly for a man his size and was next to Stephanie before she had a chance to dismount on her own. She stiffened slightly when his hands clasped her waist. All of a sudden the memory of his passionate embrace flooded Stephanie's mind and she nearly fell over when Iain set her down.

"Are ye all right?" Iain looked at her with some concern.

"Yes, yes. I am fine" Stephanie answered. "I am just a little unsteady after such a long ride." She knew her face was flushed with heat from the memory of Iain's touch. She turned away, busying herself with securing Snow.

Iain's dark brow lifted at Stephanie's behavior. He knew she had thought of their kiss when he touched her. So had he. In fact he couldn't stop thinking about it. He longed to run his hands down her long back but he wanted more to feel her bare skin. If the rest of her was as soft as her face, neck and lips, no man would ever be able to satisfy his hunger for her. Iain couldn't resist a brief touch. He reached over and tweaked a loose curl on her neck. His fingers barely touched her neck but it was enough for now.

"Come Lady, let's not dawdle. The horses will not go anywhere. They are used to this small clearing for extra fodder. They will not wander."

Stephanie's neck still tingled from the touch of his fingers. Just the slightest touch made her think and feel things she shouldn't. She felt like such a fool. She knew the boys were just to the left of where they were but she couldn't go and tell them they would be getting out today. She wanted to get as far away from Iain MacDonald as she could as fast as she could before her body betrayed her feelings.

They began walking towards the neat village. Stephanie was distracted from her thoughts of Iain, looking at how organized and clean the small area was. All the people they passed looked clean, well fed and while casting looks of doubt and suspicion at her, still looked content. They strolled through the village homes and shops. People greeted Iain as he passed he stopped often along the way to converse and make sure the people were satisfied.

Iain completely ignored Stephanie as they moved through the town. But he kept her close. Everyone knew she was still with him but as he made no effort to introduce her to anyone, they didn't have the opportunity to find out more about her. Stephanie guessed it was easier for

Iain to pretend she wasn't there than to try to answer difficult questions about her presence. So she was happy to stand next to Iain and look around her to get her bearings for her escape. She was sure she made out the edge of the burnt field at the edge of town and guessed that if she and the men could just make it through the clearing they could stay in the trees until they reached her father's land.

As she looked through the walkways of the village she saw some boys engaged in mock sword fights. She smiled as she watched their untrained moves, trying to mimic what they had seen their fathers do. Probably on Iain's own training grounds. They were no different than the boys on her own father's lands, growing up with dreams of glory on the battlefield playing with their wooden swords. In that instant Stephanie realized that one young boy, smaller than the rest, was struggling under the weight of his sword. With horror she realized that was because it was not a wooden sword, it was a real sword. Before she could speak out, she watched the boy lift the sword up to his shoulder and call out to the others. But the weight was too much and the sword arched down right into his thigh. At that moment both the boy and Stephanie screamed.

"Iain" Stephanie screamed as she ran towards the group of boys. She didn't care about anything else but getting to the injured boy.

Iain was listening to the tanner asking for more game as the leather supply was low and he wanted more to be ready for winter. He heard the boy's high pitched scream of agony, heard Stephanie scream his name and go racing between the cottages. Stephanie's golden hair was streaming behind her as she ran to a group of local boys. Iain immediately took control.

"Here now what is happening?" From the looks on the boys faces Iain knew something bad had happened. The boys started and looked at Iain with large frightened eyes. None could speak. Iain heard Stephanie's quiet gasp. She dropped to her knees beside Lachlan, one of his soldier's boys. Then he saw what the boys were too shocked to speak of. Imbedded in the young boys leg was one of his father's sparring swords. It looked like the sword had almost cut through Lachlan's leg. Iain feared the boy would lose his leg as he screamed in agony. Ian stepped forward to stop him but Stephanie was already speaking to him.

"Here now" She was bent close to Lachlan's ear but still had to speak fairly loudly so he could hear her. She had to calm him down so that he would not worsen his injury. "Quiet lad you must stop that so we can help you."

Instantly Lachlan stopped screaming and his clear blue eyes focused on Stephanie's face.

"Yer a bluidy English?" He said with some surprise.

Stephanie frowned. "Young man such awful language. Hardly the language of a gentleman. But yes I am English."

"My da calls all English 'bluidy english' and says he'd love to run them through if he had the chance. That is what we were doing. Fighting the English. Who are you?"

"My name is Lady Stephanie and I want to help you. But I don"t know if I should with such bad manners. And you will probably kill me when I am through." Stephanie tried to keep the conversation at the young boy's level so that he would not realize how serious his condition was.

He looked horrified. "Oh, no, I wouldn't. Not if ye helped me. That would be dishonorable. Can ye make this awful pain go away?"

"Yes I believe I can"

"Then I willna think of ye as English. Ye will be my golden angel. No one can hate an angel can they?" Lachlan's eyes were fearful with shadows of pain but Stephanie had managed to calm him. She spoke quietly to him as she tore a strip from her underskirt and tied it tightly on the boy's leg to stop the bleeding.

"What is your name child?"

"Lachlan, lady. But I am no child I was the only one to have a real sword." Suddenly his eyes welled with tears. "My da is going to whip me fer this"

"Now Lachlan don't fuss your father will not beat you."

"Get yer hands off my son or die English bitch." Stephanie heard the soft gruff voice whisper in her ear and for just a moment she was sure she felt the tip of a sword pressed to the back of her neck. But just as she registered it, it was gone. She thought she must have imagined it until Iain spoke.

"Rowan ye are one of my most valued soldiers but by God if ye harm one hair on her head I will run ye through where ye stand!" Iain towered behind Rowan and held the tip of his sword to the side of Rowan's neck.

Stephanie looked up and saw the man named Rowan glaring down at her with eyes as blue as his boy's were. The hatred radiating from his eyes seared Stephanie's skin.

"Iain stop that at once! I am sure this gentleman, Rowan, you call him, did not mean he would actually kill me. It is his fear for his son that makes him speak so."

"Silence English. I dinna need the likes of ye defending me from the man I am loyal to. I would rather die though than let ye near my son."

"Stand down Rowan now! If ye are as loyal tae me as ye claim, then I command ye tae cease threatening Lady Stephanie at once. She is here tae help yer son, whom if ye hadn't noticed is grievously injured and ye are preventing him from getting the help he needs right now."

"Da!" Lachlan's voice was whisper thin but cut through his father's rage "It's all right, she's nay English. She's my angel and she's going tae make the pain go away. Dinna hate her please."

Stephanie looked down at the little boy and how pale he was. At the sight of him, her own anger took over. She stood up nearly as tall as Rowan himself, looked him straight in the eyes letting him feel the brunt of her anger. She hissed quietly at him,

"Rowan, you can hate me all you like and you may even kill me one day but if you do not cease behaving like such an infant, I will knock you down where you stand. Nothing is more important than trying to save your son's leg and his life, if you prevent me from looking after him very much longer! How will you explain to your wife and your son that you let him be crippled or killed because the person trying to help is English. Stand back or get out of my sight!" Stephanie's voice was not loud enough to upset or disturb Lachlan, but there was no mistaking her intention. Rowan looked more than shocked but he was set back enough to relax his warrior's stance.

"Do what needs tae be done. But if he dies or loses his leg I will kill ye."

"Rowan go get your wife and the tanner tell them to meet us at the keep." Stephanie directed.

The tanner spoke up from behind "I am here Lady."

"Good" Stephanie said "Go and get your finest needle for stitching leather. Rowan have your wife bring the finest thread she has. Iain carry Lachlan up to the great hall. We must lay him out on the tables there."

"Are ye going tae eat me?" Lachlan's thready voice drifted up worriedly.

"No young man I need to be able to reach you so I can patch you all up. Come, Iain, we must hurry."

Iain lifted the boy his large arms made Lachlan look even more helpless and small. The sight of the small boy so vulnerable and fragile, made Stephanie all the more determined to help him. Iain barely noticed the boy in his arms except he made sure not to jostle him overly much. There was quite a crowd of people lining the path to the gates of the keep and Iain knew they would all follow them as they passed. Stephanie was certainly the focus of everyone's attention now, but she didn't even notice the people gaping at her now. All of her attention was focused on Lachlan whom she kept quietly reassuring on the entire way to the keep. Iain was amazed with Stephanie's calm strength. In the midst of a horrible crisis she had stepped forward and taken charge, directing everyone with dignified authority that brooked no argument. She held herself with such strength that Iain was satisfied to let her be in charge at this time. If all went well, then the people would simply accept Stephanie's presence here without question and that would suit his purposes.

They reached the hall. Judith met them at the entrance.

"My God!" She gasped "What has happened?"

"Judith" Stephanie sighed with relief. "Good you are here. We will explain everything later but right now I need you to get as much water boiling as possible. I also need you to find a sharp pointed dagger and keep it in the flame but don't let it get dirty. Here Iain lay him down." Iain laid the young Lachlan on the table. The boy was drifting in and out of consciousness. Stephanie bent over Lachlan's leg and carefully undid the bandage at the top of his leg. She fervently prayed that she had slowed the bleeding. It would be very hard to inspect the wound if the blood was still running freely.

"I need torches, the light is not strong enough" She spoke to no one in particular but many men rushed forward with torches. As they brought them close to the table they all looked at Stephanie with some measure of awe.

Iain then noticed Lachlan's parents were standing anxiously behind Stephanie. Rowan was bracing his wife who was clutching what appeared to be all the thread she owned. Her face was white and tears streamed down her cheeks but she didn't utter a sound. In fact the whole hall was eerily silent. The loudest sound was Lachlan's rasping breath and small whimpers. Every eye was on Stephanie while she worked. Iain saw the tanner and went to retrieve the needles from his shaking hands. He quietly walked back and stood next to Stephanie waiting for her to notice his presence. She looked at him with worried desperate tear filled eyes.

"Iain" she whispered. "I cannot fail. I will be unable to bear it if anything happens to this child."

Iain smiled gently at Stephanie, put his arm around her and leaned down to whisper in her ear.

"It is all right Lady. Ye ken what ye are doing. Ye dinna need tae fash yerself about anything. I will be right here. If ye need anything just ask." He squeezed her shoulder and dropped the lightest kiss on her forehead filled with all the confidence he had in her. Stephanie closed her eyes and felt his strength seep into her soul. Iain believed in her and she felt sure that she could do this. It was time.

"Iain I need you to lift the sword straight up as quickly as you can. I just hope it has not been imbedded in the bone or we shall have serious complications."

Iain nodded and grasped the sword. Stephanie gently held the skin away to avoid any further tearing. Iain pulled the sword out quickly and cleanly.

The whole room breathed a sigh of relief. Stephanie nodded in satisfaction. She began to work in earnest cleaning the wound very carefully. Thankfully she noticed that the wound was clean and free of any shards of metal left behind by the sword. After she had cleaned the area thoroughly it was time to close the wound.

"Where is the thread?" She asked

"Here Lady." Lachlan's mother stepped forward white and shaking.

Stephanie knew Lachlan's mother from her palpable distress. She took a moment and gave her cold shaking hands a reassuring squeeze as she took the thread. "It is going to be all right. When I am finished I will speak to you about his care. Please don't worry the news is good."

Stephanie gave the woman a kind smile, and bent over Lachlan again. Judith stepped forward and added.

"Do not worry, Rose all is well if the Lady Stephanie says so." Rose nodded and went back to stand next to her husband. Stephanie carefully threaded the needle then knotted the thread. She looked at Iain and Judith.

"I need you to press the skin together but not so much that it puckers or he will have a jagged scar. Just gently hold the wound closed and the skin still so I can stitch it. Is he still unconscious?"

"Yes" Judith said marveling at her new friend's skill and calm. "What if he should wake during the stitching?"

"It is a possibility but he is weak from blood loss, and exhaustion from the ordeal, so it is unlikely. Did you call his mother Rose?"

"Yes" Judith replied

"Rose" Stephanie called. Lachlan's mother immediately went to Stephanie's side.

"Aye mi lady"

"I would like you to sit next to Lachlan's head and speak in a gentle quiet voice so that if he does awaken while I am working he will be less likely to panic. Tell him everything we are doing as it wont be such a shock to him should he wake up. Rowan, hold his legs firmly but gently so he does not thrash."

Stephanie surprised everyone there by taking up the needle and thread and she began with the first pierce of the needle. While she worked she hummed a soft lullaby. Her quiet humming continued right up to the last stitch. Thankfully Lachlan didn't wake up. He stirred once and whimpered, but as Stephanie had predicted, his mother's soothing voice kept him calm so Stephanie was able to complete the stitching with no visible complications.

Stephanie was so relieved after she had finished she wanted to drop into a chair and cry like a little baby. She had succeeded and she was not ashamed to feel some pride in herself. But she was still ready to collapse on the spot. Not yet. First she had to speak to Rose and Rowan about Lachlan's care. Just a little longer. She had to keep going.

"Rose, Rowan. Lachlan is fine at the moment. You must keep the wound clean. Any dirt could cause serious infection and he could lose his leg. Cleanse and put fresh covering on his wound as often as it is needed. If you do this, there should be no complications."

"Thank ye mi Lady." Rose held Stephanie's blood stained hands tightly in her own. "Thank ye sae much for looking after our boy." Rose had tears in her eyes as she spoke.

Rowan lifted the sleeping form of his son. "Come woman. We shall see if the English has taken care of our son. Remember English if anything happens to him I will cut you where you stand." With that Rowan turned and pushed through the crowd of people to exit the hall.

"You are welcome you ungrateful man!" Stephanie muttered quietly at Rowan and Rose's retreating forms. Judith came around the table and put her arms around Stephanie.

"You were wonderful, Steffie! But now it is rather late so you are going up to your chamber and have a bath and some food. You have done enough today."

By the time Stephanie had cleaned up and made her way to her temporary chamber the bath had been prepared behind the screen for her. She went around it and undressed. As she lowered herself in the warm scented water she could feel her spirits picking up again. With it came her renewed determination to get back home and stop the madness between Iain and her father. She knew her father was not responsible for the damage to Iain's property and she knew that Iain wasn't destroying her father's lands either.

Her resolve was bolstered. She had to stop Iain and her father from fighting. To do that she had to leave immediately and she had every intention of doing so. As difficult as it was to get out of the soothing water, she did.

Chapter Thirteen

It was getting quite dark outside, the benefit was that she would have some cover to make her escape but the hindrance was that she wasn't exactly sure where she was going and she would have to be very careful. Stephanie dressed in the oldest dullest clothes she could find, hers still hadn't been returned from being cleaned. She didn't need to take anything with her except some of the food that had been laid out. She grabbed a cloth and wrapped up as much bread as she could hold. She also took some apples. They would have to forage along the way because she couldn't hold enough food to sustain the four of them for the journey home. Hopefully they would be able to get home quickly. She gathered her meager bundle of provisions and descended the stairs to the great hall. She stayed close to the wall opposite the huge fireplace and moved slowly through the shadows.

Iain sat quiet and still as he watched Stephanie creep in the shadows. He knew exactly what she was doing but wanted to entertain himself, toying a bit with her first. He knew she wouldn't see him as he was in his chair seated in the corner of the hall. He had come here to get some peace and reflect on the day's events. He was still amazed at the way Stephanie had handled herself and he wanted to reflect undisturbed on how much her actions had impressed him. She had been soft and yielding in his arms earlier when he kissed her. Yet, later, he watched her turn hard as steel as she dealt with young Lachlan's injuries. She had to be exhausted, but here she was sneaking out preparing to try to escape. He had to smile at her courage. He knew she was going to where she thought the men were being kept. But of course they had not been kept there. In fact they were no longer on his land. With the aid of Fergus and his other man, Murdoch, they would all be at her father's home by tomorrow to deliver his message. That thought made him smile all the more.

Stephanie had reached the door and gave silent thanks to Iain's people for looking after his home so well that the door made not a whisper of sound when she opened it. She hurried out into the dark courtyard. As her eyes adjusted to the darkness outside she was pleased to see that the night watch had not finished their rounds so the gate was still open. She waited nearby to make sure they were not coming, then ran out in the direction of the horrible mound were the men were imprisoned. She could just make out the hump in the landscape, so dark and cold. It had been horrible to see during the day, Stephanie was sure it would be much worse at night. So intent was she on reaching her goal she didn't notice, even at a distance, that there were no guards posted outside the mound.

Iain watched Stephanie slide swiftly through the darkness. Fortunately, she wasn't going anywhere. As he drew closer he watched her disappear around the mound.

He was only a moment behind her but what he saw when he rounded behind her, nearly undid him.

When Stephanie reached the door she still had not registered that there were no guards nearby. Her exhaustion from the day had clouded her mind. All she could focus on was getting the men out and escaping. She struggled with the door.

"Edmund, Duncan, Matthew. I am here." She whispered as loudly as she dared. "Come. We must hurry."

It was EMPTY! No it was not possible they had to be here. Stephanie had to be sure as she groped about on her hands and knees in the inky blackness. Maybe they were asleep.

"Matthew, Duncan, Edmund are you here? Answer me. It is I Lady Stephanie." Nothing! They were not there. Where were they? Gone, all traces of them vanished. They were dead! They had to be how else could they just disappear? Stephanie fell to the dirt, silent tears coursing down her cheeks and she began shaking with shock and such despair she felt unable to breathe.

Iain found here there on her knees with her hands braced on either side of the narrow doorway. She was barely making a sound but her shaking shoulders were evidence that she was crying. When he lifted her up and turned her to face him, the stark pain and horror on her face tore open his heart. The tears were flooding from her eyes.

"Stephanie. Stephanie" Iain spoke to her gently but she looked right through him. In her shock and pain of discovering that the men were not where she thought they would be, she had retreated deep within herself to avoid dealing with the reality that they were gone. He realized from the anguish pouring from her that she thought the men were dead.

Stephanie didn't hear Iain calling her. She wasn't even aware that he was there and holding her up. All she knew was that the men were gone and there was no sign of them ever being there. They had been killed and all trace of them erased to avoid detection or culpability. She felt like she was being crushed under the weight of the guilt, being responsible for their deaths.

Iain knew Stephanie was going into shock. He had to do something to bring her out of it. He knew he could not force her back or he might permanently break her mind, she had to be brought back gently. He lifted her carefully in his arms. She did not resist but her body was stiff in his arms. Iain quickly strode back to the keep knowing every moment was crucial to her recovery. He saw a man on watch and called to him.

"Go and wake Cook. Tell her tae prepare a hot bath immediately and bring as much food and wine as she can find readily in the kitchen. Tell her to bring everything directly tae my parent's old chambers. Run! Tell her it is an emergency."

Seeing the pale form in his Laird's arms, the man didn't hesitate but went directly to carry out his Laird's orders. Iain carried Stephanie to her 'guest' quarters and set her in a large chair by the hearth. He quickly lit a fire and pulled her closer to the roaring blaze. He watched to see if there was any change in her. Iain hoped that she would shortly begin to focus on her surroundings but Stephanie's mind still refused to acknowledge anything.

There was a knock at the door.

"Enter." Iain called and Cook entered with a huge platter of bread, cheese and some apples. Iain was pleased to see a bowl of steaming broth. He also noticed that Cook had warmed some wine as well. She came in and set the tray on the chest at the foot of the bed. Then she turned and directed the sleepy kitchen boys behind her to bring in the pails of water heated for the tub that was still standing from earlier.

"Ach, the puir wee lamb. Wha has happened to her?" Cook took a look at Stephanie and knew she had suffered a severe shock. Then she looked at her Laird and nodded, he knew what to do.

"Go ahead and call Laird if ye need anythin further. Dinna worry none about waking me. With what the lass did today fer our Lachlan I'll do anything. Just ask."

Iain nodded not taking his eyes off Stephanie's face. He still waited for her to focus on her surroundings. He heard the door close quietly and he knew he had to coax Stephanie back somehow.

"Stephanie. Can ye hear me? Ye must listen tae my voice." Iain spoke quietly and firmly "Come Stephanie we have tae try tae get ye tae eat something."

Iain had dealt with many young men their first time in battle who often went into shock after the bloody battle was over. But it was nothing compared to this moment. He actually felt fear. He pulled the chest over next to Stephanie's chair and picked up the bowl of broth. He began to try to get Stephanie to try to take some. Not much success there, most of what he tried to feed her, dribbled down her chin back into the bowl.

"Come on Stephanie ye have tae eat. Dinna make me force this down yer throat." But still Stephanie made no movement or acknowledgement that she had heard anything Iain had said.

"Right then. I'll have tae move this along a little bit shall I?" He lifted Stephanie, with no resistance from her, onto his lap. Gently he leaned her back onto his shoulder. He then took the bowl of broth and trickled some into her mouth.

"Careful lass ye have tae have something in ye. Ye have tae come back Stephanie. Ye must hear the sound of my voice. I ken what ye think ye saw but it weren't true. Ye can do it, come back tae the sound of my voice sae I can explain what ye saw. Please come back." Iain gently kept a trickle of broth at Stephanie's lips.

Then he noticed her begin to swallow. "That's it lass drink up." Iain kept feeding her knowing that soon she would begin the uncontrolled shakes. It was going to be rough on her but he would remain with her throughout the ordeal. Iain wouldn't have let anyone else do this because he knew he was responsible for her current fragile state of mind. She had no idea what he was up to and he had no intention of telling her. But he had not thought she would try to escape so soon. He looked down into her lovely face with a full measure of admiration.

"Well my fiery spirited beauty. Ye have some heart in ye tae try tae run away. But ye canna run from tonight and what is coming. Come on Stephanie ye can make it back. Try tae make it back before the shaking starts lass." Iain gently stroked her soft honey gold hair. Without warning he was struck by the sudden urge to gather Stephanie close and bury his face into her soft golden tresses. He felt his desire for her begin to surface again. And for one of the only times since they had come together she lay quietly in his arms. Her eyes closed she looked to the world to be sleeping.

"Aye ye are as bonny a lass as I have seen. But when ye use tha tongue for whipping tis no wonder men run from ye." He traced a finger down her cheek. "Ye need a man who'll nay run from ye." Iain smiled and pressed his lips to Stephanie's forehead. Her skin felt like ice.

With dismay Iain realized that the shaking was about to begin. Sure enough little tremors began to ripple through Stephanie. Iain held her close and whispered soothing words, all the while telling her to hear the sound of his voice.

She was so cold. Stephanie thought she must have fallen through the ice in the pond in her father's gardens. She was drowning in the black coldness. Then she thought she heard a voice calling her up from the dark. She felt the cold but she felt a heated restlessness run through her. She needed to move. Why was everything so dark? Why couldn't she move? Then she realized that she was being held fast. Was it her father? Why was he holding her so tightly?

"Easy lass. Dinna fash yerself. Ye are going tae hurt yerself if ye carry on sae. Come now Stephanie can ye hear me?"

Whose voice was that? It was slightly familiar to Stephanie but it sounded so warm. She needed to find out who that voice belonged to.

"Tha's it come back now. Be strong lass hear me."

Stephanie's eyes flew open. Yes she knew that voice! It was the bastard Scot that had murdered her father's men. Oh God it was all coming back to her now. Stephanie's heart was breaking. Her very soul ached with guilty despair.

"Why oh why?!" The words tore out of her in anguished sobs. She realized that she could not stop shaking and she felt as if she would never be warm again. "I am so cold."

"I ken ye are lass. Now listen we have got tae get ye into the bath. The water is verra warm and ye need tae get some warmth back into ye. Ye can survive this. Remember ye have already helped a woman deliver no one but two bairns. And ye saved little Lachlan's life and his leg. This is nothing. Come on lass buck up. Now I am going tae get these clothes off ye."

"Oh no you are not." Stephanie said through her uncontrollably chattering teeth. "You will do no such thing. I will have a bath but I will do this myself. Keep your hands off me."

"Still got some fight left in ye? All right get yerself intae this bath my Lady. Be my guest." Iain was so pleased to see her spitting at him like a cornered cat again. He thought it best to let her try to get undressed herself. He let go of her and stood back with his arms folded.

Stephanie's whole body shook with violent tremors. She could barely stand. It wasn't until she fought with the ties of her mantle that she realized she could not do this on her own. But she also knew she had to get into that bath.

"Are you going to help me or just stand there laughing at me?" Stephanie didn't even realize how absurd she sounded having just ordered Iain not to touch her.

Still in shock Stephanie lost her indignation and began to sob uncontrollably. "Please help me. I can't bear this anymore. I can't feel anything more. I am a murderer. I am a murderer. Why, why did I do it?" Stephanie rocked back and forth shaking and holding her arms around herself. Tears streamed down her face.

Iain stepped behind Stephanie and gently began undoing the stays on her mantle. He could only undo down to where her arms were tightly wrapped around herself. He carefully pried her arms loose so he could take her mantle off. Stephanie stood in her shift with her head hung forward, her hair spilled around her face as she continued to weep. Iain was afraid he was losing her again. He made short work of the rest of her clothing and took her up in his arms. He knew when she raised no alarm or objections to his holding her naked body that he was losing her quickly.

"Come lass dinna give up now. Here I am holding yer naked body in my arms. I feel yer soft skin. Ye make me burn with passion. Ah see how your soft lips part so slightly for me. Yer breath caresses me and smells so sweet. Perhaps ye want me tae taste ye again, is that it? That must be it. Ye are begging me tae taste yer sweetness again."

Iain looked at Stephanie's face for any kind of reaction. All he saw was exactly as he had described to her. Her eyes were closed, the lashes fanned against her pale cheek. Her full lips were gently parted as her breath flowed softly and erratically. He shook himself away from the thought of Stephanie's soft vulnerability. Gently and with some reluctance Iain set Stephanie into the hot water. Stephanie moaned and reached for him.

"Don't leave me Iain. Please don't leave me." Stephanie barely spoke above a whisper.

"Nay lass, I willna leave ye. Hush now" Iain gently began pouring hot water over her skin. Her skin was still cold to the touch but was turning pink. Iain continued his ministrations and hummed softly in Stephanie's ear. She leaned toward him as her breath became more regular.

After a few minutes Iain realized that Stephanie's skin had finally taken on a lovely pink glow and she was no longer ice cold. She was out of immediate danger but as he looked at the lovely lady in her bath he realized that she was not out of all danger. He looked at Stephanie exposed before his eyes and felt his eyes seared by her loveliness. She took his breath away. He knew looking at her like this was not right given the ordeal she had just gone through, but she was so tempting a feast for his eyes. He let droplets of water run over her shoulders and down between her round breasts. His eyes hungrily followed the water as it flowed down to her womanhood. He ached to let his tongue follow the same trail as the water. He wanted to taste her incredible body and fill himself with her. Iain began tantalizingly running tiny droplets of water all over her just as he imagined where he wanted to run his hands and tongue. He was getting hard and almost lightheaded in his desire to touch and taste every long inch of this spirited beauty laid out before him.

Stephanie felt so warm, finally. She did not want this languorous feeling to go away. But through her haze she felt a more intense heat building within her, rising tides of restlessness. She felt the pressure building deep inside her and it was making her want. What she wanted she didn't exactly know but she wanted to run her hands over herself to settle her skin. She moaned.

Iain watched the water catch on Stephanie's rosy pink nipple taut with his liquid teasing. He knew that she was being affected by his teasing love play. Then she moaned and rubbed her face into his hand. She began twisting in the beginnings of her ecstasy and she grabbed hold of his arm. Her sensual movements were his undoing. No more could he stand this. No more. He had to taste her again.

He leaned forward and nibbled her shell pink earlobe his breath gently fanning her as he did so. Stephanie nearly rocketed out of the water so intense were the feelings of pleasure as he kissed her. He trailed kisses along her neck then onto her chin. He pulled back and looked at her before leaning forward and pressing his lips to hers. Oh God! She tasted so sweet, better than he remembered. More he had to have more. He gently forced her mouth open with his tongue and swept it around her mouth. She was intoxicating.

Stephanie came to awareness with a start. He was kissing her and kissing her thoroughly. She should be shocked and angry but she didn't want him to stop. Her limbs were tingling and she felt like she had a fever and the only relief was found wherever he placed his hands. She needed more of him. Without thinking she wrapped her arms around his neck and pulled him closer. Her tongue mated with his. At this moment nothing felt more right.

Iain couldn't believe it when Stephanie responded to his kiss. She was wildly passionate and he growled deep in his throat. He needed more of her. He lifted her out of the tub and slowly let her slick wet body slide down the length of him. She was not shivering now; she was making sexy purring noises in the back of her throat as she stretched up and down his body. He had to stop this now or there would be no turning back.

"Lass, Lass can ye hear me?"

"Oh God, yes, Iain, I can hear you, feel you and taste you. Please don't stop, don't ever stop" Stephanie pleaded breathlessly.

He made one more attempt to do the right thing "Stephanie we canna do this. I am about tae make love tae ye. This is wrong."

Stephanie locked eyes with Iain and said "This cannot be wrong." She looked at him with her lips half parted swollen and wet from his kisses. His last rational thought was hardly that. Thank God she didn't want him to stop because looking at her now he knew he never could.

"Stephanie, ye are so beautiful I must have all of ye."

Iain lifted Stephanie up and carried her to the bed tasting her neck all the while. He never stopped running his tongue and lips over her throat while he gently laid her down. He lifted her arms over her head and began to move his kisses lower. He tasted the valley between her breasts and Stephanie felt the hot liquid heat building inside her again. She was aching for something she couldn't name. She cried out in surprise and pleasure as Iain took her breast into his mouth. He teased her nipple to its peak and kept laving it with his tongue. Unconsciously Stephanie's hips followed the rhythm of his stroking caress. She had to be dying she kept twisting her body trying to free her hands, she had to touch him. Had to, had to.

"Easy my little vixen." Iain chuckled. He began teasing her breast while he pressed and kneaded the other with his free hand. She arched toward him to get as deep into his mouth as she could. She thought she would explode from the heat burning inside her. She whimpered when his mouth left her breasts. Iain then began kissing her belly. She shivered from the touch. He dipped his tongue into her navel but he didn't linger. He moved lower. When his tongue tasted her womanhood, Stephanie was shocked but so excited.

"No Iain you mustn't."

"Hush lass." He continued his exquisite torture. In moments Stephanie was lost again in the sensation of his hot tongue branding her everywhere. His tasted her fully and completely moving his tongue in and out of her in mock mating. The ache between her legs was so intense she could find no release from the pressure. She thrust her hips up to match Iain's rhythm. He was driving her wild.

Iain could not believe all the passion in Stephanie's response to him. She was hot and wet from his touch now not the water, and he could not get enough of her taste. He wanted to thrust himself so deep into her until he was lost forever in her hot wet sheath. He had a moment of guilt with what he was going to do. But just then Stephanie began to scream out with pleasure as her hot wet sweetness flowed out of her into his mouth. He sucked her gently to taste all he could. She was like heaven.

Stephanie felt her very core ache and ache until suddenly with the magical thrust of Iain's tongue she felt herself soaring high above her body and the release crashed over her in continuous waves of pleasure. She moved against Iain's mouth hoping to find more heat and pleasure.

"God Stephanie ye are so wonderful, so wet for me. I feel I am drowning in your taste and scent." Iain moved away from her off the bed, releasing her hands as he did so. Stephanie stretched and slid over the sheets reveling in the pleasure still throbbing through her body.

Iain looked down at her with intense desire. She was so beautiful and he wanted to bury himself in her hard and fast. His breathing quickened at the thought, as he struggled to maintain his control and rid himself of his garments. He stood in front of her hard and throbbing, enjoying the delay of his final release to watch her more.

Stephanie opened her eyes. Good Lord, she forgot how large he was and standing before her totally naked his size was revealed in full. Sweat glistened on his body as he strained against losing himself to his desire for her. She was so soft and giving beneath him.

Stephanie felt every nerve tingle in anticipation of what, she didn't know for certain, but her body reacted with elemental knowledge. In her pleasure and anticipation she instinctively thrust her hips up to him reveling in how good he felt on top of her. His skin covered with old scars and coarse hair rubbed her own smooth soft skin creating a sensation beyond anything she ever imagined. Her breasts pressed against his chest and his hair teased her nipples to excited peaks again. She was on fire for him.

She felt him pressing at the juncture between her legs insistently and she knew what to do to increase the growing pleasure again. She spread her legs wider to allow Iain entry to her most private self.

Iain began teasing Stephanie's senses with his intimate kisses as he probed her entry. She was being burned alive in the fiery passion that threatened to incinerate them both. Iain wanted to drive into her with all the force of his passion but he held himself back for fear of hurting her too much too soon. As he began ever so slowly to move in the slow rhythm of mating Stephanie suddenly thrust herself up to him and took him deep inside herself.

Iain nearly exploded with need as she took him up to her maiden barrier. He was sweating trying to control his wild lust for her. She moaned beneath him and pushed her hips up again and he felt her hand grip his buttocks trying to drive him further inside of her. He could wait no more he broke through her barrier and entered her hot wet tight sheath with such pleasure he never felt before. No other woman had inspired such passion in him. The pleasure at being buried inside her to his hilt was exquisite. He was overcome by pleasure. He tried to still himself to allow her time to accommodate his size but Stephanie was clutching at his buttocks and bucking wildly beneath him.

"Be still lass let the pain pass."

"No, no Iain please don't stop."

The pain that Stephanie felt when Iain first broke her maidenhead had been so brief compared to the aching pain of desire when he stopped moving inside her. She lifted her legs around his hips and began to move herself against him.

It was too much! Iain roared with pleasure and drove himself into her again and again until neither of them could stand the torture any longer and they found their release together. Iain's shout of ecstasy as he poured himself into her mated with her own scream of pleasure and her body convulsed around him wringing every drop of pleasure from him. Both of them collapsed, spent fully and completely in a passion neither had ever known before. They were so sated and breathless in the aftermath of their climax neither could speak.

Iain eventually realized that he was probably crushing Stephanie so he rolled to his side and pulled her with him. He wanted her close. As he lay looking at the room bathed in flickering firelight he pondered the intensity of his reaction to Stephanie. He had never had a woman respond to him so openly without fear. She affected him like no other woman ever had. Now the realty was creeping in, he had compromised her totally.

She sighed and pressed closer to Iain, everything forgotten. But the blissful memory lapse lasted only moments before she remembered what had happened to the men. Her disgust with herself began a fresh. What was wrong with her? Innocent men were dead and she had just behaved like a wanton trollop with the man who had murdered them. She felt her pain return. How could she behave that way, she was a disgusting disgrace to all. Stephanie rolled away from Iain and began to cry.

Iain knew what she was thinking and feeling. He knew she must be disgusted with him and his behavior when she began to cry.

He used her so badly he couldn't bear to hear her cry he had to leave. He got up, got dressed and spoke coldly with self loathing.

"I will send someone tae help ye bathe and air out the chamber." Stephanie could hear his disgust in his voice. She felt sick. Unable to speak a word she shook her head and kept crying. Iain left slamming the door behind him.

He needed to get drunk, so he went off in search of a bottle.

Stephanie wanted to call Iain back; she wanted to beg him to stay with her. She couldn't help the drift of her thoughts. Where were the boy's bodies? Had they been dumped quickly somewhere to avoid detection? Had they been taken back to her father as a warning? How was she going to explain this to her father? She continued wondering and hating herself more and more. But then she thought about Iain. How could a man touch a woman with such tenderness and passion having just killed men known to her?

Stephanie brushed the tears from her cheeks and shored up her resolve and anger. He would not get away with this! She would make him explain himself and then she would demand retribution. She hastily dressed herself, not even bothering to fix her disheveled hair. She stormed past the bewildered maid, arriving to assist her, and went in search of the rogue laird, her mind burning with anger.

Chapter Fourteen

Iain had thought to rouse someone to drink with him since Fergus was off to Lord Rockforte's keep, but he decided against waking anyone else up just so he wouldn't have to be alone with his thoughts. He sat down in the great hall in front of the wine and goblet he had abandoned earlier when he had followed Stephanie's ill fated quest to rescue her men. How things could change in such a short span of time. In a matter of hours Iain had put his whole plan in jeopardy all because he could not control his desire for the Lady Stephanie. She was supposed to be his 'prisoner' and she was really not much more than a stranger to him. But even now with everything in ashes around him he could not forget how incredible she was. Her fiery spirit was as hot in bed as it was out and Iain didn't think he would ever be able to stop reliving the feelings he had experienced when he was making love to her. She would haunt his dreams and fantasies forever. As he thought about her soft, slick wet body Iain felt himself growing hard again. He wanted her again and again. He had to do something to stop these thoughts from taking him over again.

He grabbed his cup and emptied it in one draught hastily refilling and emptying it again. Now he had to figure out how to salvage his plan. He would be meeting Stephanie's father in a matter of days at the place Iain had arranged if he found out that his daughter had been spoiled, he would demand war. Iain couldn't really blame him; he would do the same if he had a daughter.

At a sound Iain looked up and his breath caught. There was Stephanie coming into the hall, definitely looking for him judging by the fury in her frame. Her anger crackled the air around her. Despite that or maybe because of it she was still stunning, her hair loose around her shoulders. She would probably be horrified to know that if anyone saw her in this state it was obvious she had just been bedded thoroughly. She took his breath completely away. But her anger was tangible as she stood before him like some avenging angel sent from heaven to punish him for his sins. He didn't trust himself to speak lest he tell her how beautiful she was standing before him. Lest he tell her how much he wanted to bed her again.

Stephanie waited for Iain to speak hoping that he could and would explain himself without her having to say a word. But he just sat there staring at her obviously annoyed.

"I gather by your silence that you will tell me nothing about what horrible deeds you have perpetrated this evening."

Iain's brows raised. He couldn't help but feel somewhat offended by her description of their time together. Based on her response to him he didn't imagine that she had thought it such a 'horrible deed' As beautiful as she was she obviously was a good liar verbally and physically. His tone was icy as he replied.

"Horrible deeds? Well you would be the first tae call it thus with me. Personally I found great pleasure in this horrible deed as ye call it…"

"You stupid barbarian! I don't know much about you but I never could believe that you would find such pleasure in such a senseless act. You sir are despicable!"

"Well my lady I am sorry ye feel tha way, particularly since ye seemed tae enjoy the deed as much as I" Iain leaned forward across the table "Or were ye just pretending? Were ye just lying with yer words and yer body when ye responded tae my touch with such wild abandon?"

Stephanie's jaw dropped as the heat flared in her cheeks. How could he be speaking of their intimacy and so easily dismiss the men whose lives he had taken? She spluttered.

"You fiend. How can you be speaking of 'that' at a time like this? Do you disregard human lives so easily?"

"Tae what exactly are ye referring lass? I must say yer words now have absolutely no meaning. If ye were not referring tae our lovemaking, what exactly are ye speaking about?"

"THE MURDERS OF INNOCENT MEN!" Stephanie yelled. "Innocent men… What is wrong with you? You had them killed and then just forgot all about them. Never have I met anyone as cold and heartless as you. So what was I then? A little dalliance after your noble deed? Were you feeling so proud of yourself that you had to show off your power by conquering me too?"

"What murders are you babbling about woman? Have ye lost yer mind?"

"Duncan, Edmund, and Matthew. Who else would I be speaking of? Where did you put their bodies? I want them prepared for return to my home for proper burial. Better yet I demand that you let me take them home immediately to be given a proper burial. This action means nothing short of war and well you know it. Mark my words I shall be at the front of the charge for your head!"

Iain began to laugh. For long moments he continued to laugh. Stephanie was outraged.

"This is no laughing matter you heartless bastard."

Iain wiped the tears from the corners of his eyes. "Nay tis no laughing matter for ye maybe my lady but for me I find I have not had such mirth in sometime."

Stephanie felt sure he was insane. "You honestly find your sport of murdering innocent young men funny?" She couldn't help but be shocked by the thought that someone who showed such tenderness in his lovemaking could be so heartless about ending someone's life. It was completely incomprehensible. She stood before him with such despair and confusion Iain had to speak.

"Stephanie I did not kill those men."

"What? I don't believe you. Where are they then? There is no sign that they were ever here before. It was like they had been erased from existence. They have vanished."

"You are right they are not here. But I find it interesting that your first thought was that I killed them."

Stephanie ignored Iain's comment and focused on what she had heard "Not here? But where are they then?"

"Nay lass I would know how you could think that after what we just shared that I would have them killed in cold blood."

"I thought that before we… Oh never mind." Stephanie's face flushed crimson with embarrassment.

"Mmm… Yet after what we shared, ye still believed the men murdered by me. Why?"

Stephanie was momentarily flustered by the directness of Iain's question. "Why?"

"Yes why? I have done nothing tae show you any side of violence. So yer opinion of me seems rather unjust."

"Because I don't know you that is why. I do not know anything about you. Just because you haven't shown me violence doesn't mean you aren't capable of it."

Iain frowned. "And ye my Lady just because ye profess intelligence doesna mean ye are capable of displaying any. I dinna kill those boys."

"So you have told me, yet you have not told me where you have taken them."

"I have sent them home with Fergus."

"You sent them home? Why? Why didn't I go with them?"

"Because they were required only to take a message to your father that ye are tae be kept here until he agrees tae meet with me, when and where I choose. In fact I was very fortunate they were with ye as it prevented my sending many of my men to potential risk from ambush or any misdeeds delivering my message."

Stephanie couldn't speak because she didn't know if her father would have been honest and fair with his dealings with the 'raiding Scots.' She was suddenly very tired and despondent and she just wanted to sleep.

"I am sleepy. If you will excuse me I shall retire to my confinement and hope for some respite from the double dealings of men." Stephanie didn't wait for Iain to reply; she just turned and walked up the stairs with barely enough energy to lift her feet.

Iain watched her move through the hall. Her usual lilting form burdened by what seemed to be the weight of the world on her shoulders. He wanted to go to her, carry her up the stairs and see if he could inspire in her the passion he found not so long ago but what already felt like a lifetime ago. Iain felt some of the heavy burden that Stephanie carried. He wished he could ease some of what she was feeling but his responsibility to his people came before the passion he felt for one woman.

Iain took a long draught from his goblet and wished that things could be different. He had hoped to convince Lord William to end the raids against him by holding his daughter as ransom. But his growing desire for his lady captive utterly surprised him and he felt like he had completely compromised his plan for peace.

Chapter Fifteen

"Where is she? Where is she? Someone had better speak up now. How long has she been gone?"

Lord William of Rockforte's voice shook the beams in his hall. He wanted to rip his keep down to the ground with his frustration. Someone would pay that was for sure. But his retribution would come later after he had his daughter and his men back.

"My Lord" Matilda spoke seemingly unperturbed by his fury. "We have been looking for her since she left from Anne's house where the babes were delivered. We are all very concerned in light of the events of late but raging is not going to help us find her."

"Damnit woman!" William slumped into a chair. "I know you are right but all this time I was away who knows what my daughter has suffered. I should have been here to protect her. Do you know why she took such unseasoned men with her? I told her not to venture out alone but if she had to go to take an escort. Why such young men?"

"To leave enough seasoned men behind to protect the keep. You know that Lord."

William pressed his hands to his eyes. "Exactly how long has she been missing?"

"Almost two weeks now."

"Two weeks?" William had to steel himself to remain calm. "Who has been out looking for her?"

Matilda looked stricken "We all have My Lord. But we have found nothing. Our only clue to her whereabouts was with young Mary and Anne. But Anne was not aware of anything or anyone else but her daughter and Stephanie's instructions at the time."

"What about Mary?"

"Well My Lord, that has been a problem. We all agree that young Mary must know much more than she is saying, but she will not talk about it at all with anyone. Not even her parents. When the subject is brought up she just smiles and says that Stephanie is with the angels."

"What does that mean? Did she see Stephanie die? What if Mary saw Stephanie murdered by the Scottish raiders we have been plagued with of late? I have to speak to her to see if she can't reveal more."

Lord Rockforte strode purposefully out of the hall to the stables. When he reached the door he brushed past the stable boys and went to the stall where his horse was kept. Everyone watched as he quickly saddled his mount and set off in the direction of Anne's home. He had to find Stephanie. What if she was dead? What was he going to do then? He had tried to speak to the King about his trouble with the neighboring Scots, but the King didn't want to receive him. William's neighbor Eduard had told him that King Edward was far too busy to hear of the trouble he was already aware of across the borders.

Now William had nothing to end this escalating disaster against the Scots. He did not want to go to battle, too many people were at risk.

"I shall burn them to the ground if they are responsible for Stephanie's death. God give me the strength I need to find her killers."

William reined his horse in front of Anne and Tom's cottage, determined to get some answers. He knew young Mary knew what had happened and he had to know who killed his daughter.

"Lord Rockforte, what are you doing here?" Anne stood at the entrance to her home, a new baby balanced in the crook of each arm.

"Lovely young sons you have there Anne." William spoke as he approached.

"Thank you Lord Rockforte. I couldn't have done it without the Lady Stephanie. Have you heard anything? Is she all right?"

"I have nothing new. But I am quite sure based on what Matilda told me, that Mary knows much more than perhaps even she realizes. I need to speak with her myself, please."

"Lord Rockforte, both my husband and I have asked Mary again and again. But she says no more than Stephanie went with the angels and that she is safe."

"How does Mary know Stephanie is safe?"

Anne paused "She says the angels promised she would be safe. Then she goes back to whatever she is doing as if nothing is amiss. I am sorry Sir but she will not say more."

"Anne might you and your husband; allow me to speak to her for a moment? I promise I will not upset her. If she begins to remember something terrible and shows any sign of distress, I give you my word that I will cease my inquiries."

"My Lord we are very afraid for our little girl. I know that Lady Stephanie is missing and were my little Mary gone I would do anything to find her, but if anything happens to my Mary now I don't think I could bear it."

"Oh Anne I know. I don't want to cause you any pain but I am desperate. I need help. Please I beg your assistance." Lord William felt his hope fade if Anne and her husband would not let him speak to Mary; he faced insurmountable odds to track his daughter. 'Please God' William begged silently 'I need to speak to Mary I need her answers.' The wait was almost unbearable. But William had spent enough of his life entertaining the whims of royalty, he knew how to wait. He would wait and he would have to accept the parent's decision. What he would do after that he would not think about.

"My Lord I will ask Tom and if he agrees then I agree as well. He will be arriving for his noon meal any moment now. Would you care for some mead?"

"Yes Anne that would be appreciated and I shall wait for your husband's decision."

Anne turned to go inside and fetch a mug for his mead, as she turned Tom appeared from the fields. He paused momentarily at the sight of his Lord standing with his wife and sons. While he liked and respected his liege lord it was very disconcerting to see such a great man so at ease in such humble surroundings. Tom, for a moment, wished he had better to offer. He took a deep breath and hoped that Lord William was not here to issue any complaints against him. Tom felt he had been producing much for his Lord as he had always done. Now with the two new babies he was trying to help Anne as much as possible with his very limited experience but he did not think his work in the fields had been affected.

"My Lord?" Tom bowed slightly to William.

"Tom. First of all I don't want you to worry I am not here for any other reason than Stephanie, who is still missing. I see you certainly have your hands full with your family. You should be very proud."

"I am Sir. Very." Tom spoke with some caution

"Good then I shall come straight to the point. I need a favor Tom."

"My Lord?"

"Tom I need to speak with Mary alone. I need to find out exactly what she knows about Steffie's disappearance, or possible murder. I must determine what happened. As a father you understand."

Tom was a father but here was his Lord asking him like an equal for his help. Lord Rockforte should never have had to ask twice. Tom felt conflicted between chastising his wife for delaying their Lord, and knowing as a father it was his duty to protect his family from harm. He knew Mary had suffered a deep shock. She believed she had seen angels. Lord Rockforte could have easily ordered them to bring Mary to him to be questioned but he was asking their permission. He looked at Lord William and saw every father's worst nightmare come to life in each crease and wrinkle of worry.

"My Lord of course you may speak to Mary. Forgive me for making you wait so long."

William clasped Tom's shoulder and said "Thank you so much for this opportunity Tom. I believe it best if I speak to Mary alone but if you could wait nearby in case she becomes upset you can come forth and take her right away."

"Thank you My Lord."

William couldn't help but feel a measure of relief. Now he was certain he could find out exactly what had happened to Stephanie.

"I will send Anne out with Mary." Tom said.

William sat down and took a moment to feel the warmth of the sun on his face and say a little prayer for his success. He had none with the King, as Eduard had predicted, he had to have some now. William didn't wait for long for Anne and Mary to come out of the small hut and stand before him.

Anne spoke first. "Mary, you remember Lady Stephanie's father Lord William?"

"Oh, yes, mama. Once Lord William gave me a sweet. He and Lady Stephanie always send me to the kitchen for cake or pie from Cook." Mary looked up at William and said "Good afternoon Sir. How are you today?"

"Well young Mary. I am feeling well enough but I am very sad."

"I bet it is because Lady Stephanie has gone off with the large angels and you miss her."

"Yes, Mary, that is why I am sad. But how did you know that?"

"Everyone is talking about Lady Stephanie disappearing. But I do not know why everyone is so upset. I told them all she went with the angels and they helped my mama have babies by guarding our house."

"Mary, these angels, can you tell me more about them?"

Mary looked surprised. "You believe me? No one else does."

William laughed "Mary, you have never told me an untruth before, why would you tell me one now? Especially when you know how concerned I am about Lady Stephanie."

"Yes, Sir, I know that. But everyone else keeps telling me not to tell such stories and tell them what really happened. But it did really happen, it did!" Mary got a stubborn set to her jaw and her eyes started flashing. William didn't want Tom to stop their conversation yet so he quickly tried to calm Mary.

"Mary, sweet child, it doesn't matter what others say. I am Stephanie's father and I am asking you about the angels. Please tell me what happened."

Mary looked at Lord William, he seemed to believe her. "Lord William they were angels. They said they were and that they were going to look after Stephanie and protect her. My mother and father have told me how dangerous it is to go anywhere alone. I am not allowed to. But I had to go and get Stephanie to come help my mother and the new baby trying to be born. We have two new baby brothers now. I like them a lot but they do get awful messy."

"Mary what else can you tell me about the angels?"

"Well some of the angels were good and some were bad."

"Bad? What do you mean bad?" William felt a chill in his belly. Had someone hurt Stephanie and this child had seen it happen?

"They were fighting. There was so much noise. I was very scared. Lady Stephanie was scared too but she kept trying to tell them to stop fighting. Then he came in…" Mary's eyes grew large and round. William hoped she wasn't going to panic at the memories and retreat into herself before she had finished her tale.

"Mary tell me more, was he a bad man? I mean bad angel? Did he hurt my Stephanie?"

Mary looked shocked at the suggestion. "Oh, no, Sir! He was not bad at all, he was wonderful. When he spoke the ground shook and the whole world stood still. Even the forest creatures were silent. He didn't hurt Lady Stephanie at all. He took her away to keep her safe. He promised to keep her safe."

"Mary did the angel tell you where he was taking Stephanie?" William felt the desperation rising in him. Someone had taken Stephanie and he had no idea how to find her.

"No Sir. But he made me promise not to say anything to anyone. I don't think he would be mad at me for telling you about him though. He is an angel from heaven and you are Lady Stephanie's father. I do not think he would want you to worry. I wonder if all angels talk funny like him. All the angels that were with him did. Do you think all angels talk like that Sir? You know make that funny sound especially when they say the letter r. Rrr" Mary made a trilling noise imitating the way her 'angel' spoke.

William's heart leapt, "Scots" he said. It had to be his northern neighbors. The anger in William was building. The King had to help him now. His daughter a peer of the realm had been taken. This was no longer just a border skirmish. Careful not to startle Mary with his angry realizations he thanked both Mary and her parents for allowing him to ask the questions he needed to ask.

"It was helpful then?" Anne wanted to know, feeling fear and some responsibility for Stephanie's disappearance. "You know where she is?"

"No I don't know exactly where she is but I have enough of an idea to go searching. This time was most valuable. Thank you for your assistance." William shook Tom's hand, anxious to start off.

Mary looked at the grown ups all smiling at her. "I hope the angel won't be angry I told you about him, Sir." Mary looked a little afraid.

"No Mary the angel will thank you, for now I can go and bring Stephanie home safely."

"Then you can bring her to play with me and my baby brothers." Mary said with a smile and they waved Lord William off.

William's countenance was stern and determined. The bloody Scottish barbarians would pay dearly for this. More dearly if he found Stephanie harmed in any way. He rode his horse hard back to the keep barely stopping as he leapt off the animal's back and strode inside. He was shouting orders as he went.

It took William only moments to realize that his men were not watching him closely as he entered. He stopped and looked. There before him were the three young men Stephanie had taken with her from the keep. With them was a large man with orange hair and bushy whiskers. William was so shocked, at first he couldn't speak. He knew who this man was…one of Mary's 'angels'.

"You bloody mongrel! You have the nerve to walk into my keep after what you have done. I can give my men the order to cut you down where you stand and send your head back to your clan." William spat the words at the Scottish man before him and stood toe to toe with him. Bloody Scott didn't even step back or look the least bit concerned about his present situation.

"Aye tis a fine welcome ye give yer guests there Lord William of Rockforte."

"Guest?" William spoke the word with such disgust. "You are no guest of mine. You had best be gone quickly before I give the command for my men to take you."

"Ye'll do nae such thing, Lord William, not if ye want tae see yer daughter alive again." The Scot had not raised his voice but the quiet tone was full of menace. "Now let us be civilized men sae that I may have my discussion with ye. But first it has been a long hard journey back and we are all thirsty." He gestured at the three men at arms beside him.

William noticed the men were bound at the wrists but did not look any the worse for wear for their absence. They looked very frightened but not at the burly Scot, rather at himself. William took a deep breath to regain control. He wanted nothing more than to rip the Scot from limb to limb but that would do nothing for Stephanie. He had to play the Scot's game until he found his daughter.

"Usually when I entertain 'guests' in my home I am familiar with their names. Yours sir is still a mystery to me."

With a large smile that touched only his mouth the Scot spoke. "I am Fergus MacDonald, brother tae Laird Iain MacDonald, leader of the clan MacDonald. He bids ye greetings." Fergus swept a low mocking bow to William. He felt some measure of respect for this man. Fergus knew how angry Stephanie's father was. He could also see how much self discipline he was invoking to keep from cutting Fergus down himself.

William spoke in low measured tones. "Do not mock me Fergus. You have the luxury of knowledge that I currently do not. I tolerate your presence and your life because of my daughter, nothing else."

"Tis true Lord William. I do possess knowledge ye do not. And it is on this matter that I come tae ye. I bring a message from my brother, the kind and generous leader of the MacDonald clan."

William's face mottled with barely contained anger "Kind? Generous?" He spluttered. "Your bastard brother has taken my daughter with no provocation!"

Fergus roared. "Silence! Dinna speak of Iain in such a manner."

William steeled himself. He had to gain control of his emotions. Stephanie's life was in danger. For the moment he had to go along with this Scottish brute. But when he had his Stephanie back there would be hell to pay. No matter what the cost the MacDonald clan would be wiped out. Men, women, and children, no one would be safe. He faced his enemy with cold disdain.

"Since we are not here to debate your brother's parentage, Let us set aside this baiting. What the hell do you want Scot?"

Fergus raised his brows. "It is simple Lord William. To show Laird Iain's goodwill, I have returned yer men tae ye. Although ye might want tae increase their training before sending them out alone again. They are verra unseasoned." Fergus couldn't resist the barb but continued quickly before William could object. "Laird Iain wants me tae take ye tae a meeting place where ye will learn the terms of the peace agreement between you and our people."

"What about my daughter? Will Stephanie be there? I want her home safe with me before any deals are made."

"No! Stephanie remains with Laird Iain to ensure the terms of the agreement are kept."

Lord William lost all color in his face. "No" he whispered. "NO! I won't allow it. My people have done nothing to you and yours. It is your plaids found on our land. You will not get away with this."

Fergus started at the mention of plaids found on the English Lord's lands. Iain would have to know about this as to the rest. "If ye have anything tae say, then I suggest ye come with me and speak tae Laird Iain. He is a fair man and he will listen tae what ye have tae say. But be warned if Iain doesna like what ye have tae say nothing ye say will change his mind."

"So he will let Stephanie return with me?"

Fergus shrugged. "If ye want tae find out we had best move. We dinna want tae keep Laird Iain waiting."

"Let us go then." William strode out of his hall with purpose. He would get Stephanie back home no matter what the cost.

The two men left the keep. When they got to the yard William's horse was saddled and being held by another very large Scot. His stable lads stood to the side with fear and confusion. These large men had entered the stable and demanded, weapons drawn, that their Lord's horse be readied immediately. For fear of their lives they quickly obeyed. Now they feared what Lord William would do.

Although distracted by thoughts of his daughter and her safety, Lord William did notice how afraid his stable boys were. He took just a minute to allay their fears.

"Lads my thanks for your speed in readying my horse. You have done your jobs well." They all looked so relieved and William wished he could feel better about his own situation.

The group of men rode out hard in a cloud of dust. What waited at the end of the journey had all hoping for Lord William and Lady Stephanie's speedy return. In the meantime all spoke silent prayers for everyone's safe return and for life to return to normal.

Chapter Sixteen

Stephanie sat looking out the window at the sun descending on the water. The land was so achingly beautiful here. If she were seeing this beauty under any other circumstances she might have found more peace and contentment in the surroundings.

At the moment she felt anything but peace and certainly she was not content. It had been a week since she and Iain had been intimate. She blushed to think of it and blushed at how often she did think of it. Iain had made himself scarce since they had parted. Stephanie had heard from Judith that Iain would be riding out to meet the man responsible for the raids. Judith did not know that man was Stephanie's father. She had approached Iain about going, his refusal was blunt. She remembered their brief but intense conversation days ago.

"You go to meet my father. I should go so that he can see I am alive and well."

Iain's icy eyes seared her on the spot. "Ye willna be going anywhere lass. Yer father will take my word ye are alive. Ye stay here and that is final."

Stephanie was shocked. "Do you expect my father to accept that? Would you accept that if the situation were reversed?"

Quietly Iain spoke. "Lady Stephanie ye remain here at the keep either willingly or unwillingly. But until I get yer father's cooperation and commitment tae peace, ye remain here. What is yer choice?"

"You would lock me up to keep me from reassuring my father? Why?"

"Do ye stay enjoying the freedom ye currently have or do I change yer station and lock ye up?" Iain towered over Stephanie with threatening menace.

Stephanie felt so defeated she knew Iain would lock her up if she continued to argue with him. Her shoulders braced with a confidence she didn't really feel.

"There is no need to lock me up. But don't insult me by pretending I have any freedom here. I am a prisoner but there is no need to upset everyone here by showing them my station. Remember you are trying to create the illusion of a courtship here. Have a safe journey."

Iain admired her bite but he couldn't let her think she got the better of him. "Thank you for yer concern for my safety my lady. As we are courting I trust you will have some fond memories to keep you warm at night during my absence." He bowed to her as she flushed scarlet.

It took all of Stephanie's will to turn and walk away. She wanted to scream and rake her nails down his smug face. She never believed herself capable of being so angry at another person, but she was that angry with Iain. She could barely stem the tears that threatened to engulf her. He had seemed so gentle and caring attentive to everything she was feeling. Now he was as cold and distant as when they had first met. The pain felt unbearable.

That conversation was days ago and still thoughts of him consumed her like no other man ever had. She knew when he was leaving even though she could not see him go. She felt herself pulled by an invisible string, a connection to a man she didn't really even know.

She had thought that with the tenderness that had passed between them scant days ago, he would understand her need to go to her father and show him that she was fine. But she knew that once there she would not have returned with Iain no matter how much she would have wanted to. Stephanie's green eyes widened at the realization that she wanted to stay here. She wanted to know more about Laird Iain MacDonald, this giant of a man who could show so much tenderness. Had she gone she would have returned with her father to their home but she didn't want to leave here. What could that mean? Her mind was turning over and over in such confusion she didn't hear the knocking at the door.

"Steffie? Are you in here?" Judith's lovely face peeked around the corner of the door. Startled Stephanie turned.

"I am sorry I knocked but you didn't answer and I saw you come up so I knew you were in here." Judith apologized.

"Please, come in Judith. I didn't hear you knocking I am sorry. Come sit with me I was just admiring the view."

Judith sat down next to Stephanie and for a moment both women looked out over the loch each lost in their own thoughts. Stephanie saw Judith's restlessness in her eyes

"What is it Judith? You seem…I don't know… troubled about something."

"I miss Fergus. He was here so briefly and now he is gone again. I just want him home with me for a time. Now with the raids going on I worry about him." Judith laughed weakly "He would not be pleased to hear me worrying about his safety. But I do."

"Judith any man should consider himself blessed to have someone as lovely and kind as you worried for his safety."

"Thank you. But men, especially Fergus and his brother, don't take kindly to women worrying for them. It makes them believe they are seen as weak or incapable if women are fretting over them. I always worry when he goes away especially now, but until you came I had no one to tell my worry to. I am so glad you are here."

Stephanie swallowed. "So am I." She wasn't all that glad to be here after her parting with Iain.

"So have you and Iain had time to discuss your marriage plans yet?" Judith nudged Stephanie's shoulder.

"Marriage?" Stephanie spluttered. "No, actually not at all. I am only here to see if Iain and I could be compatible. Nothing has been finalized yet."

"Don't be ridiculous. I have seen the way you two look at each other. The tension between you is palpable. You cannot deny it."

"Well" Stephanie hesitated wondering how much she should open up to Judith. Yet what could it hurt to express herself. She needed to talk to someone. She just wouldn't tell Judith everything. "I cannot deny that I am drawn to Iain and that confuses me."

"If he already occupies your thoughts you have developed feelings for him."

"That doesn't mean marriage. I have rarely been able to speak to Iain. He is so preoccupied with everything that is going on."

"Yes, but that won't take long now that Iain has gone to meet Fergus. They will strongly convince this Lord William to accept the peace agreement and then we can all go back to normal again."

Stephanie felt a little tingle of anxious suspicion at Judith's words.

"What do you mean 'strongly convince Lord William'?" She couldn't entirely suppress the fear that was beginning to well up inside her. Would they hurt her father if he didn't agree with the terms, whatever they were? What if they tortured him to compliance? She would not know. She might never know until it was too late to do anything to help her father. Until she was away from Iain, she would never know if her father was alive or dead.

"I don't know exactly but Fergus said that this time Iain has a plan to ensure successful peace and there is no way Lord William can resist the terms. It is all very vague but Fergus is so convinced that Iain's plan will work that I am sure he is right."

"He is not going to harm Lord William is he? I mean there would be retaliation wouldn't there. That would certainly ruin the peace agreement."

"Stephanie how could you think that?" Judith looked aghast at Stephanie. Her shock so clear on her face that

Stephanie almost felt a twinge of guilt for suspecting Iain. Though only for a moment. Her priority was her father not Iain or his family and whether or not she had offended them by thinking ill of them.

"Judith I am not insulting you or your family. I am only looking at the situation objectively. This is a very serious feud and if anything gets out of hand at this meeting, then no matter what kind of men Iain, Fergus or Lord William are, anything could happen."

"No! Not Iain and not Fergus. I cannot speak for this Lord William, but I know my husband and I know his brother. They are honorable men."

"Even honorable men are driven to dishonorable deeds when so much is at stake."

"Stephanie." Judith fixed her with a troubled gaze. "You are considering marriage to Iain and yet you seem more concerned about what he and Fergus might do to this unknown English Lord, than you seem concerned by what might be done to them. This man's people are carrying out some dangerous tasks for their Lord which seems to demonstrate that he is more likely to be violent than Iain and Fergus. I know them very well; they would harm no one unless their lives were under threat."

Stephanie knew she had gone too far with Judith "Forgive me. It is just as you say. I am here to see if Iain and I suit but I find myself alone here and don't know what thoughts get into my mind. Maybe I am feeling a little unsure that I should be here at all since Iain is not here. Now he is off at what could be a potentially dangerous negotiation and anything could happen. I just don't know what or how to feel." A small sob escaped before she could stop herself because she realized she really didn't know how she should feel. Iain was meeting with her beloved father who would be sick with worry about her and she couldn't be there. But Iain had treated her so tenderly when he had made love to her. He had awoken a part of her she never knew existed. She wanted to see him again; she wanted him to touch her again. It became too much for Stephanie to think about and she felt her eyes fill with tears.

Judith looked concerned and reached over to hold Stephanie's hand.

"Don't cry. This really is bad timing. Would you like to go for a walk by the loch with me? It might help clear your mind a bit?"

"Thank you Judith but I think I would rather stay here alone for a while if you don't mind."

Judith looked like she wanted to argue with Stephanie but she patted her hand "Of course. Take the time you need I will see you later."

Stephanie hardly heard Judith go. She turned and fixed her gaze off to the distance. Silently willing Iain not to hurt her father or be hurt himself in this meeting. The waiting was unbearable.

Chapter Seventeen

"Well, Lord Rockforte, you wisely chose to come." Iain towered above him with his arms crossed and legs braced. His demeanor was anything but cordial. William would not have been surprised if he had his sword at the ready, but it appeared Iain MacDonald was unarmed.

"MacDonald." William greeted him tersely. "I did not choose to come. You are holding my daughter hostage for some reason and I want to know where she is so that I may take her home with me."

"Yer daughter is at my keep and there she will stay until I am satisfied ye are no longer going to plague my people or torch my land. She currently resides there as a guest to all but myself and my brother. She has agreed to stay there as a guest for your protection and her own."

"You black hearted bastard." William spat out at Iain. "How dare you tell me what I am to do when you crossed onto my lands and kidnapped my daughter? I don't even know if she is alive or if her body has been left for scavengers. As to my plaguing your people, I have no notion of what you speak. I have never had any dealings with your people so I do not know how it is I am plaguing them."

"Liar!" Iain roared "Ye have sent yer men on numerous occasions to torch their homes, their crops and to kill their livestock. Always someone catches a glimpse of your colors or your emblem, but the perpetrators always move too quickly tae be caught. I am not here tae discuss anything with ye. I am here tae tell ye that I am keeping yer daughter with me until I am sure the raids have ceased."

"I ask the same question MacDonald. How do I know my daughter is alive and safe?"

Iain's smile was chilling "You don't. Ye will just have tae take my word for it. But, if ye continue yer raiding ye will have no doubt to her well being because ye shall find her corpse, or what is left of it, at the gate to yer keep."

William blanched. "You cannot. You wouldn't. Don't hurt her!"

"Mind my warning Lord Rockforte. I will contact you when I am satisfied you have put an end to all of this." Iain mounted his horse and turned to Fergus. "Come brother let us go home. I am sure that Rockforte will do the right thing tae keep his daughter safe. Good day."

William watched the two Scots ride away from the clearing. Anger gnawing at his heart, he wanted to go after the MacDonald brothers and get his Stephanie back. But he was one against a whole clan on their ground. He was not so foolish in his advanced years. So he would have to ride home and lose valuable time to come up with a way to rescue Stephanie.

It wasn't until William's anger had begun to cool a bit and he was well on his way home that he remembered Iain MacDonald's accusations against him for the raids on his lands and people. Damnation his daughter was being held captive for something he knew nothing about. How could the Scot be so upset with him when he was doing the very same thing he was accusing William of doing? His thoughts were in such turmoil he needed to get home and think about all that had transpired during that brief meeting.

Chapter Eighteen

It had been a long day for Stephanie. Her emotions were raw and confused. She was tempted to miss the meal but she knew Judith would come looking for her company if she didn't go down. She really had no appetite, nor any desire for company, when she reached the hall she took a deep breath and braced herself for a long tiring meal.

Judith looked up as she entered and gave Stephanie a big smile.

"Oh Stephanie I am so glad to see you. Without Fergus and Iain here I feel like such a conspicuous fool on display up here alone. I almost feel like everyone would like me to get up and dance on the table or sing a song so they don't have to watch me all alone up here."

Stephanie couldn't help but laugh at the picture of Judith dancing on the table.

"Then I am glad I came down. I wouldn't want you to fall off the table and injure yourself doing a particularly lively reel." The two ladies laughed quietly to themselves enjoying their private joke.

That was how Iain and Fergus saw them when they entered the hall. The women looked like two young lasses giggling over some very private joke. So occupied with each other they didn't notice that the hall had silenced upon the men's entry.

"So, ladies" Iain's voice pierced through their mirth "Is this how you two carry on while we are away?"

"Seems tae me we might be needin' a governess for these young lasses."

Judith spun in her seat so fast she nearly toppled over. Her entire countenance changed as she saw her husband. Suddenly she looked like she was glowing from within. Her smile lit up her whole face.

"Fergus!" she breathed. In a flash, with very unladylike haste, she flew from the head table. Stephanie watched, as did the others present in the hall, the tender scene unfolding. She watched as devoted husband and wife greeted each other with undisguised love and passion. Stephanie could not claim to be human if she did not view this scene without some longing of her own. At that moment she glanced over at Iain who was watching her with intensity. A faint blush stole over her cheeks under his penetrating gaze. He walked across the hall to stand before her at the table. Iain lifted her hand to his lips and caressed her skin with a kiss. Softly under his breath so that only she could hear when he spoke.

"Ah, Stephanie, would that ye would greet me with such a passion." His steely eyes locked with her molten green "I would share that passion with ye again lady but this time ye would be in possession of all yer senses. I want ye tae feel everything I do to and with you."

Stephanie's hand felt scorched by his kiss and his breath as he spoke. Her body was all liquid heat with his teasing words. She felt the deep aching longing in her belly as he spoke of such intimacies. She wanted to shout to him that she remembered everything he had done to her that night and remembered it everyday. She wanted him to know that she wanted all that and more again. Instead she spoke stiffly.

"Laird MacDonald, welcome home. You have been missed." Under her breath she added "Not by me mind you. You overstep yourself and your cruelty towards me."

Iain straightened. "Cruelty? This should be enlightening. Steward, some wine for me please." He pulled out his chair and sat down next to Stephanie. His large frame, while just barely touching her, made her feel completely overwhelmed. His presence was unmistakable and she was aware of everything about him. She watched as he took the goblet in his large hand. The filigree cup looked ridiculously fragile in his grip. Which was exactly how she was feeling in his presence.

"So I am cruel am I? How is it ye come tae this conclusion? While I must admit we know each other quite well intimately, I am no sure how ye think ye know me so well otherwise."

Stephanie glared at Iain's very self satisfied face. "You are cruel because you sit there making fun and teasing me, when you know full well why I am here and where you have been." Stephanie stopped waiting for Iain to respond.

He didn't speak so she continued. "You sit there saying nothing to me when you know very well that I am desperate to know what went on with my father. That is your cruelty, sitting there ignoring my only concern. I don't know how the situation fared with my father.

He knows nothing about me. You most likely told him nothing of me that would allay his concerns for my well being, did you?"

"Nae lass of course I dinna do tha. If he thinks ye are a pampered guest in my home what motivation does he have to end this torment against my people?"

"I am a guest here only in the eyes of your people and that is not my point. He is my father. He must be so worried."

"That is what I am relying on. His worry and concern for you."

"Fine then." Stephanie could not make him understand. She did want to admit to herself that as a strategy Iain was right. But she wanted to make a point; her nerves were raw made worse by not knowing any details of the meeting. "So you would keep him wondering of my condition. Well then what about my concerns and my fears?" Stephanie knew her voice was rising but she was teetering on the edge of the breaking point. Was her father alive or dead? If he was dead how could she not make it her life's work to seek retribution?

"I think that you and I should continue our conversation elsewhere Lady Stephanie. You appear to be experiencing some distress." Iain stood up and carefully but firmly put his hand under Stephanie's elbow and began to lead her from the hall.

"Iain where do you think you are going?" Judith tore her loving gaze from her husband.

"Stephanie is feeling poorly so I am going to escort her above. Just in case she suddenly feels unsteady I want to be sure she does not fall."

Judith started to rise. "Well I think I should go with her too."

"No" Iain said "Sit. Stay with your husband. All will be well. I will get someone to attend to Stephanie shortly."

Stephanie clenched her fists at her sides, wanting to slap Iain's face with all the strength she could muster. He was pretending to be so solicitous when his callousness knew no bounds.

"Well if you are sure Iain." Judith took her husband's hand as they both rose as well. "Steffie, you are quite flushed. You should get some rest."

Iain turned and steered Stephanie up the stairs of the south tower. When he reached the door of his parent's old chambers he paused but only for a brief moment before he propelled Stephanie in the room ahead of him. As he closed the door, Stephanie spun on her heel and let loose her fury.

"How dare you treat me in such a manner? I won't stand for this anymore. I am not an invalid and I refuse to be set aside every time your people's peace is threatened by me. What about my peace? You have returned from a meeting with my father and you have done nothing but try to shame me with your intimate words. I want to know what you have done to my father. I will not be put off any longer. Tell me did you harm him? Does he still live?"

Iain felt an anger grow within him to match her own. How dare she stand there speaking to him with such insolence when he had been nothing but kind to her despite her situation?

"Lady Stephanie, ye surprise me with yer hysterics."

"Hysterics?" she spluttered "Why you oaf! Answer me now! Stop avoiding my question."

Iain saw how his subtle insult had caught her off guard. He knew she was concerned for her father but damn him he wished she was concerned for him as well. It also galled him that she suspected him of injuring her father, possibly even killing him. How could her father's death possibly do anything but bring him more than full war with England?

He watched her tall statuesque form shake with anger and frustration. He felt himself become aroused by the sight of her as she stood unflinchingly before him. Her green eyes flashed dangerously and her ivory skin was flushed pink with anger. He wanted to kiss every inch of her again. Taste her unique flavor. She was so beautiful, even as angry as she was. God help him he wanted to lose himself in her softness again. He had hoped by keeping his distance from her after their first night of passion, would cool his ardor but as she stood there in front of him all he could think about was kissing her full lips. He gave in and spoke

"I will tell you everything but first I want a favor."

"A favor? What favor could I possibly do for you?" Stephanie should have seen Iain's intention but she was too angry to know until he stood directly before her. Then she knew. "Oh no!" she said and tried to push him away.

"Oh yes!" Iain replied with the barest hint of a smirk as he lowered his head.

She was lost. The minute his hot lips found hers she could no longer think clearly. She could only feel clearly. Feel the heat and power he held back as he gently caressed her lips with his. Ever so slightly he teased her mouth open with his tongue. Sensuously he traced her lips with his tongue until she opened to him. With a gasp of pure pleasure she wrapped her arms around his neck and kissed him back with all the desire she felt in her.

Iain was undone. Her reaction to his kiss was all the invitation he needed and wanted. He pulled her close to him and held her tightly. Her body molded to his perfectly. He could feel his arousal pressing right at the juncture of her soft thighs. Every sensation he had when they had made love the first time, came back to him with painful intensity. He groaned and deepened the kiss. He had to taste more of her.

Stephanie felt her nipples and belly tighten and quiver at the intimate onslaught Iain gave her with his kisses. Then he ever so slightly began rubbing his arousal between her legs. She shifted slightly to better fit him between her legs and almost screamed with pleasure as his arousal rubbed against the bud of her womanhood. She was throbbing and aching everywhere. God help her she wanted this man so much! She remembered how he filled her and she wanted to feel that full again. Instinctively she ground her hips into Iain's trying to get him closer.

Iain trailed kisses down her neck and up behind her ear. He flicked the tip of his tongue gently around her ear and spoke softly with his hot breath.

"Woman, ye are going tae be the death of me. If ye want me tae stop, ye must stop me now because if ye don't I am carrying ye tae that bed and tasting every inch of you."

"Oh Iain you can't stop! Don't stop! I will die from this ache. I need you so much. I have been so empty without you."

"Ahh" Iain roared and claimed her mouth with the full heat of his passion. He lifted her up against him, never breaking the kiss, his hands were beneath her buttocks and had she not been dangling off the ground, she would have spread her legs right there to fit his hand between her legs. She held his neck tighter and kissed his jaw. She wanted to taste him as he had her. She ran her tongue along his jaw relishing the contrast between her wet tongue and the dry rasp of his cheeks and jaw line.

Iain carefully laid Stephanie down on the bed and rested on his elbows above her. Their passion drugged eyes met and they saw the longing in each others gaze. Iain gently toyed with a loose strand of Stephanie's silky gold tresses. He gently rubbed himself against her and watched her eyes begin to glaze with desire. His reasonable self forced him to make one last halfhearted attempt to reach her before they went any further.

"Lass" He said softly "Dear God, lass, ye are sae beautiful I want tae be with ye fully again. But if ye dinna want tae ye mun stop me now because I am about tae lose myself in ye again."

Stephanie could barely think, let alone speak. She moaned and in response raised herself up until her breasts were touching Iain's broad chest, then licking her lips ever so slightly with the tip of her tongue she rubbed herself back and forth across Iain's chest.

Iain near spilled his seed on her right there. He could feel her nipples taut against the material of her mantle.

Her movements were so sensuous he could barely contain himself. He had to touch her skin.

"Sae be it. If ye agree tae this there is no turning back, lass." Stephanie's only response was to press herself to Iain more fully. "Now let me enjoy what ye are offering with much generosity." Iain took one hand and pulled the material over her shoulder until one creamy breast was exposed. He looked at her dewy skin, the proud nipple thrusting forth begging to be touched. And touch it he did. Iain bent his head and licked the rosy bud.

Stephanie bucked underneath him. She was on fire! Iain's tongue was hot on her breast as he began licking and blowing her nipple and skin. She wanted to scream with the intense pleasure. She bit her lip to keep from crying out. Without stopping, Iain slipped her other shoulder out of her dress until both breasts were bared before him. He licked and kissed first one then the other while his hands kneaded the breast his lips weren't devouring. Stephanie lifted her hips and rubbed herself against his heat and strength. As she rubbed herself Iain pulled the material covering her down over her hips in one firm tug. They heard the material tear but neither one cared. Iain looked down at Stephanie laid out before him like a feast for his senses. As his eyes traveled over her soft body he knew he intended to feast on her until he was full.

Stephanie watched Iain devour her with his hot gaze. She felt a little embarrassed to be naked before him. Then he leaned over and began kissing her again, her embarrassment was lost under his sensuous touch. His tongue thrusting deeply into her mouth, she willingly opened to him. His hand trailed down her body skimming over her breast and hips. Then he moved his hand between her thighs and cupped her apex. He swallowed her scream of pleasure deep in his kiss.

"God!" he moaned against her lips "God! Ye are such a beauty, ye are already drenched for me" He eased one finger through her wet heat and into her hot opening. "Oh yes! Wet and hot for me, ye are such a miracle lass."

He pushed his finger deeper into her feeling more of her release pulsing against him. He could take no more. He had to drink her passion for him. He ran his tongue down over her chin, between her breasts and dipped it into her navel tasting only for a moment there, the sweetness she offered him. But he moved with skilled deliberation down to the most sacred of places he sought. He raised her knees to better access her center of moisture. He gently pressed his finger on her lips to silence her protests. Then he deeply thrust his tongue into her tight passage. More, was all he could think of.

Stephanie cried out when he thrust his tongue into her. She bit down on his finger, but quickly began kissing and sucking it to show him her pleasure. His tongue was pushing deeper into her and felt so good. She lifted herself up closer to his touch. She wanted him as deep inside her as he could go. Then she grabbed his soft black hair and pressed him closer to her sex. She had to have him.

Iain lifted his head, his mouth glistening wet with her spent passion. He smiled and kissed her. She was entranced by the taste of him mixed with her own flavor. The kiss was intoxicating.

"Wait" Iain said breathlessly as she began to deepen the kiss. "Wait. Let me undress."

"No" she said "Please let me do that for you." She rolled over on top of him and straddled his thighs. Iain could feel her wet heat soaking him. His English beauty was as wild for him and he was for her. As she began undressing him he had to keep himself very still or he was going to lose all control. Then she began to mirror what he had done to her. Her small pink tongue flicked over his nipples.

Stephanie was delighted by the taste and smell of Iain. His skin was so salty and the crispness of the hair on his chest tantalized her wandering tongue as she trailed kisses over him. She felt wicked and emboldened by the freedom he was allowing her with his body. She intended to taste and touch him as intimately as he had with her. Every kiss she gave him increased the throbbing between her own legs and she knew she wanted much more. Her exploration of Iain was tormenting her as much as him. When she reached his navel and began to swirl her tongue inside he growled

"Oh God lass! I can stand it nae more. I need ye. I need to bury myself inside ye." He flipped her over and positioned her beneath him. She looked down at their bodies nearly touching. She saw his pulsing shaft with the sheen of moisture on its tip. She had to have him.

"Yes Iain, yes oh yes! Please!"

Iain thrust himself inside her as deeply as he could and she took all of him in. She was all heat and tight. Iain could feel her beginning to climax. He pressed himself closer to her bud of pleasure and ground his hips against her. She began whimpering and panting.

Stephanie could barely breathe and every nerve tingled. She felt herself drawing closer and closer to something she couldn't name. She moved with Iain's rhythm as he began to move in and out of her. As her pleasure mounted so did her moans of pleasure. Then just when she thought she could stand it no more she screamed with her heavy pulsating climax. Her body opened to take Iain even deeper within, at that moment she felt like he had reached her soul.

When the rippling of her passage in the throes of her climax began to tug and squeeze Iain's rock hard member, he felt like she was tugging on his soul. Hi didn't care he only wanted to be deeper and deeper inside her and she kept taking him further in. Then with her release he shouted to the sky as he spent himself fully inside her slick body. He collapsed on his back and rolled Stephanie next to his side. His little beauty was still moaning in the aftermath of their lovemaking and stretching sensuously next to him.

Iain watched as she fell asleep almost immediately. He wanted her closer; he wanted to always keep her close. She was so incredibly beautiful, intelligent and wildly passionate. He wanted her to stay here in his keep always. Iain sighed. It was impossible for her to stay after he had concluded his business with her father. But now he had bedded her twice that changed everything. He could not turn her out. What if she were carrying his child? Maybe he could convince her to stay as his mistress. She would have everything. But she was too proud for that.

He would marry her right away except that she was English and the daughter of the man who had tormented his people for so long. He couldn't ask his people to accept her, but he didn't want to let her go.

He had many things to think about and he knew Stephanie would be after him again to find out about his meeting with her father, but he didn't want to humiliate her by being seen coming out of her room. People would talk. With much reluctance he eased his arm from beneath her and rose from the bed.

Stephanie muttered and rolled over onto her back. The blankets fell beneath her breasts. Iain felt himself swell in response to the sight. She had one arm lifted above her head and made such as tantalizing vision he wanted to lie down and take her all over again. Instead he leaned over and rested his lips between the valley of her breasts, inhaling the sweet smell. He groaned with mounting desire. When she stirred slightly he rose and gently covered her and quietly took his leave.

Chapter Nineteen

Stephanie woke the next morning feeling very satisfied, languorously stretching. She felt relaxed yet strangely energized. Iain's lovemaking had set her body ablaze once again. She felt wickedly wanton at the thought of things she said and did. She began to feel the desire building at her core. What must he think of her? Her cheeks flushed at the thoughts. She rolled over carefully so as not to disturb him. He wasn't there! Nor was there any indication that he had stayed with her.

Damn him! He had used her body thoroughly then left her as soon as he was done with her. He had obviously meant to distract her from finding our anything about her father. She was going to throttle him.

She quickly hurried through her morning ablutions and dressed. When she picked the clothes up that Iain had discarded off the side of the bed, she remembered that they had been torn during their passionate interlude. She became further upset with her carelessness. She never treated anything with such casual disregard before. Iain was addling her brain and she needed to get herself together quickly. She strode purposefully down the stairs and caught a servant passing by.

"Where is Laird Iain?"

The servant looked at her with slight distaste and suspicion at the sound of her English accent.

"He is usually working with his horse at this hour." After this delivery the servant abruptly turned and walked away.

How rude, Stephanie thought, but she did know that while she had no place here she couldn't expect the servants to treat her as anything else but the hated English.

She walked out of the hall into the sunlight of the day. It was slightly cool and she wished she had brought a cover of some sort as the breeze bit through her clothes. Her clothes, that was another matter she had to take up with Iain. She had nothing of her own to wear and she did not want to be wearing the clothes of his recently departed mother any longer.

She walked through the yard to the stables and pushed open the great door. It was warm in the barn with all the horses and other livestock still inside. She asked a stable boy for Iain and with barely an acknowledgement he pointed to the end of the barn. Stephanie rounded the corner of the last stall. Thank goodness Iain's back was to her because she completely lost her ability to speak. All she could think was that he was magnificent.

In the heat of the stables Iain had slipped off his shirt and was lifting heavy pitchforks full of used hay and straw. There was a slight sheen of sweat on his muscular body and his muscles rippled and flexed under the strain of the labour.

"Sae, lass, are ye going tae stand there all day or did ye wish tae speak tae me?" Iain knew the minute Stephanie had arrived. After the thrilling connection their bodies had made, not once but twice, he could smell her fragrance anywhere. His ear was tuned to her approach and his body was tuned to respond to her approach with a great enthusiasm he thought wryly. He shoveled heavier loads to distract himself and get his body back under control.

Stephanie had no idea how long she had been standing there admiring his form. She had been imagining his reaction if she had gone behind him and began tasting the sweat on him. Embarrassed to be caught woolgathering in such an intimate way Stephanie reacted.

"You odious man. You might have told me you knew I was here instead of making me wait until you were finished."

Iain stopped his lifting and turned to face her casually leaning on the end of the pitchfork. Stephanie wished he would turn right back around again. He was beautiful and her body began to ache for him again as the memories of their love making assailed her. She forced herself to swallow and moisten her lips.

"Well I have noticed ye. Now what do ye want?" Iain's eyes darkened as he followed the line of her tongue tracing her lips. He found his thoughts again turning to tasting her luscious mouth once more.

"Tell me what happened with my father."

"Yer father saw the wisdom of ending his tirade against me and he agreed to end the attacks."

"What? He admitted to attacking your lands and your people?" Stephanie shook her head. The sunlight gleaming off her golden hair momentarily mesmerized Iain.

"No! I don't believe you. He never would have admitted doing something that he didn't do." her eyes narrowed. "You threatened him didn't you? You told him you would harm me if he didn't stop. You forced him to admit to deeds he didn't do."

"Of course I threatened him Stephanie. Your father was not going to end this without me forcing him to. That is why you are here to force him to stop."

"Damn you! You can't manipulate people like that. What happens when the attacks don't stop?"

"Ye speak as if ye dinna believe yer father will stop."

"No. I speak as if I don't believe the attacks will stop. Because Iain I don't think they will. My father didn't attack you or your people. But I have come to also realize since I have been here that I don't think you or your people attacked my father's lands either. Someone else is involved here."

"Come now, lass, dinna let yer mind get sae complicated. Ye canna accept that yer father is a greedy mon. Until the death of my parents yer father must have been kept away but now my father is gone, yer father seeks tae destroy us."

"That is ridiculous. My father is not so greedy. You don't even know him."

"Be careful Stephanie, because I dinna think ye ken him tha well either. Greed can turn a mon intae something verra ugly. Something that even his own mother wouldn't recognize."

Stephanie wanted to rip her hair out and scream. This man was so stubborn. He did not want to consider any other possibilities but his own misguided theories and erroneous unfounded conclusions. She had to try to get him to think. She needed to convince him.

"What is wrong with your clothes?" Iain suddenly asked looking at her with some perplexity.

Stephanie blushed profusely. "Ahem…well after last night the clothes I have been wearing were ripped and I had to put something on." Stephanie knew she was poorly dressed. His mother's clothing other than the lovely blue didn't fit her particularly well, so she had put on what ever fit. "I am so glad that you mentioned that. I want clothes of my own. It is no longer believable that my trunks are delayed."

"Go get Judith to help you. Pick what you need from my stores. Ye are tae tell her tae pick whatever ye need tae make a complete wardrobe. Then she can get other ladies tae help sew for ye."

"I can sew for myself" Stephanie huffed indignantly.

"I ken that you can sew flesh, but I dinna think tha ye performed such maidenly tasks as sewing clothes." Iain watched with some amusement as Stephanie fluffed herself up like a hen about to attack.

"I can certainly 'perform' maidenly tasks as you call it. I just choose not to because there are so many more interesting things to do than sit with a bunch of women spreading mean little stories about one another for no other reason than to entertain themselves."

"Och, careful now lass, yer starting tae show yer claws. I agree that there are many more interesting things tae do than idle chatter. Would ye like tae know what some of those other things are?"

"NO!" Stephanie began backing away realizing that it was Iain's intention to kiss her again.

"Och, come now, so many more interesting things." In two long strides he was before her and hauled her up against him. As he lowered his head slowly he spoke.

"Lass ye are sae bonny when ye are spitting yer fire at me. The heat of yer temper sets my body on fire for ye." He pressed his mouth on hers in a heated embrace.

No! This couldn't be happening again. She had to resist him. Stephanie put her hands on Iain's shoulders and tried to push him away. It was like trying to move a mountain. Iain just ignored her vain protest and pulled her closer. She tried to twist her head away, but he pinned her in place with a firm hand cupping the back of her head and holding her in place. He whispered against her lips.

"Dinna fight me lass. Ye ken ye want this as much as I do. Just enjoy."

Stephanie came undone, again, and did just that. She felt his strong lips so gently caressing hers with such a tenderness that belied his physical strength. She suddenly became aware of her hands on his sweat soaked chest, and he felt good. She slid her hands up and down his slick shoulders and gave herself up to his kiss.

Iain felt her surrender and almost yelled his joy. Instead he groaned and slanted his kiss to enter her mouth. Their tongues dueled in a frantic passionate mating that began to imitate the thrust and withdraw of two bodies mating. The erotic caress began to draw them both in. Iain wanted to throw Stephanie's skirts up and plunge himself deeply into her wet heat. He knew by her kisses that she would be ready to take him right now. But no matter what, she was a lady and she was his prisoner of sorts, he had to stop this.

"Ye see" he said as he pulled back reluctantly from her intoxicating kiss. "There is much more tae do than gossip. Now go and get Judith tae help ye with yer clothes." He turned Stephanie, still weak from their embrace, around and patted her bottom as he pushed her forward.

She came back to her senses at the affront. "Don't you put me aside like some child. As to my clothes I shall see if I feel like making anything today. Don't lay your hands again on me Iain or I might just…"

"Just what my little kitten?"

"Oh never mind. Just do not do it."

She heard Iain laugh as she stormed out of the barn up to the keep.

Iain watched her go, her backside moving so tantalizingly up the incline. He felt his hand burning with the memory of that round naked backside in his hands. Oh what he wanted to do to her naked bottom, again. He shook himself angrily. What was wrong with him? He was behaving like some rutting untried youth. His thoughts were never far from his sexual fantasies he would like to fulfill with his green eyed golden temptress. He quickly began working at an increased pace to try to get his thoughts and impulses under control. He had to figure out how to end this obsession with Stephanie and her passionate nature.

Stephanie stormed up to the keep muttering to herself all the way.

"Cad. Bastard. Who does he think he is? Ordering me about and treating me like his own doxy to grab and fondle me anytime he likes. Well he can't do that anymore I won't let him! I won't!"

Stephanie nearly ran Judith over as she entered the keep.

"Careful Steffie! You are going to damage someone or yourself storming about like that. What has happened?"

Stephanie focused on Judith standing in front of her. Once again she was struck by how beautiful Judith was, both on the inside and the out. Why should she make new clothes? Stephanie thought to herself spitefully. She was nothing compared to Judith. Which was another thing that confused her about Iain. He always behaved as if he was extremely attracted to her. But Stephanie couldn't understand what he thought was so attractive. She was too tall, too thin, with barely a figure to speak of and she was too opinionated. He must be trying to play games with her, torturing her as part of his plan.

"Hello Steffie? Where are you? Are you still not feeling well after last night?"

"Last night what do you mean last night?" Stephanie feared that Judith had somehow found out about her and Iain's tryst last night.

"Well you were so feverish and flushed when Iain took you upstairs, I wondered if you were still suffering the effects this morning?"

Stephanie thought of the feverish responses her body was engaged in with Iain's incredible love making the night before. Judith could have no idea how much she was still 'suffering the effects' of last night.

"No. I am fine. I don't know maybe it was just something I ate." A picture of herself licking and kissing Iain's naked body flashed in her mind. She shook her head forcefully to banish the images and sensations that it evoked.

"Well if you are sure you are all right?" Judith said doubtfully, noting Stephanie's strange behavior.

"Yes" Stephanie smiled at her friend. "I am all right except as you can see my clothes are not."

"Well I did notice that. What happened to the clothes you were wearing last night?"

"I ripped them in my haste to go to bed last night...I mean after Iain left I felt terrible and just wanted to get into bed so I was quite shamefully careless with them." Stephanie hastened to add "Now I am in a quandary. My trunks are still not here and I need clothes that fit me better. Iain said you would be able to take me to the storerooms and help me get the materials I need. He said I am to get enough to make a complete wardrobe for my stay here."

"Wonderful! Since we don't actually know how long you are going to be here, hopefully a very long time, we will have to make you lots of changes of clothes. I would love to be able to dress you in the clan's plaid but I think that would be too presumptuous and cause all kinds of problems. So I guess we shall have to content ourselves with dressing you in your typical English garb... for now! Let us go and see what we can find. I have some wonderful ideas already."

"Marvelous!" Stephanie thought if Iain was known to be generous she would just have to avail herself of his generosity. "Let us go and see how generous Iain can be." The two ladies set of arm in arm to begin choosing the items they would need for Stephanie's new wardrobe.

Chapter Twenty

William of Rockforte felt like a very old man. It had been a long journey home after his meeting with Iain MacDonald. Iain MacDonald was a strong leader but with the temper of untried youth. William stretched his legs out before the fire and took a sip of the brandy Matilda had brought him earlier. He had briefly told her and his senior men that Stephanie was all right. He didn't want to go into anymore details, he needed to think. He needed to plan. He was not going to wait until Iain decided to let his daughter go, he had to get her away somehow himself.

Iain was convinced that he had been staging the attacks on Scottish lands. But William had thought that Iain was attacking his lands and people. He had thought that until he had met Iain. Despite everything, William knew from his meeting that Iain couldn't have been responsible for the attacks on William's lands and people. William knew from the young man's outrage, regarding the attacks on his own people, that the young Laird would not inflict the same crime against others in the name of revenge. But, Iain was young and was not in any frame of mind to listen to anything William had to say. William knew that there was some deeper plan afoot but he had no idea what it was. With Iain convinced that William was plotting attacks against the Scots, holding Stephanie captive to ensure the attacks stop, William was at a loss about how to resolve all of this.

Since William wasn't responsible for any of the attacks it was more probable that another attack would occur sometime very soon. Especially if the real guilty party found out Stephanie was being used as assurance against further attacks. It was a heavy dilemma that William needed to think more about. Who could he speak to with any confidence? He needed help but whom could he trust? That was his problem at the moment. He didn't feel like he could trust anyone.

His daughter's life hung in the balance and any ill move by him would most probably cost her her life. As he pondered the situation, he knew he had to figure out a way to somehow stage a rescue. He had to rescue her quickly before the real culprit behind all the attacks struck again. He slowly sipped his brandy as he concentrated on the flickering flames before him.

One thing was for certain, he could not directly trust anyone with the full story of what was happening until he knew the full truth himself.

Time passed and when William had finally finished his brandy he knew what he had to do to rescue Stephanie. Now he needed time in order to put everything in place. If everything worked in order and in perfect sequence, not only would he set Stephanie free but he would also discover the true culprit behind the attacks on himself and Iain MacDonald. Lord William of Rockforte slowly eased himself out of his chair to seek his bed. Yes, he felt old tonight, but he would not give up this fight. He may not be blessed with the vitality of youth but he had an old warrior's mind full of experience and he would use it. Tomorrow his plan would begin.

Chapter Twenty-One

Stephanie and Judith went into the store rooms off the kitchen. They passed the every day items stored in front for easy access for the cooks.

Stephanie was amazed by the vast stores Iain kept. He was truly organized to provide for everyone if needs required it. She could imagine that if one farmer's crops failed Iain would easily be able to supplement that farmer's loss from his own stores. Judith echoed Stephanie's thoughts.

"Iain has much and we all help gather and prepare everything for storage. Because we all contribute, should anyone lose anything Iain will measure what was lost and replace it from here. It is a very clever system because anyone who suffers a loss does not feel they are taking any charity because they helped collect the harvest."

Stephanie felt the temperature drop even more as they worked their way further down past rows and rows of stores. Finally they reached the end of the corridor and found a large wooden door with a great lock on it.

"Ah finally. Here we are. This is where Iain stores the extra weapons, spices gold and jewels he trades for."

"Trades for? When does he trade?" Stephanie asked.

"Oh he and Fergus go to the coastal regions at least once a year to get goods we can't get locally. They trade for the goods with the wool we produce here. Iain has quite a reputation for some of the finest wool in Scotland."

"But I didn't see any sheep around the keep."

"Well between you and me that is the secret. The sheep are allowed to graze freely up Iain's slopes. Their natural diet produces our prized wool."

"Iain seems to practice many trades but master none." Stephanie said with pique in the face of Iain's continuous talents at everything.

"Never say so" Judith looked surprised by Stephanie's spiteful words. "Iain is one of the finest warriors in the area but he did not want to earn his livelihood by sword alone. Countries are not always at war and so Iain knew he would have to provide for his people during these times as well. Iain and Fergus's father made sure that his boys had experience at anything and everything that interested them. He always told them that focusing on one specific thing denied them the experience and benefit of others."

"Sounds to me that their father was quite a hard taskmaster."

"Oh no! He was very kind to his sons and never made them do anything they didn't like. Now enough chatter let's get to work on setting up your wardrobe."

With a flourish Judith took the chain of keys from her waist and fitted the large brass key into the lock. Stephanie peered into the room. It seemed cavernous.

"You know" Judith said slyly "As Iain's wife you would have the keys to all he possesses and be able to suit yourself like a queen."

"Judith, I am not here…" Stephanie almost slipped again and told her friend that she was here against her will. "I mean I am not going to force Iain to wed me. We are taking time to get to know one another and see if we suit. You know that. Besides Iain may not decide to pursue his suit if we are unable to spend time together."

"You may say what you like, but I see the way his eyes seek you out every time he enters a room. He watches you when you are not paying him any attention. No matter what you think, I believe he is seriously going to offer for you."

Stephanie almost wished what Judith was saying were true. Imagining that the passion that flowed between them was something more, was a thrilling fantasy. But Stephanie harbored no illusion that Iain was only responding to her wanton ways. He was only a man after all and she could have stopped him last night if she had tried. He touched every part of her and she hadn't wanted him to stop and, truth be told, if he did ask her to wed him, she felt sure she would say yes in order to stay with him. She was such a fool.

"I don't know Judith. We shall see. Now, let us see what is in here shall we?"

After sometime spent in wonder at the plentitude of everything wonderful a woman could imagine the two ladies emerged with many different types of materials for many different ensembles. The had taken brushes and combs and mirrors that Stephanie felt better about using since they didn't actually belong to anyone, especially Iain's recently deceased stepmother. With these items she no longer felt like she was using something she should not. They left quicker than they had arrived, eager to start working on the new wardrobe. Judith collected some extra hands along the way.

"Agatha, Margaret, get your girls and come to the solarium. We need to work a miracle and get Lady Stephanie some clothes." As the ladies hurried away to do Judith's bidding, Stephanie heard them mutter beneath their breath.

"Bluidy English, coming here and taking from us like she has some right tae it. I for one shall only do it because the Lady Judith asked, not because the English wench needs clothes."

Stephanie flushed at their animosity. What was she going to do? She had to pretend to all that she was here willingly, but she wasn't and no one wanted her here either way. She wanted to be home. Most of all she wished she had never met Iain MacDonald. Never met the handsome man who was not the least bit intimidated by her intelligence or shocked by her temper. Never met the man who awakened the most feminine feelings and longings that she never thought she possessed. No, sadly for her she was a weak minded fool, for she was glad she had met him and she was glad that she had lain with him. After all, by the time he sends her home and everyone finds out where she has been, she might as well have done all the things that everyone will suspect her of doing alone and un-chaperoned with a good looking man. Besides her tattered reputation would mean all the fops after her for so long would definitely seek their brides elsewhere. No dowry could buy back her reputation. Stephanie smiled to herself.

"What are you looking so satisfied about?" Judith smiled up at her.

"Oh, just thinking about all the lovely things we are going to make and the fun we will have making them."

They went into the south facing room on the opposite side of the keep which had windows all around it. With all the shutters open the room was filled with light. At the base of the towers it was sheltered from any strong wind but there was still a large hearth and many small braziers around the room to keep it warm all year round.

As Stephanie and Judith began to arrange the bolts of material to decide what to make, Agatha and Margaret arrived each with their young girls, the eldest of whom was just beginning to blossom into young womanhood. In fact, the girls were teasing the young woman about the blacksmith's son who kept leaving posies at her door. Then behind them came Rose, Lachlan's mother, with shy smile.

"I dinna think ye would mind if I lent a hand."

"We told her that ye were making new clothes and when she found out they were for ye she insisted she come tae help." Agatha barely looked at Stephanie but tossed the words at her derisively. Stephanie tried not to let the woman's tone bother her, instead she turned to Rose.

"Rose that is so kind of you. Are you sure that Rowan will not mind sparing you for me?" Stephanie smiled and gently led Rose into the room.

Rose said with a sweet smile. "If he minds my being here, we shall see how he minds the side of my cooking pot meeting his ungrateful head."

Such outlandish talk had the women young and old laughing and for the time they were all united in their laughter. They began chatting about which colors would go with which and what would make the best combination for Stephanie's coloring. Their fun was enhanced by making Stephanie stand while they draped the various bolts of cloth over her. Agatha and Margaret set their younger girls to making Stephanie some shifts to wear under the new outfits. Even they were enjoying the laughter and teasing enough to 'forget' Stephanie was English.

"Here now dinna ye think tha Laird Iain would enjoy seeing her in this lovely green and gold?" They said. Rose and Judith smiled appreciatively.

"Yes. You two have a wonderful sense of color. You should pick the materials to go together and set them in a pile together. Then Rose and I can begin sewing."

"What a marvelous idea Lady Judith." Rose said with great enthusiasm. "With that plan we will get at least one outfit completed for the midday meal."

Judith smiled secretly. "Let it be the green and gold then"

"Wait" said Stephanie somewhat desperately "What can I do to help?"

"Dinna ye worry lass" Margaret looked up from the floor where she was measuring Stephanie's hem "We'll keep ye right busy eno for the moment just taking yer measurements. Ain't tha right Aggie?"

Agatha laughed "Aye too right Lady. Ye willna have time tae do anything else this morning until we have finished choosing the colors and material for yer new clothes. Now stand still."

And so the morning passed in a flurry of color and laughter for Stephanie. Although she was quite tired standing and being poked and prodded and sometimes discussed as if she were not even present, the cheery atmosphere helped her to pass a pleasant morning. Even though they were engaged in traditional womanly tasks, that Stephanie always avoided, she found she enjoyed their constant teasing, laughter and harmless gossip. They never spoke of anyone with any mean spirit and as Stephanie stood there and listened she learned much about Iain's people and how much they cared, not just for their Laird, but also for each other. The teasing was all in good spirit and nothing was hurtful.

This was nothing like the girls who had come to her father's house because he had wanted her to make friends. Those girls had all thought of Stephanie as a freak with her love of books and political discourse. These women were simply having fun.

It seemed like just moments but after a number of hours Judith called an end to the sewing session.

"There. All finished." She held up the green and gold underskirt and mantle she and Rose had been working on. "Just in time to wear for the meal. Thank you ladies for being here and helping with this emergency."

"Yes" echoed Stephanie "You have all been most kind to give up so much of your time to help me. I cannot thank you enough."

All the women beamed under Stephanie's genuine thanks and appreciation. Agatha and Margaret said they would take some sewing home and then the girls would finish the rest of her shifts. When they were all finished they promised to bring the completed garments to the keep.

Rose spoke up. "We must see Stephanie try on her first outfit to see if any adjustments are required."

Stephanie felt helpless as a newborn infant as the women took her out of the ill fitting ill matching clothes she wore and began draping the new outfit on. As each article was put on her there were many satisfied exclamations from the ladies present. The clothes fit perfectly. The dark green under gown fell in luxurious folds to the floor, the sleeves fitting her arms perfectly. Then they put on the lighter green and gold embroidered mantle over top with a braided gold cord to cinch her waist.

"Oh my Lady" said one of the younger girls "Ye look just like a queen."

Judith took some of the extra gold cord and wove it into a braid around Stephanie's head. The effect was stunning. Stephanie's hair shone with her own golden color and the gold cord reflected more light so that she looked as if she wore a crown of gold. With her long hair pulled up from her face her eyes were beautifully accentuated and sparkled with all the gold reflecting around her. The material fit her figure exactly. She looked statuesque. Since her arrival this was the first time that Stephanie had clothes that fit her and were designed to flatter her own coloring and figure.

Judith smiled at the end result "Well worth the effort. We can have some other choices for you over the next couple of days. But this is marvelous. Come on Steffie it is time to eat and now that you are well and truly properly attired let us go and enjoy the meal. I am sure I will enjoy it more than anyone."

"Whatever do you mean by that?" Stephanie asked

"Oh nothing." Judith sang "Nothing. Let's go and eat I am famished."

Stephanie linked arms with Judith and could not help but feel quite a bit more self confident garbed in such elegance. With her renewed self confidence Laird Iain would take note of her wants. Suddenly the image of him kissing her flashed into her head and she saw his face over hers just before he drove himself fully into her welcoming body. Angrily Stephanie gave herself a good mental shake. Those were not the wants she was referring to. She would no longer accept his habit of setting her aside or ignoring her questions anymore.

With her renewed purpose Stephanie walked into the main hall holding herself at full height. She did not notice the looks of astonishment at her arrival. Instead she focused on all the conversations she was looking forward to having with Iain. She would have all the control of the conversation and he would dutifully answer her questions. She pinned her flashing green eyes on Iain with such determination that they took on a slightly feral glow. She looked like a large cat about to catch a very tasty mouse.

Iain felt Stephanie's stare trying to penetrate him and so he deliberately avoided looking at her until she and Judith had almost reached the table. He had noticed the level of usual noise had diminished but he attributed that to their enjoyment of a good meal, rather than the ladies arrival. For just a moment more he continued his conversation with Fergus before he noticed that Fergus had gone silent and his jaw had nearly dropped to the floor. Then Iain looked up.

Damnation! He was a fool. Here he thought he had been so clever avoiding looking at Stephanie until the last moment, yet if he had looked he would have had more time to get used to the vision before him. There were no other words to describe Stephanie. She was a glorious golden vision. He wanted to take her into his arms and hold her beauty close to himself. He knew how silky her hair would be if he unwound the braids. She was so lovely that he felt his heart swell with pleasure looking at her. He frowned.

This is not what he needed. He had to try to keep himself away from her entrancing self. Her bewitching form in front of him, drew him like a moth to a flame. Where was his warrior's control and discipline?

Stephanie saw Iain scowling at her. Whatever was his problem now? To some his thunderous glare would have them running for cover but now today his look just made her stand taller and straighter. Let him try to intimidate her or dismiss her. She was ready for him. In response she met his fearsome gaze with one of her own.

Judith was surprised to see these prospective suitors staring daggers at one another. Very unusual. "Here now Iain doesn't Stephanie look lovely in her new clothes?" Judith stood by her friend waiting for Iain to stop glaring at Stephanie and take notice of how lovely she looked. The expectant silence stretched on as Iain and Stephanie glared at one another. Fergus finally broke the silence.

"Ahem. Aye yes but the lady is a vision. My wonderful wife ye have again worked wonder with yer needles. Lady Stephanie lass, ye are a lovely vision and ye grace us all with yer beauty."

Judith shot her husband a brilliant grateful smile, while her brother-in-law sat there in ungentlemanly silence.

Fergus jabbed Iain with his elbow. "Perhaps the ladies would like tae join us for the meal Iain? Why don' ye invite them tae join us?"

Iain grunted and focused his eyes on his brother. "Of course." He stood "Would ye ladies care tae join us now for the meal?" He held out Stephanie's chair for her while Fergus pulled a chair out for his wife. Fergus kissed his wife softly when she thanked him.

"Thank you" Stephanie said stiffly to Iain. "So, are you going to continue to look at me like some distasteful object all through the meal or are you at least going to try to pretend to be civil?"

"Hrumph" Iain grunted. "Some food, Lady Stephanie?" Iain passed her some of the tempting dishes that were spread over the table. She filled her plate and spoke to Iain as she enjoyed the delicious meal.

"You know" She said with some bewilderment in her voice. "It is really too rude of you not to compliment me on my new clothes. Or if not me then at least Judith, who had a large hand in the making of them."

Iain looked at her sidelong and replied "Ye ken ye really dinna suit the coy miss. And if ye want to know why I havena said anything tis because I am astonished at the richness ye have garbed yerself in here considering yer 'position' It seems a little presumptuous of ye." Iain could not believe that those pompous words had came out of his mouth. He sounded like an ass. He would not blame Stephanie if she dumped a tankard over his head. But her newly discovered beauty affected him so. She had been passable fair dressed in the servants garb when he had first seen her in the woods. Then she had been mildly attractive when she had cleaned up and dressed in his stepmother's clothes. But she was stunning in clothes that fit her and were chosen to flatter her. Here he was behaving like such a boor because she affected him. He had to try to keep himself from grabbing her and kissing her in front of everyone.

"My position" Stephanie hissed pulling Iain back from his thoughts "My position? And what position would that be? My real position or the position you keep trying to get me to present to others? I told you before I am happy to remove myself from your hall and be locked in your awful prison. Give me back the clothes I arrived in and I shall show everyone what my real position is."

Iain raised his eyebrows at Stephanie and said "Are ye sure ye want me to show everyone yer real position. The position of last evening."

Stephanie flushed red. "If you are referring to the position you created for me to keep me in the hall, and now it seems to keep me in your bed, then I think I have done quite well representing myself as a prospective bride for you. Except that now you seem to be the one who is incapable of remembering my position, as you call it, here. You told me to get proper clothes made, which I did with Judith's help and some other ladies, who were not keen to help 'the English' at first but fortunately got past all that thanks again to Judith. And now you are chastising me for doing as you ordered. So now tell me Laird Iain who keeps forgetting my position?"

"Well done m'lady. It seems ye have found yer sharp tongue again."

"Well I am quite sure you are very satisfied with your own company, so don't let me disturb you." Stephanie went back to eating her meal. After some moments of silence Stephanie had to ask.

"Laird MacDonald, you mentioned that you have a store of books. I wonder if you would permit me to borrow one to read."

Iain quirked his brows. His icy gray eyes clashed with her warm green ones. "Lady Stephanie, I doubt ye would be asking sae prettily for my books if ye ken where they are kept."

Stephanie was confused "Don't be ridiculous. I was simply asking if I could read one of your books. I read much at home and I heartily miss it here. If it is so much trouble to get them, then I will continue to occupy myself staring out the window."

"Now lass dinna get so angry. I just tried tae warn ye. Ye may borrow one of my books but they must remain in the chamber. I have some work tae do sae ye may remain while I work. Does that suit ye?"

Stephanie huffed. "Yes thank you that suits me." Under her breath she muttered 'Warn me? Warn me about what? Just a book for heaven's sake."

The rest of the meal passed in relative silence. Stephanie was looking forward to reading again. At least when she was reading she could be alone with her thoughts. However, given her present situation, Stephanie couldn't trust her thoughts and where they might lead her. She could either focus on being kidnapped and taken from her home. Or she could focus on her kidnapper and the astounding effect he had on her senses and her body. She turned and looked at Iain, who was sitting and watching her with hooded eyes. What was he thinking?

Iain watched Stephanie's thoughts play across her face. He watched as her face had softened and her cheek bloomed with a soft infusion of color. The rosy tint so became her that it took much effort to stop himself from reaching over and caressing her face. He had taken her to force her father to keep peace between their lands. Now he found that she had brought no peace to his senses. Iain knew he had to be prepared for the possibility that Lord William might not heed the warnings and attack MacDonald lands again. What would he do then? Would he be able to hurt her as he had promised? Iain had to doubt his resolve on that point. Shockingly, Iain realized that despite his best efforts he was becoming personally involved with the Lady Stephanie. He had better start drawing some of his great warrior discipline to try to resist his fascination with her. Iain focused and saw that Stephanie was looking at him intently.

"Are ye ready? I need tae start my work now." Iain offered Stephanie his arm. As she took it he smiled. He wondered how she was going to react when she discovered he kept his books in his private chambers. At the very least she was going to be surprised. He almost chuckled aloud.

"What are you looking so pleased about?" Stephanie asked Iain suspiciously.

"Nothing lass. Just looking forward tae seeing yer pleasure at my collection."

Stephanie thought he sounded much too cheerful to be thinking just about books. He was up to something.

Chapter Twenty-Two

They arrived at the door, Iain smiled a very predatory smile at Stephanie.

"What is it?" Stephanie said with a hint of irritation in her voice.

"Welcome." Iain said as he guided her inside and closed the door.

Stephanie looked around and noticed first how masculine the room was. Dark woods and heavy draperies abounded throughout. The most dominant piece of furniture in the room was the large oak desk that stood beneath the window. Its surface was covered with papers quills and ink. There were also all manner of fascinating instruments that Stephanie would have loved to learn about.

But then she looked around the room. Massive bookcases lined the walls, filled with books of all sizes and descriptions. She stood for a moment just enjoying the sight of so many books all in one place. Books that she could read without worrying about how unseemly the content was for a lady. No fear of censure from anyone.

Then she noticed the other door at the far side of the room. There through the open door she could get a clear view of Iain's bed chamber. Her eyes instantly flew to his large bed. What could he be thinking bringing her here? Suddenly, it dawned on her. This is what he had been so amused about earlier. He knew all along where he was bringing her yet he had said nothing. The odious arrogant man! He intended to embarrass her by bringing her to his private rooms. Too angry to speak, she stood glaring at Iain.

Iain was right she was obviously angry with him for bringing her here. But before she had realized where she was her joy was a sight to behold. She was a sight to behold, shimmering and golden.

"Here" Iain spoke very close to her ear. "This is one of my personal favorites." He reached up to a shelf just above her head, causing him to place a hand on her shoulder to reach. The length of him pressed into her back. Once he reached the book, he handed it to her without stepping back or removing his hand.

"Tis a book with much adventure and bloody wars." Iain's breath stirred the loose tendrils on Stephanie's neck. His breath was so hot on her skin it was like the sun beating down on her. She shivered, as chills of desire ran up her spine.

Iain leaned in closer "Why lass are ye cold? Should I warm ye up?" He placed both arms around her and braced his hands on the bookshelves effectively trapping her within his embrace.

Stephanie swallowed and took a deep breath. Standing so close to him she could see the dark stubble already shadowing his cheeks her hands itched to touch him. She swayed closer to him, her breath catching.

"Be careful Stephanie the heat I have tae give will burn ye."

Lips almost touching Stephanie moistened her lips with the tip of her tongue.

It was an invitation that no reasonable man could refuse. "So be it" and he crushed his lips to hers. The heat was most definitely there and they were both aflame. Their passion burned as fully as it had before, nearly consuming them both and leaving them in ashes. Iain put his arms around Stephanie and gentled his kiss. Scorching her with his desire left no room for him to taste her honey sweet lips. So taste them he did. He lightly traced his tongue over her reddened swollen mouth easing some of the heat he imagined he had touched her with. He skimmed his hands up and down her slender back. She was so long and graceful this temptress melting in his arms. He fit his hands to her waist and pulled her closer fitting his arousal between her legs. He groaned at how perfectly he fit to her. Her body was designed for his. He rained light kisses all over her face and Stephanie moaned as she strained to free her arms. But Iain held her fast bending her slightly over his arm wrapped around her waist. He teased her breast through the material of her new mantle.

God, she could feel herself burning at his touch. The moist heat of his mouth seeped through every layer of clothing she wore and she felt as if her breast was weeping in turn for the pleasure his mouth brought. When her nipple pressed through the cloth he lightly rolled it in his teeth. She was on fire for this man; he could pleasure her so well and thoroughly, even fully clothed. Bent slightly over his arm, his arousal pressed tightly and intimately against her womanhood she began to feel the feverish restlessness of her own arousal. She felt him quiver and pulse with pleasure in his thick shaft. She spread herself open just slightly to pull him closer to her. The throbbing in her most private places was tightening and building to a hot climax. She licked her lips and bit on her lower lip as she moved her hips against Iain's.

Iain thought he was going to die here on the spot feeling her come alive under his touch. She was going to climax here fully clothed and he had no part of her exposed to himself. She was so ready for him she was going to come apart in his hands.

Suddenly, the reality of their situation doused his ardor. What was he thinking? He could not play with this woman. She was too full of passion. He had to stop this before he was gone beyond all reasoning. "That is the kind of heat I have, Lady Stephanie, and it is tae hot for ye. Take yer book and go tae yer chambers before ye do something ye will regret." With regrets of his own he set her gently away from him. "Go on now" He said this with more gentleness than he was feeling. He wanted nothing more than to strip her bare and devour her on the spot.

Stephanie's passion glazed eyes cleared and flared in confused indignation. "No! You wouldn't dare end this. You know what is between us."

"I ken tha we are both warm and willing, some more than others, but this is just the available moments. We would not succumb to such passions if others were present. Or if we had met under different circumstances.

I dinna think we suit." Iain tried to straighten himself up and remain calm.

"You know sir your tale might be believable had you not held me in your arms and I had not felt your attraction for me, or seen it for myself. You lie and we both know it. For what reasons, I do not know, but I am not going to forget so quickly." Stephanie turned on her heels and left Iain's study with considerable force.

"God's blood!" Iain swore aloud in the echoing silence of his chamber. He looked disgustedly down at his 'lack of interest' displaying itself proudly for anyone to see. She was right his body betrayed him but his mind knew he was right to keep away from her and all the wonderful promises she presented. No good could come of their continued affair.

Stephanie was still seething by the time she reached her temporary chamber. It took all manner of self control not to resort to the most childish of behavior in light of Iain's callousness. She longed to yell at the top of her voice and throw something, anything to release a fraction of the frustration she was feeling. Breathing a sigh of resignation, Stephanie knew she could not indulge in such behavior. Wouldn't she make a grand impression on Iain's people? Yet there was no way she was going to let Iain get away with igniting such passion between them and then try to pretend it didn't exist, or meant nothing.

She looked down and realized she still held the book Iain gave her. 'A Warrior's Strategies' Wasn't that an interesting title Stephanie thought with a growing smile.

Perhaps she could gain some insight on how to win her own battle with Iain. That is it. Stephanie's smile grew broader. She would employ all her efforts to proving to Iain he was not unaffected by her. He would admit he wanted her as much as she wanted him. Let him try to remain distant. If she kept igniting the passion between them, he would have to admit his desire of his own free will or she would make him admit it by her own sheer will.

Chapter Twenty-Three

Patience, Lord William thought to himself. He must have patience. William hoped the plan he had devised would be an effective one culminating in Stephanie's release.

What he was currently having problems with, as he rode to one of his closest neighbor's homes, was the amount of time this would take to set in motion. He had already visited other neighbor's within a day of his own keep and had lost three days with the beginning of his plan.

However, as he reached Eduard Stockton's keep, William prepared himself for the final recitation of his speech, imperative to his plan. He was showed to Eduard's parlor. Eduard himself was not long to follow.

"Why William, this is a surprise. I did not know you had planned a visit. What entertainment can I come up with on such short notice? Shame on you for not telling me of your arrival in advance."

William shrugged off the feeling that Eduard really was annoyed with him and began his rehearsed speech.

"Lord Stockton, this is not a social call I make to you."

"Oh? What is the problem then Rockforte?"

"It is Stephanie, sir."

"Mmm, well, yes, she is a bit of a problem is she not? A tad willful and disobedient but, not to worry, a husband with strength will be able to train her."

William forced himself not to react to Eduard comparing his daughter to a naughty dog that needed to be taught. "No you misunderstand me. Stephanie is gone. She has been taken from me."

"Do not say so! Who did it? We must ride out and find the brigands then cut them down for their audacity."

"Stockton you are too kind and generous with your support. However, I am not entirely sure who took her. Witnesses' accounts lead me to believe it is the Scots across the border but I cannot be certain."

"Well then, why do we not ride across the border and find out? Or perhaps we should find these witnesses and question them again. Perhaps they require more persuading to remember what happened to our lovely Stephanie."

William shuddered at Eduard's tone and implied threat. Always he spoke cryptically like that; speaking the right words to chill a person but never coming right out and threatening them.

"No, no Eduard I have spoken at length to those who were there and they know nothing more than they have told me."

"If you are sure. I of course accede to you in this matter."

"Eduard I know you may think that riding fully armed and mounted across the border is the best course of action but I don't know for certain that it is the Scots who have her. She could be being held by anyone. God forbid she might even be dead."

William paused for a moment then continued. "There has been no demand for ransom so I cannot even be certain she is still alive. I must go to the King because if he takes up my petition with all his men, resources and power, I will have a better chance of finding her whether she is alive or dead."

Eduard looked tight lipped and angry at the mention of William's plan to ask the King's aid but he replied. "Of course if that is what you prefer. I stand with you if you have need of me."

Eduard's reply was the same as all his other neighbor's after William had spoken of his plan.

"Thank you Stockton." William turned to leave.

"A moment, Lord Rockforte, if you please."

William stopped. "Yes?" Please he thought hurry man I need to get home and get to rescuing my girl.

"Well, I realize that you are rather preoccupied at the moment but I would like to make something clear before you retrieve your daughter from…whomever has her."

"Yes?"

"I wish to make your daughter Stephanie my wife upon her return."

"Your wife?" William was shocked at Eduard's words. Eduard had spoken of wedding Stephanie before, he often made frequent comments about her lack of proper womanly traits. "Your wife? Well that is something. Yes Eduard I know you have asked often but you never seemed over fond of my girl so I did not take your intentions to be so serious. But now that she is missing; I find I cannot give your offer the consideration it deserves. Bringing her home is all that I am thinking of now."

Eduard quickly covered the scowl at William's words, and smiled a cold smile that didn't touch his eyes. "Of course good neighbor, friend, there is time to speak of such details when Stephanie is found. I only mention this now because if she is found alive, we both know as men of the world, that it is highly unlikely she will be untouched. I would just like to tell you of my intentions before that time is revealed."

It took much for William to reply cordially. "You are too kind. I am honored by your suit. But you must understand that I will not speak of this anymore until Stephanie is found. Surely you understand?"

"Of course Lord Rockforte. Are you sure I cannot assist you with your petition?"

"Thank you but I will move much faster and attract less attention if I am alone."

The men parted company and William rode with all haste back to his keep. Once he arrived he called his sergeant at arms and told him what he wanted him to do.

"John, I want you to wear my cloak and ride my horse in the direction of the King's current residence. Make sure you are well concealed in your appearance but it does not matter who sees you pass. Let anyone see you but stop for no one. All who see you must think it is me on the way to see the King. Make sure that no one follows you. Once you are well past and know for certain you are not followed, discard my cloak and sell my horse to buy a ride home."

"Forgive me, sir, but why do you need me to pretend to be you?"

"I am going to rescue Stephanie and I need you to do this to help me."

John was glad in any small way to help, no matter how strange his task may have seemed.

"When should I go Sir?"

"We will both be off at first light. God speed."

After John had left and William was sitting before the fire with a glass of brandy in his hands; he pondered his next steps.

Tomorrow it was his goal to reach MacDonald's land and present himself as prisoner in exchange to Iain MacDonald. He hoped his plan would achieve two goals. First, by offering himself in place of Stephanie as Iain MacDonald's prisoner, Stephanie would be allowed to go free. Second, he hoped that being Laird Iain's prisoner when the raids began again, Iain would see that he, Lord Rockforte, was not responsible for such cowardly attacks.

William admitted to himself that the plan was not perfect but he was desperate to get his daughter free and avoid war. Long into the night he watched the fire burn, praying that he would succeed; his daughter's life depended on it.

Chapter Twenty-Four

Stephanie was getting very frustrated. At every turn Iain seemed to be thwarting her plan to get him alone and seduce him. He was quite determined not to be alone with her anywhere where she might be able to take advantage of him. It was quite un-nerving because she didn't have any idea how to seduce someone properly. Her noble upbringing was proving to be very vexing when she was trying not to be very proper. Who could have imagined the thrill of wickedness could be overwhelmed by the inordinate amount of effort It was taking to convince an obstinate man he really wanted to have an affair with her. The more he resisted the more determined she became. Truthfully, if they had not succumbed to passion more than once Stephanie would have taken Iain's apparent disregard as he true feelings. But she had felt and seen his desire for her and she had experienced something so wonderful she wanted more. She knew he wanted more as well, but, getting him in a situation where he would finally admit that, was not as simple as she would have liked. A warrior's fight was not done until the opponent concedes defeat. She was not going to admit defeat, so, Iain had better be prepared the true battle was still on. With determination she went off again in search of her foe, Laird Iain MacDonald.

CLANG! The sound of metal on metal reverberated from the exercise yard of the keep. Fergus deflected a potential stunning blow from his brother, who had of late seemed to become rather demanding on Fergus's time and attention in the yard.

"All right brother while I enjoy thrashing ye on the grounds, I have tae ask wha has driven ye tae try tae best me or at least try tae match my skill level?" Fergus teased his brother.

"Och ye are a funny mon Fergus. Ye ken full well I can trounce ye soundly on any field in real or mock battles." Both men locked swords and stood toe to toe. Iain cracked a devilish grin.

"Care tae go another round?"

"Nay brother. My wife would kill me were I tae return home with any more wounds from our skirmishes. I have no desire tae incur her ire just tae distract ye from whatever is driving ye of late. Speaking of that, would ye care tae tell me what is troubling ye rather than trying tae damage us physically out here?"

Iain sighed and sheathed his sword. "I ken ye are right brother, but I canna seem tae find any peace anywhere else in my keep."

Fergus raised a bushy red brow. "Peace from what?"

"Not what…but whom."

"All right then. Peace from whom?"

"HER!"

Fergus let loose with a loud belly laugh. After a moment he managed to compose himself long enough to say. "Ah brother, ye got more than ye could handle with yer little hostage eh?"

"Ye have the right of it brother. As much as I hate tae admit it, the woman is driving me tae distraction. I dinna ken what has happened but she dogs my every step and vexes me at every turn."

"Well ye ha tae be more specific than tha. What exactly is she doing tae vex ye sae much?"

Iain ran his hands through his hair so that it almost stood straight up. "I dinna ken if I can sae for sure. But she is always right next tae me standing sae close and pressing herself against me. She doesna say anything but unless I go out of my way tae be where she is not then every time I turn around there she is."

Fergus looked intently at his brother for a moment or two until suddenly a look of comprehension crossed his face.

"Good God mon! Have ye bedded the lass? Never mind brother, dinna bother tae deny it. Everything ye are speaking of is proof enough that ye have."

Iain had the look of a very guilty young boy. "Aye, tis true, brother. I dinna ken what has come over me but I have bedded her thoroughly and more than once."

"God's blood brother, have ye gone mad? Thank God she was no innocent miss or we would be facing serious retribution."

Iain said nothing and didn't look at his brother.

"Och, Iain, mon. Say it isna sae. Ye bedded a virgin?" Fergus looked appalled.

"Aye, brother, I did."

"How could ye? She is the daughter of an English Lord. She is lady born. Ye canna bed her like some tavern wench and be gone."

"Aye, I ken tha too brother."

"Well, ye ken full well ye have tae marry the lass now."

Iain looked shocked. "Now just a minute, Fergus. I dinna have tae do no such rash thing. No one who sees her and her advanced age being unwed would believe that she had been a virgin. She is on the marriage shelf. Sae by now she would not be expecting anyone tae offer for her. Her virginity isna an issue."

"Marrying the woman whose innocence ye took isna rash, brother. Bedding her in the first place that was rash."

"Aye, I ken that, brother. But I have nae worries that when she is returned to her father I can pay him and pay some English man to take her without her innocence. Ye ken I have the means tae pay them both well."

"Och, Iain, that is just too heartless. Tis not like you brother tae be sae cruel. Tis not Lady Stephanie's fault ye couldna control yerself either. I am verra surprised tha ye could talk so." Fergus shook his head sadly and walked away from Iain, leaving him standing alone in the practice yard full of self recriminations.

Fergus was right and Iain knew it. He was to blame for all this, not Stephanie. He took advantage of her terribly every time he bedded her. But she responded to him so fully it was impossible to imagine that she had been a complete innocent that first time he took her. As he contemplated all this it never once crossed Iain's mind that Stephanie reacted this way to him because she felt more for him than any other man she had ever met.

Chapter Twenty-Five

Stephanie finally found Iain alone on the practice yard. She stood for a moment watching him as he put some practice pieces away.

The wind playfully tousled Iain's shiny black hair. Stephanie's fingers itched to do the same. As if teased up by the wind Stephanie felt her desire for Iain rise up unbidden, and beyond her control. Without any thought she moved closer to him.

Iain knew Stephanie was there. He could feel her like a cool breeze on his skin. He turned and saw her moving in his direction. Damn his eyes! He knew she had seen him looking at her. He could not pretend he didn't know she was there. Iain hated himself for it, but he felt like a trapped mouse being stalked by a ravenous cat. A very sleek elegant cat but deadly nonetheless.

What was she doing here? So far he had managed to keep distance between them because he knew he wouldn't be able to think clearly with her so near. Already he could smell her faint smell, just strong enough for him to catch it on the breeze but just faint enough for him to want to move closer to breath in her scent. As he looked down at her the wind picked up and playfully tossed her shining gold tendrils around her face. He had to clench his hands in fists at his side to keep from reaching out and catching one of those strands of hair to tuck behind her delicate ear. He remembered how soft her hair and her skin were. He could barely stop himself from reaching for her. Instead he looked at her and spoke.

"Lady Stephanie what brings you down tae this very unladylike area of the keep?"

Stephanie turned towards him and pressed herself closer to him. She turned her green eyes to him and gently placed her hand on his arm.

"I came to see you of course. It has been some time since we managed to have some time alone together, so I thought I would find you and we could make time."

Iain's mouth nearly dropped. "Lass" he said sternly "Wha are ye playing at?" She was so very irresistible looking up at him all softness and golden glowing light in the sun. His hands and lips ached to touch her again. She just smiled up at him. "Ye mustn't speak like that or people's opinion of ye might be affected."

Stephanie struggled to keep her smile in place. She wanted to slap Iain across the face. But she knew that he was being rude because he was not so unaffected by her. Also their precious lovemaking proved without a doubt how attracted he was to her. He may not love her but he was obviously attracted to her and she had to focus on that.

"Iain, you are kind to be so worried about my reputation. But this conversation proves I need you to help rid me of the last vestiges of my ignorance in the matter of relationships between men and women. I mean, after all, I will be married someday I suppose and since I will not be wed on my innocence I had better be well educated and experienced to attract someone."

Iain's expression darkened. "Should ye decide tae marry there is no way ye'll have tae sell yerself tae any man." He leaned forward gray eyes storming and blazing. "Do ye understand me, lass? There is nae way ye'll have tae buy a marriage I willna allow it. Do ye ken me full well?" Without waiting for her answer Iain turned and stormed off to the stables.

Stephanie knew he would go and throw himself into any physical labour to work off his frustration. She beamed at his back and whispered. "O I 'ken' you full well Iain MacDonald. I just don't think you 'ken' me full well at all." Stephanie hurried back to the keep smiling as she planned her next strategy.

Later that day Stephanie descended the tower stairs carefully. She had spent a long time getting ready. The red and gold gown and overcoat deliberately chosen from the clothes Agatha and Margaret had sent to her room earlier. They had spent a long time putting together a rich wardrobe for her.

She knew that her outfit was too formal for the meal but she didn't care, that alone would draw Iain's notice to her as would the fact that she looked radiantly lovely. She drew a deep bracing breath reminding herself that Iain was fighting their attraction and her attempts thus far to seduce him, so this evening would be no different. Strength and determination had to be her companions now, just until she managed to convince Iain to continue their affair.

As Stephanie entered the hall everyone was already seated and food had begun to be served. Stephanie fervently hoped she would not cause much of a disturbance with her entry. Fortunately, only a few people glanced up and for the most part no one gave her much attention. She stepped up to the dais and took a seat next to Iain. Judith and Fergus didn't notice her at first. But when they did, they both took a second look and Judith smiled knowingly. When Fergus began to speak Judith place her hand on his arm and shook her head. Iain didn't even look at her. He just scowled at the glass in his hand ferociously. With some nervousness Stephanie sat down.

"Good evening, Iain. How are you?"

Iain had known the moment Stephanie had descended the tower stairs. Up until the time of her arrival he had been continuously glancing over and watching for her. The vision she presented stole the very breath from his body and his palms began to sweat. She had no idea he had watched her adjust her appearance before entering. She was so appealing as she stood there mustering the courage to enter the hall. She was a fiery vision in red and gold, as she came to the table. She was the flame and he felt as though he was about to be drawn in and burned. And she did draw him in, he could not seem to get enough of the sight or sound of her when she was near. When she was near he just wanted to wrap his arms around her and carry her off to make love to her thoroughly. At times recently when he felt himself longing for her, Iain felt like he was more the prisoner than she was.

"Are ye not a wee bit over dressed for the meal lass?" He noticed Stephanie braced herself at his words.

"I suppose it might be a tad too formal but Agatha and Margaret worked so hard on my clothes, I had to show my appreciation by wearing this for all to see. I chose this because it is so stunning. Don't you think that it is lovely?"

"Humph, I ken or care not for ladies fashions because ye all tend tae change yer tastes as often as you change yer minds."

Stephanie laughed loudly "Oh Iain you really are very amusing."

Fergus turned towards them and then looked back at his wife. "What is going on there?"

Judith laughed and leaned in closer to her husband. "She has the obvious good sense to have decided."

"Decided what?" Fergus asked

"Why decided to marry your brother of course. Isn't that wonderful?"

"Are ye telling me tha truth wife?" Fergus looked at his wife "Ye are, aren't ye? Oh my bleeding hell. This is tae much!" Fergus turned to his brother laughing, and pounded him on the back. "Well done, brother, well done!"

"Are ye daft mon? What the hell did ye do that for?"

"Oh nothing; just admiring yer great plan tae deal with the raids. The latest word is that nothing has happened in some time. Well done." Fergus smiled broadly and turned back to his wife.

Iain looked at his brother's back in astonished confusion and muttered. "Ye have gone daft, mon."

"Is everything all right, Iain?" Stephanie put her hand on Iain's arm. He thought he was going to explode. His brother's crazy outburst had momentarily distracted him from Stephanie and all her temptation. He carefully, as if handling a dangerous animal, lifted her hand off his arm and placed it on the table.

"Everything is fine Stephanie. Thank ye"

Stephanie gave Iain the brightest smile she could muster, in spite of her nervousness. "Wonderful. So tell me what is good this evening?"

"Stephanie, lass, what are ye talking about? This doesna sound like ye."

"Don't be silly." Stephanie put her hand lightly back on his arm "I don't sound any different. I am just hungry but I don't know what we are having. Now, what is good? What do you suggest?"

Iain looked absolutely dumbfounded by her. He sighed heavily "Lass, I am not sure what it is exactly that ye are playing at but I just canna try to figure ye out right now. So ye ask what is on offer and what is good? There is some wonderful venison in a mint rosemary sauce. Would ye like some?"

"Why yes that sounds lovely. You seem to know quite a bit about the recipes. Do you know how to cook?"

Iain sighed again. Stephanie was behaving most odd. "Nay lass, I dinna cook but I do ken what flavors I am tasting."

"That is so interesting. Most men do not pay any mind to such subtleties. Yet here you are tasting the subtle flavors in the food."

"Thank ye for yer appreciation for my talents." Iain said with some sarcasm.

Undaunted Stephanie continued with what she hoped was going to be a successful seduction. "You know, if a man can appreciate the subtleties of food, surely he must fully understand the subtleties of women." Stephanie gently traced his forearm with her finger.

"Nay, Stephanie, dinna do this. Ye are better than this, lass." Iain stood up quickly "I must go."

Judith looked up with surprise from her meal. "Iain, where are you going in such a hurry you have barely eaten?"

"I must go. I shall return later. I am going tae take a patrol out and make sure everything is all right around the keep."

"I'll go with ye brother." Fergus started to stand up

"Nay, tis fine. I will go alone." Iain walked away before anyone could say anything to delay him any further.

Fergus kissed his wife. "I will go and see if I can talk tae him love." He left to catch up with Iain before he rode out.

Judith moved into the chair Iain had vacated just moments before. For the most part Stephanie seemed fine but she wanted to be sure. "Oh, Steffie, why didn't you tell me you were interested in Iain?"

"Well I do not know. I guess I thought I could make him interested in me." Stephanie gave a thin smile. "I will be fine. I only feel slightly foolish. I think I will go up to my chamber now."

Stephanie left the hall with her head held high. But once she reached the chamber she roughly dismantled her carefully arranged ensemble and laid it aside.

"I am such a fool!" She spoke out loud in the empty silence. "Insufferable man! He knows he feels something for me but he won't acknowledge it. I keep making such a fool of myself trying to force him." She changed into her nightshift and brushed out her hair. Suddenly as she brushed her hair she remembered Matilda and how she would sometimes, even now, brush out her hair at night.

The brief memory reminded her she was alone. She missed her father, her nurse and everyone at home so much it hurt. All the loneliness filled her up, coupled with her growing feelings for Iain, Stephanie curled up on the bed to try to shrink the pain and wept until she fell asleep.

Chapter Twenty-Six

Just a little while longer and he would be there. It was such a long journey for William to Scotland. He was alone but he had to keep stopping to make sure he was alone. He listened and scanned the trees behind him and dragged a large tree branch behind his horse to cover his tracks. Soon he would arrive at MacDonald's keep. Fortunately, Eduard, his neighbor, remembered where the keep was from previous dealings with the young lord's parents. It made sense that they would be in more contact as more of Eduard's lands bordered the Scot's than William's. Strange though that Edward had never mentioned any problems with cross border raids.

Oh well, right now his goal was to get to Iain MacDonald as fast as possible, to trade his own freedom for hers. William could only guess what peril she was in or how badly she had been made to suffer. Just a little further to go William kept silently repeating to himself as he rode on.

Chapter Twenty-Seven

Iain was suffering, there was no doubt in his mind about that, if he could even trust his addled brain anymore. He thought back to the conversation he had had with Fergus after he had left the table. Fergus had found him in the stable saddling his horse.

"Seems a bit of a waste tae take a warhorse out on a patrol that could be handled by a few of yer men, Iain." Fergus leaned against the stall casually twirling his bushy red beard. To most it would seem casual, but Iain knew his brother well and he knew Fergus was concerned. He sighed.

"I ken Fergus. I ken ye think I am acting strange. That is probably because I am feeling strange."

"What is it that is making ye feel sae strange Iain?"

"I dinna quite ken. Well, I think I do, but I amna sure."

Fergus raised a brow at his brother.

"Och I ken Fergus. I sound daft. I need tae go out and get some clean air. Maybe then when she is nae everywhere I turn I might be able tae think straight."

"If ye are speaking of the Lady Stephanie, tis highly unlikely ye'll ever be able tae think straight. She's a bit of a whirling top that one. But my Judith is right fond of the lass sae there must be some good in her."

Iain jumped to Stephanie's defense reflexively and vigorously. "Oh there is nothing but good in the lass. She is good and kind and verra beautiful. Surely ye saw her this night? She looked like bright firelight."

Fergus was surprised to her his brother speak so vehemently about Stephanie. It seemed Judith was right, there was something between them. It appeared though that Iain wasn't willing to accept it or do anything about it. Maybe if he just pushed Iain a little.

"Well she is tha I suppose tis true. But she can certainly let fly with a tongue I dinna think I have heard from any lady in her same station."

"Of course she has a tongue. She has a strong mind as well. She may be a little spoiled but she is a verra bright woman and hasna been able tae speak her mind as freely anywhere until I brought her here against her will. Now she is acting so unlike herself. She is as frivolous as all those other girls whose mothers have been throwing at me in hopes of marriage. Stephanie has already told me she doesna really want tae be married yet now she speaks of having tae buy a husband when she returns. She canna do that. No one will make her happy." Iain shook his head in bewilderment of his outburst and turned to his brother. "I am sorry brother but I need tae go. I will return late." Iain swung himself up onto the back of his great horse and set out.

Fergus stood and watched him go. He knew his brother would be safe, no one would dare attack Iain on his own lands. Then he thought about Iain's words about Stephanie. It seemed that no one would make Stephanie happy but his brother. Fergus knew his brother was taken with Stephanie and after this evening it seemed she was developing a tendre for him too. He just couldn't see how either of them would be able to overcome the situation and circumstances they found themselves in to come together.

Iain rode thoughtfully for sometime. He thought about his brother and, of course, Stephanie. Iain wished that he had never thought to cross onto William's lands in such secrecy. If he had just approached William directly things would be different. Stephanie wouldn't be his prisoner. In fact he probably wouldn't have met her. That thought hit him with a small measure of sadness. He couldn't imagine never having met the bright, funny, beautiful passionate woman that so beguiled him. He had thought he would be able to forget her by bedding her. Now his own selfish desires and fascination for her had ruined her. It angered him to think of her having to buy a husband and it was worse that he was the reason she would be forced to buy a marriage.

What struck him even more was that he could barely stand to think of another man being with her. Iain felt quite sure that no one would appreciate how appealing she was when she was mad or arguing with him. Her temper turned into the most sensual passion he had ever experienced in bed with any other woman. She responded to him with such wild abandon and had held back nothing in her inexperience. She was never trying to get something from him like other women, she just wanted him as much as he wanted her.

She was liquid heat running through his veins and it tore him up inside that he would have to let her go eventually. He could not keep her here to keep the peace forever. It had not been one of his better strategies but, then, he had not counted on his prisoner completely capturing him. Iain shook himself back to attention to his patrol he had to get the golden haired temptress out of his mind.

Chapter Twenty-Eight

It was late when Stephanie woke up. The moon was high in the night sky and she realized that she was hungry. Slowly she remembered that dinner had been a sorry affair and hadn't lasted that long. She hadn't even eaten a bite. As she cleared the sleep from her swollen red eyes, she knew she had to have something. Her stomach was rumbling and it felt like it had cleaved to her ribcage. No one else would be up, she could go down to the kitchen and get some food. She didn't need much, just a bite to tide her through until morning.

Stephanie got up and put a wrap around herself. Fortunately it was a fairly mild evening so she wasn't too chilled as she made her way down the stairs. Although the stone was quite cold on her bare feet she didn't mind. She quickened her pace into the kitchen.

The fire was out but it was still warm in the room as Stephanie set about finding something to eat. There was still some venison left, but after the memory of her conversation with Iain, she quickly set it aside. She needed something to eat not something to ruin her appetite. She still felt so foolish after her ridiculous attempts to seduce

Iain with all sorts of nonsense about recipes and women. She quickly found some chicken, a bit of bread and some cheese. As an added surprise she found some sticky sweet honey cakes to finish her midnight snack. She put the meal on the table and fetched a cool cup of water.

The small meal was delicious and Stephanie felt comfortable and giddy with her freedom. She tucked her feet up underneath her and enjoyed every morsel. She felt like a naughty child sneaking around while no one was about. A full contented smile settled on her face as she sat at the table.

It was there that Iain found her when he came in. He had not thought to grab an apple or something earlier before his ride and since he had run like a frightened hare during dinner he felt the pangs of hunger. Fortunately, everything had seemed quiet and still on his tour around the keep. It seemed that Lord Rockforte had decided to suspend the attacks to keep Stephanie safe. Smart man! It made Iain's life a little more peaceful.

But peaceful was not what he felt when he found Stephanie in the kitchen. She looked like a guilty child but Iain knew the womanly curves that lay beneath her modest amount of clothing and the memory stirred him again. She had herself all tucked up on the chair with her golden hair streaming down her back. Her green eyes shone with happiness as she licked the drops of honey from her fingertips.

Iain nearly jumped out of his skin as he watched her small pink tongue flick delicately around her fingers and he imagined what it would feel like should she do that to him. Her movements were all the more sensual as she believed she was alone and so showed no signs of inhibitions. Iain wanted to grab her and taste the honey that had just sweetened her mouth.

What was wrong with him? Just moments in her presence and he wanted to ravish her. He was no better than an animal in heat. How could he feel this so intensely all the time? Poor Stephanie didn't even know he was standing there wanting to do all sort of wicked things to her body. He should be gelded.

Stephanie suddenly felt Iain's presence in the room. His large frame filled the doorway. Somehow he looked even more forbidding in the moonlight, but she had forgotten how large he really was. When she looked up at him Iain was scowling at her. He was certainly looking very angry and formidable glaring at her that way. She couldn't believe he could be so angry about her taking some food, she wasn't stealing. Stephanie jumped up of the chair and faced Iain's imposing countenance.

"Well what are you so angry about now? I suppose I am not allowed to eat except at designated mealtimes? That is what happens with prisoners, right?"

"What are ye on about now woman?" Iain was sorry to have spoiled her moment.

"That is why you are standing there trying to intimidate me. I just had some leftover food since dinner was such a fiasco. That cannot be wrong of me."

Iain crossed his arms and leaned against the doorframe as he let Stephanie have her outburst. She planted her hands on her hips and continued.

"You know I didn't ask to be here. You brought me here. You did. Do you remember?"

"Aye, lass, I remember." Iain spoke softly as his breath caught. Stephanie stood there blazing at him and she was completely unaware that the moonlight made her nightshift almost transparent. He could trace the outline of her body with his eyes. He saw her legs clearly reflected in the light and once again his thoughts turned to ravenous desire as he imagined her legs wrapped around him as he drove deeply inside her. Even though Iain was ashamed of the train of his thoughts he was unable to stop them. No matter how hard he fought his desire, she continued to draw him in as no other woman ever had.

"Damnation woman! What are ye doing tae me?" Iain pushed himself away from the door and crossed the floor in two long strides. Stephanie saw him coming purposefully towards her and she was powerless to move. Had she crossed a line with him? He looked very angry and no matter that she was intimidated, even a little fearful, of him as he strode to her. She couldn't move. She was like prey frozen at the sight of a predator moving in for the kill. He stood in front of her so she had to crane her neck up to look at him. His eyes were a swirling gray storm as he grabbed her and pulled her closer. He spoke as if he were in some pain.

"Sae help me, lass, I ken twas me that brought ye here. I dinna know if I thank myself or hate myself fer doing it. Ye are in my mind constantly and I canna lose the scent of ye or the memories of yer touch. Sae help me I canna."

Before she could speak he pressed his lips to hers. She instantly melted herself against him. For however long the kiss would last this was what she wanted. The kiss was intoxicating. She knew how upset he was with himself but none of that mattered his kiss was firm and possessive, but so tender she nearly wept with the flood of emotions that poured through her. His tongue delved deep into her mouth. She opened willingly to him. Her heart filled to bursting with the love she felt for him. LOVE? By God she loved him! The moment she recognized her heart's desire she abandoned herself completely to Iain.

Iain felt the intensity of her passion escalate but he didn't know the full cause of it. He only knew that he nearly came undone with the sudden intensity he felt flow through her kiss. He had to have her here and now. He didn't care that they were in the kitchen. He just felt so heavy with his passion, he wanted to explode inside her.

"Christ's blood, lass, forgive me! I canna wait, I canna wait."

Stephanie barely heard him but moaned in despair when his lips left hers to speak. She grabbed his hair and dragged his head back down to her. Iain lifted Stephanie off the floor and set her on the table. She was so consumed with love and passion she could have been on the softest bed in the world she wouldn't have noticed. She loved how her hips were directly level with his pulsing arousal. She could feel him pressing urgently against her and she opened her legs wider to bring him closer. Iain lifted her shift, loving the softness of her thighs as he freed himself from his britches. He hesitantly teased her entry. God in heaven his little English lass was so wet and ready for him, he wanted to shake the rafters with his shouts, He thrust deeply into her and pulsed deeper and deeper as Stephanie dropped her hands to the table and lifted herself to meet each of his powerful thrusts.

Stephanie was sure she was glimpsing heaven through her passion glazed eyes. Little spots of light danced behind her eyelids. She dropped her head back praying that Iain would never stop and she thrust her chest and hips forward to meet his every move.

"Ye are sae beautiful" Iain ran his hand up between the valley of Stephanie's breasts then back down to caress her seductively through the thin material of her shift. He leaned over her arched form and sucked at her breast, soaking the material through. The heat of his breath with the cool moisture of the air, peaked her nipples instantly. Stephanie bucked wildly against Iain's hips.

"Oh Iain! Please! Please!" Stephanie wanted more of the pleasure that rocked her through to her very core, but she felt sure if he didn't stop soon she was going to shatter into a thousand pieces in his hands. She bit her lip as Iain teased her breasts. She wanted to scream at the throbbing that pulsed through her but she bit her lip to silence herself. It was a useless endeavor the passion he brought to a climax in her had her breathlessly exclaiming her joy.

"Yes, yes oh God yes!" She breathed. She pushed her hips against Iain's hips with all the force of the powerful climax that tore through her. As she reached her soul shattering peak she screamed his name. "IAIN!"

Her cries mingled with the pulsing of her muscles inside her brought Iain to a higher, fuller climax than he had ever known before. With one last desperate thrust he exploded inside Stephanie's wet warmth and collapsed against her chest.

"Iain?" Stephanie spoke very softly and with a small hesitation in her voice.

With the tremor of hesitation in her voice Iain feared she was going to chastise him for his lack of self control, again. He had forced her to yield to him again, he spoke with his own hesitation. "Yes lass?"

Stephanie swallowed and took a deep breath. "Iain, please don't leave me tonight." Iain lifted his head and looked into her shimmering eyes so full of uncertainty. He knew that no matter what happened tomorrow he was powerless to deny her soft plea. Iain caressed her cheek and traced her lips with his thumb.

Stephanie was afraid that he would walk away like he had every time before, so she continued quickly. "I mean you usually leave right away once we have... finished." She blushed furiously as Iain just let her go on and get her emotions out. "I just want to be with you tonight. All night."

"Aye lass, and I want tae stay with ye. If ye want me tae stay. I will stay." He leaned over and kissed her forehead so tenderly she could have cried. As he withdrew from the warmth of her body she felt the loss of him keenly. Maybe he would just leave her again. But he didn't. Iain picked her up off the table and carried her through the hall, up the tower stairs to his rooms. Stephanie was astounded. When Iain saw her look he said.

"Ye are right lass. I want ye with me this night, sae ye shall stay with me."

"What will people think or say?" Stephanie didn't really care about others, but if anyone found out what they were doing that would be different.

"They will say nothing lass if they are wise." Iain walked into his bedchamber and laid her down reverently in the middle of his bed. "Are ye sure this is what ye want?"

Stephanie didn't hesitate. She wriggled out of her nightshift and lay there in naked splendor. Feeling the enticing wickedness of her behavior she opened her arms to him "You are what I want. More than anything."

Iain groaned and fell on her raining her with kisses and love nips all over her body. Then he quickly stripped himself naked. He was wonderfully handsome and Stephanie felt her body begin to heat up at the sight of him. Once he was naked he came to her with more passion than either thought they would ever experience.

As he ran his hands, tongue and lips over her he whispered. "This is what I want. Ye are sae beautiful. I dinna think that I can ever satisfy myself of ye."

But he did satisfy himself and Stephanie again. They gave into the passion with no regard for tomorrow. Their passion was all that mattered and hours later when they were both fully sated, they both slept in a tangle of damp limbs, smiles hovering on their lips.

Chapter Twenty-Nine

The lone figure moved silently through the forests. Anger welled up inside his black soul. Fools! He had hired useless fools. They were incapable of following his instructions, so he would have to do the job himself. He was getting impatient to reach his goals over the last few months. His heart's desire was just beyond his grasp and something, or someone, always managed to thwart his ends. Well if he wanted his plan to progress, obviously he had to do the work himself.

The shadowy figure reached the outskirts of the village and slipped into the first barn he found. Inside it was tepid with the smell of livestock heavy in the air. God, he hated barns. He looked into the stalls for a likely candidate for his purposes. He found a dozing docile ewe with her two new lambs. He quickly grabbed one of the lambs and hefted it out of the stall before the ewe could awaken. To ensure his success he squeezed the lamb under his arm and held its mouth closed.

Once he was outside he quickly grabbed his dagger at his side and with one motion slit the lamb's throat. He dipped his finger in the warm rivulet of blood and wrote his message on the barn door before stealing away back into the dark night.

He would have success no matter what the cost.

Chapter Thirty

Stephanie stretched languorously. Her body felt thoroughly spent and relaxed. She rolled over and saw that she was alone in Iain's bed. Damn him he had done it again! Here she was alone after their night of lovemaking. She may have discovered that she loved the man but his behavior was becoming rather annoying.

She loved him! The memory of the revelation washed over her again and she felt her body tingle with the memory of her full abandonment to her feelings. Stephanie Rockforte, old maid, had fallen completely in love with Iain MacDonald, her captor. She must be crazy but she didn't care. And now he had gone off and left her again without a word. Well let him try to get away and avoid her this time. She threw the covers off and stormed about muttering while she tried to find something to wear.

"Cad, bounder, scoundrel. How dare he walk away from me after last night. He needs a good swift kick in the…"

"Mmm seems someone had sparked yer ire. I am sure it couldna be me."

Stephanie turned, and there Iain stood with a tray of food in one hand, and some her of clothes in the other. Immediately Stephanie forgot her pique and in her newly discovered love for him she raced over to him. Abruptly she stopped short in front of him. She tried to appear unaffected as she spoke "Oh. You are here."

Iain smiled seeing her obvious pleasure at his arrival. He laid the tray and clothes down on the bed and pulled her close to him. "Of course I am here. Did ye think I would just leave ye? Come here and say good morrow tae me properly, lass."

Iain kissed her so deeply she felt herself go limp in his arms. This man could kiss her very sense away.

When he released her, Iain laughed at her struggle to try to regain some composure as she stood before him gloriously naked. She seemed to have forgotten her nudity.

"Well, it is what you have done every time we have lain together. You cannot deny that."

"Nay, I suppose I canna deny that. But I am here today sae let us not begin the day by arguing. I took the liberty of fetching ye some clothes and bring us some food."

Stephanie's anger dissolved as he showed her what he brought. "Did you get my clothes yourself?"

"Aye I did. I got everything I thought ye might need. If I forgot something, tell me an I will go and get it."

"Thank you." Stephanie took the clothes and dressed. Once she had finished dressing she took some of the bread and fruit Iain had brought and ate it thoughtfully.

"Ye know lass tis early eno that we could sneak out for a ride before anyone else awakens. Would ye like tae do tha?"

Stephanie's eyes shone "Yes, Iain that would be wonderful."

"Do ye have a cloak or som'at? It might be a wee bit chilly out yet." Iain paused "Sorry. I ken ye wont have one since I dinna bring one with me. Here one of my shorter cloaks should do for ye."

Iain pulled the cloak from his chest and draped it around her. Even his short cloak was quite long enough on her.

He took her hand and they crept downstairs out into the stables. Storm and Snow were quickly saddled and they rode out.

The ride was wonderful. Both of them forgot everything but each other. They talked deeply of many things. Many things except for Stephanie and her current situation. Iain was so wonderfully intelligent. How could she not love him? She thought to herself as they rode along. He never talked down to her or told her she was foolish. Now that she had come to realize how she felt about him, she wondered if he could ever come to love her too. No she had to stop herself from thinking such things. She would just have to be happy to love him while she had the chance and be prepared to hide the love away when she had to go.

It was enough for now that they were laughing and enjoying each other's company. As the keep came into view Stephanie felt her heart sink a little bit. Back in the reality of the situation Stephanie had to try to convince

Iain to continue their affair in secret. With her love for him she needed to be with him while she could.

As they rode up they saw a large gathering of people looking angry and upset. Fergus rode down to meet them.

"What is it?" Iain asked bracing himself for the tale.

"It is bad trouble Iain. The folks are verra angry about som'at that happened in the village and they wont say what it is. Douglas, the leather maker, says he is the one who discovered 'it' Trouble is he wont say what 'it' is except tae ye."

"Well I guess I should see what the trouble is."

All three of them rode into the crowd. Everyone started talking at once when Iain arrived.

"Silence" Iain said, settling the crowd instantly "I ken that Douglas has something tae tell me. Do any of ye ken what it is?"

Murmurings rippled through the crowd. Iain continued "Good then I should no be hearing any voice but his."

From the crowd a voice cried out. "He dinna tell us what he found, but he did say the English were at it again. Damn them!"

"Well let me have some quiet sae that we can all hear what he has tae say. Doug where are ye?"

"Here Laird." Douglas stepped forward his hands stained with the oils of his craft clasped before him.

"What is it that ye have discovered that is sae terrible?" Iain queried.

"Well Laird, if ye dinna mind I think ye should se it for yerself."

Iain dismounted "Well lead the way mon."

Everyone followed as Douglas went around to the back of the furthest barn in the village. Stephanie dismounted and followed as well until Douglas stopped and said.

"Laird my reading is nae sae good but the message is no complicated." Iain saw what was written and judging by his thunderous glare the message wasn't good. Stephanie looked as she came around the corner. She staggered with shock. There written in dried blood were the words. 'Death to Scottish bastards'. Pinned to the wall beneath the message was the slain lamb.

Stephanie felt sick and her ears started ringing. Who could do such a thing? She clutched her heart as she realized that Iain would believe it was her father. She whirled to face him. What would he do to her?

"Iain, my father…" Iain silenced her with a look of warning. By now, most of the village had gathered around the barn. The message was deciphered by those who could read and it was told to everyone. The angry murmur of the crowd was growing.

"There must be retribution" said one angry voice

"We should go and kill them afore they have a chance tae come back and start murdering us." another one yelled.

"Aye!" shouted many more angry voices. "Aye death tae the Sassenach devils." People were getting quite vocal.

Suddenly Stephanie felt someone clamp her arm in an iron grip. "Let us start with her. She's English we dinna even ken who she is. She was probably sent here to give us this message and now she is living in the keep. She could poison us all."

Voices clamored, most in anger but a few in shock and denial. Many still viewed her as a stranger and possible enemy. Others knew her better and knew she would never do such a thing to them.

Stephanie noticed that Iain was talking to Fergus and Douglas a little further away and so wouldn't hear what people were saying to her. Worry began to build in her.

"Aye let's start with her. She's a bluidy English bitch. Let us spill her blood as she did the innocent lamb."

At that threat Stephanie began to panic. The crowd of people were frightened and panicky and one still had a firm grip on her arm. Their anger and bloodlust for revenge were growing and she couldn't free herself.

"IAIN!" She cried "Iain help!"

Iain heard Stephanie's cry and turned to see her completely surrounded by the mob of angry people. His people. They looked threatening, moving in a slow circle around Stephanie trapping her in the middle. He felt sheer terror when he saw Stephanie's golden head shimmering above the dark mob. Her eyes were wide with fear and her complexion was death white. Suddenly she was gone!

"NO!!!" Iain roared. He broke through the crowd, pushing people out of his way to get to her. God he prayed let her be all right. He finally reached her. She had stumbled and had curled up where she had fallen. He could see her body shaking. He knelt down and spoke to her softly with a soothing tone.

"Lass? Oh lass tis all right I am here. Come now get up." Stephanie loosened her position enough for him to grasp her and he lifted her up into his arms.

She turned terror-stricken towards him. "Thank God! Iain I was so frightened."

"Hush now I have ye lass" Iain turned to his people. "What in the name of Christ has gotten intae all of ye? Ye are behaving like animals. This is nae how the clan MacDonald behaves in the face of such events. By God ye should all be ashamed of yerselves" Iain cast his furious glare around the crowd "What were ye thinking? If ye were thinking at all?"

Still braced by the gathering of the crowd a voice piped up. "We are under threat of death by the English. Why shouldna we protect ourselves?"

"We dinna even ken if an English wrote this or no." Iain said calmly. "We are looking at everything carefully before we make an uninformed decision and go charging off to war and bloodshed. But that still doesna explain why ye were terrorizing Lady Stephanie."

Stephanie kept a tight hold of Iain's physical and emotional strength. She couldn't lift her head away from his chest. She didn't want to see those angry faces again. Another voice spoke up

"Laird Iain, we dinna even ken who she is or where she came from. She could have done this terrible deed. How do we know for sure?"

"First of all" Iain said looking around the crowd. "The fact that she came home with me is all ye need tae know, especially if ye are nae going tae be making any effort tae know her. She is here with me and that should be enough for all of ye. But perhaps ye dinna trust me enough. Ye should be seeking another clan leader if I dinna have yer trust." People were visibly shocked by Iain's words.

No one wanted anyone but Iain to be their leader. Iain continued.

"Secondly, I ken that Lady Stephanie could no and dinna do this terrible thing." People had begun to calm down in the face of Iain's logic. They seemed more willing to accept what Iain, was saying. At that moment Iain could have walked away but he didn't. When he spoke Stephanie could not believe what he said.

"Do ye all ken what I am saying tae ye? I ken she dinna do this and I ken because she was with me last night. Stephanie was with me ALL last night." Iain spoke the words and he knew he probably shouldn't have but he didn't care. He wanted to make sure that everyone knew Stephanie was innocent.

Stephanie would have collapsed if she weren't already in Iain's arms. "What are you doing?" She hissed under her breath. "You are going to tell everyone what we did. Are you mad? We are not affianced. You cannot tell everyone we are engaged in an illicit affair."

Iain looked down at her blushing countenance and smiled faintly. "Ye are absolutely right lass." Iain called out to the crowd. "Yes the Lady Stephanie spent the night with me as she has graciously consented to be my wife." Iain squeezed Stephanie tightly so she could not argue with him in public. It wouldn't have mattered even if she could speak as the crowd erupted into well wishes and congratulations. Suddenly words could be heard above the cheers.

"Our future Lady couldna ha done this. Some terrible person was trying tae defame her name and turn us against her. But we willna. Hurra for Laird Iain and our Lady Stephanie."

The people parted as Iain carried Stephanie away. Fergus was laughing as he clapped his brother's back. "My hearty congratulations brother. Well done on yer pending nuptials. I must go and tell my wife."

Iain kept walking, seeming to ignore everyone around him. Once they were away from the crowd, Stephanie managed to speak.

"Iain MacDonald, you put me down this instant!" Iain stopped and set Stephanie on her feet. She put her hands on her hips and glared furiously at him.

"Have you lost your bloody mind?" She all but shouted at him.

"Now, lass, such language is nay becoming of the future Lady MacDonald. But nay I dinna think I have lost my mind."

"But don't you see what you have done? Not only did you tell everyone what we did last night, but now you have gone and told everyone we are going to be married. What were you thinking?"

"I was thinking of your safety, lass."

"But marriage Iain? Why did you tell them we were going to be married? Now everyone expects us to go through with a wedding." Stephanie started pacing back and forth, her skirts swirling around her legs as she moved.

"Ye ken even as ye are sae upset by the fact that everyone thinks we are affianced, I find I am verra attracted to ye Stephanie." Iain reached for her. "Why not be married?"

Stephanie slapped his hand away. "Don't be mad. We have to come up with a plan now to make sure this 'wedding' doesn't take place."

"Ye worry tae much lass. Everything will be all right. But for now I have tae go see if we can find out how all this happened. Come inside with me."

They moved inside the keep where Iain stopped a passing servant and addressed her. "Maggie, please get some help and move my possessions into the south tower, my father's old chamber."

"Really Laird? I mean aye of course I will. We will get that done right away." Maggie fairly flew to do Iain's bidding. Stephanie watched the beaming girl go.

"What are you doing? If I am not mistaken I am currently staying in your mother's rooms am I not?"

"Aye."

"And so the south tower were your parent's rooms correct?"

"Aye"

"So haven't you just given that girl the impression that you are moving into your position as head of the clan and with me being there already further strengthening the notion that we are going to be wed?"

"I suppose most people will want tae believe that."

"But Iain this is not possible. You cannot let your people believe that."

"Stephanie, lass, ye worry tae much." He leaned over and kissed her nose. "Stop worrying, as yer future husband I command it."

"As my what? You command what?" But Stephanie was already talking to Iain's retreating back.

Never had she felt so out of control. Surely Iain had lost his mind. She had to think. What was she going to do now?

"Steffie. Oh my God is it true?" Judith came running "I can't believe it! We are going to be sisters. This is too wonderful!"

Stephanie listened to Judith's overjoyed exuberance at the thought of the wedding. She cringed inwardly. How would people react when the wedding was called off. Surely there would be more anger. She had to get Iain to put a stop to this farce before it got out of control.

"Well, actually…" Stephanie began but Judith was so excited she didn't let Stephanie finish.

"I should have known this was going to happen. I mean I knew you were trying to seduce Iain. Sorry." Judith paused at the blush on Stephanie's cheeks. "But we are going to be related. I can talk to you as a sister now not just a friend. This is wonderful. You have to tell me everything."

Judith kept up a stream of chatter as she led Stephanie away. Stephanie, still in shock from the whole morning's events, just followed mutely along. Eventually, when Judith had settled Stephanie would be able to speak to her plainly.

Chapter Thirty-One

After Iain had left Stephanie, he decided to start a search for signs of whomever had perpetrated this crime. By the time he reached the scene most people had already left. Only a few children remained, each trying to frighten the others with tales of how the message got there. Stories of ghosts, goblins and devils of the night coming with the intent to make mischief and start stealing young children, flew around the group.

Iain chuckled in the face of the seriousness of the situation. Trust a child to turn such horror into a game.

Iain watched the children for a moment longer then turned to the task that lay before him. How fast had everything progressed since this morning? His night with Stephanie was the best he had ever had. But it was also a joy to wake up and have her wrapped in his arms sound asleep. She was so lovely and angelic in her sleep and he liked that about her. He liked it even more when he had come back and found his angel storming around the room angry because she had thought he had left her alone again.

He hadn't had a choice about announcing their engagement to everyone present had he? No. It was for the best. It was the only way to solidify the truth in his people's minds. She was with him last night and the engagement gave validity to their lovemaking. After all it wasn't unheard of for affianced couples to share a bed before they were wed. It certainly wasn't common but it was not unheard of.

But then there was Stephanie. She was quite adamant that he call off their engagement before people started expecting and planning a great wedding for their Laird and his Lady. Iain told himself that until he could find out who had committed this terrible act last night, keeping his pending marriage would keep Stephanie safe. Hell it might even allow him to have more nights like last night with her. He felt his pulse quicken at the thought of bedding Stephanie again. She drove him to the brink of madness with his desire for her, all of her, her body and her mind. For now, she would have to accept their engagement. Finding out what was going on and protecting her and his people, that was his priority. He set off to begin his investigation.

Chapter Thirty-Two

Man and horse stood dozing in the trees when the band of men found them. The three were painted in traditional war dress, battle hardened and battle ready. At closer look they were definitely a rag tag bunch barely surviving. Their desperation for survival made them dangerous men. So when the group came across this old man, obviously an English noble, it was accepted without speaking that they should rob him, kill him and leave him for the forest predators to hide their crime.

The air was still and quiet as the group moved in for the kill. It didn't even matter if this man had nothing of value on him, they could still get something for his horse. Closer they moved with the practiced stealth of trained fighters.

Then just when it seemed success was at hand, one of them stepped on a twig and startled some birds in the trees. The ensuing cacophony woke both man and horse and stirred them into action.

William's horse tried to bolt so he was momentarily distracted and did not see what was happening until he reined his horse in.

Then he saw the rugged painted faces and knew his luck had run out. Now he needed to use his wits. He was so tired he wanted to give up but he had to keep thinking of Stephanie at the mercy of the huge Scottish Laird. He had to think fast.

"Wait! Don't kill me! I am bringing important news to Laird Iain MacDonald, are you his men?"

The largest of the three men spat on the ground and spoke. "Och nay English, we arena the MacDonald's lackeys and ye are no on MacDonald land. Ye are on the Campbell's land. Now what news do ye bring the MacDonald? Perhaps if it is as valuable as ye say we shall let ye live a while longer." He laughed at his own joke, the others joined in.

Damn! William thought he had been going the right direction but he had strayed off course. This was not a welcome delay. He needed to use all his courtly ways to escape this deadly situation.

"Excuse me, kind sirs" William began "I mean no offence or disrespect but the news I bear is for the MacDonald's ears alone. I have been charged with this duty and I must obey to the letter. Scotland's safety depends on it." William eloquently exaggerated his speech.

"Why, in the name of all that is holy, would ye, an English cur, be trying tae save Scotland? Seems verra suspicious tae me. Maybe ye should go to our Laird's keep first an' he can decide iffen yer message is sae important."

This was not good, William was afraid more delays would hinder his plan, but it did not look like these men cared much for 'important messages' It looked like he would be much safer to accede to their wishes and go with them. William had to hope that he would be allowed to deliver his message to Iain.

"Well, sirs, if you believe that is the best course of action, then lead on. This message must get to Iain MacDonald and I must deliver it to him personally." William had a sudden thought to add. "But be warned if Iain does not receive my message and provide a response by the allocated time, England will launch full war on Scotland until there is nothing left."

"Bah! I would like tae see yer English try. Nothing but a pack of limp milksops. But we will take ye tae Laird Campbell and he can decide yer fate. Come, men, let us go. Lead the English dandy's horse and ye willna try anything, do ye ken?"

"Yes I understand. My task is too important for all of us to risk death in a foiled escape. You have nothing to fear from me I go willingly." William was seething and wished he could skewer all these men for keeping him from reaching Stephanie. He wanted blood for all this. Please God he prayed look after Stephanie, keep her safe until I can reach her.

The small band headed off to the Campbell keep and William's fate.

Chapter Thirty-Three

Stephanie spent most of the rest of the day of her engagement trying to appear sincerely grateful for all the well wishes she received. Judith's excitement was so great that Stephanie almost wished her wedding was going to be real. But the wedding wasn't going to be real. It couldn't be real. She had to stop Iain from continuing this charade.

During the quiet moments of the day, Stephanie found herself wishing this was all real. Her love for Iain only young and newly tender in her heart made her entertain the notion of being his wife. She couldn't deny that she would like nothing better than to be at his side day and night, but she knew her desires were folly. He didn't love her; but he did desire her. She felt a warm flush at the memories of all the ways he desired her. But desire was not what mattered here. Desire was too temporary. Marriage was for good and she did not want to be in a marriage where she loved, but was not loved in return. How happy could she be?

Stephanie gave herself a mental shake. She had to stop thinking this proposal was real. None of this was real. Stephanie sighed. These last weeks were taking their toll on her. She felt like a child's spinning top going everywhere all at once but going nowhere. Her life, since being taken by Iain, had been taken over by Iain. She loved Iain and wanted to stay with him but she wanted to go home as well. Back to her home with the people who loved her. Before she had known such passion. Such wonderful passion.

"Why so glum, bride to be?" Judith interrupted Stephanie's thoughts as she chanced to find her there alone.

"Oh, I am not glum" Stephanie forced a smile "Maybe just overwhelmed by all that needs doing. I mean, while we haven't set a date yet, there is still so much to do."

"Don't worry. Weddings have a way of bringing out the helper in everyone. You will be surprised how many people want to be involved in this wedding. It is not as if the Laird gets married everyday. Many people will want to be part of the special day, and be a part of making the day special."

Stephanie muttered "It certainly will be special when everyone finds out it isn't going to happen."

"What did you say?"

"Nothing, I am just a little overwhelmed and emotional."

"Well don't neglect your rest." Judith smiled broadly at Stephanie who blushed. Suddenly, Judith leaned forward and hugged Stephanie.

"Oh Steffie, I just knew when you came here that Iain wouldn't let you go. He never would have brought a woman all this way if he were not already seriously considering marriage. That and putting you in his parent's old chambers, told me how serious he was about you."

"I don't know about that."

"I do." Judith said firmly "Don't fret. All this doubt and worry is normal. Whenever we women marry the men we love, we can't help but feel insecure. But we just have to remember that our men love us too."

"I can't fully feel that confidence since Iain was forced to reveal my whereabouts last night, he had to reveal our engagement."

"Steffie are you suggesting that Iain bedded you without a proposal? Don't be absurd, he would never be such a cad." Judith looked indignant.

"Do not be so quick to believe the best of everything." Stephanie said darkly. She quickly realized that she had better be careful yet. It wouldn't do for her to ruin Iain's plan to catch the culprit. Nor would it be a good idea to reveal her true circumstances. She couldn't risk such a move. "Oh don't mind me" Stephanie said with a tight laugh. "You are right it is just the jitters."

Judith took Stephanie off to set about creating the menu for the eventual wedding feast. There was no date set yet, nor would there be, so Stephanie didn't think it would do any harm to begin the planning. As long as nothing was actually undertaken it would be all right to pretend. Perhaps even enjoy the fantasy for a short time.

Iain had spent most of the day with Fergus and a select few of his trackers, looking for clues as to who had left that violent message. The only fact they had discovered so far was that who ever had committed this foul act, was skilled in the art of treachery. They found few broken branches and no obvious tracks on the ground. But Iain's trackers were very skilled and they knew the importance of what they were seeking. So they all redoubled their efforts.

When they found a broken branch, they got down as low to the ground as they could without disturbing anything. Through slow meticulous effort they were able to discover some useful bits of information.

"Here, my Laird" one said

Iain and Fergus left the copse of trees they had been searching to walk over to the tracker. The man was examining something small in his hand. When Iain arrived the tracker placed the object in his hand.

Iain looked at it and recognized it. "This is Rockforte's emblem which was attached to the sword belt of the men we found with Stephanie." He spoke directly to Fergus while the trackers continued looking for signs and trails. It wasn't their job to speculate on the origin of what they had found only to discover the trail of the one, or many, who left it behind.

Fergus took the small metal pin from Iain to look it over.

"Aye, ye have the right of it. I recognize it from that day as well. D'ye think tha he has sent more men over tae begin raiding us again?"

Iain took the scrap of metal back and worked it over between his fingers. He thought of Stephanie. Then he thought over his meeting with her father, Lord William. The formidable man who was more concerned about his daughter's safety than his own. Meeting with the supposed enemy alone in a field all he wanted was assurances of Stephanie's good health, not his own. This man would not come back onto Iain's land to threaten him while Stephanie's life was still in the balance.

Iain was an experienced enough soldier and had spent enough time with his father, watching him deal with clan betrayal to know that something was very amiss here. After meeting with William it was all too neat to find a sword pin right around the scene of the crime. Iain's instinct was to keep looking even though the evidence told him that it was Stephanie's father. He could still be in the area after all and it wouldn't take much for him to have found his way back here after the meeting. Particularly, if he had been on the land before on any or all of the previous raids against the MacDonalds. Iain decided to keep going further to look for more evidence, after all his instinct had served him better than well in the past. He, also, didn't want to give Stephanie any cause to be angry with him when he tried to approach her with the prospect of continuing their liaison under the premise of their engagement. Then after a time he was sure he could convince her to go through with the actual marriage.

"Iain come look here." Fergus called Iain's attention. When Iain reached his brother and the trackers in the small clearing, he saw what they were all looking at. An area of brush had been tidied to look as undisturbed as possible, yet there was a half a boot print missed. Iain studied it.

"It seems we are dealing with one man but that is all we can be sure about for now."

"But sir" one of the trackers spoke "Isna the bit o metal from that English, Lord

Rockforte?" he spat as he spoke the man's name.

Iain had forgotten all his people had followed his lead in believing Lord William had perpetrated the crimes against them. He would have to guard Stephanie's identity carefully to shield her from their animosity towards her father and his family. This was getting more risky as the person responsible for these events appeared to be getting bolder.

"Now, dinna be hasty. I ken that the pin points tae Rockforte, but every piece of evidence now appears tae be carefully planted so that we only see the obvious and not ask ourselves why." Iain turned "Fergus, a word." The two brothers separated themselves and Iain again stated his belief about the situation.

"It seems tae me that all along someone has had us chasing our tails like dogs, brother." Fergus waited for Iain to continue

"Right from the start of the raids we were led to believe it was Rockforte who was raiding us. As the raids began almost immediately after the death of our father we did not have time to investigate everything that was happening. So when we were offered the easy solution as to who the guilty party was we jumped on that did we not?"

"True, brother."

"But we dinna consider where this evidence was coming from. None of our people saw Rockforte or any of his men specifically, they just reported what they had been told by 'witnesses' who were drifters or captured clansmen from Campbell. The chaos on our own land distracted us from examining these sightings any further."

"Iain, I think I ken where ye are with all this. But I am afraid that ye are possibly denying the truth because of yer feelings for Stephanie."

"Och, dinna be daft mon! I dinna have 'feelings' for Stephanie." Iain snapped. Feelings? Did he have feelings? Well other than the obvious desire. He couldn't say at the moment but he was more concerned with presenting his brother this theory he was working on. "Fergus, we both ken I amna governed by emotions. Something is just nae right with all of this. Can ye honestly say that after meeting Stephanie's father, ye think he would be willing tae sacrifice her safety by engaging in the raiding again? He is more likely to try to mount a rescue."

"William is a warrior like us brother. Who is tae say he wouldna have stayed behind after the meeting tae test whether or nay ye meant yer word."

"I might have believed that brother had I not seen how much he loves Stephanie. His love was reflected by his fear for her safety. Aye he might be a seasoned warrior but it seems he prizes his daughter above any ill gain or ill will he might have against us. I sense now with this last event that we have been looking for the wrong man."

"God's blood mon! Never say so for then we are guilty of kidnapping a lady. An English lady, our lives will be forfeit."

"Och, mon, that is nothing, after all she is going to be my bride. I can easily embellish the event of the day we took her to make everyone even the English king if needs must, believe I spied her then and there and had tae have her."

"Ye mean tae go forward with the wedding then?" Fergus looked at Iain intently.

"Aye, but only after I have cleared her father of these crimes and I have a feeling brother that I will in time."

"Tis the 'in time' that has me concerned. I dinna think Stephanie believes ye want this marriage and she herself does no seem sae inclined."

"I am going tae marry the lass. Her father's land will make the perfect protection against any clan or English Lord looking tae squeeze out more for themselves. Tis a verra strategic marriage."

Fergus put his arm around his brother's shoulder and laughed. "Good luck tae ye brother! I think ye have a job ahead of ye tae convince Stephanie tae proceed."

"Oh she'll proceed all right. Dinna worry about that brother." She'll proceed if I have to carry her in front of the priest myself; Iain thought to himself. Yes, the match would work out perfectly all around and Stephanie would see the wisdom in it. He would take it up with her after the most recent events were resolved. Iain whistled a tune as he went back to the keep. Yes, Stephanie would see the wisdom.

Chapter Thirty-Four

Upon arriving at the Campbell keep, William was still given no rest or reprieve. He knew full well this grueling ordeal was meant to keep him at a disadvantage. In his younger years he would have been able to better handle this strategic game but he had to admit he was older now and combined with his worry for his daughter he felt sure he was going to fall face first in front of the Campbell leader.

William distracted himself from his exhaustion by taking in his surroundings. One thing was for certain, the Campbell's were not a lucrative or well organized clan. The keep was run down and in dire need of repairs to its outer structure. Inside, the hall was covered in sooty grime from the fireplace and all the rushes under foot were rotted, full of decaying bits of food and dog excrement. The odor was strong. It seemed the general state of disrepair and disregard extended to the tenants of the keep as well. There were still men sprawled around the benches that had not been cleared away, snoring and obviously still drunk from the previous night's revelry.

The servants were apparently trying to clean up but they were not very enthusiastic about any of their efforts.

All in all William thought as he took in the sight, this was a clan of mercenaries. They grabbed what they could take and didn't make any kind of future plans for themselves. That meant that everyone else relying on these men to provide for them were sorely disappointed and had no hope for themselves. This did not bode well for William because none of these men, least of all the clan leader, would be interested in the fact that he carried an important message for Iain. He had to start planning his release in more appropriate detail. It was obvious that what would really appeal to these brigands would be the promise of easy money. He wouldn't offer that up first though, he had to lay his plan out in order to be sure that he ended up at Iain's keep no matter what the outcome.

One of his William's 'escorts', looked around the hall for their leader. When he sighted the man in question, he walked over and gave him a solid kick in the ankle.

"Oy, wha the bluidy hell is going on?" William was appalled at the insolence shown by the clan leader's men. But given the state of affairs it seemed as if no one cared about anything anyway, let alone giving the man they called leader any respect. He watched the 'leader' slowly and painfully unfold himself from the position he had passed out in the night before. When he finally stood, William noticed he was not an overly large man and certainly not a very attractive man. His nose was large and crooked from being broken too many times, his eyes were bloodshot from the excesses he obviously engaged in. William could see his dirty gray black locks hanging in greasy strands around his head and his beard full of stray bits of food. Not the picture of a man in command. William imagined that this man was the current leader of the clan Campbell solely because he must have been strong enough to beat anyone who challenged his authority.

The filthy man scratched at his groin and glared at the man who kicked him. "Daniel ye must ha' some kind o' death wish tae ha' woken me. What the bluidy hell d'ye want?"

Daniel spat on the already filthy floor, looking unconcerned and said "Angus, we found an English Lord for ye."

"Wha? Ye dinna say." Angus Campbell walked over and peered bleary eyed at William. "Well he's righ' puny ain't he? 'Ow am I supposed tae have any fun wi' tha'? He'd be dead afore I had any sport."

"Nay mon. We dinna bring him here fer sport just yet. He has some news that might be of some interest tae ye."

"Interest? Wha' could a Sassenach say tae me tha' I might find interesting? Except maybe tae beg me fer his worthless life. Is tha' wha' ye brought him for? Is it?"

Angus Campbell grabbed a passing servant "Oy ye, fetch me ale now." He stood silent and studied William while he waited for his drink. William remained still and unwavering under the glare and stench emanating from the man. When his drink arrived Angus took a long deep draught. William was quite disgusted as ale dribbled down the man's beard and the front of his tunic. This must have been a usual occurrence because once he finished the servant refilled his tankard and Angus sat down.

"Ahh!" Angus sighed as he settled himself . "Well no' wha' is this great news I am tae hear? Speak English cur!"

William raised a brow but didn't react to the insult. He had to win this man over to get him safely to Iain.

"Well, Laird Campbell, as I explained to your good men…"

Angus roared with laughter. "Ay my men have been called many a name afore but I canna rightly say I've heard them be called good men."

William continued "Be that as it may. As I told your good men I have been instructed to deliver a message to Iain MacDonald."

"Iain? That scoundrel? Wha' message do ye have fer him?"

Daniel spoke up "Eh tha's wha we asked him but he wouldna say."

"Here, ye shut yer mouth! I dinna ask ye tae speak. Keep silent." In the face of Angus' anger Daniel and the other men cringed. It seemed Angus ruled with a temper. He turned his blazing countenance back to William, who refused to balk at Angus' fury. "Now wha' is it ye were goin' tae tell me?"

"With all due respect, Laird Campbell, I was not going to tell you anything else." Angus's complexion turned an unhealthy mottled purple.

"Wha?! Are ye daft, mon? Who is playing games wi me? I dinna like games. I want some answers now dammit! I am fast losing patience with ye."

"When your men found me on your land, I informed them that I had a very important message to deliver to Iain MacDonald and the message was only for him.

No one else. I also informed your men that it would be unwise to proceed with their plan to slit my throat and make off with my meager possessions, as the message requires a response be sent back. Should such a response not be delivered within a certain time, these lands will be invaded by a large English force."

Angus listened to William's tale intrigued, but not affected. He then spoke.

"Did any of my 'good' men ask who the hell ye are?"

"They did and I told them that it was of no importance who I am. Only my message is important and its timely delivery."

"We disagree there. I think it is important who ye are because I'm no believing what ye are saying. I will tell ye what I ken is going on. Ye are an English spy sent tae find out what ye can about our lands up here for yer bastard king tae steal. While on your mission ye were discovered by my men here sae ye concocted this tale about an important message tae try and save yer own hide." Angus completed his theory with a stream of spittle onto the floor, much to William's disgust.

He said "I suppose it would take no great effort to come up with that notion, but why would I 'create' a tale of important time sensitive messages, if you were not going to be inclined to believe me anyway. Would it not make more sense for me to be begging for my life right now, rather than being secretive and difficult?" William hoped to confuse the increasingly inebriated Scot and judging by the glazed expression in Angus' eyes it seemed to be working.

"Ye know this is why I hate ye English 'Lord' scum!" Uh oh, William thought, perhaps not. Angus continued

"Ye always think ye have an answer tae everything. If ye were a true Scot ye'd be fighting me tae live. If ye were a poor English peasant ye'd probably be beggin fer yer life. But ye English Lords think we Scots are fools and tha ye can talk around us in circles. Tha is what ye are doing here an' I dinna like it one bit. Tell me why I shouldna run ye through with my sword where ye stand eh?"

Think fast! William thought now was the time to fasten on the man's greed. "Well I suppose you could kill me but I still repeat what I have told your men and now you. Stopping me from delivering my message will ensure an invasion on your lands and people. However, there is something I haven't told you or your men. I will tell only you and only in private for once I tell you this I guarantee you will regret letting anyone else hear." William looked expectantly at Angus.

"I do grow weary of this game ye are playing. But ye are either verra brave or verra stupid tae keep on with yer game. It is for pure amusement I will allow ye tae speak with me in private. Come follow me."

Angus turned and grabbed William's arm propelling him forward with just a slight twisting pressure. Angus' grip told William that he wasn't taking any chances with him or underestimating what William might do out of the reach of Angus' men. He led William to a small storeroom just off the hall and closed the door.

"Here we are here. What is it ye have tae say that is sae interesting?"

"First of all, let me say I do apologize for having to deal with all this secrecy." William nearly choked on his sugary words. He had no regard or respect for this filthy drunken lout in front of him. But he had to rely on convincing Angus to go along with his plan to get to Iain and Stephanie. "I had to keep this piece of information secret from your men. You and I are men of intelligence and position, so I can share this with you if you will help me."

"Ye ken I amna sure I will help ye until I hear wha ye have tae say. If it is as interesting as ye say then we will see."

"As I said we are men of intelligence. I truly do have a message for Iain MacDonald and it is a matter of life and death. But the interesting part is that I am not a fool, I demanded payment for being reduced to a common messenger. After all I am a peer of the realm, I can hardly be expected to exact such common activities as delivering messages without some sort of compensation for my time."

"Mmmm, keep talking mon."

"Well I have two messages to deliver to Iain MacDonald. One is the message of import and I can tell no one but Laird Iain that one. The other identifies me as a messenger requiring payment, handsome payment, at the least due to my position."

"Ye are right this does sound interesting. Wha is the message?"

"Come now, Laird Campbell. Don't make me re-evaluate my first impression of you. I said you were an intelligent man but really that is a very foolish question."

Angus laughed deeply "Ye canna blame a mon fer trying."

"I suppose not so long as we are clear."

Angus stopped laughing instantly "Actually we are not quite clear yet. What is it ye are wanting from me and why did ye tell me about the payment ye are expecting from Iain?"

"It is abundantly clear to me that unless I have someone to guide me to the MacDonald keep, it is doubtful I will be able to deliver my message on time at all. So, what I would like you to do is escort me to the keep and I will give you a cut of my payment."

"Now who is insulting my intelligence? If ye want my escort, then I expect a full half of yer payment."

"Half? That is quite greedy, don't you think?"

"Greedy? Nay, if I were as greedy as ye think I would take all yer payment. But I amna a greedy mon, I will settle for half and ye will get yer escort."

"All right then. You drive a hard bargain Scot. But you will get your half only after I have delivered my private message and received my payment. Oh yes, and after you receive your payment I am sure never to see you again. Agreed?"

"Agreed"

"Then we should be off. As I mentioned this message is time sensitive." William followed Angus as he exited the small room. Intelligent ha! He thought. The man is a drunken buffoon. All William had to do now was get to the keep and speak to Iain alone. Once he explained the situation to Iain, William felt sure he could get Iain to loan him some coin to pay Angus. William would have to pay Iain back once he got Stephanie home safely. That would satisfy everyone William was sure.

"All right men" Angus bellowed "We have a job tae do"

"Ere now, what are ye talking about?" The others looked startled as Angus strode into the hall.

"Ye heard me, ye lazy oafs! Get up and get a move on!" Angus delivered quite a few well placed kicks to various men's behinds that didn't move out of his way fast enough. All those that were sober enough to move got up and readied themselves muttering and growling all the while.

"Mark my words. There's coin involved here." Daniel muttered, reasoning that that would be the only incentive to get Angus interested or involved in the English mon's foolish errand. It didn't really matter one way or the other, if Angus was getting paid to take the English dandy, they would all see their part of the spoils as Angus always spent any unexpected windfall on a lavish feast. There would be food and drink a plenty when the job was done.

"Come on, ye lazy curs! Let us be off. We have some miles tae cover before we get to MacDonald's keep."

"Aye we ken how fare we have tae go…we travel it often eno." A swarthy man grumbled.

"Ey keep yer foul tongue in yer mouth, Ye filth. Or I'll cut it out fer ye!" Angus clipped the man with force on the back of his head for his words.

William wondered what that was all about. But didn't spend too much time thinking on it. He just had to get to Iain, explain his situation and his plan to set Stephanie free.

Chapter Thirty-Five

Stephanie worked diligently to keep the smile on her face as plans progressed towards her 'wedding' It had been a couple of days since the announcement and she hadn't stopped hearing about it since then. What had upset her the most was the fact that she had not even had a moment to speak to Iain about how they were going to end their engagement. He had been so busy trying to track down the man or men responsible for the message on the barn, that he only arrived at the keep very late. He would enter her room and before she could speak he seduced her so thoroughly and made love to her with such passion that she couldn't speak and fell into a deep dreamless sleep after reaching glorious satisfaction Then he was gone the next morning.

Stephanie endeared herself to his people by ensuring that the kitchen staff sent out plenty of food with Iain and the men he took with him, so they could continue their search without having to stop and return for food. Everyone thought her such a solicitous fiancée. But she knew that Iain would not end their engagement until the perpetrator was caught so she didn't want him to waste any time finding those responsible. So she found herself now in the kitchen listening as the cook fretted about food preparation for the wedding feast.

"M' Lady We havena got any time. We must start preparing."

Stephanie tried not to roll her eyes in frustration. "Really there is no rush. Laird Iain has not even set a date yet. You mustn't get too upset about planning anything yet. I am quite sure that once this man or men are caught, Iain will announce the date and give everyone plenty of time to prepare."

"Och, but we canna know that for sure. We must begin slaughtering the animals to cure the meat. We need to get more sugar if we are tae serve sweets to everyone. Someone has tae go to the trade ships for more sugar, that will take time."

Stephanie tried to maintain her composure when she just wanted to yell out that the engagement was fake and she was here against her will, but she smiled. "We do not want to get too far ahead of Iain's plans or we may end up causing some unnecessary expenses. Just imagine if you get the supplies for a feast now and it doesn't occur for maybe a month or two. What a waste."

The cook looked at Stephanie with horror. "Nay Lady! Laird Iain wouldna wait that long tae have this wedding. He needs tae settle his home now. It will be soon. Mark my words."

Stephanie was feeling trapped again and she snapped out her frustration. "Whatever anyone may think we will not be ordering any supplies until Iain sets a date for the wedding. No!" Stephanie held up her hand to stop the cook's protests. "There will be no more discussion about this. We will wait until Iain has made a decision and we will make do with what we can gather together in that time. That is the final word."

Stephanie knew the cook wanted to argue but couldn't. After all that would mean arguing with the new Lady of the keep and that was unheard of. That at least was one benefit to this sham engagement, at least everyone knew who she was or, more importantly, who she would be and that stopped all the speculation and whisperings about her.

After Stephanie left the kitchen, she decided to take a walk. She had precious little time to just look at the scenery since she had arrived only weeks ago. Mere weeks. How had her life changed so much? It was amazing and frightening at the same time. In that time she had fallen in love with a man, who may not regard her as enemy anymore, but still regarded her only as his instrument for peace. Her life seemed planned out but shrouded in uncertainty all at the same time. Stephanie knew that Iain would send her back to her father after everything was solved and resolved. In fact she didn't think he really believed her father was the instigator in the attacks anymore. So she knew eventually she would go home. How would she go forward from there? A part of her would have loved to insist on the marriage to Iain just to stay with him. Perhaps he might even come to love her in return.

Fool! Stephanie chastised herself. She couldn't marry Iain, it wouldn't be possible. She didn't really believe he would ever love her. He desired her, there was no question about that, but she was still English after all and there was no love between their people. Some would always regard her with loathing and suspicion and that would not do.

Stephanie found herself in the little grotto by the moss covered pond and sighed. This is where he kissed her the first time and she had become drawn to him. She sighed heavily and sat down looking at the depths of the pond dappled in the sun. It would seem she would return to her father's home and spend the rest of her life thinking about the man she loved and who had kindled such passions in her. Stephanie sighed again.

"Ye ken when I first saw ye I thought of this verra spot in my mind's eye." Stephanie spun around on her rock perch to see Iain watching her from between the two boulders. He casually strolled over to her and sat next to her on the stone.

"I could hardly speak tae ye the memory was sae clear in my mind. I thought maybe ye were some wood sprite come from this spot to play tricks on me."

"What are you doing here?" Stephanie immediately regretted her abrupt tone.

Iain slowly came out of his reverie. "I saw ye heading this way with much weighing on yer mind, sae I thought I would come and see if ye were all right. Are ye?"

"Yes I am fine." Stephanie turned her head and looked at Iain's gray eyes, gone soft silver with concern. She didn't realize he was sitting so close to her. She felt the heat rise up in her again at his close proximity.

"Are ye?" He asked softly leaning closer.

Stephanie gave Iain a rueful smile "I have to be." she simply said.

"Ah, lass, such heaviness. Let me lighten ye" He gently took her chin in his hand and pulled her towards him.

Stephanie knew she should resist but she didn't want to. She wanted to feel his kiss, breathe his breath and just draw some strength from him. She moved forward and met his kiss. The softness of his lips on hers was the balm she needed. It was a sweet and tender kiss as they slowly caressed and tasted each other.

Iain loved her sweet mouth. The innocent kiss was driving his desire for her higher because he knew what simmered below the surface for both of them. That passion subdued made him continue the gentle exploration of this fiery woman's mouth. He gently nipped and tugged on her lips with his teeth. The breathless moan that escaped her parted lips made him chuckle.

"Ah, lassie," he whispered against her mouth "We have a fire between us that never seems to get banked does it?"

Stephanie wrapped her arms around his neck "I don't care what it is between us. I just want more." She looked at him shyly with passion drenched eyes.

Iain could have shouted his pleasure to the heavens at that provocative invitation.

"Ye are such a wanton woman, Lady Stephanie. I like tha about ye." Iain pressed her to him as he bent and kissed her again with all the passion they were both feeling. The moment their lips touched their mutual desire tore through them like lightening. The attraction split through them in almost visible streaks. Hands and lips touched everywhere and they barely had time to breathe.

Stephanie was dissolving from the inside out. Iain's lips on her mouth, her neck, then soaking her nipples through her dress. All the while a hand rubbing and pressing her between her legs. With every touch Stephanie pressed herself closer to Iain. Her small gasping moans rang louder and louder as her desire reached its climax.

"Oh, Iain, don't stop!" Stephanie felt her climax rip through her as she came apart in Iain's arms.

Iain looked at the glorious woman limp in his arms. A shimmering sheen of perspiration made her skin glow. He gently swept golden tendrils of her hair back from where they had clung to her face and neck.

"God, ye really are a beauty! Yer passion takes me over and it is all I can do not tae take ye where ye stand." Iain leaned over and nibbled at her neck.

"Ahh!" She cried out "Iain, you make every part of me cry out to be touched by you. You know that. But now look at me, I am a mess and it is so hot."

"Well then" Iain said in a husky voice "Let us go for a swim lass eh?" He started to remove his clothing.

"What are you doing?" Stephanie squeaked in shock.

"Oh come now lass. Ye just came undone in my arms. Dinna be turning the prude on me now. I am saying let's go for a swim and maybe play a little more."

"Here? Out here where anyone can find us?" Stephanie unconsciously crossed her arms over her chest.

"Who is going tae find us out here? This is my place and as ye can see from the state of it, I am really the only one who ever uses it now and again. Come now, ye said ye were hot." As he spoke, Iain had been drawing Stephanie closer and closer to him.

He took nipping kisses at her while he ran his hands up her arms. Stephanie felt her desire blossom again. As he suckled her lower lip he gently tugged the neck of her mantle over her shoulders. His undressing of her was slow and sensuous. He licked the sweat touched skin as he exposed it. First her shoulders, then the swell of her breasts. He trailed his tongue between the valley of her breasts.

Stephanie groaned at his onslaught. She felt the liquid heat pooling again between her thighs. She had to brace her hands on Iain's shoulders as he dedicated himself to lavishing her breasts with such passionate attention. She nearly lost her balance as he pulled the gown past her wrists and exposed her navel. He swirled his tongue around her indentation. The sensation was gripping her again as she began to move her body against him.

"Lass ye are such a minx. Lord help me but I canna get enough of ye." He buried his face in the folds of her gown at the juncture of her thighs and breathed deeply the scent of her desire for him. "Ye canna imagine how much I want ye, how much I need ye." Iain quickly divested himself of his clothes and stood before Stephanie's heated gaze.

Stephanie finished undressing herself, her eyes never leaving Iain's naked form. Hungrily feasting on his full arousal, she held his hands at his sides. It was a useless gesture. Both knew he could move his arms at any time with the flick of his wrists. But he enjoyed her bold curiosity and did not move as she slid herself up to him and placed a deep kiss on his mouth. She sucked his tongue into her mouth then slowly drew back releasing it. She slid her body down his length until she reached the object of her desire. As she took his length into her mouth, she looked up at him, her sultry green eyes melting in passion, her golden hair around her face, she looked like an angel.

A very sexy angel. Her tongue circled his shaft and Iain bucked at the incredible sensation.

Stephanie watched Iain break out in a sweat as she laved him with her tongue. He was perfection, made for her body and that was what she wanted, to have him fit right inside her.

Iain threw his head back and when he could take no more he grabbed Stephanie's head and stroked her hair. He wanted to thrust himself forward to continue and further the ministrations of her exquisite mouth. But he wanted to be looking into her eyes as he buried himself inside her. He wanted to see the green depths cloud over with her climax. He gently pulled her away. At her protests, he didn't speak. He lifted her up and gently slid himself inside her as he wrapped her legs around his waist.

"Oh!" She exclaimed. This was a new sensation as he slowly entered her. Stephanie could feel the pressure building as she wrapped her legs around his waist and clung to his neck. Iain gloried in this position as her breasts were now at the perfect height for him to kiss. As he moved slowly to tease them both their heady passion was building at a feverish pace. Stephanie tilted her head back and her long hair, unbound in the tousle of their passion, caressed his thighs. She was hot, wet, tight perfection, and Iain was going mad from watching her.

"Iain, please!" Her breathy plea undid him as he impaled himself fully into her. They both climaxed instantly. Their cries of release mixing into one. The release was so intense that Iain was shaking slightly as he set Stephanie down in front of him. She was glowing with desire and she ran her hands down her body, luxuriating in the sated satisfaction she felt. He laughed and leaned forward to kiss her nose.

"What? Oh!" Stephanie's passion soaked eyes focused and she blushed to realize how forward she must seem to Iain. "I'm sorry…" she started but found Iain's calloused fingers pressing her lips.

"Nay my little beauty. Never apologize tae me for yer passion. Ye inflame me like no one else and I dinna want ye tae think ye owe me any kind of apology for anything we do together in passion. Do ye ken?"

"Yes" She said, suddenly feeling shy again.

"Come on then let us refresh ourselves." Iain tenderly took her hand in his and helped her over the slippery rocks into the cool water of the pond. It was only waist deep so they were able to stand next to one another. The water was soothing on their heated skin and Iain tenderly washed Stephanie as she stood gladly for his touch. It didn't take long for their desire to build again and they made love in the cool water. After they had finished they dressed in satisfied companionable silence. Then they sat together on the stones.

Chapter Thirty-Six

"Iain, we must talk." Stephanie turned and looked earnestly at him. He looked over at her. He knew what she was going to say, but he was going to do all he could to get her to see the wisdom of their marriage.

"This sounds serious. After such a memorable afternoon ye want tae spoil it with serious talk."

"No, I don't mean to spoil anything but we must talk." Stephanie had to swallow the tears she felt welling up. What was the matter with her?

Iain heard the distress in her voice. "Hush now I was only teasing. What is it?"

"Iain, I know you don't want to do anything about this sham proposal but we must. This cannot go on anymore. Too many people are becoming too involved with the planning of a wedding that is never going to take place. These people accept me now because they think we are going to be wed. Imagine how much they will despise me when the wedding is revealed as a hoax. Please, Iain. I don't think I can bear such hostility and humiliation."

Iain looked at her she was visibly upset, not because she wouldn't be marrying him but because of the people that she felt would be wasting time on something that would came to naught. He turned and looked out into the still green pond and said.

"What if it wasn't for nothing?"

"I beg your pardon?"

Iain looked at her again. "What if their planning wasn't for nothing. What if we did marry?"

"Are you daft?" Stephanie felt torn wanting to shout her agreement to wed him and knowing she couldn't. She wouldn't marry Iain knowing he didn't love her.

Iain watched Stephanie struggle to understand what he said. "Listen tae me, lass. I am thinking that we should go ahead with our wedding. Make it real, make it official. There are sae many reasons tae go forward. Our actual wedding would be the perfect strategy tae end what brought us together in the first place. I mean your father can hardly continue to attack if his only daughter is wed tae me."

Still stinging from being referred to as a strategy Stephanie lashed out. "My father is not carrying out these acts. How many times do I have to tell you that? I can't marry you for that very reason. You think he is guilty, but he isn't and I couldn't live with you knowing you always believed my father guilty."

"All right then. Let us say I dinna believe he is guilty, if we wed we would both look after our duties in a very pleasant way. I would like tae be able tae have my wife running my keep and hopefully beget some heirs from our union. For ye, ye would marry as ye ken ye must, but ye would not have tae buy a husband tae make up for yer loss of maidenhead."

"I already told you I do not want to be married."

"Ye may have mentioned that aye. But ye also acknowledged that ye were going tae have tae buy a husband."

"That was said in a moment of frustration and anger of which I seem to have a lot with you! Be that as it may. I won't pay anyone to marry me because I am not going to marry."

"Such a noble sentiment, but ye ken yer father needs family tae maintain his lands and his title. And if he dies with no heir by you through marriage doesna yer king receive his lands and title back. Does the king also not inherit ye as well as part of the property to be dispensed?"

Stephanie clenched her fists at her sides. Damn him! He was right. Once her father died, she would become a chattel, a piece of the lands and titles to be disposed of as the King saw fit. She spoke through gritted teeth "Yes, I suppose you are right on that score. Heaven forbid a woman could be left in peace on her family's lands to maintain it in her father's place. No, only a man is clever enough to do that."

"Here now. Dinna be blaming me fer the law lass. I ken full well how smart ye are but if I may continue?"

"There is more you must taunt me with?"

"I am only explaining the wise legal reasons for us to be wed in truth."

"Very well, then. What more do you have to tell me?"

"Well if ye become part of yer father's property to be dispensed with upon his death, how are ye going tae explain yer lack of innocence? When that is discovered do ye not become worthless to the King?"

"Worthless? Why you…" Stephanie spluttered

Iain was enjoying presenting Stephanie with the undisputable facts, she would agree to be his wife but he would make sure she had no argument to disagree. "Now, now. If I may. If ye are of no value tae the king, does he not just send ye out tae be 'earning' yer keep. Essentially a servant to him or someone else perhaps? Ye have nae value on the marriage market after all."

Iain knew a woman of Stephanie's intelligence would be nothing short of livid at her inability to be allowed to govern people and property after her father's death. He hoped that her frustration at the potential loss of her independence would push her into agreeing to wed him. He needed her to agree. He told himself it was to further ensure the raids stopped. It surely didn't have anything to do with knots in his belly at the thought of her leaving. Or about how he wanted to be able to grab her and kiss her senseless anytime he wanted. Iain told himself his desire for Stephanie was not what drove him to push for this wedding. His desire was just a benefit. He would desire his wife and enjoy her company, how many men could boast the same? He waited for Stephanie to speak.

Stephanie didn't think she was capable of speaking without yelling. She had no notion why Iain was insisting on the marriage. He didn't love her, but despite that he argued a strong case to go forward and get married. She wanted to be his wife. She loved him. She did. But there was so much between them she did not see how they would overcome those issues. And here he was speaking of marriage so matter of factly, so coldly, so precisely. How could she condemn herself to such a thing?

She would have to keep her love caged like a bird and Stephanie wasn't sure she could do that. But she knew in her heart of hearts that the cold truth was she would not be able to go home and live her life with her memories of Iain. She would be sold to someone. And if she had to be sold she knew the man would not be the best of men if he had to pay for a 'spoiled' wife. Who knew what sort of life she would be condemned to. The thought of it made her want to weep. But she didn't want to believe she did not have a choice. She choked out.

"I can't do this. You do not know what you are asking of me!" Stephanie couldn't look at Iain as she spoke. She did not want to look into his eyes and lose herself in the notion that she should proceed with the marriage to be with him.

"Stephanie" Iain took her hands in his and spoke gently "Ye ken I am right about this, lass. Everything I have said is true and you canna deny it. Ye said ye dinna want tae be married but since ye will have tae eventually, why not marry me? We both know we are well suited."

Stephanie removed her hands from Iain's clasp "I cannot say yes right now. Let me think about this. I just don't want to speak of it right now."

"We both know I am offering ye the most advantageous solution to our present situation. We willna speak anymore of it now. Come Stephanie it is getting late let us go back to the keep."

They walked back together in silence. Each knowing what the other was thinking. Stephanie knew she had to accept Iain's proposal if she wanted to escape what fate awaited here upon her father's death. But the marriage was not any kind of a peaceful solution for her. For all the practical reasons, having the marriage take place only made sense, but it wasn't all practical. She loved the man and wanted to be a true and proper wife to him. How could she possibly open herself to that if he only viewed her as an instrument for a purpose? How could she live in a loveless marriage when she knew now the passion that could exist between two people? In that way she would be much better off to take her chances on an arranged match. At least then the marriage would be truly loveless and she would not be suffering alone.

God! She was so embarrassed by what a simpleton she had become in her love for Iain, moping because he didn't love her. He wanted her there was no doubt about that. Why couldn't she be happy with the physical pleasure they shared and shared often?

Because she wanted and deserved more! She wanted to share her life with Iain body and soul. She had to figure out a way to get him to agree to be husband truly, not just for the sake of the raiding or for her honor. It was ridiculous to be wed for just that. There was no way they could pretend to be happy. Passion could only last for so long before it too would be diminished by an emotionless union. She needed to sit in quiet and think all of this through.

"Iain, go ahead without me. I need to be alone."

"I hope ye are nay thinking of calling off the wedding. Tis going tae happen and ye ken it, lass. There is too much at stake. I will give ye the time tae come tae realize and accept what will be. But make nae mistake, lass, it will happen." Iain gently took her chin in his fingers, leaned in and brushed his lips over hers.

Stephanie felt the lightening bolt of desire run straight through her veins again. "Ohh" she sighed "That is what I mean. I cannot think clearly about all of this when you keep kissing me like that."

"Well thank ye for the advice. I do believe then I shall keep kissing ye." Iain spoke with a smile and wrapped his arms around Stephanie, proceeding to kiss all rational thoughts from her head. His tongue deeply swept the inside of her mouth and she grasped his arms tightly to keep her balance. Then she responded with all the feeling in her heart.

He set her away from him with a smile "Remember lass, time to accept what will happen and nothing else will do." He turned and left her standing there dazed and completely without a thought in her head.

"You see" Stephanie called after him. "That is what I mean you infuriating man!" Iain didn't turn around but he waved at her over his shoulder.

After he disappeared Stephanie found a nice large tree and sat down beneath it. She leaned back and closed her eyes. Her lips still burned with the memory of Iain's kiss. What was wrong with her? A lifetime of kisses like that was nothing to dismiss lightly. And what usually followed those kisses was just as marvelous. He knew how she felt about politics, education and her own independence. Iain would never hinder her from pursuing those things that interested her. In fact he was, by going through with the marriage, not condemning her to the loss of her independence but a guaranteed opportunity to develop it. He was ensuring she could be who she was without any worries. And since she loved him he would not be sacrificing himself to her. She would continue to love him with everything she had and then he could at least be content with the choice he made. They could be happy with this marriage.

Stephanie felt the heat of the sun and the buzzing of the insects lulled her to sleep with a smile on her face. She dreamt of the happiness she and Iain could share together as husband and wife.

Chapter Thirty-Seven

Iain walked back to the keep with a smile on his own lips. He knew Stephanie would agree to all this because she really had no other choice. He felt a small measure of guilt for emphasizing how she could be used should she refuse to wed him, but he knew that would seal his plan. Kissing her also proved beyond a shadow of a doubt how smart his plan was for both of them. His little English lass was full of passion and it would be a sin to let it die out in a loveless marriage. Iain didn't give a second thought to the fact that theirs was, in essence, a loveless marriage, all that mattered was that he could settle in and enjoy her at any time and in any manner of ways. Yes, this would be a wonderful union.

He didn't notice his man of arms until he was almost on top of him, so engrossing were his fantasies of Stephanie, his soon to be wife.

"Here now" Iain said "What are ye doing mon?"

"Excuse me Laird Iain. I canna believe what I have tae tell ye but tis truth. I have just seen it"

"Aye what is it?"

"Ye willna believe it. Maybe ye should just come tae see it for yerself." The man said shaking his head.

"Out with it now!"

"The truth of it is that Angus Campbell is standing in yer hall in all his 'glory if ye can call the trail of filth and stench that follows him glory."

Iain listened to the news with surprise. Angus Campbell in his keep. He hated the MacDonald clan and vowed to plague the clan for as long as he drew breath. So far Angus had lived up to his vow. He and his ragtag bunch of followers and kinsmen were always causing problems for Iain and his people. Generally though, he had proved to be harmless for the most part. But here he was now standing in the keep of the family he swore he despised above all others. Iain was curious but only cautiously so. Too much curiosity could get a man killed in the company of one such as Angus. Iain knew he had to beware but he would find out what this turn was all about.

Iain strode inside his hall and was none too pleased or surprised to find Angus slouched at the head table making free with Iain's own ale. It took all of Iain's self-control not to walk over and beat Angus before tossing him out on his ear. Clearly, judging by Angus's demeanor, he felt he had something of interest for Iain for nothing else would have brought him here. Iain spoke in a low tone but there was no mistaking the menace lurking beneath his words.

"Angus Campbell. Well, well, auld mon. What has dragged ye out of your usual drunken stupor and brought ye in tae my home?"

"Auld! Hrumph I could still beat ye senseless and well we both know it young one so dinna be trying tae prick my temper." Angus leaned forward and glared at Iain. "Ye won't like it if ye do."

Iain was completely unperturbed by Angus' bluster. And while he was quite sure the two of them might be evenly matched in a fight, despite Angus's age, Iain was in no mood to tear apart his home trying to best the old warrior. "Mmm as much as I would like tae take ye up on yer challenge I find I shall wait tae see what ye have tae tell me before deciding what to do with yer useless hide. So, auld mon, speak yer mind and let us get on with our day without having tae spend anymore time in each other's company than is necessary."

Angus leaned back as Iain took a seat next to him at the head table. "Well, now, dinna be sae hasty. I have traveled with great speed tae bring ye this news and I have a powerful hunger, and oh aye a powerful thirst as well. Surly ye canna be such a puir host as not tae offer a weary mon some food and drink?"

Iain wanted to throw Angus out right then but something stayed his hand. His instinct told him he should play this game out. "But of course how remiss of me." Iain beckoned a gawking servant over and requested more ale and some food. The two men sat in silence studying each other until the small meal arrived. At the arrival of the food Angus dove right in and began feasting on everything he could lay his hands on. Iain watched with disgust at the spectacle next to him. Yet he did not want to interrupt Angus during his masticating, in case that should delay the meeting. So he waited until eventually Angus had slowed his eating down enough to remember where he was.

"Ah, yes." He said to Iain grandly "the purpose for my visit. Well, it is certainly an interesting one to say the least. I am currently in possession of an item reportedly to be yours."

"Well Campbell as ye ken I have many things that belong tae me and it is sometimes hard tae keep track of it all." Iain hoped to goad Angus a little. So as he delivered his comment to Angus he smiled benignly.

But rather than reacting Angus just smiled right back. "Is that sae? Tsk tsk. Must be sae difficult for ye, ye puir mon." Angus made a sucking noise through his teeth. "Tae have sae much of everything that ye can keep track of nothing. I am here, out of kindness, tae return what belongs tae ye."

Iain raised his brows and waited for Angus to continue. He didn't want to give Angus any satisfaction so, he just sat back looking very bored and waited.

Angus' face, already mottled from the alcohol he had consumed, grew even more so at Iain's lack of interest. "Right" He thundered "Down tae business. I am a fair mon and since I canna be sure that the information provided tae me is reliable, I willna ask ye fer payment until ye have inspected what I brought. If it does in fact turn out tae be valuable, I want tae be rewarded and rewarded well. Are ye agreeable tae that?"

Iain looked amused. "This is verra interesting. Ye have something ye claim is mine yet ye dinna want any reward until I judge for myself what it is worth? Come, Angus, what are ye playing at?"

"Well, truth be told, I am here more fer interest at this point than for reward, but should this be valuable tae ye then I want payment."

"Verra unusual but if I think reward is warranted I shall give ye my word that ye shall receive it. Fair?"

"Done" said Angus "All right men bring it in."

Two of Angus's men reached around the door outside and pulled someone in. At first the figure was not recognizable but then when he made eye contact with Iain, he was recognized. It was Stephanie's father! What the devil was he doing here? Iain schooled his features with great discipline. Something was a foot here. He watched as the men brought William Rockforte forward. As William moved forward Iain could see his eyes pleading with him. So Iain contented himself to wait patiently until the plot was revealed.

Angus stepped down and shoved William forward. "Well, MacDonald, here 'it' is. Says he has some message fer ye."

Iain saw William begging him with his eyes as he stood up, "Aye, my message. Well come along then, mon, I havena got all day let us be quick about this."

Neither Iain nor William spoke as Iain led them away from everyone else, to his study. He sincerely hoped that Stephanie had not returned from her walk and was still composing herself after their passionate afternoon tryst. Certainly having her father here was going to complicate matters but Iain would fix that soon enough, once he knew exactly what was happening. They arrived at Iain's study door without encountering Stephanie and Iain closed the door behind them with some considerable relief.

William spoke first "Thank you Lord MacDonald. Thank you so much for not forcing me to speak in front of that awful barbarian."

Iain waved the gratitude away. "Keep yer thanks and tell me just what the hell ye think ye are doing?"

"It is quite a long tale." William sagged wearily into a chair. "I am sorry but I have been traveling hard to get here to you and this boor managed to capture me before I got to you. So my plans had to change. I am telling you true it is a long story."

"I am waiting"

"Well it begins after our meeting. I went back home sick with worry over Stephanie's well being because despite your assurances she would be fine, I could not be certain. This is because I am not the one responsible for the raids on your people. But you are so convinced that I am, that if anything had happened you would have harmed Stephanie as you promised. I could not let that happen so I began to try to figure out how to ensure her safety and perhaps try to figure out who is the real guilty party in these attacks on both of us. Incidentally I don't believe you or any of your people are attacking me. I think it is someone else." William paused to judge Iain's reaction.

Iain just spoke. "Continue"

"I thought if I could make my friends and neighbor's believe I was off to raise an army to attack you to get Stephanie back I would then come here and offer myself as your hostage in exchange for Stephanie. Once doing that and seeing her safely home, you would see who came to attack you while I was 'away.' Then you would know it was not me responsible for this cowardly behavior."

"And what of Angus. Did ye tell him all of this?"

"Angus thinks I am bringing you a very important message for which you are going to pay me handsomely. But I had to tell him that the message required a reply within a certain time so he would bring me quickly. Also I told him that the message was for your ears alone. So thankfully you sequestered us here so I could inform you of what is going on."

"Well, nae offense, Lord Rockforte but the panic in yer eyes told me ye dinna want tae speak freely in front of Angus. And now I see why." Iain sat down across from William. "Now, let me respond tae all ye have told me. First of all there have been some developments here recently that have forced me tae alter my own plans since we last spoke. I will explain that later. I do have tae say that I agree with ye. I dinna think ye are the one responsible for the attacks."

William interrupted. "Wonderful! So you will let my daughter go then. I will stay until we flush out the true guilty party but first I can see to getting her home safely."

"Dinna interrupt me sir. And no Stephanie definitely canna go home now."

"But…"

Iain held up his hand "Let me finish. As I said recent events have forced me to change my own plans and now yer being here may further both our plans to catch the culprit. We had someone slaughter a lamb and write a death threat on a barn door a few nights back. Unfortunately, because Stephanie is English suspicion fell on her immediately. In order tae protect her I had tae announce that Stephanie was with me that night and could nay have done the deed."

William paled visibly beneath his beard. "And tell me Laird, was she with you?"

"Aye, sir, she was."

"Oh my God! This cannot be happening. What have you done to her? You have seduced her." William jumped to his feet seething with rage.

Iain rose up with his own anger and spoke in quiet deadly tone. "Because ye are my betrothed's father I shall take no offense with yer manner and tone. But kindly remember ye are in my home, show some courtesy."

"How can you stand there and speak to me in such a manner? You have seduced my daughter when she was at her most vulnerable and you expect me to take direction from you?"

"Sit down Lord William and let me finish." Finally, after a moment's hesitation William sat down with barely controlled anger. Iain continued. "As I said she was with me that night and since I was forced to reveal that publicly I had to rescue her reputation. So I told everyone that she had just consented to be my wife. That way all suspicion was removed from her and her reputation was not destroyed. In fact, it seems to have been raised somewhat and I find that my people are very excited about planning the wedding."

"I am in shock." William put his head in his hands. "First you take my daughter hostage and threaten me, then you seduce her and now you tell me you proposed to her? Did she accept you truly?"

"Well, nae exactly. I dinna actually propose tae her, I had tae tell everyone I did to protect her. She was under threat by the angry mob" Iain realized how mad the whole situation sounded and he felt some measure of pity for Stephanie's father trying to understand it all.

"What? A mob? And you haven't proposed? Christ, man, are you trying to kill me?"

"Well there is more tae tell. I may not have actually proposed tae Stephanie but I have decided that we will wed regardless."

"So she has accepted then?"

"Nae exactly."

William laughed "Ah now I know she is all right if she is still as stubborn as always then she has not suffered at your hands. I should thank you for that at least. So she won't accept you?"

Iain sheepishly admitted "No" He looked at her father and said "Lord Rockforte, I amna proud of what I have done. But I did everything as I felt was best for my people. I am even less proud of taking advantage of yer daughter at a time, as ye say, when she was most vulnerable. But after all that I find that I want verra much tae marry yer daughter. She, however, is adamant not tae wed. With yer presence though she will surely now wed me."

William looked carefully at Iain. "My being here is not likely to change her mind if she doesn't want to marry you. And I cannot force her to."

"I dinna expect ye tae. But if the marriage has yer blessing then she may see some reason. Look I ken full well that my taking her maidenhead has made her nigh useless in the marriage mart."

"True, rather crude, but still true."

Iain went on "And I know that her age combined with her loss of maidenhead has ensured that you would have tae pay a hefty price for her tae be wed. At first I thought I would buy her a husband because we both know she has tae wed for the sake of yer lands." Iain paused

"Go on." William said

"Then I found I couldna stand the thought of Stephanie being sold tae someone else. Someone who doesna understand or appreciate her spirit, but is wedding her only for what she brings tae his purse. I couldna do that to her even tae protect her. I have lain with her, yes, but I also know her to be intelligent and kind. I wouldna see that be taken from her because of my weakness where she is concerned. Forgive me for speaking sae plainly but I feel ye should know."

William said nothing. He just sat and studied Iain until finally he stood up and clapped Iain on the back. "So that is the way of it then. I wish you luck." At Iain's confused look William continued. "Listen MacDonald, I will not force Stephanie to wed you. But the fact that you are willing to wed her to right the wrong you have done to her, makes me see that you will look after her. Also it comforts me to see that you understand my daughter more than any other man who has met her. And rather than being put off by her intelligence and independent spirit, you want to marry her to protect her from harm from another man who may not see the value of her qualities. Although I think this is admirable sentiment, I know you are going to have a hard time convincing her of this. So if you are truly serious I gladly give you my blessing but if she really refuses you, we shall have to accept her refusal. Do you agree?"

"Aye, I shall agree. But she will accept the marriage if ye give yer blessing. She isna a fool."

William laughed again. "Good luck to you then. So what do we do now? I have to pay Angus off. We have been here too long for him to believe that what I had to say wasn't important. Before you say anything though know this, I have nothing to pay Angus with at present but if you could provide the reward I will repay you as soon as this affair is sorted and I can get home again."

Iain shook his head. "I will pay Angus and ye willna pay me back."

"MacDonald… Iain you are marrying my daughter I can't allow you to pay for my foolishness in getting caught by these brigands."

"It is precisely because of the fact that I am going tae marry yer daughter tha ye willna pay me back. I need ye tae help me convince Stephanie tae wed me. I ken ye willna force her but surely ye can assist me in swaying her."

"I love my daughter but she does not always know what is best. First can't we agree then that I shall pay you half what we know Angus is going to be stealing from you? Agree to half and I will help you with Stephanie as much as I can."

Iain laughed "Ye are as much a brigand as auld Angus. Fine we will agree to half but only because it is more important for me tae convince Stephanie tae wed me than it is tae argue a few coins with ye."

"Good then what is it you need me to do?" William rubbed his hands together because no matter what had gone on before, Iain was committed to marrying Stephanie. William could also see that she would be safe with Iain, since he already treated her with kindness. What did it truly matter that they had lain together before marriage.

What mattered now was that his lovely daughter would be, safely and happily William suspected, wed.

"Nay much really. I just want ye tae agree tae what I tell yer daughter in her presence. Can ye do tha?"

"Agree to what you say? Well that might be all right but I wont agree to anything that might hurt her."

"Of course no' I am quite sure that if ye give her yer blessing she will agree."

"Come then, let us be rid of Angus and then go in search of Stephanie. I have not seen her for so long and I have been so worried and anxious to see her face."

"Actually, sir, I would like ye tae remain here until the evening meal. Ye can amuse yerself here for a while, can ye no?"

"You ask much young man. You stole my daughter once from me and now you are attempting to do so again. But since I am asking much of you I will remain here until you fetch me."

"There is more I need from you."

"More! What do you mean?"

Iain knew William was not going to like what he was about to say but he had to say it anyway. "I need ye tae remain here with the doors locked."

"Locked? You jest I hope?"

"Nay I dinna jest. But that is not all. The doors must be locked from the inside so that Stephanie canna happen tae find ye before I am ready."

"Locked from the inside did you say?"

"Aye. But I would need yer vow you wouldna open the door should she come by looking for me."

William scowled "You have my word. Now let us get this over with. I want to see my daughter as soon as possible."

"Good then I will get rid o' Angus and find Stephanie."

Iain turned and locked the door leading to his bed chamber handed William the key then left the study. He waited at the door until he heard the key turn in the lock.

With strength of purpose he went back downstairs to get Angus out of his keep. Once Angus and his men were gone Iain would be able to focus on his renewed plan to wed Stephanie.

Not surprising, when he reentered the hall Angus was exactly where Iain had left him. Filling his face with food and ale at a rate that had many of Iain's people staring in disgust. With barely contained relief Iain addressed the pathetic man before him. "Angus, well mon as much as I have sae enjoyed yer company, I am thinking tis time for ye tae leave."

Angus barely glanced at Iain as he continued to gorge himself. He spoke with his mouth full. "So am I tae understand that yer lost item was worth yer while?"

"As a matter of fact aye." Iain replied

"Good then. What are ye going tae give me for safely delivering it tae ye?"

"Mmm. You are a big fighting mon, aren't ye?" Iain smiled coldly. "Shall we duel? If I win, ye leave here with nothing and ye dinna ever come near my lands again."

Angus rose to the challenge. "An if I win?"

"Ye can name yer price tae what ye think the auld mon was worth tae me."

There was no reason for Iain to engage in this course other than the satisfaction of putting Angus down. The man was vile and Iain hadn't had an opportunity to deliver a good thrashing to anyone lately. He just wanted to do it. He hoped Angus would accept the challenge in his usual arrogant way. Iain watched as Angus rose from his seat and with a great belch he replied.

"Hah! Would be my pleasure tae trample ye. An' I am looking forward tae naming my price. I am thinking ye'll have a hard time paying it." Angus strutted himself off the dais drawing his sword as he came.

Iain continued to smile his same big smile. "Dinna fear Angus, I can pay yer price whatever ye name it."

Servants hastily drew up benches and chased the men watching to the side of the hall. None of them doubted what the outcome would be. They just hoped Iain would not spill much of Angus's blood in the victory.

The two warriors met in the center of the room swords drawn. Angus spoke first "Tis going tae be a fine day today tae lay ye out upon yer arse, lad"

"We shall see who is on their arse, as ye sae eloquently put it, when this is over, auld mon. Begin when ye are ready."

After a moments pause metal met metal with a sonorous clang as the two men wrestled each other for victory.

Despite his age and recent feast, Angus was still a decent warrior and fighter. Mostly he had many years of experience to draw from rather than any particular skill. But he was still not as good as Iain who had youth, his own experiences and a fine skill level with his sword. Iain met every stroke of Angus's sword with his own and managed to keep Angus moving, watchful of where his next point of attack would be.

Many people had gathered to watch, drawn by the sound of warriors in battle. The men pushed and drove each other back and forth. At some moments one obviously held the advantage over the other, but neither wanted the sword play over too quickly. So they toyed with one another.

Finally, after some minutes Iain decided he had had enough playing with Angus. He wanted to teach the man a lesson and get him out of his home as quickly as possible. With a quick motion Iain twisted Angus's sword arm with the point of his sword so Angus was forced to drop his sword and suddenly found himself with the tip of Iain's blade at his throat. Sure enough he was just enough off balance that when he stepped back away from the sharp point, he landed squarely on his rump. Iain repositioned his sword at Angus's throat again and said.

"Sae it seems ye are on yer arse auld mon. Now I am going tae let ye up but ye are going tae get out of my hall and off my lands right now. Ye and yer men have ten minutes tae clear out of here and anyone taking longer is taking his life in tae his own hands since I will be sending my own men tae follow ye out. Should ye take tae long my men are free tae cut anyone where he stands. Now go before I change my mind and cut ye down right now."

Angus hauled himself to his feet. "Ye are a bastard Iain MacDonald. This is nae the end of this."

"Maybe not but I will end it if I see ye on my lands again Angus. Get out!" Iain watched as Angus lumbered out of his hall with his rag tag bunch of half hearted followers. He then motioned some of his own men standing nearby to follow them out to make sure they left quickly. It was a task the men were glad to do, as they left, each one smiling, hoped that they might have the opportunity to spill some Campbell blood. With only the briefest of thoughts Iain hoped that Angus and his men moved quickly.

Chapter Thirty-Eight

Fergus strolled up to Iain as he sheathed his sword. "Quite a display brother. Feel better?"

"A little but nae much. I am as frustrated as ever. But, recently, I have had some good news and hopefully this will help me proceed with my wedding much quicker than I hoped."

"That so? Ye may be feeling better about things but I see someone who is not." Fergus looked over Iain's shoulder pointedly. When Iain turned he saw her. Damnation what was Stephanie doing here now? Then he took a closer look at her. She was as pale as death and frozen in place, eyes wide with fear a half eaten apple forgotten in her hand.

"Och, hell!" Iain exclaimed.

"Good luck with yer speedy wedding plans." Fergus chuckled at his brother's retreating back.

Iain stood in front of Stephanie. "Lass? Lass? Tis over now. All is a right." She made no acknowledgement "Sweeting can ye hear me?"

Slowly, ever so slowly, Stephanie focused onto the sound of Iain's voice. Then she acknowledged him full force. "You bloody bastard!" She said in a thin voice just before she collapsed in a faint in his arms.

For only a moment Iain was slightly confused. Then he gathered his intended and carefully bore her upstairs to her chamber. He placed her on the bed and gently lifted a stray strand of hair from her face.

Was this the woman he had made passionate love to only hours before? Now here she was looking so frail and achingly beautiful. He wanted to touch her all over again. Ruefully he sighed and lay down on the bed next to her. Cradling her in his arms he began to sing old folk tunes his mother used to sing to him. As he sang softly he stroked her head.

It wasn't long before Stephanie began to stir. She opened her eyes and it took her a moment to see Iain looking at her. But when she did, she came awake full of fury.

"You beast! What was the meaning of that awful display in the hall?"

Amused at his fiery bride to be, Iain replied "Well I dinna think it was sae awful. I think I displayed my great skill as best I could fighting one such as Angus. Dreadful man that he is, it is hard to look one's best when one's opponent is drunk and stuffed with food."

"How dare you make jokes?" Stephanie hissed jumping off the bed, her green eyes flashing fire. "I could kill you myself for what you did."

"Come now love, dinna be sae angry. What has got ye sae upset?"

Stephanie hesitated. She was so upset because the damn fool man could have got himself killed. She wanted to shout that at him and see what he thought of that. But she couldn't let him know how much she cared for him. She couldn't.

"Stephanie?"

"You want to know why I am so upset?"

"That is what I asked ye"

"I am so upset because you and that great oaf have torn up the hall as the servants are readying for the meal. All for a bit of sport you have made extra work for those who have enough to do already. That is what I am so upset about."

Iain laughed "Liar"

"I beg your pardon?"

""Ye heard me lass. Ye are lying. I saw yer face before ye fainted ye were scared."

Iain held up his hand as Stephanie began to protest. "Dinna bother tae deny it because no matter what ye say I willna believe ye." He stood up and moved in front of her. "Besides, I dinna want tae fight. Not today. I have a wedding present for ye."

Stephanie's jaw dropped. In shock she spoke very slowly. "What…are…you…talking…about?"

Iain cupped her face and pulled her closer as he imitated her speech. "I…have…a…wedding…present…. for…ye."

Stephanie stared in disbelief "Are you mad?"

"Why does everyone keep asking me tha? No I amna mad."

"You can't have a wedding present for me. We are not going to be married. Why won't you listen to me?"

Iain could see how frustrated Stephanie was but he was not going to give up. "Careful, darling, ye look like yer about tae start stamping yer little feet and throwing things around."

"I do not have tiny feet nor am I going to start throwing things around. No matter how much I want to. And we are not going to get married."

Iain lifted the hem of Stephanie's dress. She slapped his hands away. "Ye are right, ye dinna have small feet, my mistake. Now listen ye are nae tae worry about a thing. Ye will get yer gift at the evening meal. Ah, dinna interrupt. Right now I have tae go and make sure Angus has gone with his men."

Iain didn't give Stephanie a chance to respond he kissed her possessively on the mouth and was closing the door behind him before she even knew what had happened.

"Ooh! That man!" Stephanie couldn't care one bit how ridiculous she sounded talking to herself. Iain made her just mad enough to do many things she wouldn't normally do.

"Who does he think he is ordering me about? Carrying on like we are getting married, when we are not. All this after nearly getting himself killed." Stephanie stopped and leaned heavily on the back of a chair. He could have been killed today! That was one of the worst moments of her life, seeing him there fighting in earnest. She had felt like her heart had stopped beating. Iain with sword drawn was not what she had expected to see after her return. She was planning to find him and tell him again that it was not an option for them to wed and there was no way he could force her to go through with this insane plan.

Then, seeing him there, she knew she couldn't wed him as much as she loved him without dying more each day trying to protect her feelings from the lack of his own.

But Stephanie could not understand Iain's insistence they were to be wed, even going so far as to get her a gift. He would not listen. As leader of a clan he could not sacrifice himself to her out of a sense of duty and obligation. She couldn't allow it. She would have to be more insistent and persistent than he.

Stephanie decided to go and see if Iain had returned to his chambers. She left and made her way to the door of his study. The door was locked. What was going on? Stephanie rattled the knob and pounded on the door. Nothing. Then she thought to go into his bedroom and try the entrance there. Same thing. She began calling to Iain to open up.

William heard his daughter's voice and almost wept with relief. As he listened to her William was amused to hear how riled up she was and getting more so by the minute. It took all of his discipline not to run out the door and hold her to him. But listening to her go on he realized she was in a fine temper about something.

The fact that she was just like her old self made William wonder if this strange marriage wasn't really the best thing for both of them. Stephanie obviously felt comfortable enough with Iain to show her true self. She was not cowering or intimidated, not that she would be by any man. But she was certainly allowed more freedom than any prisoner he had ever seen. That made him realize that Iain didn't actually consider her a prisoner anymore. Although judging by his daughter's current mood and by the fact the two had already been intimate, William wondered if Iain had ever really considered Stephanie a prisoner.

It seemed like too much to hope that these two could marry and be content. Iain certainly wanted to marry Stephanie. William was anxious to speak to his daughter and find out how she felt. He walked over to the door as she was still calling to Iain and laid his palm on the door.

"I love you my girl." He mouthed so that she wouldn't hear him. Then he went back to the chair to sit and wait for the moment to make his presence known to Stephanie.

Stephanie felt as though her voice was going hoarse calling to Iain. He was ignoring her, she knew it. She had heard him moving on the other side of the door and fancied she had heard his breathing. She pounded on the door one last time before calling out again. "This is not over Iain. You cannot ignore me forever. I will have my say and you will listen. Just see if you don't!"

After delivering her message, she thought she should really go and see what she could do to help prepare for the meal. Maybe she could find Judith. She always managed to cheer her up.

As Stephanie entered the hall she saw Iain coming in with Fergus and Judith. He was so handsome he stopped her breath. She wished she could go to him right there. But such a display of affection would not be well received while they were only 'engaged' even so she longed to do it.

Iain saw Stephanie standing there staring at him. He could almost feel her drawing him over. With a sense of mischievousness and wickedness he decided to tease her a bit.

"Excuse me a moment please." He said to Fergus and Judith. Without waiting for an answer he crossed the hall barely stopping he picked Stephanie up and kissed her deeply in front of all who were there.

"Oh Fergus, that is so marvelous" Stephanie heard Judith exclaim.

"Hello, my sweet." Iain drawled.

Stephanie flushed pink. "What are you doing?"

"Kissing my bride to be."

"I am not your fiancée, well I guess I am but only in name."

"Soon to be my name."

"Stop being so exasperating." Stephanie hissed. "We are not going to get married, make no mistake. You can't force me."

As the two wrestled verbally back and forth everyone thought they were witnessing an intimate tete a tete between the betrothed couple, so they all smiled.

"Come now, lass, we musna get too carried away here with yer emotions. Remember people are watching."

Stephanie quickly schooled her features. "Fine, then. I would like to have a moment of your time if you don't mind."

"Of course, my darling. What can I do for ye?"

"Stop that!"

"What, darling?"

"That…calling me darling and sweetheart or any other endearment."

"Why shouldn't I address my lovely wife to be with tender terms of affection?"

"Because I am not going to be your wife, you oaf! Now stop that right now!"

Iain laughed and led Stephanie into the solarium. "Okay, lass, ye wanted tae speak tae me. What would ye like?"

"I want to know what is going on?"

"With what exactly?" Iain asked innocently.

"Why are your chambers locked? At first, I thought that you were in there ignoring or avoiding me."

"But then ye saw me in the hall. Tha' must have taken the wind out of yer anger."

"Well yes as a matter of fact. Wait that is not the point. I was certainly going to let you know how rude you were being but of course seeing you there you obviously weren't ignoring me. So why are the doors locked? What is going on?"

"Nothing is going on. But if ye must know, I told ye I had a wedding gift fer ye."

"Yes, yes, I know."

"Yer wedding gift is in my study."

"Locked in the study? But why?"

"Obviously you were walking right into the study so if I hadn't locked the doors ye would have discovered yer gift before I had the chance tae present it tae ye."

"What exactly is my wedding gift?" Stephanie asked suspiciously.

"I want tae surprise ye sae I canna tell ye."

"Iain, listen, as I stood at the door I was sure you were ignoring me because I heard someone in there. I heard movement and I am sure at one point I heard someone breathing."

"Ye did?"

"Yes, I did and I was so sure of it I was coming to find someone with keys to let me in so I could give you a piece of my mind."

"Well, then, I guess we can both be happy that I am not locked in there. For sure that scene would not have been verra pleasant, especially for me. So all is well, let's go."

Stephanie grabbed Iain's sleeve as he walked away. "No, all is not well, Iain. Who is locked in the study?"

"I told ye it is yer gift."

"You can't keep someone under lock and key for my amusement, because I am not amused."

"Who said that it was 'someone' locked up there?"

"Don't tell me that no one is locked in there Iain. I heard the breathing."

Well his wife to be was nothing if not persistent. He knew she would never guess that her own father stood on the other side of the door. But he did need to distract her from even potentially figuring out anything. He had to come up with something fast.

"Come now, ye dinna want tae spoil the surprise?"

"Iain…" Stephanie's tone was akin to a mother warning her child of impending trouble and that was exactly how frustrated she felt. It was as if Iain was a young boy caught in the act of doing something wrong yet not admitting to anything.

Iain let out a large sigh of disappointment. "All right then, ye have ruined my surprise. What is upstairs locked in my study is…"

"Well go on. Stop this nonsense."

"It is a dog!" Iain flung his arms wide and split a large grin.

"A dog? Impossible. What I heard breathing was no dog. It was way too large to be a dog!"

"Of course, it is a large dog. I got ye a verra large dog for protection at the times when I am away."

"Iain, please tell me you are teasing me."

"Nay lass. I amna teasing ye. Yer gift is a verra large, verra hairy dog." Iain chuckled to himself at the thought of her father and comparing him to a dog. If Stephanie believed she was getting a dog just wait until she saw her new 'pet'. This was all too much fun.

"What am I going to do with a large hairy dog? I don't really like dogs. I don't mean to sound ungrateful but Iain you assume too much." Stephanie began wringing her hands. On top of everything else now she had to worry about a new dog. Well, no use complaining she had better just start coping.

"Iain" she said matter-of-factly "You cannot give me a dog as a wedding gift because I have to keep reminding you we are not going to be married. So you need let that poor beast out of that room. I mean really what if the poor creature needs to relieve itself. Oh my goodness! What if it has already done so?" Stephanie was appalled at how absolutely thoughtless and careless Iain seemed to be about her 'wedding present' She continued pleadingly. "Iain please you must let the poor dumb animal out. What is the matter with you?" Stephanie was shocked as she looked at Iain and saw him laughing so hard tears were rolling down his face.

"Iain? Are you all right?" Iain did not seem in his right mind as far as Stephanie could tell. She couldn't believe he was carrying on so. Finally when he caught his breath he reached out for her and pulled her into his arms.

Stephanie tried to push him away but he didn't loosen his grasp. She looked up and him her eyes blazing green fury.

"Iain MacDonald, you are such a cruel brute! I cannot believe you would find an animal's discomfort funny. Animals are completely at the mercy of the people taking care of them. And you are not taking care of the beast." Stephanie could still sense Iain's amusement. He looked down at her his eyes twinkling in merriment. But he said.

"Stephanie, I promise ye the puir dumb beast is well taken care of. Ye will see. Can ye trust me in this?" He cupped her face with his large hands and leaned in close "I promise ye lass, ye will see for yerself this evening how well cared for yer gift has been." Iain leaned in and kissed her.

He meant only to give her a reassuring kiss but his desire for her quickly became inflamed and he deepened the kiss. Her taste intoxicated him, but made more so by the fact that she would soon be his wife. Stephanie quickly relaxed into his kiss and her own ardor was aroused making Iain wish he could take her right then and there. Reluctantly, he broke off their heated embrace.

"Lass, go now and get dressed for the meal. But go now before I take ye where we stand."

Stephanie slowly focused and brought her reeling senses under control. She was disappointed Iain had ended that glorious kiss, but he was right no one could eat until Iain was seated. So if she didn't arrive he wouldn't start without her. His final words penetrated her haze.

"Iain don't be ridiculous."

"Make nae mistake lass, I could make love tae ye here and now."

He set her away from himself and gently pushed her to her chamber. "See ye at the table, bonny one." Now he had to go and speak to William about their plan. Whistling as he went down the stairs to reach his own chambers, he thought for certain that this would be a night to remember.

Chapter Thirty-Nine

Stephanie didn't waste time dressing for the meal. She needed as much time as she could get to remove her 'wedding gift' to a more appropriate area of the keep before everyone started eating. She was still worried that the animal had suffered from its confinement. Even though it would not remain in the keep, she wanted to make sure it was all right. She was so busy worrying about the dog that she ran straight into Iain's chest at the base of the tower stairs.

"Lost in thought?" Iain asked teasingly

"As a matter of fact, I am very worried about the dog if you must know."

"Never fear, lass, after ye have had yer meal ye can have him."

"After?" Stephanie exclaimed incredulously. "Oh no Iain! Surely you cannot mean to keep it shut in that long. He may get distressed and tear up the room."

"Hardly" Iain snorted "If he tore up the room I would tear him up."

Stephanie's eyes widened in shock. "What?! Have you completely taken leave of your senses? This is an animal not a human. It doesn't know any better. The beast is in an unfamiliar place with unfamiliar smells and sounds. It may have already begun to mark the territory. But you cannot blame the animal for acting on its instincts."

"I can and I will. This animal knows better." Iain insisted stubbornly. "Now this talk is foolish. If ye must have the beast slobbering all over ye at the meal then that is up to ye. I just dinna think ye would want the dumb animal beggin' ye for food at the table."

"No. It is all right. It is better to begin training it now rather than waiting. Animals need repetition so the simplest tasks can penetrate their ignorant heads."

"I couldna agree with ye more. I will go and fetch the beast once ye are seated."

Iain led Stephanie to the table and seated her next to his chair. Fergus and Judith were already there. Both greeted her cheerfully as Iain seated her. Then he went to free the 'dog' from his study. Iain returned a large smile on his face.

"All right, my darling" Stephanie shot him a warning glare but Iain continued "I have released the dumb animal. But it is not too late for me to go and tie him up outside or put him out with the other dogs."

"No, it is fine. I had best begin training him now." Stephanie braced herself for the large gift in store for her.

"Here boy" Iain whistled "Come"

From around the corner Stephanie's father appeared looking rather perplexed at his 'summoning' Stephanie's heart stopped in shock. She was sure she must be dreaming so she sat still so as not to wake up. William had no such delusion he strode straight over to her chair, picked her up and held her as tight as he could.

"My girl"

Stephanie gasped and came back to herself. It was his voice and it was his smell. It was her father! "Papa" She could barely breathe the word as the tears started flowing. She fell against him and breathed deeply. But she didn't think she would be able to let go of him or stop crying. Gently her father sat her next to him. Iain said nothing. He just sat down and watched them. Throughout the meal Stephanie could barely touch all the wonderful food as she kept stealing glances at her father. She rested her hand on his arm the whole meal afraid to let him go.

Once the meal was finished people began leaving and Stephanie was able to steal some private time with her father. Iain hoped that William would do what he could to convince Stephanie to go forward with the wedding. Reluctantly, he took his leaving saying.

"Lass, Lord William I am sure ye both have much catching up tae do sae I take my leave of ye. Stephanie try not tae keep yer father up tae late he is probably verra tired after the journey he has had."

Stephanie replied tersely "I haven't seen my father for such a long time, but I do not think I am so ignorant or cruel to keep him awake should he need to take his bed."

"Now, sweetling, dinna be sae prickly. I mean nay offense." He kissed the top of her head and stroked her hair. She felt a twinge of shame for being such a shrew to Iain. But she really did want to talk to her father alone. After Iain had left she also received a scolding from her father.

"Come, now, Steffie. I taught you better than that. You were quite rude to your betrothed."

She sighed. "I know father. I know you did but I was just so anxious to get time alone with you. And, by the by, you must know by now that Iain is not really my betrothed."

"I do know it started out that way. But I also know that the lad does want to wed you."

"Father, you have to help me make Iain realize the foolishness of this. He will listen to you."

William snorted "Steffie that is the last thing he will do. He is a stubborn Scot and he wants to marry you."

"Never mind that foolishness for now. Papa, how did you get here? What are you doing here?"

"I was coming to help you my girl, but I am afraid I didn't exactly do the best job of it."

"What happened?"

William related his movements of recent weeks events since returning to find Stephanie missing from the keep. He finished up "I was coming here to offer myself as hostage to let you go. Then I would stay here in your place so Iain could see that I was not responsible for any attacks against him."

"Oh, father. How could you be so reckless? You could have been killed traveling alone through Scottish lands. I hear tell of many Lairds who kill or maim strangers just for entertainment. If they had also discovered you were English you are most definitely lucky to be alive."

"Very true, my girl. I was actually caught by the Campbell's but fortunately their greed is much stronger than their desire to kill for sport. I managed to convince them to bring me here instead."

"Father! How could you? What would I have done to find out you were killed trying to save me?" Her eyes glistened with unshed tears as she reached out and held his arm.

"Sweetheart, you cannot be so concerned with what I or others are doing. You must look after yourself. That brings me to some other matters we need to discuss. I want to tell you that I think you should reconsider your opposition to this marriage."

Stephanie jumped up out of the chair. "What? Father, no you cannot be serious."

William put his hand on her arm. "Calm yourself. You need to look at this proposition from a more practical sense, girl."

"Father how can you say such a thing? He kidnapped me to force you to do his bidding." Stephanie was shocked to hear her father speaking like this. Of all people, she felt sure her father would support her refusal to wed Iain. She had thought he would be her ally to break the sham engagement and take her back home. Her father took her hand.

"All that may be so my girl but we have talked in depth upon my arrival. Let me tell you no one could have been more shocked and appalled when MacDonald told me he wanted to wed you. But then he told me that you two had to announce yourselves for your protection. That seemed reasonable enough but Iain wants to wed you even when the puzzle of this raiding is solved and the matter laid to rest."

"You see then it is absolute nonsense for me to wed the man based on the fact that he had to tell everyone in order to protect me. When there is no more need for protection then there is no need for a wedding. It is utter nonsense to continue with this."

"No, not utter nonsense, anything but, in fact. Your marriage would solve so many outstanding dilemmas. First of all, if our families were to be united through marriage then whoever is behind the attacks would have to stop. It would no longer be an option to try to convince everyone that families were raiding each other."

"Wait a minute, father." Stephanie held up her hands to speak. "You mean to tell me that after your talk with Iain both of you finally realize that the other is innocent of the raids?"

"We both realized that we had come to the same conclusion, once we had a chance to speak, yes. But we both had our suspicions after the meeting he arranged when he took you hostage."

"Well there you are. You said it yourself I am a hostage. It is completely irrational for me to marry a man who took me against my will."

"That is not so, Steffie. Men have often taken brides by force or stealth when it seemed prudent to do so. After all a wedding forced or otherwise in the eyes of the church is sacred. But, my girl, he took you, though not by force as you suggest." At Stephanie's blush he continued. "Come now, Steffie, you are no young miss anymore, but I do think you are willing. Am I right?"

"Father I cannot talk about this with you it isn't proper." William pulled his daughter into his embrace.

"Sweetheart, I am sorry you do not have your mother to speak to about such matters but I think we are both old enough and intelligent enough to discuss the important matter of your future candidly."

Stephanie hid her face in her father's rough tunic. "This seems so strange. However, even if I have been a willing participant that does not make the marriage right."

William set Stephanie back and looked into her eyes. "Daughter, I wish only the best for you but you have to realize how you have compromised yourself with MacDonald. You cannot hope to make a match for wealth and status, you are no longer a virgin and you cannot lie about that. That does not leave you with many men that I would like to consider you to be married to. I would only agree to a match with someone who would be kind to you. I know you have thought about the results if you are not married before I die. I neither judge nor condone what you and Iain have done but there are consequences that cannot be ignored. I have spoken to him and he genuinely wants to do right by you Stephanie. He does care for you."

"He cares for me only out of an obligation for these events and his seduction of me." Stephanie paused and dared to utter the words she really felt. "He marries me out of duty not love."

"Love?" William snorted disbelievingly "Love? Come now, we both know how unrealistic love matches are. Sweet girl, I do not mean to be unkind but you are unlikely to find many men who will love you for your intelligence and knowledge. That is my fault. But MacDonald, admires your intellect and does not feel threatened by it. Truly, my girl, you two could not be better suited."

"Father, I know I sound foolish but I want a marriage like yours and my mother's"

"You are still so young. Ours was not a love match. Not at first."

"But I thought you both loved each other deeply. You were so happy together."

"Not at first, no. The marriage was arranged by our parents. I had no desire to be saddled with a shrew and she had no desire to be with a man she knew nothing about. But we were more than fortunate that we did not fight our parents' will and we came to love each other very much over time. Your mother was a remarkable woman and I cherish every moment we had. You could have that with Iain you know."

"No, father, I don't know. And your story is not enough of a reason for me. He receives nothing for wedding me. You know that."

"He will receive my lands when I die and once you have a son he will have an heir. That is not nothing. Ah, why do you not see reason? I think you are just being stubborn. But I tell you this, if you do not wed the man you would be a fool indeed. I do not want to force you but if you are refusing because you want love then I may be forced to change my mind."

Stephanie was shocked. Her father usually let her make up her own mind. But he was convinced Iain would make a good match and was willing to go so far as to consider forcing her to wed despite his promise not to. Her affair with Iain obviously had changed her father's mind about forcing a marriage. Maybe both men were right. Iain wasn't a cruel man. He seemed to enjoy their conversations, when they weren't arguing. They were most definitely attracted to one another. Perhaps this is what she had set herself up for at best when she went to Iain's arms so willingly. Would another be so kind, especially knowing she had given her body to someone else? Deep down Stephanie knew she couldn't hope a stranger would accept her as Iain had, despite their unusual meeting. But the whole affair seemed so hard to accept she didn't want to settle and she didn't want Iain to just settle as well.

She looked at her father. "I know you feel strongly about this but can you not see how I feel about it? I do not want Iain to come to hate me because he felt he had to marry me."

"Do you know what I believe? I hear you talking about him and his feelings but you have not once come out and said you didn't want to marry him because you couldn't stand him. Nor have you offered any of your own feelings. It seems you already care for him at least a bit my girl. Don't you?"

Stephanie's shoulders slumped. "Yes, father. I cannot lie, I do care for Iain. But that makes this all the worse knowing he doesn't care for me. I am going to have to hide my feelings and live in a one sided marriage."

"Again, I remind you what you would face marrying anyone else. But now taking your feelings about Iain into account marrying him could not be better. You already have a tendre for him, and he for you or he would toss you aside and not give a thought to your future prospects. Come, girl, don't be so stubborn."

"I know you are right, father, but now I can't do this to myself or to Iain. Surely one of us is going to end up miserable." Stephanie wailed.

"Or you can choose to be happy and maybe make your husband happy as well." William took Stephanie by the shoulders and continued, "Steffie, you can make this a happy marriage if you choose to and in time Iain will come to care very much for you, maybe even love you but that is all up to you."

For a moment Stephanie considered continuing this circular argument with her father but there didn't seem to be much point anymore. He was for the marriage and so she would have to be as well. She would simply have to make the most of it. So she offered a small smile.

"Father, we could continue to say the same words to each other all night but you must be tired. So I shall marry Iain as you both seem so determined that I do and as you say it is up to me to make the best of it."

William beamed at his daughter. "That's my girl. This is the perfect answer to everything. All will work out in the end. You will see. You are right though I am sorely tired so I will retire and see you in the morn."

"Do you have a place to sleep? He hasn't put you in the prison has he?"

"Come now, child, put your suspicious animosity to rest. He has given me his old chambers as I understand he has recently moved."

At Stephanie's blush William laughed "Tis all right now, especially since there will be a wedding. I am very happy now and am looking forward to the celebration. Now you go to bed. I imagine your Scottish Laird is anxious for news from you." He leaned forward and kissed his precious girl on the forehead. "Rest well, my child. You will come to believe, in time, that this was the best choice for you. Not because you are no longer valuable in the marriage mart, but because you have someone who cares for you."

"If you say so, father" William watched his grown daughter head up the stairs to her chamber where he knew Iain would be waiting. He smiled to himself at the innocence of the young. These two would do very well together and he suspected their feelings for each other were much stronger than either realized.

Chapter Forty

It was driving him mad! Iain wanted to go down to the hall and demand to know what Stephanie and her father were talking about. He hoped to God that William was aiding his cause with Stephanie and not weakening it. He couldn't be sure. But he decided he would marry the stubborn woman even if he had to lock up her father until she agreed. He was almost ready to call some men to secure William when Stephanie finally entered.

She did not look happy at all and it tore him up. Iain thought it best to let her tell him what had transpired in her own time.

Stephanie was a little surprised to see Iain in the room but he had said he was moving to her chambers. Her chambers, ha, all the rooms were his and he could be anywhere he wished without her agreement. As she entered the room she noticed he had stoked the fire and lit some tapers so the room was warm and cozy. It touched her that he had done such a small yet thoughtful thing. His voice interrupted her reverie

"Would ye care for some warm wine lass?"

"Mmm? Uh yes please." Stephanie jumped as he spoke. Now that she knew she was going to wed him she suddenly felt awkward in his presence. Everything had changed. It was up to her to inform him and she guessed it would be better to let him know now rather than later.

"My father and I have talked in depth," she began, Iain held his breath and his hand stilled bracing himself for what followed. He just knew he would do whatever he had to, to proceed with the wedding. It all depended on her.

Stephanie still couldn't look at Iain as she spoke. "He is completely in agreement with you."

That was good Iain thought as he waited. William was a voice to Iain's cause, but was he effective that was what Iain still waited to hear. He wanted to shout to get her to speak but she seemed very reluctant. She sighed

"So it seems there will be a wedding after all." Iain released his breath and found he wanted to rush to her and scoop her into his arms. He was so pleased. Outwardly he remained nonplussed.

"Tis a good thing lass." He said quietly as he handed her the wine. Stephanie forced herself to meet his gaze as she took the cup. The glow of the fire warmed his eyes to molten silver. She couldn't really tell what he was thinking though.

"So you and my father say; but I don't feel that way."

"Lass, I know yer father said he wouldna force ye. So, if ye agree tae the wedding, what is it that makes ye so sad?"

"Actually you will be glad to know that my father says ours is a perfect match. So perfect a match that he told me he would force me to marry you if I did not agree."

Iain put his arm around her and pulled her close stroking her head with his large calloused hand. "Ah, sweetling, I am sorry tae hear that. He swore tae me that he dinna want tae force ye. But if he finally agrees the marriage is right, why do ye not see it too?"

Stephanie couldn't help it, she started to cry. She couldn't speak, she just kept crying.

"Hush, Hush" Iain stroked her face and kissed her head. He showered small kisses all over her face gently wiping the tears from her cheeks.

It was too much for Stephanie, she just wanted to be with him. With a boldness she didn't know she possessed she grabbed Iain's face and pulled him into a deep bone melting kiss, into which she poured all her unspoken love for him. For as long as he would have her she would give all of herself to him.

Iain was taken aback by the passion in Stephanie's kiss. But only momentarily before he returned her kiss with matching heat. In just seconds the two were so lost in each other they were oblivious to all else. They made love with such intensity they nearly devoured one another. When both reached their climax simultaneously, they were breathless with emotion. Both knew that what had just transpired was more than just the physical act.

It was a desperate need to be connected instantly and intimately once the decision had been made by both of them to carry forward with the wedding. It was as if they were branding each other with their passion to make their union bindable with their bodies. Spent with satisfied exhaustion both Iain and Stephanie were rocked to the core with what had just taken place.

Chapter Forty-One

Stephanie awoke the next morning her body slightly sore from the many times Iain pleasured her. A blush rose to her cheeks remembering the seemingly endless number of times they both found their release so exquisite it seemed other worldly. That must be what heaven was like. Stephanie giggled at her irreverent thought but secretly, she was convinced there was some truth to it.

She rolled over as she stretched the stiffness from her muscles. Half hoping to find Iain stretched out beside her, she wasn't really surprised to find he wasn't there. It was a foolish notion to expect him to lie abed with a full keep to run. Reluctantly, she knew she had to rise as well.

Stephanie slid out from the warm bed. As she dressed for the day her skin tingled at the memories of every one of Iain's caresses each time the material brushed her skin. The memories of their lovemaking made her smile and luxuriate in how alive Iain made her feel.

And now her father was here. He was here! Stephanie half feared she imagined seeing, hearing and touching her father last night. All the joy though was scarred slightly by his words about the marriage between Iain and herself. Did he really believe their marriage would work or had he also seen the political advantage to the union? Stephanie sighed as she finished dressing. It didn't matter what her father's reasons were, all that mattered was that he said he would make her marry Iain if she tried to refuse. That hurt since he had promised he would never do that to her. But Stephanie knew he did have the right as her father to force a union, and rather than ruin their relationship she had agreed. In some respects it was a good thing she loved Iain since she would not have to bear living with someone she couldn't stand the sight of.

She snapped out of her thoughts. She had taken too long, everyone would be waiting. Stephanie hurried down to the hall, hoping that she had not held anything up. When she arrived many people were still eating. Iain and her father were talking very jovially together. Their easy camaraderie shocked Stephanie for a moment as she remembered Iain's hostility and suspicion towards her father at their first meeting. She was amazed at how easily miscommunication could cause wars among men, but how easily reasonable dialogue could end them.

Her father and Iain noticed her entry. Iain stood and spoke.

"Good morrow lass" Iain walked over with a large smile, leaned over and kissed her possessively in front of everyone gathered there. He started to guide her to her chair when Judith sprang up and spoke.

"Oh, no, you don't Iain. Stephanie stays next to me since we are going to be busy with the wedding so soon. Congratulations, Steffie. I welcome you as my new sister."

Stephanie could feel Judith's happiness in the strength of her hug. "Now sit. We have work to do in short days."

Stephanie was slightly bewildered. "What do you mean days?" She looked at Iain and her father, who were smiling broadly at her.

"I have got permission from the church tae wed ye on Sunday lass, sae that yer father may be present with ye at the service."

"That is right my girl. I want to see my only child wed and the church has granted permission."

"Wonderful" Stephanie said with some sarcasm. "But can we be ready that quickly?"

"We will be lass. Watch this." Iain turned and faced those still gathered in the hall "My good people." He called until everyone's attention was on him expectantly "Excuse my interrupting yer good feast, but I have some news. Joyfully I announce tae ye all that the church has granted me and my lovely fiancée special license tae wed on Sunday."

There wasn't a moment's hesitation as the whole hall erupted into cheers and shouts of congratulations. It took a few moments for Iain to gain their attention again and for the cheers and murmurs to quiet.

"I thank ye good people for such kindness. But there is a problem. The Lady Stephanie's father is here for only a short time and it would please me tae show him what kind of feast and celebration we can honor his daughter with, tae show him true Scot's hospitality. But I canna do it in such a short time without yer help. Can ye help me?"

Again the rafters shook with the people's enthusiasm. Stephanie was still bewildered with their seeming acceptance of her. She was overwhelmed at how excited and keen they all seemed to be, now lost in conversation with each other about what they were going to do for their Laird and his new Lady.

Iain continued "As this celebration honors both Lady Stephanie and her father Lord William, I shall sit tomorrow with my brother Fergus and make note of any contribution ye wish tae make sae that everyone may contribute without any confusion. This shall be a day tae remember!" Amidst the shouts and toasts Iain sat down and gently pulled Stephanie to her seat next to him. He looked at her and smiled before he turned to speak to Fergus and Stephanie's beaming father. It was only a moment before Judith's voice penetrated Stephanie's daze.

"It is rather overwhelming isn't it?" Judith was smiling broadly. "Steffie, I am so excited! Your wedding will be magnificent if Iain's people's happiness is any judge."

Stephanie could only smile at Judith as she continued on about the plans for Stephanie and Iain's upcoming nuptials. Judith began describing what needed to be done for Stephanie's dress.

As all the excitement and revelry continued through the evening no one noticed the dark figure in the corner by the doorway. Poised to slither out quickly should anyone notice. As people spoke of the Sunday wedding the menacing man's eyes narrowed in cruelty. His plan was not going as he had hoped. It seemed he was going to have to take more serious actions. He needed to take action quickly though, before the wedding took place. At any cost there must not be any kind of alliance between Rockforte and MacDonald. He had worked too hard to see all his efforts laid to waste. Suddenly the shadowy figure knew what had to be done. There would be no wedding if there was no bride. It was a damned nuisance though, he had wanted to marry the chit himself to secure his position and claim. But there was naught to be done about that and perhaps he could work this new course of action to his benefit. Yes he could still get what he wanted he just needed more patience. It was getting so much harder but the prize at the end would be worth it. Once his plans were complete he would be as powerful as the King himself but more so because he was not going to be afraid to 'deal' with anyone who stood in his way, friend or foe.

Smiling to himself he turned and slipped back into the night to finish his dark plot.

Chapter Forty-Two

The fire glowed warmly in the chamber but Stephanie couldn't see or feel it. She was getting married in a few short days. Should she be as excited as everyone else seemed to be? She knew she should be happy to be marrying the man she had grown to love, but it was all happening too fast. She could not seem to grasp everything as quickly as it was occurring.

Iain came and stood behind her wrapping his solid arms around her. "Hie lass. What is the matter? Ye seem miles away."

Stephanie leaned back into the warmth and strength of Iain's embrace. "I just feel like this is all a dream and I am going to wake up any moment in my own bed, all of our time together existing only in my dreams."

Iain turned Stephanie to face him. "Well, then, do ye think this is a dream?" He leaned down and kissed her with such fervent ardor Stephanie was sure her blood had stopped flowing to everywhere else except the core of herself. Iain broke away suddenly watching Stephanie sway in dazed passion.

He asked again "Is that a dream then, lass?"

"Oh, Iain, no, but if it were I would just hope to die now so I would never have to wake from this feeling."

Iain laughed. "No minx, ye canna die until I have finished what we began here."

There was a knock at the door.

"What?" Iain growled and went and threw the door open. A buxom serving girl stood there holding a tray. "Excuse me, Laird, I've just brought ye some wine before ye retire."

"Thank ye, now be gone tae bed." Iain had the feeling that he knew the girl from somewhere. That was ridiculous. Of course he knew her, she was a servant. He laughed inwardly at how his desire for Stephanie seemed to dull his own wits. He poured them each a goblet and they drank in silence. Finally Stephanie spoke.

"Iain, I want you to move to the chambers next door." She braced herself for his displeasure which came soon enough.

"What? Nay, lass, I willna. I will stay here." He looked rather like a sullen boy, but Stephanie continued

"Really Iain. I am going to marry you on Sunday. But I do not feel right sharing a bed with you until then. My father is here and it doesn't feel proper."

"We have shared more than just a bed since ye got here, lass. It doesna make sense for us tae be apart now. Yer father knows full well I have bedded ye an' done so more than once."

"Ohhh" Stephanie groaned and turned very pink. "That just makes it worse! What must he think of me?" She grabbed Iain's tunic. "Please Iain, please. I know that you think I am being unreasonable, but I just want to do this properly."

"Well we havena been proper yet, why start now?"

"Because, Iain, I am my father's only child and I do not want him to think less of me or you."

"Me? Why would he think less of me?"

"Since you cannot sleep in another chamber until we are wed, he might think you weak and undisciplined."

"If I sleep anywhere except by your side, I think he will consider me weak, knowing what he knows of us." Iain grumbled knowing he would have to relent before Stephanie became any more upset. This was important for her for some reason. He had to keep his eye on the fact that she was going to be his wife on Sunday. Then on that day he would never let her sleep without him as long as he could help it.

"Please, Iain." Stephanie laid her head on his chest. "Please." She whispered.

"All right, lass, dinna fash yerself sae much. It is not good for ye." He stroked her hair until she had quieted. Then she looked at him with her beguiling green eyes.

"Thank you, Iain. I will make this up to you. I will be the best wife you could hope for. I promise. Dutiful, obedient..."

"Now, lass, let's no get carried away. I will be content tae have ye as my wife. Warts and all. Now go tae bed." He kissed her sputtering indignation and turned to grab the flagon of wine grinning sheepishly. "I suspect I shall need some assistance tae get tae sleep myself."

"Thank you Iain. I lo..." Stephanie stopped herself just in time before she made the biggest mistake of her life and blurted out her feelings to Iain. She looked down. "Good night. Sleep well."

Iain sighed. "Good night, lass." He softly closed the door behind him.

Stephanie walked over to the door separating the two of them on shaky legs and leaned against the closed door. Suddenly, she felt rather dizzy and heavy limbed. She thought it must be due to the stress and upheaval of the last few weeks. She willed herself to remain steady. Surely this strange feeling wasn't all just stress. Something was wrong but she didn't know what.

With increasingly unsteady legs Stephanie stumbled over to the bed where she lowered herself slowly on top of the blankets. She lay completely still in the hopes that the dizziness would pass. But the swirling continued until her ears were ringing and there were points of light dancing on the inside of her eyelids. She felt truly terrible. Just as the blessed relief of total blackness swallowed her she whispered Iain's name.

Chapter Forty-Three

Iain sat with his feet propped on the grate staring at the flames. He idly swirled the wine in his goblet. He had the flagon by his side with the intention of getting blind drunk. But somehow he just didn't think that was going to help his situation. Sunday could not come soon enough. Then he would teach his stubborn wife that she would not be able to keep him from her room, or most especially her bed.

He stared into the flames. His head was feeling foggy and he was having trouble concentrating. It seemed ridiculous to imagine that he was being physically affected by his separation from Stephanie. Surely his unrequited desire was not addling his brain. Regardless he was feeling groggier. He guessed it was probably time to turn in anyway since he and Fergus would be organizing the mayhem tomorrow of everyone trying to contribute to his wedding. It was heart- warming that his people were so genuinely happy about his upcoming marriage. But more importantly they appeared pleased with his choice of bride. Everyone wanted to show their love for their Laird and Lady with their participation in the wedding preparations. He hoped he would be much more clearheaded for the crowds in the morning. That was his last thought as he fell onto the bed and complete blackness enveloped him.

Chapter Forty-Four

The night was still and black like the thoughts of the figure on the bed. The ominous shadow slithered through the door and over to the sleeping form. Ha! What luck! Only 'she' lay there. This was going to be even simpler than he had planned.

Deep in her sleep Stephanie stirred. She felt the malice in the room and began to waken. Quickly, the figure brutally covered her mouth with a gloved hand. The impact on her face brought Stephanie to full consciousness. What was happening? Someone had her pinned. She began to try to cry out and struggle against the bruising pressure on her face.

"Be still or I will have to strike you." The cloaked figure hissed in her ear.

Stephanie recognized the voice! It wasn't possible! But as he pulled back she looked at his face. Good God it was him! It was her neighbor Eduard. What was he doing here? And what was he doing to her?

"Keep still it is time for us to go. I had hoped you would still be sleeping but, no matter, you will cooperate, wont you?"

Stephanie's eyes flared glowing green as she determined he wouldn't take her without a fight. She drew as much strength from within herself to struggle against Eduard's cruel grip. She had to get away.

"Not going to cooperate, my little pigeon?" Eduard whispered, momentarily taken aback by her earnest struggles. "No matter you will cease this behavior at once. Thank God I do not have to wed you now. You are much too troublesome." Stephanie didn't see the first blow coming but she surely felt it. The pain in her face stilled her struggles.

"Ha! That is much better you bothersome wench. One more well placed blow and you will be silent." This time Stephanie watched as Eduard balled his fist and struck her full force in the face. She lost consciousness before the real pain washed over her.

Eduard didn't waste any time binding her hands behind her, then binding her ankles. He flung Stephanie over his shoulder and peered into the hall. Thankfully the keep was silent. Nothing was moving except Eduard as he crept down the stairs barely moving he slithered out the hall and through the door.

He made his way to the gate where the guards still slept having tasted his drugged milk. He spat on them as he passed. Disgusting heathens. None of his men would dare neglect their duties or they would feel the whip.

He paused a moment to deal the men a sharp blow to the head with the hilt of his sword, to be sure they didn't awaken too quickly. Eduard continued down the hill, his unconscious burden unmoving on his shoulder. He flung Stephanie over the back of his horse and mounted behind her. He knew exactly where to go next. Angus would not dare betray him for the money he would be paid. Also, Angus knew that Eduard's cruelty ran deeper than his own and that Eduard wouldn't hesitate to destroy Angus should anyone find him before he was ready.

Chapter Forty-Five

Iain woke the next morning with a monstrous headache. Surely, he couldn't have had that much wine to drink. When he checked the flagon, it didn't seem he had had that much. Strange. He shook himself awake, washed and dressed. He wanted to go and wake up Stephanie but he resisted the impulse. She was probably exhausted, poor lass. Best let her sleep as much as possible before their wedding day.

He went down to the hall feeling better at the thought of the day ahead. He was one day closer to being married. He met Fergus in the hall and they sat down together to begin the 'list'

"Ye ken I am going tae bash ye on the practice field for this, don't ye?" Those were Fergus's words of greeting to his brother.

Iain grinned unashamedly. "Ye can try but it is unlikely ye'll do anything but take my beating."

"Hrumph. I owe ye a sound thrashing for making me participate in this pre-wedding escapade. Why are ye doing this anyway?"

"Everyone wants tae help I am hoping that this will keep the event organized. Without that we will end up with confusion and hurt feelings. So this seemed like the most sensible approach."

"Well I am not sure how ye think I should be involved in this. Where is your bride to be anyway? Isn't this what she is supposed tae be doing?"

"She is resting and nay she is not supposed tae be doing this. I just want her tae focus on getting herself ready and nothing else."

"Seems tae me that since she is sae reluctant tae wed ye, it would be better tae occupy her mind with details like this sae she doesna have tae reflect on how little she wants tae wed."

Iain glared at his brother. "Ye are helping me, end of discussion."

Fergus sat heavily down in his chair. "Lucky me." He grumbled.

The two men sat and listened as people came forward and stated their intended contributions. Iain then recorded their names on the list he was keeping. It was a long and rather tedious task, but they didn't let their frustration show as every person who came forward was full of cheerful enthusiasm, without exception. Iain was about to call a break when he saw Judith coming towards them, looking frantic.

"Iain! Iain! Something has happened." She said breathlessly as she came to the table. She looked near to tears as Fergus put his arm around her shoulders to comfort her.

"What is it love?" Fergus asked her gently.

"Oh… Stephanie is gone!" She wailed.

At everyone's startled gasps Iain spoke quickly. "Nay, nay, dinna worry, she's fine. I let her sleep this morn. She was right tired out last night. She is probably still sleeping."

Judith looked around at all the people crowded there and said softly "No, Iain, something has happened. Can we go somewhere so we can speak in private?"

Iain wasn't worried but apparently Judith was so he called out to all gathered that they should have a break. He asked servants to serve people where they stood or sat so everyone could keep their place in line. Once his people had settled and were served some refreshments, Iain led Judith off to his study. There they found Lord Rockforte peacefully reading some of the books.

"Ah, good." Iain addressed him. "Ye are here. This concerns ye sae ye should stay and hear here this as well."

William looked up from his book. "What concerns me? What is going on? Did you find the bastard responsible for the raids?"

"Find who?" Judith asked "No we are looking for Stephanie."

William still did not look bothered. "Oh well, she is around here somewhere I am sure. But she is not here with me."

"What is wrong with you? Men." Judith said with great exasperation. "She is gone and no one knows where she is. No one has seen her since last night. We need to search for her. Something bad has happened. I can feel it."

"Come now, sweetheart." Fergus said soothingly

"Don't you sweetheart me you obstinate man. Now all of you sit down and listen. No one is to interrupt me until I finish or there will be hell to pay."

Seeing Judith so riled up the three men sat down and waited for her to speak.

"This morning I was supposed to meet Stephanie to do her dress fitting. I have been working on her gown since you first made the announcement of your engagement. Anyway I waited for her but after an hour I thought I should see if she was even out of bed yet. I went into her room but she wasn't there. No interruptions I said." Judith held up her hand as Iain began to speak.

"The blankets had such a disheveled look to them but the bed was not slept in. I am sure that she struggled. I think she has been kidnapped."

William jumped up red with anger. "What? Again? What is going on MacDonald?"

Judith looked stunned. "Again? What does Lord Rockforte mean again?"

"Never mind love it is not important." Fergus said hoping to divert his wife from the topic.

William continued to glare at Iain, who was still in stunned silence and not paying his betrothed's father any attention.

"Oh my God!" Judith suddenly exclaimed. "Now it all makes sense. You kidnapped Stephanie and brought her here against her will. No wonder she didn't have any belongings nor looked like she had traveled to meet her husband to be. She was a mess that day if I recall. How could you?"

Fergus knew his wife was furious but there was no time for recriminations for past regrettable actions. "See here. You speak of such things you know nothing about Judith. Keep silent we can speak of the matter later once Stephanie is found."

"Don't you dare take that tone with me Fergus MacDonald. I just cannot imagine you doing that to someone. It is just too cruel. What were you thinking?"

"I was doing what was asked of me by the clan leader and if Iain asked me I would do it all over again. He had his reasons and at the time they were the best under the circumstances. Now stop this at once until we find Stephanie. If she has been taken, as you suspect, then she is the priority nothing else. Is that understood?"

Judith and Fergus angrily turned from each other to see William demanding answers from Iain. But Iain was still deep in thought.

"You bloody well speak to me now, man! I want to know what has happened to my daughter. Are you involved in this again? Answer me."

Putting aside his frustration with Judith, Fergus went to William and tried to calm him.

"Here, Lord Rockforte. Just wait a moment, Iain is thinking. He is no ignoring ye. Sae dinna get sae angry. This is nae the time tae be fighting one another if Stephanie is truly in trouble."

William was settled somewhat by Fergus's words. Though everyone could see he was still simmering with rage. After a couple of moments more of silence, Iain finally spoke out.

"Damn me. That was what was wrong last night. Dammit! How could I have not realized?" He turned to face everyone, his face a mask of anger.

"Fergus we need to suit up the men and start a search."

"Right." Fergus turned and left without slowing down.

Judith spoke out. "Iain I think everyone should be involved in the search. Why just your warriors?"

"Dinna get upset again, Judith. It is simple. Stephanie was most definitely taken against her will last night and when I find her I expect a serious fight tae get her back."

"A fight? Then you can count on my presence." William said. "But I just have to ask, you really had no hand in this at all?"

Iain frowned. "Nay. The only hand I had in this was being careless and unobservant."

"What do you mean?" Judith asked.

"Last night Stephanie and I were brought wine by a servant. At the time something bothered me but I dismissed my misgivings. It wasn't until just now that I remembered. She works at the tavern. She was not a servant but I have seen her on occasion when I have been in the establishment. When I left Stephanie to sleep, I sat up and drank the wine, which had to have been drugged. I didna have that much but I felt stone dead drunk and barely managed tae make it tae bed last night."

"You were both drugged?" William asked "Did my Stephanie have much? What if it was too strong and killed her?"

"I dinna mean tae be cold but if Stephanie had died, whoever it was wouldna have taken her. They would have just left her where she lay. Sae in my mind the good news is she must still be alive."

"Fine. Now where do we find her?"

"Come, I want tae go outside tae see if I can find any clues tae where she might have been taken."

"Do you think they will return?" William asked as the two men hurried outside.

"Well tae be honest until I ken why Stephanie was taken I canna be sure what these people will do next."

"I suppose so. Yet something tells me if this event was directed at you there would have been more damage done. This is all very strange."

Iain stood and surveyed the landscape. Finally, he spoke,

"I can tell ye whoever did this dinna want tae be found. There is no sign of their exit here."

"So how would they have left?" William asked.

"I'm afraid they will have left out the front gate, which after morning activities will make the track nigh impossible to follow."

"Ahh. There must be something we can do." William groaned in frustration.

"I dinna ken if this is good news or bad, but since Stephanie was taken out the front, I am quite certain she is with only one person. I shall have tae find the guards who were on duty tae find out what they saw. Are ye ready tae go? After we speak tae the guards, we will begin our search around the outside of the keep into the village."

"I am ready to go lad. When we find Stephanie I want someone to pay for this. I am ready."

Iain finally understood the anger that fueled Lord Rockforte. He felt it himself. It would be hard to explain to Stephanie's father at the moment how Iain fully intended to kill the kidnapper and anyone else involved, personally. First they had to find her. God help those that took her. If there was one hair harmed on her head, Iain was prepared to tear them apart with his bare hands.

Both Iain and William strode with angry purpose through the keep, leaving startled people in their wake. The muttering of speculation as to what had made the Laird and the bride's father so angry had some curious. So when Iain and William arrived at the gatehouse they did not notice the small crowd that had followed them.

"Who was in charge of the gates last eve?" Iain bellowed without pausing for breath. The men gathered there turned and felt a frission of fear at the Laird's tone and demeanor, so they were struck silent for a moment.

"Well?"

The sergeant came forward. "Laird MacDonald I was about tae send for ye. A situation has arisen and coupled with yer unexpected arrival, I think something is verra wrong."

"What do you mean mon?" Iain asked

"Well, sir, this morning we found last night's gate sentries unconscious in the guardhouse. Judging by the over turned jug and cups, I suspected they had gotten drunk. But upon closer inspection the jug contains only milk. However I think tha once they were unconscious they were both hit on the head. Look at the swelling."

Iain noticed the two men sprawled on the ground and looking at where they lay it did not look like they had just collapsed from too much drink. They had been dragged and dumped in the corner. True enough when he looked further he could see how they had been hit.

"Come with me." He said to his sergeant as they stepped outside. It was then that they saw the crowd gathered there.

"On second thought." Iain said "Let us go back inside and keep the others out and away from the door."

""Ye two heard the Laird." The sergeant barked orders at the two closest guards.

"There are some foul deeds afoot here and I dinna think yer men were at fault."

"What do ye mean Sir?"

"Lady Stephanie has disappeared."

"WHAT? From the keep?" The sergeant was visibly upset with the news and briefly Iain felt a swell of pride that Stephanie had already inspired his people's loyalty. The sergeant continued. "Then we must go and find her!"

"I agree." William spoke up. "So let us saddle up and move quickly. We are wasting time here."

Iain stood before William and laid his hands on the old man's shoulders. "Nay, we dinna waste time here. I need tae know before we ride where tae go. There is too much land tae cover. We must take some time tae get as much information as we can before we start looking. Looking in the wrong place is going tae be the real waste of time."

William locked eyes with Iain. "Yes" He sighed "You are right. I know."

"We will find her sir. I give you my word."

"Right then. I follow you."

Iain was relieved and sincerely hoped that William would remain patient. "Now sergeant, what can ye tell me of what transpired here?"

"Well, Sir, as ye can see two guards are down and no one else saw anything untoward last evening."

"I dinna ken sergeant if these men will regain their senses tae tell us more. Both were hit verra hard after they were drugged."

"Who would do such a thing?"

"I suspect the same person who drugged the wine Stephanie and I drank before we retired."

"By God! We must find the culprit and get some answers."

"Well I ken who delivered all our drinks but what I dinna ken is why, or on whose orders. Come we need tae go tae the tavern. Ah Fergus, brother, yer timing is impeccable."

Fergus arrived with saddled horses and men at arms behind him.

"Sergeant" Iain said. "I need ye tae stay here with yer men and guard the keep. I dinna ken if there is anyone else in danger here but I need tae know they are protected while I am gone."

"Aye Sir. Ye have my word. We will protect the keep."

"Good mon. I hope tae see you soon with my bride. We have a wedding tae celebrate."

"Hurrah" said the sergeant as he went to tell his men of their orders.

Iain turned back to Fergus. "Thank ye, Fergus. We need tae ride down tae the tavern and seek out Rosie."

"What for?" Fergus asked as Iain got onto his mount. They all quickly headed for the village.

"Because for reasons unknown as yet, she drugged the guards' milk and my wine. She is somehow connected and might be able tae provide some clue as tae where we need tae go to find Stephanie."

"How do ye ken she was responsible?" Fergus asked

"She brought the wine to our chamber last night. When I saw her I knew something was nae right but I couldn't put my finger on it."

"Why would she take the risk? It is verra unlikely that ye wouldna have recognized her eventually. Why wouldn't she have had one of yer servants deliver it?"

"My guess is tha she was acting on someone else's orders. Orders that carried some sort of threat to them if they were not carried out precisely and successfully. Only that would have made her take the chance herself. I am just verra angry with myself that I dinna recognize her sooner as I could have helped her and ended this all before it happened. When I find those responsible Fergus, I am going tae kill them."

They arrived at the tavern and were dismounting when they heard a woman's shriek from within. As they barreled through the front door the barman pointed through the kitchen out the back.

"Ere Laird. Rosie's just caught sight of ye and run straight out the back."

"Go!" Iain said to Fergus as he sprinted out the back. Iain saw Rosie running. When he called out to her he saw her hesitate then fall to the ground weeping.

When he reached her he could see she was a sobbing heap. She looked up at him and cowered. "Oh please, Laird Iain, have mercy. Dinna kill me. Please dinna kill me." She kept weeping and repeating her plea over and over as Fergus lifted her to her feet and held her in front of Iain.

"Kill ye? Why the bluidy hell are you carrying on sae Rosie? Ye must tell me what has happened sae I can find Stephanie. Why would ye think I am going tae kill ye?"

"Because I delivered the drugged wine tae you and the milk to the guards. I helped the man who has taken your bride to be."

"Rosie ye need tae tell me what happened. We have to find Stephanie."

"Well it was the about a fortnight ago, just before that message was found on the barn, when I noticed this stranger come in tae the tavern. He was always cloaked, kept tae himself and sat so's that ye could never get a verra good look at him. In fact he always took great pains no tae be in good viewing light."

"Damn!" Iain said with frustration "Go on."

"Well as I said he always kept tae himself. Oh and he was a good tipper. Nae sae much as tae stand out but still left some good coin. Then one evening on my way home, he stopped me. He told me he had a job for me tae do tae earn some extra money. I told him I wasna that kind of woman and tried tae pass him. He seemed rather disgusted with the notion of bedding me but he stopped me nonetheless." Rosie looked beseechingly at Iain. "I tried tae refuse him I did. But that was when he threatened me."

"Again he is predictable with his tactics. Rosie ye get ahead of yerself." Iain said gently "What did he ask ye tae do?"

"He asked me tae give the guards and ye some drugged draughts. I refused repeatedly. He said that he would drug the drink but he wanted me tae deliver them.

I wanted nae part of that and I told him so." Rosie's voice caught in a sob.

"He said since I was nae clever eno' tae do it for coin, then he would have tae resort tae more distasteful means tae convince me. But when he told me what he would do he surely dinna seem that disgusted at the thought."

"What did he tell ye he would do Rosie?" Iain asked

"He told me what he would kill my babies if I dinna deliver the milk tae the guards and the wine tae ye and Lady Stephanie."

"Hush Rosie. I amna blaming ye. But I do need tae know who I am dealing with. He and possibly others took Stephanie. I have tae know what may be happening to her." Iain tried to calm Rosie but she was too upset.

"I'll tell ye what kind of mon ye be dealing with. No man at all, he is a devil."

"Rosie, did ye see him again?"

"Aye, last night after I had delivered the drinks, he was waiting for me here at the tavern."

"Did he say anything else? Perhaps mention anything about his plans?"

"He did not say much. Only that he was surprised I had been successful, since the last Scot he had hired turned out to be a drunken old fool."

"Rosie, thank ye." Iain absently patted the woman on the shoulder. "Take yer children up tae the keep an stay there. Tell Lady Judith all ye have told me and tell her ye need protection until I have caught the man. One more thing. Did he ever mention any partners or people working with him?"

"Nay Sir, nothing more than complaining about the drunken Scot."

"All right go then and dinna leave the keep. Ye most of all here could still be in verra grave danger."

Rosie's eyes welled with tears. "Thank ye Laird Iain. I am truly verra sorry for this and for nay coming tae ye sooner. I was just afraid of what this stranger would do. Wait I remember one thing. This beast spoke with an English accent."

"Thank ye Rosie." Iain said as the woman hurried away to gather her children and get to the keep. "Well that last bit of information is exactly what we were looking for." Iain spoke thoughtfully.

"Why is that Iain?" William asked.

"I ken of one 'drunken Scot' in this area, who has always had that reputation. Fergus I think ye ken who I mean, do ye not?"

"Aye brother, tis Angus Campbell ye think of."

"Aye Angus Campbell. Come on we ride tae Campbell's keep ad end this once and for all."

All the men cheered and rode forward with grim determination glowing from their eyes.

Chapter Forty-Six

Stephanie came to consciousness slowly. Her head ached horribly and she felt queasy. She was disoriented, and when she tried to move she found herself bound and gagged. With a groan the memories of the night washed over her.

"So the princess awakens does she?" Stephanie's eyes flew up to see Eduard standing over her. She furiously tried to kick out with her feet but he stood just out of her reach.

"My, my such a revolting display of temper from a 'lady' who is supposed to be manor born. I guess I should be glad that I have decided not to wed you." Eduard leaned forward over her. His face became ugly and twisted as he spoke to her.

"Your father teaching you the ways of a man's world. You may be beautiful in body but you are ugly as a woman."

Bastard! Stephanie thought to herself. It was all fine for him to insult her when she couldn't speak back and let him know what she thought of him. She wondered what he was going to do now.

"Ere now. Dandy mon, we need tae finish here." Stephanie's heard the Scottish burr but didn't recognize the voice. That was a good sign. She supposed whoever it was in league with Eduard and his plot was not associated with Iain. Eduard turned

"Listen Angus you had better keep silent. Do not provoke me. If you hadn't made such a mess of the jobs I gave you to do, then you and I would not be standing here now would we? Just follow my instructions, that was all you had to do. Then I find you had Lord Rockforte here, in your keep, and you let him go! Fool!"

"Fool!?" Angus roared as he jumped unsteadily to his feet, trying to draw his sword.

Eduard laughed scornfully. "God yes Fool! Look at you. It is not even midday and you are already drunk. What a noble accomplishment."

"No one calls me a fool and lives." Angus roared.

In one quick move Eduard had Angus pinned back into his seat at sword point. "I do!" Eduard said in a deadly quiet tone that made Stephanie shiver in dread. He pressed his sword point into Angus's cheek drawing a thin rivulet of blood, then stood back and sheathed his sword.

Angus wiped the thin line of blood from his cheek and said. "Ye ken tha' the MacDonald is nae going tae let his bride tae be disappear. He will search for her until he finds her."

"I am counting on that." Eduard said casually.

"Are ye counting on the fact that he will tear ye apart fer this?" Angus smiled, relishing the thought of this disgusting English bastard being brought down. This inhuman creature before him reminded Angus once again how much he despised the English and their arrogant ways. This little fop would get what he deserved, Angus thought as he left, maybe not from him but Iain would surely kill him with his bare hands. He derived great pleasure in that image as he left the room smiling.

Alone with her captor Stephanie wondered what she was supposed to do. How long would Eduard leave her on the floor like this? How could she convince him to at least remove the gag?

"E' uar, E' uar?" Stephanie tried to speak around the gag. At first it seemed he didn't hear her, then slowly he turned to glance at her.

"What is that, my pretty? Wait let me guess. You would like me to untie you? Remove the gag?" Stephanie nodded. Eduard laughed "Not likely. I rather enjoy seeing you like this. Helpless, quiet at my feet like all women should be."

Stephanie was shocked. She had known Eduard all her life but she never knew him to be so dreadful. He was evil. Masking his true self behind the guise of a nobleman. She always considered him to be rather arrogant oft times more than most. He always seemed to tolerate her presence but barely.

Eduard could barely rein in his temper. Damn her and her father! If he had wed Stephanie she would be his and her father already would have met with an unfortunate accident.

"Perhaps I shall remove the gag. It will be amusing to hear your inevitable tirade, yet have the satisfaction of knowing I can silence you should I wish it."

After the gag was removed it was all she could do not to let loose a torrent of rage against him and tell him exactly what she thought of him. But she held back, he was obviously hoping for the opportunity to show her how much control he had over her. She wanted to try to get more information from him, but her mouth was too dry to speak. She swallowed a couple of times and spoke in a hoarse whisper. "May I please have a drink of water?"

"Only a meek plea for water? Where is that fiery Stephanie who speaks her mind for all to hear, whether they would like to or not?"

She ground her teeth together and didn't give him the reaction he so desperately wanted. "Just a drink of water, please."

"Fine" He walked over and grabbed a cup not bothering to check what was in it. He all but shoved it in her mouth. Relief welled through her. It was at least water. The coldness hurt her lips but the water soothed her dry throat.

"Enough?" Without waiting for her response Eduard took the cup away.

It was not nearly enough but she knew he wanted her to ask for more. She wouldn't do it, even though she nearly wept as she watched him deliberately pour the water on the floor.

"What, still not going to show me your temper? Have it your way. If you wont speak, I might as well put the gag back in."

She couldn't let that happen. She had to take a chance on conversing with this monster. "I do not know what you wish to speak of. Perhaps if you were to give me a topic for conversation we could manage polite conversation. Or perhaps you might permit me to ask a question?"

"Ah there is a little of your usual misplaced arrogance. You want to ask a question, what would you like to know?"

"Why?"

"Why? Why what, my dear? You are not very clear."

"Why did you kidnap me?"

"Kidnap you? Well quite simply because it suits my purpose to do so."

"That is no answer, sir. I heard you talking to that man who was just here. He was saying that Iain would find you and kill you. Why would you want him to come?"

"Because I want to kill him."

"Is there any particular reason you want to kill Iain? Or is this just a little diversion for you?"

"This is no diversion! This is the culmination of everything I have worked so hard for. Iain MacDonald's death and yours will set in motion all that I have been trying so hard to accomplish for the last year."

"What have you been working so hard to accomplish? Sounds like with my death and Iain's you will have your hands full with war." Stephanie paused, then was suddenly struck by the awful truth. "Oh my God! You want war! But why would you want such a thing? Never mind the waste of human lives, because I am quite sure you don't care about that, what about the financial burden of war? Surely you don't want to empty your coffers?"

"Listen you sanctimonious miss. You accuse me of the same arrogance you suffer from yourself. You think your manly education has made you think like a man? That you can possibly know what I am thinking? I truly hate to disillusion you but you know nothing! NOTHING!"

Stephanie listened as Eduard ranted on like a child. It was so tempting for her to let loose all her own emotions and frustrations. In actual fact, Stephanie thought, it was a very good thing her hands were still tied because she felt like giving into her very unladylike instinct and raking her nails over Eduard's face. Instead she maintained her calm and tried to continue to get the information and answers she needed.

"War is a costly venture and where there is no clear 'prize' to be won, the drain on your coffers will be immense."

Eduard had gathered his emotions under his cool facade again, "I repeat that you do not know anything of which you speak. After all it is only yourself speaking of war. I have not engaged in that discussion at all. Once again you prove your misplaced arrogance."

Eduard barely glanced at Stephanie except with thinly concealed disdain. Stephanie was pleased that he was no longer so emotional. If he was in such a state for very long it was unlikely she would learn much. However he was now more controlled with his responses. She had to keep him talking.

"You keep mentioning how ignorant I am. Why don't you enlighten me? If you don't want Iain to come here to start your own war, what is your plan?"

"That will be revealed all in good time."

"Do you think you are going to kill me with suspense? That my curiosity will kill me?"

"No actually Lady Stephanie I will kill you" Eduard smiled.

"Kill me? Why would you kill me?"

"So that I may claim what is mine. Since that old drunk Campbell made a mess of everything I worked for, then that barbarian Scot kidnapped you, I have had to alter my plans slightly. The end goal is still the same but I have had to modify my schedule somewhat."

"If you are not trying to wage war then, this is about wealth. All you want is money."

"You whore! How dare you even suggest for one second you know anything? You do not, believe me! You are nothing more than a witless trollop. Why?" He bent over her peppering her face with spittle as he raged on. "I'll tell you why. I am not so mundane to go through all this for money. No, I am going to get what I have always wanted and what is mine by right. Your death is only part of the catalyst to get me to the place where I can get back what is mine. That is the problem with all women. You think you are worth so much. Your only value is what property you bring to a marriage and the brats you can squeeze out to keep it. No place for their arrogance and self importance." He looked at Stephanie with loathing. "I do not need to listen to you anymore." He roughly shoved the gag back into her mouth.

Stephanie was too shocked to resist realizing now how demented Eduard was. His hatred for women ran deep. She couldn't help but wonder where it came from. God, but this was an intolerable situation. Stephanie felt her bravado slip. Her arms, shoulders and legs were aching from being tied so tightly. She was helpless at the hands of a mad man. Stephanie knew Eduard was watching her closely to see how she would react to being gagged again. So even though she felt like screaming, crying, and raging against the impossible, she tried to school her features to look bored.

Eduard was indeed watching her, but he was more concerned with how his plan was coming together, than with how Stephanie felt or looked. It shouldn't be too long now before the stupid Scot arrived. Then finally he would set in motion all the events he needed to finish this. She nagged him about his end goal, well that was simple. He would finally get his hands on the lands he deserved but which had been denied him because he was descended from so many women. Each generation saw less and less land left to be passed to him by the time he was born. Finally after generations of losing lands through useless women and their dowries, he would get his ancestors lands and titles back.

Stephanie watched the anger and disgust mar Eduard's usually placid face as he played the memories through his head. She wondered what he was thinking. One thing was for certain, she was not going to die at the hands of a lunatic without a fight!

Eduard collected his thoughts and stood before Stephanie. "Well, my dear, I don't expect we have long to wait now."

As if on cue Angus came into the room. "Well, Sassenach, it seems ye are going tae have yer war after all."

"What makes you think I am looking for a war? You are as stupid as this woman here." Stephanie glared at Eduard.

"Since rumors from my men and spies around here tell me that Iain MacDonald is heading this was with a full contingent of fully armed warriors, Ye may not think yer going tae have a war. But I think ye'll get one just the same."

"What do you know? War is what you barbarians on either side of the border want. You think that only large scale bloodshed achieves your ends. Not so. I am here to tell you that some well placed bodies will achieve the ends I seek and I will not have to engage in any war."

"And my money?" Angus said sucking his teeth. "My money ye promised me?"

"Bah! You will get your money when I am finished and not a moment before." Eduard spat at him.

Stephanie watched the two men argue back and forth about Angus' payment. What mattered most to her was the news that Angus had brought. Iain was coming! She allowed herself to feel the fluttering of hope. Iain would not let her die at the hands of this monster.

"Thinking of him are you?" Stephanie didnt notice that Eduard had come over to her until he spoke. "Imagining his great rescue are you? Don't bother. Rather imagine how distraught he will be at the sight of your dead body." Eduard removed Stephanie's gag as he spoke. The minute she could speak she replied.

"Iain is not a bloodthirsty man like yourself. You place a great deal of faith in the notion that Iain is a foolish emotional man. He is a warrior and he will not lose control at the situation even if he does find me dead."

"Believe me, he will do just that. Your barbarian Scot wants you and when he sees you dead he will stop at nothing to punish those responsible."

"Well you are the one responsible so I guess you realize he will be coming for you."

"Actually I am quite sure he will not be coming for me. Angus fetch me some wine."

"I amnae yer servant. Get it yerself."

"No. If you want to be paid you will go and fetch it and bring three glasses. Should you not wish to do as I ask then you can forget the money you so desperately want."

"I could kill ye where ye stand ye English Bastard."

"Yes if you didn't want or need the large fortune I have promised you, you would probably try to do just that. However since you want the money so much, you will go and get the wine. Your best please not the swill you and your drunken men swallow like water. Be quick and be gone."

"Bluidy bastard. Someday ye will find yerself at the wrong end of a sword. I hope it is mine." Angus muttered threats as he did Eduard's bidding.

"You must be very proud of yourself. Ordering a drunk Scottish barbarian around. But I don't see any of your men. Did none of them wish to follow you into this fool's plan?" Stephanie taunted Eduard.

"In fact none of my men are aware of anything other than what I have told them. It is imperative that I not be seen to be involved in this."

"You are about to murder me and Iain in cold blood. How do you think you will not be discovered in your involvement?"

"Shh. I wish silence for the moment."

Angus came in with the wine and three glasses and set the tray next to Eduard. "Anything else mi'Lord?" Angus asked sarcastically.

Eduard seemed unaffected by Angus's words. "Leave us now." Eduard dismissed Angus with a wave of his hand. Angus left muttering curses all the while.

"And that is why he has been so perfect up to now. He is truly stupid." After he toyed with the cups a moment, Eduard poured himself a glass of wine. "Now we wait."

Chapter Forty-Seven

Iain arrived at the edge of Campbell property and called everyone to a halt. "All right, everyone, we set up camp here."

"Camp? Aren't we going in to get Stephanie?" William was a little confused and very frustrated that they had arrived where Iain believed Stephanie to be, and yet they were not storming the keep, nor tearing it apart stone by stone to get her.

Iain replied. "Steady Lord William. I have brought you to where I believe Stephanie to be but I amnae sure who took her."

""That doesn't make a hell of a lot of sense. We are here. Are you telling me we are going to sit and wait? Wait for what?"

"I am going tae wait for my arrival tae get noticed and acknowledged. I want whoever has Stephanie tae think they have the upper hand and the control. As I find out who we are dealing with, then I will plan my strategy. Besides if I enter full force after Stephanie I am quite certain that she will be killed before we reach the gate. Make nae mistake Lord Rockforte, I want tae tear this place apart right now and right quick. But what is more important is that we have a wedding in a few days and I intend tae get Stephanie out of that keep, take her home and make her my wife. That is my only goal. Patience, we must have patience."

William sighed heavily "Let us set up camp then."

Later when the men were settled around the various bonfires, Iain sat at the fire nearest his tent lost in his plan to try to free Stephanie.

"Ho brother." Fergus interrupted Iain's thoughts and sat down next to him. "So tell me how ye are faring?"

Iain sighed. "I amna quite sure. I fear I may have been tae hasty brother."

"Never say sae. I am quite sure ye will find a way. Ye ken this is much the same as any battle we have fought before. There is an enemy tae fight and fight we must. We fight tae protect our loved ones and it is nay different today. Ye will think of something tae get Stephanie back. She will be back safe and sound in short order."

"Tis true what ye say Fergus. I ken that but it is harder this time fighting the enemy that has Stephanie and I dinna even ken who he is. I have never felt sae frustrated before a battle than I do today."

"Believe it or not yer frustration is a good thing Iain. It will make ye more aware of the decision ye make. We will be successful. I know ye well and I have confidence in ye."

"Thank ye, Fergus, I just hope I can get Stephanie back tae safety soon."

Fergus gripped his brother's shoulder tightly. "Ye will. We all will Iain. Ye should turn in"

"Aye I will shortly" Iain sat alone as all around him men began turning in for the night. He only had a suspicion that whoever took Stephanie would be here at Campbell's keep. What upset him most was that he was unsure of everything at the moment. He could be losing valuable time by being here if Stephanie had been taken elsewhere. Precious time would be lost. No. He had to hold fast to what his warrior's instinct told him. Every bone in his body was convinced that she was here after what Rosie had heard. Whoever had taken Stephanie needed a place close by but that didn't really concern him. He just wanted to get her back. She meant everything right now. If anything had happened to her... He didn't want to think of that possibility. If the worst had happened he would make any who were involved suffer and beg for death.

Suddenly Iain's thoughts were interrupted. Someone was behind him and trying to approach quietly. Iain casually slipped his knife from his belt and began to stand up. From the person's movement whoever it was, was just to his left behind some brush. Quick as lightening Iain reached in and pulled the man out twisting him around so his blade was at the stranger's throat.

"Who are ye? What do ye want? Speak quickly before I gut ye." Iain growled

"MacDonald, tis me."

"Angus? Angus ye auld bastard. What the hell are ye doing here? Shouldn't ye be protecting yer keep from me?"

"My keep needs protecting but not from ye."

"Tell me Angus. Is she there? Is my bride inside?"

"Let me go an' I will tell ye what I can."

Iain let Angus go but kept his knife ready. Angus rubbed his neck and shoulders before he spoke.

"Aye tis much I have tae tell, but I am powerful thirsty. I am likely tae be more so before my tale is done."

"Angus, ye'll be lucky tae be alive and feeling thirst if ye do not speak quickly."

Angus showed mock surprise. "Why, Laird MacDonald, I do believe yer hospitality is slipping."

"Pray that it is just my hospitality that is slipping and not my hand which wields this blade. Now are ye going tae speak of what ye know or am I just going tae rid the world of your loathsome presence?"

"All right, all right. Tis about yer lady. But I must begin at the beginning."

"How long is this going tae take?" Iain felt his frustration rising. "Never mind just tell me is Stephanie in yer keep?"

"Aye she is."

"Is she all right?"

"For now."

"What the hell do ye mean for now? Ye had better speak now Angus or I am going tae kill ye where ye stand."

So Angus began his tale.

Chapter Forty-Eight

After what felt like hours Stephanie barely had any feeling left in her feet. Her shoulders were throbbing from being wrenched behind her for so long. Stephanie wished she could walk freely for even a few minutes to get her limbs moving again. She also had a powerful need for rest. She was so tired from all the tension, she could have slept anywhere except…

"Ha! Finally my patience has been rewarded!" Eduard's gleeful chortling woke her instantly and instantly her nerves were on edge. She was now so tired she found everything about Eduard aggravating. She supposed she should be in fear for her life but she was so tired and angry. Fearing death seemed ridiculous and pointless.

Eduard continued "I knew it. I knew he would come. And now it will be finished. Finally I can eliminate all competition to land that rightfully belongs to me and my family."

"Wha?" Stephanie choked around the gag. Eduard walked over to her and removed it. "What are you talking about?" She asked again.

"My plan to start with, was actually brilliantly simple. I originally hired the bumbling Scot to conduct raids on both sides of the border. The end result was meant to be, that our King would be involved and come to assist in subduing MacDonald. His lands would be confiscated and given to your father to govern. In the meantime, I was courting you to get the lands through marriage into your family. Eventually the land would be passed to me and my son that you would bear me." Eduard looked pensive and then he scowled. "And that plan would have worked if this drunken fool hadn't ruined everything. With everything that has gone wrong I am now faced with a more direct route to my goal. We wait now for your Scot to come and challenge me and once he sees you are dead, I will then kill him and burn this whole place to the ground.

Of course your father will be inconsolable for a while. I will be there to offer my support and sympathy until an appropriate time. Then I shall do away with him as well. At such time I shall petition King Edward for your father's land to keep it in Britain. Despite this lout ruining everything, I will still end up with my lands back. Brilliant!" Eduard held up a goblet of wine and toasted himself.

"You demented bastard!"

"Now, now. No need to be so unladylike."

"I don't care. No matter what the reason, killing people is wrong and killing people for your own gain is the vilest thing you could do. You will never get away with this! Iain will stop you. He is no fool to fall for your weak plot. He will see right through you and then you will be left with nothing. Less than nothing because Iain will kill you for what you have done."

"That may be hard for him to do since he will be dead."

"You will never win against Iain in combat. He will cut you down before you can even draw your sword."

"Not so my dear. There are other ways to kill a man rather than hand to hand combat."

Stephanie's eyes widened in shock. "You coward you are going to give him poison aren't you?"

Eduard said nothing just smiled a mirthless smile. His eyes looked coldly dead. Stephanie was chilled to think that Iain, who was bound by honor and duty in his actions, didn't stand to fare well with a worm like Eduard. She would have to warn him when he arrived, but how? Eduard planned to kill her before he arrived. Stephanie felt so ridiculously helpless. She wanted to scream. But what could she do? Nothing at the moment, she had to hope that an opportunity might present itself for her to change the course of events.

While Stephanie battled with her predicament, Iain was about to be treated to the whole sordid tale by Angus.

Iain and Angus were seated by the fire, Fergus and William, awakened by the disturbance had joined them.

Iain turned to Angus "All right let us hear the whole story, start tae finish."

So Angus began. "Some months back I received word from a ruffian traveling through that there was an English dandy putting out word that he would pay coin to hire some men. Men who would not ask questions, just carry out orders and collect the pay. Seemed tae me and my men the perfect way tae make money quickly." Angus paused. "Right from our first order, it became clear that this was nay going tae be easy money."

Iain broke in. "How did ye receive yer first order? Did ye know who it was that hired ye?"

Angus continued "Our first order actually came from the traveler. Once my men and I agreed that we would like the money, this unknown man handed us a packet with instructions and some coin. Said more money would come upon successful completion of the task set out."

"What was the first order?"

"We were tae sneak onto yer lands, at the time yer father was still alive, do some damage and leave yer parents a message."

Iain knew from Angus' vague narrative what the answer was but he needed to hear what happened. "What damage?" He asked quietly.

Angus looked somewhat worried. "We were tae loosen the bolts on yer father's carriage so as tae make it verra unstable at a high rate of speed. But still steady enough tae travel."

Iain's fist clenched and he felt his heart race. "Then what happened?"

"We left a note that there was some trouble at the border. Some of his people had been trapped by raiders who would kill all the women and children if he did not come and ransom them immediately. As ye know yer father left that day without word tae ye or yer brother. I dinna ken if it was the Sassenach's plan or nay, but yer mother went with yer father an' that is when their carriage missed a turn and flipped over."

William couldn't believe what he had heard. The MacDonald's had always been peaceful neighbors despite the King's hatred for the Scots. William had always lived peacefully with them. But he had no idea that Iain's father and stepmother had met such a tragic end. "Why? Why did you do it?"

Angus rolled his eyes "Are ye all daft? Fer the money. I didna ken the plan was tae kill the MacDonald. But it was tae late tae do anything about that. We just collected the money from the prearranged place and picked up our next order."

"An those orders were?" Iain asked.

"Tae wait fer confirmation that yer father was dead and begin raids against ye. An while conducting the raids we were tae be sure tae leave rumors it was Rockforte's men moving in on the death of yer father. Folk will believe anything they hear. So we raided frequently and it appears ye all believed it was the English as soon as everyone said it was Rockforte without us having tae say a word."

Iain sat disbelievingly as Angus continued his horrific tale. "We never had any contact with a person other than our first meeting with the unknown traveler. Nor did we care tae. We got our orders and our money. Once yer people were accusing yer English neighbors, we began tae cross over the border and raid the English Lord's lands. Our orders were tae cause disruption and animosity between yer two families where there was none before." Angus stopped.

"For what purpose were ye tae do this?" Iain asked trying to put together the pieces Angus had scattered before him.

"Never knew and never cared tae ask. The job was simple enough and the money was regular. But then ye made a mess of everything." Angus stared accusingly at Iain.

"Me?" Iain asked "How did I do that?"

"I dinna presume tae know what this man was up tae. But when ye snatched Stephanie all I ken is the orders and the money stopped. Then not tae long ago this English fop appears at my gate yelling at how I had ruined everything. How I couldna do the simplest thing. Then he said he would take over and he paid me tae 'borrow' my keep for a while."

"Did he say how long he wanted tae borrow it and for what purpose?" Iain felt they were getting close to discovering what was going on and who was behind Stephanie's abduction. But he was afraid that he was taking too long to discover all he needed to know. How much time could he risk without jeopardizing Stephanie's life?

Angus took a healthy swig from the flask of water. "Well that's just the thing. He never said anything specific about anything at all. All I can say for certain is that he is basing everything on ye and the Lady. I dinna ken everything for sure but if I had tae guess, I am quite sure he is planning tae kill the both of ye."

"What would that possibly gain him?" Iain wondered out loud.

"I amna sure. All I ken is that I want that English bastard out of my keep and out of my life for good. If that means I have tae have an alliance of sorts with ye then I will do it."

Iain frowned. "Angus, ye realize that I would rather eat fire than trust ye with anything as important as this. But under the circumstances, I am forced tae reconsider my wishes in Lady Stephanie's interest. I am guessing that yer foray into my camp was for more reasons than tae tell me ye hate this English fop ye allied yerself tae for nothing other than fast money."

"Nay, I dinna come here just tae tell ye my tale. I ken tha the only possible way tae beat this cur is tae take him by surprise."

"Ye have a plan?"

"Of sorts. I am here tae offer ye the way inside the keep but after that ye are on yer own. I dinna intend tae get involved in this at all."

"So ye are proposing tae show me another way inside rather than opening the main gate?" Iain asked.

"Aye. He will be expecting ye tae use the main gate and is anticipating yer arrival. Ye might be able tae gain the upper hand if ye arrive by means of our secret entrance."

"It seems rather like a good idea; but I canna take many with me that way. We need speed and stealth tae maximize the element of surprise."

"She is my daughter, so I am going with you." William stated.

"Ye are my leader sae I am going with ye." Fergus spoke with as much finality as William.

"Nay" Iain said. "Ye both canna come with me."

"Brother, ye will nay go in alone I willna agree. Ye will have tae tie me up and knock me unconscious first."

"And me." William added.

"Nay, men. I have a plan but ye each must play yer part and agree tae it or all will be lost. Lord Rockforte, can ye trust me one last time?"

"If I must. What is it you want me to do?"

"I need ye tae stay here."

"Oh, no!" William broke in. "No. She is my only daughter. I will not be left behind like some weakling."

"Easy, mon. I dinna want ye waiting here. I want ye tae mount an attack on the keep while Fergus and I are inside."

"An attack? Won't that threaten Stephanie?"

"Not if we move quickly and carefully. I am going tae the keep with Fergus and Angus. We shall get inside, find and secure Stephanie. Give us an hour then ride our men forward tae the main gate and challenge our enemy tae battle. If he is distracted by yer appearance at the gate, Fergus and I can probably manage tae subdue him during the confusion."

"It is very risky."

"I am counting on his surprise and confusion with an attack at night, when we have no clear idea who and how many men we are facing." Iain turned to Angus. "Exactly how many men are we facing Angus?"

"Not that many. Most of us have left the keep while this English dog is there. I suspect nay more than fifty and I doubt that any of them will be sae willing tae help the Englishmon."

"Well that isna sae bad. We just need tae spread our men out some tae make our number seem larger and the cover of darkness will help disguise that we are not many more."

"Ah." said William "That does make some sense. I think I see where you are going with this plan."

Iain smiled. "Good then we should be on our way. The sooner we go, the sooner we can bring Stephanie back. Come, Angus, ye must show us in."

"All right then let's be off. Mind ye be silent though. We must not let anyone know we are coming."

Iain called a man over to spread the word that they must follow Lord Rockforte. "Follow the English Lord as if he were me. The Lady Stephanie's life depends on your loyalty."

"Aye, mi Lord, have nay fear. We shall do as ye ask tae a mon." The young man saluted Iain and went to spread his Laird's command to the other men present.

Angus spoke up. "Come, Laird MacDonald, we canna waste any more time or we will lose the cover of darkness."

Angus, Iain and Fergus left quickly, disappearing into the darkness outside the circles of the bonfires. Everyone was tense and ready to do whatever was needed. Whatever happened Stephanie would be returned to Iain tonight.

Chapter Forty-Nine

Eduard stood looking out the window trying to survey the situation. He could see the bonfires but at night he could not see the number of men that sat at each one. Not that it really mattered he cared only to get one man in the keep. Once he accomplished that he could kill Stephanie and then kill Iain. Then he could weave the tale that Angus did it all. Of course he would have to kill the old drunk as well. But that wouldn't be so difficult. Eduard couldn't help but feel some euphoria that soon, very soon, everything he wanted would be his.

Stephanie watched as Eduard smiled and knew he felt he had won. That would never happen. She promised herself she would die first. Though her arms were still bound behind her, she kept wiggling her hands and fingers to keep them from numbing altogether. She would be ready for any opportunity Eduard gave her. She was so restless and taut her eyes never stopped surveying her opportunities. She was surprised to hear Eduard speak.

"Now we wait. But the sooner he comes the better."

"At least we agree on that much. I, too, will be glad when this is over, the sooner the better to see you dealt with squarely."

"I will be just as glad to finally be done with you and your endless prattle. I should thank God your father did not consider my marriage proposal. For I think I would have killed you sooner in our marriage than would have been wise just to end your incessant nattering." He turned from her and looked out the window. Stephanie glared at Eduard's back.

Angus led Iain and Fergus to the small opening at his keep. It was nothing more than a drainage hole with a movcable grate over it. The grate however moved silently and easily. Iain suspected that Angus and his men used the opening frequently for all their own private, nefarious reasons.

"All right MacDonald follow the drainage opening until ye reach a door. Go through that door and that will get ye tae the kitchens. Then just go through tae that hall and take the stairs tae the rear which will lead ye up tae the apartments above. Ye will find the bounder in the first door tae the left at the top of the stairs. An' this is where I leave ye." Angus closed the grate behind their retreating forms. He turned and slipped back into the dark shadows.

Iain and Fergus moved quietly and quickly through the tunnel, watching for the door. They dared not speak in case there were people nearby and their voices carried. They did not want to risk detection. Finally they reached the door. It was the only one they had come across so far, so both men hoped it was the correct one. The door opened easily. Iain motioned to Fergus to stay behind him. He looked around the room but all was quiet in the great kitchen. The fire was out, no heat radiated from it so it had been out for quite some time. Judging by the unkempt appearance of the room it seemed no one had been there for a while. The room was dirty and disorderly. But Iain was careful enough not to believe what he saw. He knew Angus was as unkempt as the room they now stood in. So there was no way to know for sure how long the kitchen had been empty. They had to move carefully. The two men ran into no one as they made their way through the kitchen, out the door to the yard that lay between them and the great hall.

When they reached the entry to the hall, Iain motioned Fergus close and whispered in his ear. "When we enter I will go straight tae Stephanie. I want ye tae remain behind and find and subdue anyone inside. If ye can do it without killing anyone it would be best. But do what ye must."

Fergus nodded and they entered the hall. Still they encountered no one. They parted and Iain followed Angus' direction until he reached the door. He disciplined himself not to throw the door open and rush in. He had no idea who was on the other side, nor what kind of condition Stephanie was in. He knew he had to proceed with great caution. But it was so hard. He wanted to storm through the door and destroy anyone and everyone until he had Stephanie back in his arms again.

Slowly, he opened the door a fraction to peer in. Damn! The man was in a chair, Stephanie on the floor in front of him with a knife to her throat. Worst of all the bastard was looking directly at the door and smiling mirthlessly.

"Come in, come in, Laird MacDonald. We have been expecting you. Haven't we my dear?" The man yanked Stephanie's head back so Iain could see the gag in her mouth. Iain could also see the pain in her eyes. He raged inside to run to her and get the beast's hands off her. But he knew that Stephanie's throat could be cut long before he made it across the room. He called upon every ounce of self discipline he had to enter the room slowly with an air of casualness that belied his true feelings.

"Ye have been expecting me, have ye? For what purpose?"

"Why to watch your fiancée die of course." Eduard waited for some reaction but Iain showed no emotion whatsoever that he could see. In fact he suddenly looked decidedly bored as he spoke.

"Let me see if I have this right. Ye kidnapped the woman I am tae marry only tae get me tae come here and watch ye kill her? That is rather foolish is it nay?"

"No, it is not foolish!" Eduard snapped. "It is quite ingenious actually."

Iain shifted his weight and barely glanced at Stephanie. Eduard might have believed that Iain was unaffected by this revelation but Stephanie could see in the lines around Iain's mouth how angry he really was. She prayed he would not give in to his anger. She didn't want Iain to get hurt and Eduard was just insane enough to be capable of doing anything. She caught Iain shifting again. Then she realized he was moving ever so slightly closer to them with every shift.

Iain saw Stephanie's eyes widen in shock and fear and he realized she knew what he was doing. He willed her not to give anything away. He spoke again to distract this monster from seeing his movement closer.

"Sae then, English, tell me. What is sae ingenious because quite frankly I see nothing genius before me. Only a coward hiding behind a woman's skirts for some secret purpose."

Eduard snorted "Yes, I can see how your limited Scottish intelligence would only see the obvious. However, there are always more layers than meet the eye. My plan is ingenious, as you and your doxy here are the instruments for me to get all my ancestor's lands and more, given to my care for good."

"Is that sae?"

"Yes, that is so. Upon your deaths there will be some chaos and confusion but in the end I shall have yours and Rockforte's lands."

"Mmm seems tae me this is all verra confusing. How are ye, English, going tae take my land?"

"The King shall entrust the land to me."

"Really?"

"Yes. Here why don't you have a drink?"

"Nay. I need nae drink. Just tell me yer schemes." Iain still edged closer but his movements were so small Stephanie didn't think he would ever reach her. Eduard's knife was biting into the tender flesh on her neck and she could feel the small trickle of blood running down her throat.

Iain saw the blood and heard his own roaring through his veins in fury. When he got his hands on this man he would surely rip him apart. For certain he did not want to drink anything to dull his senses.

Eduard's eyes narrowed at Iain's refusal to drink. The poison in the goblet had to be ingested so that Eduard could get rid of Laird MacDonald and Stephanie. He spoke to Iain with steely intent.

"Really, Laird MacDonald, I have a cup just for you to hear my tale. I would find it a grievous insult for you to refuse my offer to your comfort. Join me."

Iain could tell this man was closer to breaking so he had better play along. He walked over to the table and picked up the goblet. "Sae, what should I call ye?" Iain asked idly toying with the goblet.

"Eduard Stockton as your service." Iain noted his mocking tone but resisted reacting.

"Well then, Eduard, share yer tale for I find I am getting weary standing her for nothing."

"Drink up, my Lord, then I shall begin." Iain noticed Eduard's determination that he should drink. Somehow his wine must be drugged, so he only pretended to take a swallow, careful not to let any liquid pass his lips.

Eduard gleefully laughed "Oh marvelous, so we begin. Suffice it to say that Lord Rockforte's lands used to belong to my ancestors but after years of bearing only daughters my land has been packaged out to others to secure good marriages. Now as the first born male in a very long time, I have researched what lands are mine and I am going to get them back."

"Ye are certain of this?"

"Oh very. Today both you and Stephanie shall be dispatched and I shall have to bear the sad tidings to Lord Rockforte. Telling him also how I had to kill you to protect Stephanie. I shall then fuel Lord Rockforte's ire and have him go to the King to petition for war again the Campbell's and the MacDonald's, for this heinous crime against English nobility. It is no secret what the King thinks of you Scots and he is looking for just such a reason to mount full scale war on your people. Naturally William will receive all the lands as recompense for his lovely daughter's untimely demise. Then after a year or so William shall take his own life, having never fully recovered from his beloved daughter's death."

"And I suppose ye shall be instrumental in his death as well?" Iain pretended to take another drink and noticed Eduard's eyes gleam as he moved. Iain risked a glance at Stephanie and saw the stark naked fear in her eyes. She too had figured out Eduard's plot to have Iain drink whatever concoction he had made. He smiled at her ever so slightly and shook his head. He was so proud to see the light of understanding flare in her eyes. She knew he wasn't drinking anything. His wife to be was a credit with her quick intelligence.

"But of course no one will know because no one will suspect." Eduard was so pleased with himself. Iain's fingers ached to wrap around his throat and squeeze. He mentally shook himself and concentrated on the task at hand. He truly hoped everyone was moving into position soon before this crazed man realized Iain was only pretending to drink. Eduard glanced out the window and saw men at the gate, and stretching beyond. He was momentarily concerned at the numbers. But it soon wouldn't matter. Their leader would be dead.

"I wonder Eduard how ye are going tae get rid of Angus Campbell? Hating the English as much as he does I canna think he has agreed tae yer plan."

"No matter. He shall be dealt with once you two are dead. A simple matter of finding him around here somewhere drunk and asleep. Then I shall run him through with your sword. Such a shame to have to kill your own countrymen but you will do whatever is necessary to rescue your bride. Right?"

At that moment William called out "Ho there the keep. Whoever you are surrender now and your life may be spared."

Eduard looked shocked. "What is he doing here? He can't be here? Ow! Damn you, you bitch!"

In that instant when Eduard was distracted Stephanie turned her head slightly feeling the knife bite into her flesh, she bit down onto Eduard's hand. He dropped the knife but before Iain could reach him, Eduard dealt such a blow to her face that she fell to the floor and hit with such force she lost consciousness.

Iain watched this happen helplessly. "No!" he roared barely seeing Stephanie all his hate and fury pouring into his hands he began pummeling Eduard with his fists.

Eduard cried out and begged like a coward as Iain's fists hammered into him. "Please stop. Don't hurt me I am nobility."

Eduard's pleas pierced through Iain's blind fury. He took a deep breath and forced himself not to look at Stephanie. He couldn't help it. She was so pale and fragile lying on the floor. He clenched his fists and took deep calming breaths.

"Come on then ye great mon of nobility. Fight like a true gentleman."

Eduard spat blood onto the floor. His eyes filled with pure hatred, but Iain wasn't worried. On the contrary, he could hardly wait to seek his own justice against this animal. Eduard spoke.

"Fine. We shall fight with swords but I warn you I spent much time studying the art of swordsmanship through my life. I am something of an expert."

Iain's steely gray eyes flashed like his sword as he brought it down towards Eduard. "Congratulations my Lord." Iain said sarcastically "But ye should ken I perfected my ability with a sword by actually using it not just reading about it."

Their swords met. Their disgust and fury with each other fuelled and prolonged their fight. The end came much too soon for Iain. Eduard turned to perform a ridiculous impractical thrust, as useless in this fight as it would have been in battle. His left side was exposed and Iain quickly thrust his sword right into Eduard's black heart. All too soon the light of life left his eyes. He died so quickly he did not utter a word as he dropped to the floor.

Iain didn't even spare him a glance as he rushed to pick Stephanie off the floor. His heart sank to see her so pale and lifeless. But when he gathered her up and cradled her in his arms he found she was still breathing faintly. Tenderly he began to try to take stock of her injuries. He untied her hands from behind her back. When he saw the state of her wrists he fervently wished Eduard was alive so he could kill him again. Her skin was red, raw and bleeding from where the rope had cut into her. Iain was glad she was unconscious only for the fact that the pain in her arms would be excruciating when the feeling returned. Then he saw that the wound on her neck was still bleeding so he wrapped a strip of cloth around her neck to try to slow the flow of blood.

Fearfully and gingerly Iain brushed her hair from her brow to look at her face and head. These injuries worried him most. He had seen many men die from a simple blow to the head with no mortal flesh wounds. Stephanie's face was absolutely white except for the purple bluish bruises that were starting to show on her stark colorless face. Iain's heart sank when he felt the two large swellings on either side of her head. One from Eduard's blow and the other from where her head had struck the floor. This was serious and Iain feared she might not wake up from the sleep she was in. He held her close to his chest and rained soft whispers and kisses into her hair as he gently rocked her.

Chapter Fifty

It was thus that Fergus found them.

"God Iain is she dead?" Fergus asked as he rushed over and stood beside his brother.

"Nay Fergus. Not yet but I fear she may not wake up from this sleep." Iain spoke very matter of fact but Fergus could see the depths of anguish in his brother's eyes.

"Her head is swollen?"

"Aye. Once from where the bastard struck her down and once from when she hit her head on the floor. I couldn't reach her in time." Iain looked up at Fergus self reproach shone from his stormy eyes. Fergus looked at Stephanie again. He didn't hold out much hope for her recovery but his brother didn't need to hear that from him.

"Dinna worry Iain, she will be fine. We will take her home and all will be well. Ye will see."

"The keep." Iain suddenly realized where they were and the possibility that there may be more threats still to come before they were safely out of here. Even though Eduard was dead, Angus or any of his men could pose a fresh danger to them.

"Easy, brother. All is well below. Angus' men dinna seem tae care one way or the other who was giving the orders. I told them tae surrender their swords sae they did. I sent one of the men out tae open the gate, I suspect William will be arriving soon."

As if on cue William came through the door. He stopped short when he saw the two men's faces.

"My girl. Is she dead?"

Iain found he suddenly couldn't speak he just held Stephanie closer willing her to wake up.

"Nay sir." Fergus rushed into the silence. He went over to William and led him aside. "Nay she isna dead but I canna lie tae ye, she is grievously injured. Two hard blows tae the head."

William blanced. "No!" he choked out "Where is the bastard who did this. I will kill him with my bare hands."

Iain looked up briefly but didn't let go of Stephanie. "I am verra sorry sir tae rob ye of that satisfaction. But I killt him myself. That is him over there."

William walked over to the crumpled heap representing the evil that had befallen his daughter. "I am glad you are dead you vile worm!" He dealt the body a swift hard kick to the ribs and gasped as Eduard's face was revealed.

"Oh, my God, no! It cannot be!" William staggered back as if struck.

"What. What is it Lord William?" Iain asked. William turned his shocked face to Iain.

"It is my neighbor Eduard Stockton. It could not have been him. I cannot believe that he could be capable of such evil."

"Believe me, sir he, was capable of this and much more. He was mad." Iain told William of the plot Eduard had conspired against him. Once he was finished William still remained in shock. "That he could be capable of devising such a crime against all of us that required such a long time to come to pass. It defies the logical mind." William spoke disbelievingly.

"Aye tha it does. But that was his plan. Right from the murder of our parents to ultimately your own murder."

Fergus swore as he poured out the tainted wine onto the floor.

"Mind yerself Fergus. I dinna think the wine was tampered with as he had consumed some already. I think the cup contains the poison meant tae kill me." Iain warned his brother.

"God! The man's depravity knows no bounds. Are you all right? How did you know?" William queried.

"He told me he meant tae kill me and I knew he wouldna do that honorably. When he continued to insist that I drink, I knew the poison was in the wine. No wine passed my lips yet I am feeling rather ill."

Concern flushed onto Fergus' and William's faces. Iain quickly reassured them. "It is all right. I willna die but as unwell as I feel, we must see tae Stephanie. She needs tae be resting and still. Hopefully then she will come out of this."

William spoke first. "What do you suggest, lad? Do we set her up here or risk taking her back to your keep?"

Iain replied without hesitation. "I want tae get the lass out of this hell hole as soon as possible. I want her home safe and sound as soon as we can possibly manage."

"I will ride ahead with the men and get everything ready." Fergus said as he rushed out the door. William and Iain could hear him shouting to the men to ride home at once. William broke the silence first.

"What should we do about Campbell?" He was pleased but sorry to see Iain holding his daughter so close and so tight. Pleased because every father hopes his daughter finds someone to cherish her. Iain obviously cherished Stephanie. But he was sorry that she might never wake up to know how loved she was by Iain. He laid his hand on the younger man's shoulder. Iain didn't look up when he replied.

"Tae be honest I dinna care one bit about Campbell, his men, or anything he has done. I just want her safe, ye ken?"

"I know. You should know that Angus came back and stood with us at the gate. He was just opening the gate when Fergus arrived. But I don't believe he should be allowed to get away with this. I would like to speak to the King about suitable retribution."

"Nay." Iain said. "Nay. I am sorry William but if ye let yer King in tae my country, he willna stop until everything is gone. I will deal with Angus Campbell. Just not until Stephanie is better and we are wed. I want her tae decide as well, the fate of the mon who brought her to such a place."

"I still think the King should deal with Angus, but I respect that you care so much for my girl that you would let her stand by your side when punishment is met out."

The words tore through Iain's throat and soul as he looked up at the English warrior. "I love her. God help me! I love her sae much. I dinna know what I will do if she dies."

"I know. Come, let us get her back home, your home."

Chapter Fifty-One

No one would believe such hardened warriors would be capable of such gentleness as they maneuvered Stephanie inert form out of the keep and onto Iain's horse.

William stayed by Iain's side on the long slow ride back to the keep. Neither man spoke but each took turns singing gentle songs to Stephanie, hoping that she would hear them and awaken.

When they arrived at the edge of MacDonald land, the way was peppered with people standing and silently watching the two anguished lords pass. Most were shocked and fearful when they caught a glimpse of Stephanie, seemingly lifeless in Iain's arms. Judith stood next to Fergus at the keep when they stopped. She rushed forward and cried out when she saw her friend.

"Oh God no! Steffie, Steffie can you hear me?" She gently brushed her friend's face. Then she saw Iain's face. "Oh, Iain, I am sorry. Come inside, take her straight to her room. We have prepared everything."

Iain carried Stephanie up to the chamber and was touched by how lovingly it had been arranged. He prayed with all his heart that she would wake up and see all the flowers brightening the room. Then he saw hanging at the end of the bed, her wedding gown. She had to get better, she had to wear it. He had to believe that.

Gently and reverently he laid his beautiful bride to be on the bed, cushioning her on pillows. Then he stretched out beside her, laying her on his shoulder.

All present exchanged glances. Judith spoke first. "Iain, she will be fine. She just needs to rest and recover from the blows. Fergus has told me all that happened and we are all praying for her speedy recovery. But you must be exhausted why don't you seek your own bed? We will come to you the minute anything changes."

"Nay" Iain spoke with finality. "I willna leave her side until she is awake or...dead. I stay with her and that is my final word."

William stepped forward to stand next to him. "If that is what you need to do, we will all respect your wishes. I just hope with all my heart that you do not hold yourself responsible for any of this."

"How could I not? If I had not kidnapped her none of this would have happened." Iain felt as if he were being ripped apart. He held Stephanie closer. William smiled at the man who loved his daughter and said.

"Iain if you had not taken my daughter she would be dead already. Dead at the hands of that monster I thought to be my friend and ally. I blame myself. I was going to give her to him in marriage when she returned because he said he would take her despite any hint of scandal. Now I know he would have killed her and me just to get my lands. I cannot thank you enough for saving her."

Everyone in the room smiled and nodded at Lord Rockforte's astute observation. He was right and they all knew it. William continued. "If I do not blame you, then you have no grounds to blame yourself. If you want to stay with Stephanie then you must do so without any self recriminations. She needs your positive strength and your love to bring her out of this. If you give her those heart and soul, I believe she will come back to you."

The room fell silent when William finished. He could not tell if his words had reached Iain but he felt he had done all he could do for now. With one last look he and Fergus left to go and speak to the men and update them on what had happened. Judith then gathered the ladies and ushered them out of the room.

Iain smiled his thanks at his sister in law as she softly closed the door. Once everyone had left he was alone with his soul mate. He kissed Stephanie on her lips grateful to still feel warmth and life in them. Then he began his long vigil with her.

Hours and some days passed without a variance in routine. Iain was true to his word he didn't leave Stephanie's side. He constantly spoke to her of their future. He sang songs he remembered from his childhood.

The morning of the fifth day dawned. Iain was stiff and unrelenting, sponging Stephanie with cool cloths and tending her healing hands. He kept his conversation going but he was tired and beginning to lose hope.

"Oh please, lass, dinna leave me. Ye ken I canna do this without ye. I thought I had everything before ye came tae my life, now that I have found ye I ken I have nothing without ye. Stephanie lass, I love ye with all my heart. Ye must wake up sae I can prove tae ye how much I love ye."

Judith and William entered in time to hear Iain's heart-felt plea. They each felt for Iain but he had to take a break or he would make himself ill. Judith spoke in a firm no nonsense tone.

"All right brother, you must get up now and get out of this room to tend to yourself."

Iain could not help but feel some anger at this interruption. "Nay" He said with just as much firmness.

"Oh yes!" Judith countered with equal determination. "Iain, you cannot stay in here like this. You have not eaten a full meal in five days and even worse you have not bathed. You smell rank, my Laird."

Iain blinked in surprise at Judith's tone. "Aye" he whispered. "Ye are right but I canna leave her. I just canna."

William spoke up. "Yes, you can, my boy, because you need a break and I need to sit with my girl. I won't leave her alone for a second but you must promise me to eat and have a thorough wash. Can you do that? Because it just might be your stench that is keeping my daughter from waking up."

Iain's head snapped up to deliver a scathing remark, but he looked into William's sparkling eyes, rimmed with concern and he realized that everyone was just as concerned for him as they were for Stephanie. He smiled ruefully, "Yes, sir, I shall go. But not for long. I promise I will eat and wash but then I shall come right back."

William knew better than to argue with Iain. He wished Iain would get some sleep. But he knew that his battle training was keeping him awake now. Still a break would do him the world of good. "Don't worry. I wont leave her until you get back. I promise."

Iain went to his chamber and found Judith had already prepared a bath, fresh clothing and a nice selection of food for him to eat. Suddenly away from the urgency of Stephanie's condition he realized he was famished and so he ate almost everything. With a belly full of food he climbed into the steaming tub. He groaned with relief. Every aching muscle loosened in the soothing water. He made good use of the bath scrubbing himself repeatedly until he was as fresh as a newborn babe. Once he got out and got dressed, he thought it couldn't hurt him to shave. Once he had completed that he suddenly felt a little tired. He didn't want to spend another moment away from Stephanie but he didn't think his feet would carry him one step further. He thought if he just closed his eyes for one brief moment he would feel better. Iain's tireless vigil had taken a toll on him and he was in a deep sleep before his head hit the pillow.

William sat stroking his daughter's hand and after some time had passed without Iain's return, he guessed the poor man must have finally fallen asleep. That was good. Iain needed some rest. William had no doubt that his daughter could sense people around her. He hoped she sensed the love poured on her the last four days and nights.

In the stillness of the room William let his mind wander back to Stephanie's childhood. She was such a lovely child and she had grown into such a lovely woman. He couldn't believe how fast she had grown. Yet she was about to wed and start a family of her own. He choked back a sob. Surely her life couldn't be over so soon. Eduard couldn't have had the last moment. As William thought of all that was and all that might not be with Stephanie he couldn't help himself as he broke down. He cried for all that had happened to his beautiful brave girl and he cried that they couldn't save her.

William's quiet grief still filled the room and he gave vent to his feelings. After some moments he felt something, a butterfly light stroke on his head. He didn't dare hope. But raised his head. Stephanie's eyes were still closed but her fingers were brushing him ever so weakly. Tears of pure happiness replaced those of grief.

Stephanie felt like she was drowning in the darkness. There was no light anywhere and all she knew for sure was that her head hurt so badly she felt sick from the pain. She had no concept of time, nor did she really remember where she was or what had happened. All that was certain was that Iain had stopped speaking. From the moment she no longer heard his voice, she had struggled and strained to try to hear him. Her mind pulled out of the darkness she began to hear other sounds as well; birds, her breathing and someone crying. Then she realized it was her father crying. She tried to speak but her throat wouldn't work. So she tried to touch him and help him through the pain he was so obviously in. It didn't dawn on her in her waking haze that she was the cause of his tears. She just hoped he felt her comfort.

"Steffie? Have you decided to come back to us?" Stephanie heard her father's voice. She was confused. Had she been somewhere? She couldn't remember because her head hurt so much she wasn't able to concentrate. She needed a drink of water. "Water" she croaked.

"Of course sweetheart." She felt her father's hand behind her head and then the soothing trickle of water slid down her parched throat. "What is happening Papa?"

She asked sounding so much like a little girl. His little girl.

"Well you have given us all quite a scare."

"I have?"

"Yes you have."

"What did I do? I don't really remember. My head hurts so. Tell me what happened" Stephanie sounded small and frightened.

"It is all right. You have just been taking a long nap after you bumped your head."

Suddenly in a painful rush, she remembered everything. The kidnapping, the pain, the wait and Iain.

"Iain." Stephanie exclaimed as she struggled to sit up ignoring the pain. She had to see him.

"Settle down, Steffie. You have to move easy." William gently set his daughter back on the pillows which was quite easy given her weakened state.

"No, papa. Let me up. What has happened to Iain? Is he all right?" Stephanie started to cry.

"Hush, my girl. Iain is fine. In fact he hasn't left your side these past five days."

"Five days?" Stephanie exclaimed. "I have been unconscious for five days?"

William stroked his beloved daughter's hair as he kept her in bed. "Yes you have, that is why you must take it easy. You could still be suffering from serious injury. You must move slowly!"

"Iain is all right?"

"He is fine. I hope he is getting some rest. He hasn't slept in five days. Let him rest. Lie back and we will quietly wait for his return."

"Yes, Papa." Stephanie felt truly awful but it was so hard to lie still as her father related the events after she had fallen to the floor and been knocked unconscious. She just wanted, no needed, to see Iain.

Suddenly, as if he had heard her call, she looked over and there he was in the doorway. She wanted to fly out of the bed into his arms, never to leave them again. After the ordeal she didn't care if Iain loved her as she loved him. She just wanted to be able to love him for the rest of her life.

Iain was sure he was dreaming. Stephanie was awake. Perhaps he was still asleep and this was a dream. He wanted to run to her and take her into his arms but he wasn't sure how he would be received after all that had happened to her.

William looked at the two young people and smiled. "I will just leave you two alone. Call if you need anything." He looked at his daughter and said "It is so good to have you back." He kissed her forehead softly before he left. Once outside the door he made sure that no one was to enter the room for any reason until the following morning. He knew Iain and Stephanie had much to talk about and he wanted them to finally get around to speaking of the love they felt for one another.

After Stephanie's father left, she suddenly felt very shy and uncertain. She touched her hand to her hair. "I must look a fright."

Iain didn't know how to approach her. He was certain she would not welcome his declaration of love after all she had gone through from the moment of their first meeting.

"Nay lass, ye dinna look much of a fright." He moved to the end of the bed. "How do ye feel? It is sae good tae see ye awake. Are ye all right?"

"I have the worst headache I have ever experienced in my life but other than that I do feel fine. And you, Iain? Are you all right? Eduard didn't hurt you did he?"

"We are all fine. Eduard, is dead ye know."

"Yes Papa was telling me. I am sorry to say I was very glad to hear you had killed him. He was a sick, evil man, plotting so many deaths for nothing more than a memory."

There was an uncomfortable silence until they both spoke simultaneously.

"I should go, lass"

"Why don't you sit next to me?" Stephanie feared Iain would walk away and she would never see him again. He would probably send her back with her father so she spoke again.

"No Iain. Please don't go. I wish you would sit here next to me." As she looked at him she noticed the wedding gown at the foot of her bed. "Is that my…"

Iain moved to the edge of the bed next to her and saw what she was looking at. "Aye, lass, it is your wedding gown." He hastened to add "But dinna worry I willna make ye wear it. I dinna want ye tae marry me if it will make ye unhappy. I can fully understand why ye would want tae leave now and never set foot here again. But ye canna leave until ye are fully recovered."

Iain's words came out in a rush. But he had to say them. He couldn't blame Stephanie for wanting to get away from him. He had done awful things to her and led her to this place. Her words penetrated his musings.

"Iain stop scowling so. I am surprised to see the wedding gown here but that is not because I don't want to marry you. It is because I realized we were supposed to be married before all of this happened." She reached out and touched his hand. Now was the time she either had to tell Iain exactly how she was feeling or she could run away from his possible rejection of her love. He seemed quite anxious to send her away. No. She would tell him and if he tried to send her away then she would just keep pretending she was too unwell to travel until he accepted her love. With iron determination she said.

"Iain MacDonald, ours has not been a traditional courtship in anyway. You kidnapped me and forced me to stay here under false pretenses. You threatened my father's untried men if I didn't comply. You lied to everyone about my reason for being here."

Iain winced and felt more and more despondent about being able to convince Stephanie they should be wed as she catalogued his offences against her. He had behaved abominably. How could he ever convince her he loved her heart and soul, in light of all she had suffered because of him? Stephanie continued.

"Despite all those events you treated me with tenderness and respect. Never trying to stop me from speaking my mind. And for that Iain MacDonald." Stephanie paused, swallowed and took a deep breath. "I love you."

"What?" Iain couldn't believe he heard right.

Iain's look of shock gave Stephanie a moment's hesitation But she had said it so she might as well keep going. "You heard me I love you with everything I have in me to give. I will not leave this place until you realize that you might be able to love me, too." She lifted her chin defiantly. She dared not look into Iain's eyes, afraid they would be ice cold at her declaration. She didn't care. She meant what she said. She wasn't going to budge.

Iain wanted to shout for joy! She loved him! She said she loved him! It was unbelievable. She had been through so much and here she was declaring she would never leave him. Lovingly he tilted her chin to meet his eyes.

"Lass, ye make me the happiest mon in Scotland, because I love ye, too." He caressed her chin marveling at how soft she was under his calloused fingers. He chuckled as his words dawned on her.

"You do? Truly?" Her face lit up with joy. Iain couldn't resist, he leaned over and kissed her lips with such love in his heart he felt like he was racing through the air on the wind. He wanted to kiss her more but she was only just awake. He saw her eyes glaze with passion and he nearly ravished her there. He had to hold himself in check.

"My bonnie English lass. I love ye and have loved ye fer quite sometime now."

"Oh, Iain" Stephanie breathed his name like a caress. "When can we marry? Now? Can we wed now?"

He laughed. "Easy my love. Ye have tae be stronger. We have much tae talk of first."

She sat back and pouted slightly "I feel fine and I want to marry before anything else happens to stop us."

Iain stroked her hair. "Dinna worry lass. I promise ye NOTHING will stop us from being man and wife."

Stephanie didn't know if her desperation came from her nearly dying or fear that Iain might change his mind. "Iain please. Can we not wed today? I promise I am well enough."

Iain kissed her again deeply "Stephanie, we will not be wed until ye are strong enough. Is that clear?"

"Perfectly. Now kiss me again" She threw her arms around Iain and poured all her love into returning his kiss

Chapter Fifty-Two

The day of their wedding dawned sunny and bright. Everyone said their day was blessed by heaven. The wedding was beautiful and no one could miss the love that passed between the Laird and his Lady as they spoke their vows. The church walls shook with cheers when Iain finally got to kiss his bride.

After the wedding feast Iain rose and addressed his people. "My friends and family," he began, toasting each with his cup. "I want everyone tae know that my wife, Lady Stephanie, is standing by my side for everything and for always. If she speaks ye are tae take it as a command from me. Tae show ye I want ye all tae witness. Stand lovely wife. Let me give you my wedding gift."

Stephanie didn't understand what Iain was doing. He had just validated her to all his people, giving her such authority. What was he up to? She stood hesitantly. Iain pulled her close and whispered in her ear. "Fear not lass. I love ye and want tae show ye how much."

She looked up and saw Angus Campbell being brought in, in chains." He did not look terribly well, but he was alive at least. She looked at Iain. "What is the meaning of this?"

Iain spoke for all to hear "Ye all ken that Angus Campbell is the cause of all that has befallen ye an our English neighbor. That he raided our lands and led us to believe each other was the enemy. For causing the death of my and my brother's parents he should die." People cheered in agreement. Angus paled beneath his beard. Iain held up a hand and continued. "But he has wronged my lady wife more than he has wronged any of us. For that my gift tae ye my love, is that ye shall decide the fate of this mon. Ye decide the punishment he is tae receive."

Stephanie couldn't believe her ears. Her husband was charging her with a Lord's duty. She stood dazed as everyone waited for her decision. She suddenly knew what she had to do.

"Good people. This is a day of celebration and new beginning. I would therefore like to keep the joy of this day. It is my wish that Angus Campbell be released and sent back to his keep." She heard some mutterings of discontent. "Wait. Angus is to go back to his lands and his keep and begin to build up his charge so that all the folk under his protection shall suffer no more."

There were scattered cheers at her kind generosity but she held up her hand to continue. "That is not all. Should any man, woman or child come to this keep complaining of anything ill on Campbell land, you Angus will lose everything! Iain will choose a new Laird to control and manage your lands. You will lose everything for good."

Iain raise Stephanie's hand to his lips marveling at his wife's tempered kindness. Everyone cheered their approval.

"Ah wee lassie, ye are a jewel tae be sure." Angus praised Stephanie "Ye'll nay be sorry fer yer kindness, ever. May God bless yer marriage and yer kind soul."

With that he was released to go and begin rebuilding the Campbell clan.

Iain spoke again. "Now, good people. Enjoy yer feasting. But I take my leave of ye with my wife that we may feast with each other."

Stephanie blushed as Iain lifted her into his arms and carried her out of the hall with boisterous cheers following them.

They reached the chamber and suddenly Stephanie felt shy. She was a married woman; and this was her wedding night. She shouldn't be nervous but she was. She glanced at Iain from under her lashes. He stood there staring intently at her.

"What is it?" She asked.

"Are ye truly my wife?" Iain spoke with hushed tones.

Stephanie laughed nervously. "Of course, you silly man. We just spent the day being feted for our wedding."

"I just canna believe that ye are mine."

Stephanie felt her love give her strength and confidence as she moved towards her husband. Gently she cupped his rugged face and locked eyes with him. "Yes Iain MacDonald I am your wife and I love you with all my heart."

Iain gathered Stephanie in his arms. "Thank God! We have waited long enough. Sweetling ye truly have captured my heart."

As Iain caressed Stephanie reverently with lips and hands, she smiled to herself. Little did her Scottish 'captor' realize they were both well and truly captured. By love.